GROUND CONTROL
TO
MAJOR THOMAS

A novel of the Foundry

J. Fitzpatrick Mauldin

This book is for those who know that doing what is right
is not always black and white.

It is for those who are willing to protect the weak.
It is for those who are willing to make space for the misfits.
It is for those who are willing to stand up to bullies,
no matter who they might be.

You are heroes.

PERIDOT – TAMBORA CLASS ROCK HAULER

UEI DESIGNATED UNDER CONTRACT TO KTS MATERIALS

>SOL<

YEAR: 2095

[1] – Darnell

Darnell loved blowing shit up.

Didn't matter if it was big or small, colorful or just a flash, but seeing chemical energy converted into pressure and heat was a soul-trembling delight; a kind of alchemy that brought him closer to creation, closer to God. When he was a kid, it might have been a past-time to use legally questionable fireworks to make anthills blow sky high, but now, he got a paycheck for it. Three years had passed in the black of space, thousands of pounds of explosives triggered cracking dark rocks and digging out the shiny bits.

Boom.

Boom.

Boom.

Kaching.

It never got old.

Being a rock hauler was great work, hard work, but exciting or not, it sure didn't keep him from getting a little homesick. Space tended to do that.

If his time out here had helped him come to appreciate any one thing, it was that dawn in Texas was a far cry better than dawn on a spinning rock like MT-996—or anywhere else, for that matter. Central Texas was home, a touch outside San Angelo to be exact. It was warm and dry there, even in the mornings, with fields that stretched into forever, ranches untouched by city development making up one of the last run of wilds in the United States. The wind was often heady with the smell of sage, the sound of white-winged doves and warblers calling out that *Morning is here, Morning is here.* And in that calm place of gentle anticipation, the sun came when it was good and damn ready, sky shifting from black to orange, shades of pink and purple spilling across the stratus overhead. Darnell imagined himself standing, silent and watching, a steaming cup of black coffee in hand, a horse whickering at his side in anticipation of a ride. He knew that before him lay a beautiful day of meaningful work, of brothers and fathers, sisters and mothers tending the range. A day of purpose and honest fulfillment, dirt under your nails, sweat down the back of your shirt.

Yeah, blowing shit up was fun and all, but he missed home.

He missed his family.

He missed Texas.

Nothing was the same on this godforsaken, city-sized hellscape floating one hundred and fifty million kilometers off Jupiter. MT-996 did not conjure any visions of days gone past. It did not stir the heart strings or inspire works of music. It was like every other damned rock Darnell had clung to over the past few months—near absolute zero on one side, hot enough to fry your eyeballs in their sockets on the other. Dawn came to this lump in binary, not beauty, arriving once per hour as the rock spun on its axis, the light of the sun hidden, then in its fullness, like a cosmic light switch.

Darnell winced as the ancient light of Sol washed over him and burned into his retinas. Eyes shut, he flipped the visor of his vacuum suit down, shielding his vision with a thin layer of polycarbonate and gold. Damnable gold. His eyes readjusted, purple artifacts fading, and a light flickered at the corner of his perception, breaking his reverie. He twisted around, peering back at the cone-shaped tin can that wasn't Texas, but the next best thing he had for now.

Their flyer, the *Peridot,* a Tambora class mining vessel, was fastened to the surface of the asteroid with a scaffold of carbon nanofiber. Around it and Darnell, a catch net was deployed like a bubble, ensuring that nothing broken free of this rock would be lost. This craft was just a tiny speck of white and silver equipment among a great gulf of nothingness. It was a canoe in a sea devoid of life and vast as creation. At sixty meters in length, it resembled nothing more than an oversized Orion capsule fixed to the top of a habitation cylinder, that was then strapped with several cargo containers painted in safety yellow and black. At the aft of its HAB, a Falkor engine was fixed, a thick ring with four spherical fuel tanks and nuclear thermal propulsion drive, the device capable of accelerating them damn near anywhere in the known solar system so long as they had the reaction mass. Solar panels stretched out from its center of gravity like arms, keeping low power systems active while the drive itself covered the majority of their power needs and kept the Lindvolt cells charged. It was a dirty thing, scuffed and scarred, a bit ugly in most light, unless you've had a few drinks, but it was tough, and it was home for now.

Ten years back, if you'd told teenage Darnell, who at the time was crushing it as a middle linebacker and grinding his way onto the Dallas Cowboys, that his aptitude at science and a little dumb luck would put him on a flyer chasing asteroids, he'd have called you crazy. Screaming through deep space on a tumbling rock of rare metals ain't nothin' close to wrangling lost cattle at night with Gramps. They're sure as shootin' weren't no cows out here neither, but hell, at least there was a cowboy.

"Should be good, that," his helmet channel squawked. *"Ooo, all the shiny bits. Kaching. Kaching."*

He ignored comms for now, focusing instead on his delicate work, trying to ignore his intrusive, nostalgic thoughts.

It was awkward using his hands in these bulky vacuum gloves, as if his fingers had been replaced with summer sausages. These digits were his money makers, dexterous and steady, able to thread monofilament through the eye of the tiniest needle. If only he could do this delicate work within the flyer, first prepping and positioning explosive materials. If only. But no, no, he'd seen the results of that level of laziness, a good friend of his spaced by a pressure shift soon as he stepped out into the void. Explosives didn't play nice with atmospheric transition, and so that meant working with the dangerous bits in hard vacuum.

"Only fools take the easy road, and most of them end up dead," Gramps had always said.

Darnell was no fool.

A song popped into his head; one they might play at the dueling piano bars in Austin. Was it by Parallax? Dolly? Keith Urban? He began to hum its country western baseline, occasionally singing a word or two, but could not remember. He'd have to look up who it was later, not knowing would drive him nuts.

He wasn't sure why he was so nostalgic when he was out here, given how little like home it was. Maybe it was the quiet, his mind left to wander, maybe the absurdity of it all, the audacity of mankind to step foot in such a place. Nevertheless, his girlfriend, the lovely Lexi Carver, had placated this homesickness by having his vacuum suit decorated in such a way as to bring a little Texas into the void. While on leave at Stratus Base, she'd commissioned a local artist had painted a serpentine Chinese dragon down his suit's helmet and spine, its design curling around the stomach and down the thighs, its mouth open, ivory teeth barred. Riding the dragon bareback was a cowboy sporting a giant KTS belt buckle, their hat swinging in the air, a smile on their sun worn face. This suit was his pride and joy, a proper Void-Strider's ensemble shining in the light of cosmic dawn. A cowboy in the black.

"Richardson, are you done yet?" his captain, Katia Cho, called to him over his helmet speaker. *"We don't have all fucking day. If we don't get off soon, you might as well toss those explosives in the airlock and space us all. Get your ass in gear."*

He shook his head and took a deep breath, a bead of sweat rolling down the right side of his face. Cap was always busting his balls. He knew they were up against a tight production window, one that would allow them to sell their goods at a twenty-five percent premium in Pan-American Exchange Notes, even in a down market. Hopefully, they'd turn a profit on this job, but he could only work so fast. Maybe *she* should be the one to come out here and do this next time, see how it feels to be verbally cattle prodded while *she* set enough plastic explosives to blow them all into star dust.

His options were limited in this moment. The survey was done, this was the play. Their engineer, Keelin, had scanned this rock from can to can't and this here was the nugget. He wanted to be a team player, but a selfish part of him just wanted it all over with. He wanted to earn the working man's fortune he'd been promised by the company, and in turn get all the things in life he dreamed about. Too bad a nice house, a big family, and a modest collection of fine whiskey were things only the richest Void-Striders had the luxury of enjoying. You either slummed it on Mars when you were done or lived high on Luna. No room for middling folk.

All he wanted was what all Richardsons wanted. Work hard. Be tough. Buy yourself a house and have a whole mess of kids. If the good ones don't, the bad ones will. It's how America wins.

This was how it was. How it always was. And that was alright by him.

The HUD on his suit displayed an augmented reality model of the nugget in wireframe, which was what he had to go on. Often times these models weren't entirely accurate, especially those with surveys of less than two days. A bad model meant bad returns, a puny load no matter how he set the charges, and by extension, a hungry, angry crew. It was a delicate balancing act between taking your time and getting it right while staying in sync with KTS Materials' deadlines. The UEI, United Exploration Initiative, sure needed a hell of a lot of gold and platinum to prepare for outer planetary colonization, and KTS was the company to get it done.

Darnell ignored Katia, focusing all his attention on the white and gray box before him, sliding a remote trigger deep into the soft putty of S-35 explosives, guessing if it made solid contact or not.

"Okay," he told himself. "Looks good. Need to tie a wire back here. Put another block here. Let's shape the charge and focus the blast down." He kneaded the plastic explosives into a dome.

The survey's model was lining up nice with his charges, but for him to cover the circumference of the nugget would take too long.

"Mr. Richardson."

"Don't get your panties in a twist, Cap," he replied. "We're almost done."

"We are nine hours behind schedule because of Miss Carver's bad burn."

He rolled his eyes and kept working. It sure pissed him the hell off when Cap picked on Lexi like that. She was the best pilot this end of the UEI's operations—didn't matter what anyone said about her, or what kind of reputation she had. Folk make mistakes, okay? It's what you do after 'em that matters.

"I'm done," he growled, pushing off from MT-996 back towards the *Peridot.* "Coming in."

Lexi was waiting for Darnell on the other side of the airlock, her dark eyes patient as the atmosphere cycled. He looked at her through the view port like she was a piece of fine art, a statuesque form in her short-sleeve jumpsuit with chestnut skin, her black and blonde curls a perfect undercut with a lightning bolt stenciled down the side.

As always, she helped him back inside the flyer, over the lip of the hatch where he usually banged his shins. He was unable to see below his chest in the unwieldy suit without contorting his body into an awkward position that made his back pop. She reached around his neck and unfastened his helmet at the collar, twisting it off and holding it with her right hand, the two of them floating in null gravity.

"So glad you're safe, booboo," she whispered beside his ear, then pressed her full lips to his. It didn't matter how many times she did this, it was just as good as the first.

"Miss Carver," he said between kisses. "Must be careful now. Crew might become suspicious of our sordid relationship."

"Then I may just leave the door open tonight. Let them get an eyeful of something good."

"You know, if you ain' careful, that might inspire a bit of third-party participation. Does get lonely out here, and you are quite the fine specimen."

She crossed her arms and put a finger to her lips, thinking that over for a moment. "Then again, on second thought, maybe I'm the jealous type."

"I know I am," he said, smiling.

"Still... Keelin is a pretty fine engineer, and I don't just mean her professional abilities. She is pretty, and a little bit, well, you know... She doesn't just like the boys."

"You serious?"

"Are you that dense?" Lexi raised an eyebrow. "We've been on this flyer with her for almost two years, and you've not picked up on it? What do they teach young boys in Texas?"

"Well, I mean, you know, I try not to give other ladies too much attention. I know what side my bread is buttered on."

Lexi patted herself on the chest. "Get enough drinks in that firecracker, and she can get real friendly with yours truly. It's happened before."

Darnell rubbed at his beard, imagining that proposition. "Well then..."

"Richardson," the captain growled from up the hall, her coiled frame cutting an imposing silhouette sharp as a blade across the pressure hatch. "May we get this over with, please?"

"Aye, aye," he said, rolling his eyes in the direction of Lexi. She gave a chuckle and helped him stow the rest of his suit.

"Alrighty, friends," he said, floating into the bridge section, the rest of the crew waiting on him. "What do you say we crack us a few rocks?"

Atticus, the flyer's psychologist, gave a tired moan as he lowered the tablet he was reading. "Lovely, Richardson. Maybe we'll get back before the six of us murder one another out of boredom."

He watched Darnell take his place with his blue, hawkish eyes. Atticus Prescott was a pale man in his mid-forties with male pattern baldness. Darnell wasn't sure how, but he could make anything he wore, even their KTS Materials jumpsuits, look pretentious. Perhaps it was the scarf around his neck, the way the man held his wrists or perfectly pressed his rolled-up sleeves, or perhaps the tailored cut of the jumpsuit with hand stitched darts placed along the back and side. Who in the hell did this to their standard-issue uniform? Really was too bad there was only one other man on this flyer, and Darnell had almost nothing in common with him. Atticus didn't care for sports, he didn't play cards, he didn't even play video games. He was no fun. No fun at all.

It sure would have been nice to have another guy to hang out with.

"Whatcha readin' today?" he asked Atticus.

The psychologist glanced at his tablet, acting as if he were surprised to find it in his hand. "Oh, this? *Anathema and the World Tree, a*

Comparative Journey of Occidental Myths and Public Discourse, by Lanquist."

The back of Darnell's brain itched at the title. "Some light readin', huh?"

"Mmmhmm. Helps me relax under pressure."

An instant later, Logan Tomlinson, their ship's doctor, shot through the rear portal and settled into their acceleration chair. They gave a smile and J rubbed the back of their right hand. The skin flashed red beneath the surface, and a series of lights blinked up the length of their arm to the shoulder. Darnell shivered. It was Logan's latest upgrade, some sort of machine that allowed them to touch EM radiation and feel music as a direct connection to their nervous system. Darnell made no secret that this kind of biohacking and body modification freaked him the hell out. Why would Logan put something like that under their skin? Weren't natural.

Still, he supposed, to each their own. Their body and all.

"We ready to go?" Logan asked, rubbing their hands together. "I've got people to see. Money to make. And, you know, I'd prefer not to live on Exo-Bites for another month. Might have plenty of nutrients and cost next to nothing, but they have all the flavor of a brick of cardboard."

"The space-man's Ramen," Lexi said.

"I kind of like them," Captain Cho added. "Acquired taste, I guess. Like puff cakes."

"Didn't get hurt out there did you, Richardson?" Logan asked. "Tell me you didn't bang up those shins."

Darnell raised his hands. "Not this time, Doc. The blind man has a handler, and I promise she's more cattle than hat."

"Very well, then. Very well."

Their engineer, Keelin O'Connor, floated beside the net and scaffold controls. Her body was curled into a ball, her red hair sticking out in all directions like an urchin in null gravity, the collar of her jumpsuit wavering back and forth from the pressure of the life support system. Lexi winked at Darnell and back at Keelin. His face flushed. He hated to admit, even to himself, but the idea of his Lexi and this slender, freckle painted, porcelain firecracker locking lips was an interesting thought. A very interesting thought. Shit. God would not be happy with him for considering such sinful things.

"Those charges best not be actin' the maggot," Keelin said after a moment, then sucked on her teeth, her slender fingers nervous as they hovered over switches along the wall. "I'm eager to split these stones and turn 'em in for drinks, fookin' things. Let's wrap it up before I 'ave to pinch off a loaf. Come on, now, give me your riches, *Meal Ticket 996*. Kaching. Kaching."

And just like that, Darnell was reminded for the tenth time today, that when it came to Keelin, the audio often did not match the visual. She was a picture of grace and youthful beauty with a mouth full of mud.

Atticus let out a half-hearted, "Kaching," echoing Keelan's sentiment.

A familiar alarm began to chime, a notice that there was a leak in the life support interchange.

"Logan?" Keelin said, spinning her head around.

The doctor shook their head and slipped out of their acceleration chair. "Okay, okay. I'll fix it this time."

Keelin shouted as they left the room. "Just tape it up!"

"How much do I use?"

"Keep going till it stops beepin'. Can't be spending a fortune in time and coin to take the entire assembly apart."

Darnell shook his head. Always something breaking on a flyer.

"If there's enough after this haul, O'Connor, we'll split a bottle of premium as payback," Captain Cho replied to the engineer's earlier statement, picking back up as if a dangerous alert with the potential to kill them all hadn't just gone off. "Go ahead and hit it, Richardson."

Darnell gave a grunt. "Ready and rarin' to go, Cap." Now came the part he enjoyed most. "Three. Two. One."

He depressed the button and watched the view screen as a puff of white expanded on the surface of the asteroid, a gentle shockwave translated back up the scaffolds into the hull of the flyer. Boom goes the dynamite. An involuntary smile took over his face, his right foot tapping with excitement.

From the center of the blast came a shower of dark rocks, some of which glimmered in the rising light of Sol.

"Drawin' it up for capture," Keelin reported, and the dozen dog-sized robots which anchored the carbon fiber net to the rock began to crawl towards the center, capturing the loose pieces of raw ore.

"Wait!" Darnell shouted, catching a flash of color on the view screen. "Wait, wait, wait! I think I see another nugget under the surface."

The Captain leaned forward, fingers steepling. "How big is it?"

"Who can say? It was bright. Could be big."

"O'Connor?"

She started flicking switches along the wall. "Take me twenty minutes to get set up an scan. Can' see shit right now with all the debris."

"I saw it," Darnell said, pointing to the hole he had just made. "A flicker of white and gold. There's more in there." Maybe it was enough to get him closer to his financial goals, *their* financial goals. Sure would fix a lot of problems.

"Are we sure?" The Captain licked her lips. "I'll back your play to go again if you are absolutely sure. But we're running close on the production queue. We only have a margin of about one hour or we lose the bonus."

"Pretty risky," Atticus commented. "Better a bird in the hand."

Logan flashed Atticus a nasty look. "But what if there's more?"

Darnell stared at the screen a bit longer. He couldn't find the glimmer now. Had it just been wishful thinking? Or had light from the sun reflected down into the hole? He cut on the external lights and focused one of the floods into the crack. The angle was too steep, and all he saw in turn were shadows. Instinct told him to go for it, that there was far more gold or platinum in that hole than the survey had uncovered. Damn production queues. An extra couple hours wouldn't cost the UEI shit, but it would cost his crewmates dearly. Contracts had no empathy.

"I'm not seein' it," Keelin said.

Darnell exhaled, "It's there. I saw it."

"Your call, Richardson." The Captain gestured at the back of the flyer with a thumb. "You'll have to be quick."

He looked down at his hands, chapped and tired. Could he be as quick as he needed, not to put the rest of their pay at risk? He wasn't sure. What if it turned out to be nothing? He couldn't let his crew down. They were counting on this just like he was. No one wanted to live off Exo-Bites, not when their thirties were looming. They needed cold hard cash, wallets full of PAEN.

"Let it go," he said with a sigh.

"Are you sure?"

"Yeah. Let it go. Not confident I can crack it in time."

Lexi put a hand on his shoulder and smiled. What was another few years on the job? Did God not reward the patient?

Once the load was in a neat bundle, the robots bound themselves together and Keelin drew the haul back into the cargo bay. "Looks to me you didn't fook it all up," she said as measurements filtered back onto her display. "Good break, even if we didn't get a second. Won't know purity till we go back to the station."

"Estimate?" the captain asked.

"Four tons, give or take a donkey. Enough for fuel an' then some, if we're lucky."

"That's all?" Logan commented. "What bullshit. If we are even a minute late for that stupid production window this trip will be for nothing. Literally nothing."

"A bit less than last time," Atticus added. "Perhaps our cowboy should have spent more time wrangling the cattle."

Darnell rubbed his face. He had placed the charges where the survey suggested. The survey was Keelin's job, not his. But what he saw… No. What he thought he saw. It wasn't the end of the world. He was just being young and restless.

"Alright now, alright," Captain Cho said, waving a hand. "It is what it is. We've got to get back to meet our delivery window, whether it's the load we wanted or not. Carver?"

Lexi nodded and took her place at the pilot's seat. "If everyone would be so kind to get strapped in, I'll fire up the drive and take us back."

"Buckle up, buttercups." Atticus gestured at the various acceleration chairs in the room.

"You're not my daddy," Keelin replied.

He rolled his eyes at her. "I'm not so sure you had one."

"Aye," the engineer's tone became wistful. "Suppose mom was a bit thirsty. She had herself a dozen or two. Never knew what baker made the dough rise."

Darnell floated into place, clicking his harness and securing himself in his chair. He reached out and squeezed Lexi's shoulder. Her body relaxed and without looking he knew she had smiled.

"Stratus Base here we come," Lexi said.

Once the scaffolds were secure, the *Peridot* jostled and spun around, their course locking in. As the Falkor NTP engaged, a weight as heavy as a city of lost gold came down and rested itself upon Darnell's chest. It was hard to breathe in the moment as he tensed his muscles and grit his teeth on reflex.

He was tougher than this. Today was a setback. Just a setback.

"We got bills to pay," Lexi whispered beside him, her attention focused on the controls. "We got shit to fix, and the math ain't mathin'."

"I know," he replied. "I know."

"Is this all there is? Please tell me. Is this it?"

He sure hoped it wasn't.

[2] – Lexi

Once the *Peridot* was free of MT-996, Lexi turned the flyer towards Stratus Base and burned. After the Cap's scolding for her inefficient intercept and ingress of this asteroid, she didn't want to take any chances her egress might get the same scrutiny. For nearly eight hours she pored over the numbers again and again before being satisfied that this course would allow them to intercept Jupiter's moon, Ganymede, in the least amount of time. Two weeks, three days, nineteen hours, five minutes... four minutes... three minutes. There was no other way to slice it. They'd be cutting their production window close. She considered an additional burn to make up some of that time, but they'd risk using too much reaction mass and find themselves below the recommended safety threshold. She'd done her best with what she had, a balance between time and Delta-V. A cautious approach, sure, but caution was the only approach she could take for now.

Course set. Burn complete. The *Peridot* was in freefall.

Lexi let out a yawn, unbuckled from her acceleration chair, and retired to the six-by-six-by-seven foot box she and Darnell shared halfway down the main corridor. She was exhausted, wagged out like a puppy who'd been begging for treats and needed some shut eye. As always, space was at a premium inside a flyer, but this little box had a door and some basic sound proofing, and that was what passed for privacy in deep space. Along one wall hung their personal belongings in soft bags, a null gravity treadmill was mounted on the relative floor of the space, and a computer workspace glowing opposite of their sleep sacks. To make the space feel homier, the bulkheads of one half of the cramped room were decorated in tricolor cowhide patterns, Darnell's idea, the other half in muted geometric shapes shaded with sangria, charcoal, and cinnamon, hers. Like their personalities, these styles and aesthetics were different, and so this had been the compromise. Darnell had wanted a wrought iron Texas Star by the door. He got it. Lexi had wanted a mixed-media abstract by the early 21st century artist, Jolley. She got it. And while it all might have clashed stylistically, it worked in some weird way, a blending of two lives, a blending of two sets of experiences.

Opposites did tend to attract, so they said.

The lights were turned down, and Darnell was already asleep, snoring as he floated in place on the right bulkhead between wall duffels and wires, his body wrapped in the two-person sleep sack that hung from the wall, arms spread wide within. The video display was still on, its menu music playing on a loop.

She slid the privacy door shut, for what good it did, then turned off the screen and stared at him. He was a good man, a compassionate man, the kind of man she wanted to grow old with, maybe even more... He wasn't really her type, no. She normally went for rakish boys who never wore their hat straight. The boys who talked a big game and broke every rule given them. The ones who were wild like an oxygen fire in null gravity, unbridled, unpredictable, and dangerous. Then she met this big, dark skinned man from San Angelo, of all places, with a heart as big as his belt buckle, half cowboy, half philosopher, all principle.

It was over.

Darnell had been the first of those to hear what had happened over Deimos on that fateful day and shown her any kindness in return. It was her fault, she knew it. Entirely her fault. An impulsive mistake that had cost the lives of her crew. And despite it all, he accepted her.

Why? Why had he accepted her?

Everyone makes mistakes, he'd told her many times. *God looks into the heart.*

Had he just been trying to be nice so he could get some? No. That didn't feel right.

But that day... that fateful day... she could never get it out of her head. May 19th, 2092, Lexi was flying too close to the gravity lifters of Mars's smaller moon. Up against a deadline much like the one she faced now, she'd decided to shave off a few minutes with a dangerous maneuver that took her through active shipping lanes. By the time she detected the load another flyer was towing by tether, it was too late. She zigged when she should have zagged. Her flyer explosively decompressed as it hit the load, giving her crew only an instant to realize the horror of their situation before they asphyxiated.

The UEI had wanted to end her career then and there, sending her to jail for what had become a lethal disregard for safety procedures. Negligence. Manslaughter. But in the end, once the dust had settled, it appeared that there was no legal precedent. Exploration of the deeper solar system was a new frontier, in both navigation and the courts. She got away on a technicality and was still flying.

Cho must have been desperate for a recruit to hire her; it's not like her court records were sealed. Had she been the only pilot available? Questions to ask on the next interview. Given how lackluster her performance had been as of late, that might be as soon as they hit Stratus Base at Ganymede.

Without Darnell, she didn't know where she would be. Depression and regret had hit hard. For several months after the incident, she'd drank herself into a hole, unable to leave Mars. A few old friends from her childhood had even helped connect her with some pharmaceutical goods that were quite a bit harder. She'd spent weeks alone, crying, losing herself in VEs, virtual environments, trying to convince herself none of it had ever happened. No matter how many drinks, no matter how many pills, the pain just didn't go away.

She was lost. Worthless. A shambling apparition of grief and remorse.

She was so alone. Her family, no help. They weren't there; not that any of them could relate anyway. Her parents had all but told her she was trash for making such a stupid mistake, though that wasn't much different than childhood. She was stranded on Mars without work and a dwindling bank account with no idea what would come next. More than once, she had stood by the airlocks looking out the windows at the rusty expanse beyond, high out of her mind on chemicals with names too complicated to pronounce, and considered taking a step out onto the plains beneath Olympus Mons without a pressure suit. Death would be quick this way. She would pay for what she had done and no one else would get hurt.

Then a chance encounter at a Noodle Bar in Olympus Mons changed all that. A bit of swagger from a big man, kind words from an empathetic soul. She'd never once told someone her life over udon noodles, but she did that day. They often argued over how the conversation had started. He said it was over her Parallax T-Shirt, a band from Detroit they both loved which played a weird mix of country and synth-rock. She said it was when she got caught up on her own feet and spilled her hot lunch on his crotch. Both were good memories that ended up at a table by the window overlooking the Martian plains and talking for hours.

It didn't hurt that he had a job lead.

She never wanted to be alone again. Not like that. She couldn't do it.

Lexi stripped out of her jumpsuit and undergarments, stowing them in a soft bag attached to the wall. Her skin was bare in the flyer's recycled air, goosebumps covering her arms and legs. Where the reflection of her flesh was caught in the mirror, she could see that her muscle tone was not what it once was. Four years ago, when she had gone up the well and started this crazy adventure, she had been athletic, well defined. She had once worked out five days a week, both cardio and strength training. Now? Null gravity was eating away at her one bite at a time.

How many more years could she do this before she was no longer strong enough to even bear Earth's gravity?

Her naked toes against cold metal, she pushed off and floated over to their bed, unzipping the side of the bag and squeezing up beside her man. He responded to her arrival, letting out a soft moan, then turned and put his arms around her. Cuddling in null wasn't the same as it was under gravity, but this was the next best thing. It had been a long time since she'd felt the weight of her cheek against his muscular chest. Space was what they knew, null gravity and the grind.

"You get us on track?" he mumbled, nestling his face against her neck, the tip of his cold nose sending a chill down her spine.

"We're good. I'll live to get yelled at another day." His bare skin was warm against hers. Comforting. She laid her head on his chest and caught a glimpse of his quirkier personal effects, a collection of Hot Wheels cars glued above their heads arrayed from high-performance sports cars to classics like Mustangs. Despite their rough day, this made her smile, warming her heart that the kid within him had come along for the ride.

"Bless your heart," he said, shaking his head and clicking his teeth.

She let out a chuckle. "Don't patronize me."

"Look, if you don't like the weather, wait a minute. Cap is one capricious lady."

"Oh, trust me, I know." She drew back and met his eyes. "And keep your voice down. These walls don't stop that much."

He sighed and nodded. "So, what comes next?"

"What do you mean?"

"After this haul is done and all," he said. "I know we've been saving. More goes in the bank, right? After bills."

"Yeah," she said, slow to reply, collecting her thoughts. "I want to put more in. Just seems like we won't ever get there. Cost of everything keep getting higher. Inflation is out of control. We have expenses to pay. And have you checked the prices on Mars recently? Even a small place is gonna be a struggle. Sure won't be a retirement once that's paid."

Darnell raised an eyebrow at her. "Could go back down the gravity well. We might can find some room on the ranch."

"No." She shook her head, and felt her muscles ache with phantom pain. "Things are bad enough back home, what with the coastal flooding and wildfires. You see the camps outside Chicago? People just standing around looking for work, or food, or anything to give them a scrap of hope. Looks like a damn war zone out there. And what's more, shit didn't grow this fall in the Midwest. Besides, I believe in what we're doing out here. Humanity has to find a way to live outside of Earth. That takes infrastructure. That takes people just living their lives. So here we are. Good, bad, ugly."

"I agree, I agree. That, and well, you know I got legal reasons I can't go back myself," he said, sounding disappointed. "Which is why I've been thinking."

She narrowed her eyes at him, suspicious. "Yeah? About what?"

"Look, we've been together now for about a year, and well, I don't see myself going anywheres else when we settle in. I was thinkin', maybe we make some plans beyond just getting a place of our own. Mars ain't bad, just not sure it's where we should settle."

She cocked her head to the side and took a deep breath. What in the hell was he on about, and why did her hands sweat when she thought about anything lasting more than a year? Hell, was thirty too young to settle in? "What kind of plans you got in mind?"

"Maybe it's time to have a family," he ventured.

Lexi's stomach dropped like a flyer plummeting to the surface of a rocky world, her heart thundering in her chest. What in the hell kind of man asks for this? Scratch that, she knew what kind. And scratch thirty being too young to start, maybe it was too old.

"I'm sorry." She blinked. "What did you say? I think I might have just had a stroke."

"Family," he said, exhaling. "It's all that matters to me. Wouldn't be here without it. When the UEI saw my test scores, and my physical, they pursued me hard. Gramps encouraged me to go for it, be more than just a rancher, and so I aim to make the family proud. I want to add to it as well. Once we find our way out of doing these short hop intercepts, why not have a baby? One's a good place to start."

"Hang on, hang on. A good place to start?" She stared him in the eyes. "You been drinking, beau? Bump your head on that airlock too many times?"

He willingly wanted to have a big family. This wasn't the case in the Carver house. Lexi and her sisters happened by pure accident, and as a result were dragged along to every party their lush parents ever attended. It was cool when she hit her teenage years, sure, but when she was a kid, all she wanted was a bit of love and a regular meal that didn't come from a drive thru.

"No, ma'am," he said with that Texas drawl. "No whiskey for me tonight. And don't worry about my head, it's the damn shins you gotta keep an eye on. Babe, you know I have a big family, nine brothers and eleven sisters on the ranch. I want the same experience, got a responsibility."

"Responsibility to who?"

"To my family. To our country. To the feelings I have for you. I think you'd make a great mom."

Her face flushed with heat. This was too much. There was so much to consider. The money? The responsibility? Did she even deserve it?

Mistakes... Mistakes... Mistakes...

Was she even a good example?

Those eyes of his pierced her soul, patient and searching.

"I, eh, like the idea, mostly," she replied after some time, attempting to break the tension. "Maybe I am a little scared, a little excited. You know how I am about marriage."

"Don't have to worry about that," he said, his tone softening. "Marriage—it's just a word. We can be life partners, or whatever it is you like to call it. Don't have to be my wife. Don't have to take my name."

"Your name is fine," she said, chuckling. Why was she burning up? Sweating? "A family..."

"A family."

This was no simple discussion. Whatever her response would be, it would have everlasting implications for their relationship. If she said no, he'd be heartbroken. If she said yes, there were her own fears to address. Who could blame him for asking? Who could blame him for wanting this so unequivocally? She couldn't. She might not feel ready, but who was?

"I think I'd like that," she said after a moment. "A family."

His eyes glittered in the dim light of their room, lips splitting into an ever-widening grin. "Which is why I think we need to consider something other than Mars. It's still a bit wild out there, know what I mean?"

"If not Mars, then where?"

He fished out his hand terminal, cleared his voice, then began to read, taking on the tone of a narrator on television:

"Located just two miles from the Sea of Tranquility near Luna base, the *Gardens of the Moon* is a planned community designed with you in mind. Over a thousand units have been added in phases two and three, connecting fifty additional acres of open green space beneath habitat domes.

"Take a walk on our endless garden trails through canopies of dense foliage from the deciduous forests of Earth, over foot bridges and burbling streams. The garden is populated by wild birds of many species, such as cardinals and blue jays, as well as non-biting insects to close the ecological cycle and complete the nature experience. While taking a stroll in the afternoons, you'll forget you're on the moon as your mind is transported to the temperate lands of the Southeastern United States.

"Enjoy the view from your state-of-the-art home overlooking the swaying trees of humanity's first self-sustaining garden planted outside of Earth. Make use of the community's amenities with top-rated schools, restaurants, and music venues, as well as a public mall and private space port.

"Spots are limited to Void-Striders only, be sure to get on the wait list today. Prices start at 2.2 million Pan American Exchange Notes for three-bedroom apartment homes with proper credit and income validation. Financing available through Rocket City First National.

"Contact your agent today."

Their quarters fell silent. This boy had gone stark raving mad.

"The Gardens of the Moon?" Lexi hissed. "You are kidding me, right?"

"Not at all, ma'am. Best schools. Safest community. Good place for kids." He stared off into nothing as if imagining himself being there, strolling through its parks, eating at its restaurants, walking their kids to school. "Besides, the view ain't bad."

The choice was so easy, if you were only reading the advertisement. The Gardens of the Moon was the premier place to live. But at the same time, never in her life had she imagined being wealthy enough to live in a place like that. But the thought of it... It was compelling.

"Hold up," she said, raising her hands, reeling back from this beautiful vision. "Let's be realistic for two seconds. At the rate we're earning we'll never save enough. Olympus District on Mars, mid two hundreds, maybe, but The Gardens? 2.2 Million PAEN and up. What Void-Strider can afford that?"

His smile drooped.

She pulled a hand terminal from a pocket on the outside of the sleep sack and opened her banking app. Why did the practical part of her brain always have to squash these moments? "We have fifty-nine thousand PAEN. For us to be where we need to be, it'll take another four hundred jobs easy. Shit, we'll be elderly by then. Not to mention, sickly. Our time up here is ticking."

"Come now," he said. "*Stella's* crew hit a thick platinum deposit two months back worth enough almost all of them were able to retire. Kaching. Kaching. Same can happen to us. I just have to find the right spot to crack. I got a plan for next time."

"Ever the optimist."

He gazed off into nothing, thinking. "I keep tryin' to tell myself there was no way to know that what I saw on 996 was real, but my instincts say we might could have already paid for our future."

"Can't live in the past," she said, then felt sick for it. How often do we give people advice we won't take ourselves? "We are rock haulers, necessary but expendable. Chances of us hitting a mother lode like that just aren't good. Not just about the gold, but platinum, rare isotopes."

He raised his chin in enthusiastic defiance. "It's not outside the realm of possibility, though."

"I know. I know. It's just." She let out a long breath. Damn if her stomach wasn't doing flips. "Not that likely."

"We shall see. Good people are rewarded for doing the right thing. God still watchin' over us, even out here."

Lexi kissed Darnell on the lips and gave him a smile. While she didn't share his beliefs, she respected him for it and would never mock them. "I'd like to believe that. I really would."

"Besides, Miss Carver, the divine plan is with me." He began to run his fingers up and down her naked spine. Kisses were placed on her neck just below the ear soliciting a set of electric vibrations in her head. "I already found my own mother lode. Got a good woman right here at my side. I do believe she needs some good things in life."

She reached between his legs and licked her lips. "Oh, you're right about that. I need good things, baby. I really, really do."

A family...

Yeah. Maybe she could do that. But it all seemed so far out of reach. The real question was: Did she deserve it?

[3] - Darnell

Darnell waited in the refinery of Stratus Base, floating in place with the rest of the crew, Lexi's hand in his, their focus fixed on the dock's thick windows as their load was drawn out of the *Peridot's* cargo bay into processing. Keelin worked a set of lifting arms as if they were her own, a pair of 3D goggles on her face and WALDO gloves slipped over the backs of her hands with open fingers. She grasped nets of ore and forced them down a mechanical chute, ten cubic meters at a time, the bulkhead vibrating with each new load.

The question hadn't left his mind. It was even amplified after his conversation with Lexi. Had he made the wrong call? Should he have pushed Cap to let him stay and go for that extra nugget?

It had been a long time since he'd found himself praying. Sure, he'd been born of a red state where church was a major focus in the community, but out here? He just wasn't sure. It felt sometimes as if the Almighty didn't have any reception once you got past low Earth orbit.

A Bible verse came to mind.

...Neither height nor depth, nor anything else in all creation, will be able to separate us from the love of God...

Repeating the words in his head grounded him. He was a man of faith, damn it. Nothing to worry about when his fate was in God's hands.

Lexi squeezed his hand. "You okay?" she asked.

"Fine. Fine." He shook his head. "Just got lost in thought."

"Stratus is weighin' it out now," Keelin said, her tone upbeat. "I know they say get all your wishes but one, but in this moment, I don't want much of life."

"Come on, come on," Captain Cho pleaded, a fist to her lips, eyes focused on the weight display beside the view port. The numbers on the screen began to climb as the rocks entered the centrifuge and were crushed into powder, the first step in heavy metals refining.

"Clock says we missed the window," Logan reported. "Hooray for us! Maybe we should have just gone for Darnell's hallucination. It would have made no difference."

The Captain scowled. "I'll talk to the station admin. It was only by fifteen minutes. Let's see if they'll show some grace."

"Won't do much good. A contract's a contract."

"What a positive attitude you've got today. Maybe I should model my own after that?"

"If we haven't been stuck in that traffic queue," Lexi mumbled. "We'd have docked on time."

"If only they hadn't captured 16 Psyche," Atticus mused. "We wanted rich deposits of gold, sure, but not that rich." He paused and looked around at his silent crewmates. "You know, it seems like a perfect time to tell an economics joke, too bad there just isn't enough *demand*."

"Seriously?" Lexi said, rolling her eyes.

He shrugged. "If not for that stupid event, we wouldn't have to live and die by production window bonuses. A bonus should be a bonus, not something you depend on. I should file a complaint with the company."

"That asteroid put a bullet in the head of the market." Logan crossed their arms. "Raw materials commodities is a bad place to put your money. Just ask the machine that *was*, and I stress, *was*—my stock portfolio. Insert an Aston Marten in one end, get a Toyota Corolla and a smile out the other."

Cho glared at the two of them. "How many times do we have to go over this? The price is based on local supply and demand. The majority of 16 Psyche is being shipped back to Earth and Luna. Don't worry your pretty little heads."

"Not like it was." Logan raised their hand terminal and began pushing buttons. "Not anything like it was."

"It's an honest living," Darnell said, leaning in. "An honest living for honest times. Serves a real need here in the outer planets. Microprocessors and a thousand other things use gold."

"Whatever," they said and pushed off. "I'm headed to the bar. You can break the bad news when it's over."

"Can't blame them," Keelin said, watching them go. "Whole heap of work for naught but a few pence."

Captain Cho glowered at her. "If you have a better opportunity before you, feel free to make use of it."

"Ain' sayin' a word that hasn't already been thought," she watched the refinery's counter, chewing on her bottom lip as the scale did its work. "Been six months at least since we had a good run at it. Rubs like that tend to wear the fabric thin."

"Do you all feel this way?" the captain looked to each of them in turn, her arms crossed. "Jobs aren't paying what they should?"

Atticus scratched at the back of his head for a moment then shrugged. "Pretty obvious, isn't it? I do wish I could be spending a bit more time on leisure. Being out in the black all the time makes it a challenge to have, shall we say, romantic entanglements that aren't with the crew. And while you are all fine, fine people, you lack what I find—well—stimulating in that arena."

The mood in the collection center had shifted from hopeful to defeated. At this point, none of them expected much out of the haul, just like their other recent excursions.

"Null is getting to us, Katia," Lexi said. "If you asked Logan, they'd say the same as a medical professional. We can't stay out here like this forever. Being outside a gravity well is killing us slowly. We're all past the two-year safety limit. And unless you guys have options I'm not aware of, it might be too expensive to go home."

"What about the null gravity protein?" Captain Cho said after a moment. "The science team on the *Vasco Da Gama*, one of the ships bound for the Foundry, I heard they almost have it solved. There's a promising candidate at least. Certainly would give us more time up here to do what needs doing."

"I wouldn't bet on it," Atticus said. "Scuttlebutt is that those in the trial were turned blind by the treatment. I'd rather keep my eyesight, even if I do have a slight stigmatism."

"Well then, what do you want out of me?" She pounded the bulkhead beside her, face turning bright red. "I'm no magician."

The panel beside Keelin chimed. Analysis was complete. She checked the numbers several times before reporting the final tally. "Looks like the fine folks at the station will pay us just enough to top off our reaction mass and fill up the pantry."

"No splits?" Lexi exhaled.

"Oh, there's splits, but it'll be best served gettin' you pissed than anythin' else. Like they say, what butter and whiskey can't cure, there's no cure for."

Darnell felt like a balloon whose air had been let out by a pinprick. He didn't want to admit it, even to himself, but this was the outcome he'd expected all along. They'd done the proper surveys; found the richest location they could hit. Or had they? Had he messed up? Had he placed the charges in the wrong spot? Shaped them incorrectly and not gone deep enough into the rock?

And the nugget below the break. The nugget. It had been real. He was sure of it. Could have turned it all around.

"Let me see that," the captain said, pouring over the data on the panel. "Shit." She closed her eyes, took a clarifying breath and pinched the bridge of her nose. "Okay. I'll get refit estimates and dispute this total. It's going to cost a fortune to replace the bearings that went out on the last grab, re-stripe the seals that are going weak, not to mention the air scrubbers are up for maintenance. Our Lindvolt backup cells could use reconditioning as well. Don't suppose any of you can go without breathing, can you? No? Okay."

"Cap?" Keelin asked, appearing uncharacteristically sheepish in the moment. "There's another matter at hand."

"Yeah?"

"You see… well… as it is… the Falkor drive here… It um, has a crack in the lining of its uranium storage. Not dosing the flyer with radiation and givin' us extra arms yet, but heavy use could cause serious problems in the near future. It's expensive to fix, as you know. We're grounded till it is. No kaching."

"Dear, God." The captain pinched the bridge of her nose. "It's always something. Why now?"

Keelin shrugged. "Can't say. Shielding wears out. With this haul as the tally stands now, I'd say we might need to take out a loan, if even we can get one. We're stretched out like an old rubber band when it comes to finances."

They were all silent for a moment. This was the kind of damage that could leave a flyer stuck at dry dock for months, if forever.

The captain growled, "I'll meet the rest of you at the bar when I'm done. Let me see what I can figure out so I don't have to call in too many favors from my family."

Keelin grinned at the captain, playing off her worry. She hid her feelings well, but everyone could see she was upset.

"Drinks on you till then?" she ventured. "Ye promised me a bottle as it were."

"Fine, fine. Put it on the account."

Atticus took hold of the engineer's arm, an amused expression on his face. "Would you mind escorting this gentleman to the house of ill repute? I'd rather not think upon our troubles for a while."

"I'd be honored, good sir," she said, resting her free hand on his arm. "Can't have a soul that's too bright and shiny around here."

"Perish the thought."

"Cracked uranium storage," Darnell mumbled, shaking his head in disbelief. Always something. Can't be ignored.

He replayed the job in his mind, step by step. Next time, he'd make them stay longer surveying the rock, no matter how hard Cap bitched about it. There had to be a way out of this. His mother lode was out there just as sure as his dream to start a family. It could have paid for these repairs and so much more.

Lexi took hold of Darnell's hand. He hadn't realized he'd balled them into fists, and so it took some effort for her to uncurl his fingers.

"Come on, beau," she said, her tone soft. "I could use a drink. So could you."

"Won't change anything," he mumbled. Never changed a damn thing except in giving you a headache and a bad night's sleep. "We've come up short and now we're dead in the water."

"Who knows? It just might change things for a minute."

As they were heading towards the bar, three men in blue and white UEI uniforms came shooting down the corridor with tasers in hand, a man in orange ahead of them. Someone was making a break for it, running for their life. Where he thought he'd go was hard to say. They were on a closed station and there was no exit, nowhere to hide.

The officials caught up with him at one the docks, shocking him in the ribs. His body went limp, a dribble of vomit leaking from the side of his mouth and floating out into open air.

"What happened?" Darnell asked a UEI official floating at the end of the hall, her rank patch that of a Police Sergeant.

"Got caught ferrying artifacts," she said, tone off handed. "Two space probes left behind by the Americans. Still has to go to court and all that, but it looks like the Russians were buying."

"Pretty serious offense, I suppose."

"Sure as hell is." The woman crossed her arms and watched the guards haul the man off. "I wouldn't be caught dead doing something like that out here."

"Cause it's wrong?"

"No." She thumbed her nose and fixed her hard eyes on his. "Because we don't have the infrastructure for prisoners. UEI Charter countries come down hard on scavengers who try to sell space exploration artifacts. It's treason, depending on the buyer. And we don't exactly have room for a prison out here." She gave them both a nod and narrowed her eyes. "Have a good day now," she said, and disappeared.

"Well shit," Lexi commented. "Did she say what I think she said?"

"Treason," he mouthed, throat dry. From what he could remember of history, treason typically involved a rope and a short drop. And while there might not be a lot of ropes out here, a fall from an airless dock would end just as bad, an eternal journey kicked off by several seconds of intense agony and terror. "I'd never do it. Only bad folk make those choices."

Lexi's expression scrunched; attention focused on some place beyond the station. What was she thinking about?

"Never judge another's path till you've walked it," she whispered after a silent moment. "It's easy to do what's right when you have the means."

"I stand by what I said. Stealing is stealing."

Lexi shrugged. "Come on," she said, leading him in the direction Keelin and Atticus had gone. "Let's put our mind elsewhere."

It didn't matter to Darnell. There was no situation that would make this right. If the law deemed it a crime, it was a crime no matter how you got there. Laws were made to protect society, not the individual. Right?

"Maybe I am a bit parched," he agreed. "We best hurry. If we take too long, Keelin will spend all the captain's money before we even get a sip."

[4] – Lexi

The bar at Stratus was crowded and hot, with bass-heavy music rattling the bulkheads as countless clusters of Void-Striders laughed and played games. A cursory glance revealed that the *Peridot* wasn't the only flyer whose crew had been splitting rocks over the past weeks. There were dozens of other crews burning off steam. Recent years had turned the outer planets into a hive swarming with activity, support stations churning out equipment by the ton in preparation for colonists to the tune of two million over the next ten years. The work was tough. Those doing it, twice so.

Lexi, her crew mates, and the rest of these brave folk were frontier's people, setting flags in unclaimed dirt and building wooden forts to keep wild animals or aggressive natives at bay while they cut trails for the soft-skinned pedestrians at their backs. They were hard so that others didn't have to be. For most of them, it was a worthy trade, but she wasn't so sure.

There were two types of people these days. The ones who the world had made into stone through trials, and the ones who feared everything and had gone soft. This wasn't just Americans either, no, it was happening in every country in the world. Climate change and economic shifts had created an even deeper disparity between the haves and have-nots.

Those with the means had taken to lives of endless distraction, to binge and prime their way into obesity and frailty. Growth in consumer goods had been driven by manipulative marketers who made purchasing practically addictive, and with society-wide isolation, depression, and loneliness as common as hashtags, many fell into an endless loop of anesthetizing their pains with buy-it-now and instant delivery. The healthcare industry had become a monstrous machine that allowed Earth's citizens to ruin themselves with bad habits, only to put them back together to do it all over again. Drink too much for years? Here's a cloned liver from your own stem cells. Have a donut and mocha subscription daily direct for another round of diabetes? It's okay, we've got outpatient pancreas replacement. Don't worry, we'll bill you later, just another debt to hang around your neck. Forget preventative care, live for today. Treat yo' self. Because you're worth it.

But was it worth trading her body, her life, to save a people who didn't even care? She wasn't sure. They were spoiled. Too much comfort and too little struggle. A soul was forged in the struggle, not on the couch with a mobile in hand. All the while, these same people would pop out babies they didn't even give the time of day, only to stretch the world's resources further.

And then there were the rest, those without the will or means to change their lives. There were far more of them than the others, which is why major cities tended to look more like refugee camps than shining symbols of human triumph. Not enough to go around. No jobs to keep them busy. Little or no opportunity for a better life. It was a bullshit dichotomy their leaders had been unable to correct, and so it didn't matter if Coke or Pepsi were in office when it came to this. Soda was soda.

Floating into the bar with a gentle push, Darnell at her side, she groaned under her breath. She was brooding and she knew it. If they had hit a big nut, she wouldn't have given these old thoughts even a moment of her time. Darnell's sour mood, along with the crews, was infecting her like a virus. They were dead in the water till they figured this out. Not fixing uranium storage just wasn't an option. This would almost certainly spell death. Every time they cut on the Falkor drive it would be like playing roulette, the tiny window in storage opening wide, accelerating their chemical reaction mass as it initiated fission, intense stress applied to the whole assembly. Would it crack? Would it not? And what if that tiny little door didn't close properly?

Click.

Click.

Bzzt.

Game over.

"Five whiskeys, neat," Keelin shouted over the rumble of bass at the bald-headed bartender suspended behind the counter. "Charge to Captain Cho. *Peridot*." She waved at Lexi and the rest of the group.

The bartender gave a shrug and collected five bulbs of mid-priced whiskey. Lexi hoped it wouldn't leave her with a headache in the morning.

"You know," Atticus said as he took his bulb. "It's a shame we can't drink from a glass. I miss swirling a couple fingers of Elijah Craig around a tumbler while sitting on my porch, kicked back in a rocking chair at dusk, watching swarms of fireflies dance in the summertime."

"Ey? Too bad they're all gone now," Logan said, then put their own bulb to their lips and squeezed. The lights under the skin on their arms flashed and they smiled. "God, this bass frequency makes me feel things you wouldn't believe. Better than sex."

"No thanks," Keelin said. "Prefer to take music in through me ears, not under me skin." She gestured for them to take a spot around what could be called a table in appearance only. It didn't seem right thinking of it as a real table without gravity. It was a meeting space where they could hook their feet on straps and talk, as well as stick the magnetic bottoms of their drink bulbs to its surface if they needed to free up their hands.

Lexi raised her bulb in a toast. "To a safe return, if we ever get to leave again."

"Safe return," Logan echoed, and the rest raised their own and took a drink except for Darnell. Logan gave him a smile and stared, attempting to discern what he was thinking. "You okay?"

"I'm fine," he said. "Nothin' to worry about. We've been in worse."

"Well... Thanks for the drink, team." They peered over their shoulder, and a group of people in black jumpsuits with neon piping waved at them.

This made Logan's back go straight. Lexi couldn't tell if it was excitement or concern. "Well... I see a few old friends here. I'll catch up in a bit. Make bad choices."

"You too good to spend a minute with your mates?" Keelin leaned in. "Take in a drink or two?"

Logan narrowed their eyes. "We've been on the same flyer for over a month. What I need, is a break from you lovely mates."

"'Aight then," Darnell said, giving a nod.

Logan vanished among the crowd.

"How much do you think the load will be worth?" Lexi asked Keelin. "Do we have a chance?"

She gave a shrug. "Maybe ten large a piece if we kill the elephant. Ain' much. Not to me at least."

Ten large. What bullshit. If this was the new trend...

"Better than last time," Atticus commented, his attention on swirling the whiskey around in his bulb. Didn't do much good, being that liquids formed spheres in null gravity. "Pales in comparison."

Lexi shrugged in a halfhearted attempt to seem unbothered. "I keep telling myself, we don't determine the market. We just work in it."

She checked her hand terminal and flipped through her accounts. Bills had come in, taking more than she would earn from this haul. There was no getting ahead. By the time you paid taxes, old loans, air allowances, insurance, and the mandatory UEI Human Salvation contributions for the FICSE mission, there wasn't much left. She had to not only work her ass off to save humanity, but also give up the lion's share of her earnings to pay for it.

"Might just swing back around," Darnell said in a half-hearted attempt to be positive. "Seen it before, right? All kinds of markets boom and bust. Might be worth piling up while it's low and sell when it's high."

"These aren't stocks, beau. We have nowhere to put the ore, and the company wants it sold now. That's what the whole production deadline bonuses are about. It's to keep supply steady. Besides, no telling how long till it rebounds even if KTS let us stock it up. Could be five or six years."

"Has to be a way."

In this moment, Lexi felt nothing would work out. She was in no mood to agree with anything positive. But what good would taking that position do? Would it serve her goals in any measurable way? No. Got to fake it till you make it.

"Where there's a will, there's always a way I guess," she said. "We just have to look for the opportunity." And while it was weird to admit, just saying this made her feel a little better, even if it was total bullshit.

"What a shining beacon of optimism we are," Atticus mused, his tone dripping with sarcasm. "I for one believe we might be… well, screwed."

"I've got me some debts to pay," Keelin said, scowling into her drink.

"Don't we all," Lexi sighed. "Pretty sure I'm still getting collection calls over a mobile I skipped out on ten years back."

"Yeah, but mobile debt collectors don't try and break your knees if you don't pay. I can't be takin' on more."

"Boohoo." Atticus took a sip. "I have research to do, people to impress. Hard to do this on a budget."

"Folk should like you for who you are," Darnell said.

"Oh, my good friend, if only it were so simple."

He scowled. "Maybe it is if you let it be."

"Was earning the respect of your family something you had to work at? Or did they give it naturally?"

Darnell went silent at this, his bulb of whiskey spinning before him.

Across the room a news broadcast played on a widescreen television, subtitles scrolling across the bottom. North Korea, of all countries, had decided to join FICSE, a mission funded by the citizens of Earth to pursue a set of alien signals originating from Sol's galactic neighbors. UEI leadership hoped, as all humans did, that maybe we'd find some help from a species more advanced than humanity. Things must have been getting pretty bad for heavy-handed militaristic dictators to take this so seriously.

Other news stories flickered by. The stock market was reaching an all-time high and experts warned of a bubble like the one in 2062. Relations were tense once more between Pakistan and India, two nations on the brink of war due to water shortage and land rights. James Carlisle of the Holy Word of Calvary Church, a right-leaning Pentecostal organization, waved to a crowd after announcing that he was building ten new mega churches in the most liberal cities of the US as part of the Fifth Great Awakening, a movement that declared only God could save us from climate change.

It was just another news day. Same shit, different solar cycle.

The crew of the *Peridot* floated in silence for a time, allowing waves of bass to wash over them, each lost in the maze of their own thoughts. Ten large a piece. This wouldn't do. There's no way this would give her and Darnell what they wanted, a home with solid ground and gravity beneath their feet. A place, a real place to raise a family. There had to be another way. This dream of a mother lode Darnell held onto wasn't entirely farfetched, but of the hundreds of jobs completed each year, only one or two percent had that kind of luck. Was she one in a hundred? Maybe in bad luck. The incident over Deimos had been a one-in-ten-thousand mistake, and it had brought the future of three bright souls to an abrupt end.

No. She wasn't going to go down that road in her head, not tonight. It was all in her rear view, events at her back with nothing but a drive flame to compete with. Eight hundred nineteen days and billions of miles separated her from that fated moment, yet there were times it felt like yesterday. The human mind's portable time travel abilities really pissed her off.

Keelin brought over another round of drinks, which were promptly put away. She gave a shiver as the alcohol settled into her stomach, then pushed off from the table, joining a series of beautiful young people in tight fitted body suits who were doing their best to make a null gravity dance floor on the opposite end of the bar. A big breasted, dark-haired woman began to give the engineer a set of hungry, drunken eyes. Keelin responded in kind. They began to kiss, deep and passionate, more tongue than lips, before one of the woman's friends, a slender man with soft features and a silver coif of hair got a turn. Keelin had been part of their group for all of two minutes and already summoned a bit of sexual action. To be young and gorgeous. Lexi had been there once.

Darnell glared at them as they entertained themselves, his lip poked out in interest. Lexi slapped him in the stomach with the back of her hand.

"What?" he stammered. "What did I do?"

She glowered at him. Even the good guys were wired the same. "Why not take a picture? Hmm? Slip out your hand terminal. Go on. It'll last longer."

"Picture of what? I wasn't looking."

"Sure you weren't."

"Look, ma'am, I do apologize for the fact that the good Lord gave me eyes."

"And sense in where to put them," she said, two fingers raised, pointed at herself.

He smiled at her, wide with teeth flashing, and a place in her chest flushed with heat. "I know where to put them alright."

"Stop it." She blushed. "Don't give me that look. That's for later."

Several minutes passed and Keelin returned, sweat drenching the back of her jumpsuit, fingers twitching at keys on her hand terminal. The man and woman had left the bar, but Lexi had a feeling the conversation was continuing. Keelin looked to be a woman with a mission.

"Let's get pissed," Keelin declared, and waved one of the servers over. "Two rounds for the group."

"Captain Cho is going to stuff you in the airlock when the bill comes in," Atticus said, attention focused on his nails. "The price here is almost ten times what we get from the supply room."

"Fuck her. That geebag hasn't put an ounce of proper coin in me pocket in almost a year."

"Not a very nice thing to say about boss woman."

Keelin bowed up, fists balling at her sides. "Let her come and fight me then. See who's left with a bloody face."

Lexi shook her head at them.

The server returned with an arm full of whiskey. She put the bulbs on the table with a smile, the magnets on their plastic bottoms sticking in place. Keelin emptied two before anyone could reach for a fresh drink.

A woman with a clear, clear mission.

Atticus took his bulb of whiskey and gave Lexi and Darnell a glance. Keelin was starting to rub him the wrong way, and it wasn't the first time.

"Why do you always have to act so tough," Atticus began. "Why put up such a foul, vile front?"

"Excuse me, gobshite?" Keelin's face went red. She tossed one of her empty bulbs over her shoulder and it spun away towards another table, a patron flicking it off towards the bar with a finger as it neared their face.

"You want to know what I think about you? What I really think?"

"Two years we've known each other. Never held back your opinion before, even if it makes you a langer."

He raised his eyebrows and pursed his lips. "Think? What do I think... Well, I think you're just a sad girl who makes stupid choices because she feels she has to, it's all she deserves. Grew up without a daddy because her mom couldn't make money any other way than to vibrate her pink taco on a live stream. I believe the reason you're always looking for sexual comfort is to drown out the fact that you don't feel you deserve anything real."

Darnell choked on his drink and began coughing, his right palm slapping against his chest. Lexi blinked. Where in the hell was all this coming from?

"I'm warning you, Atticus," Keelin said. "It's often a man's mouth that gets his nose broke. I told you those things in confidence."

"Then what am I afraid of? Go ahead, make me stop."

Keelin's eyes had become glassy. Tiny balls of water oozed from the edges. Lexi had never seen her like this. Darnell put out a hand to hold her back.

"So, you want to play the psychology game?" she went on. "You get your jollies sizing people up and sliding their brains in neat little boxes. Let's see how you like it."

Atticus threw his arms wide. "Be my guest."

"Okay then." She downed the rest of her bulb of whiskey and took a deep breath through her nose. "You're a pretentious asshole who grew up with a tiny prig and had a silver spoon between his teeth. You were the golden child meant to carry on the glorious Prescott family name and pedigree, a bunch of rich, inbred nitwits with too much class and not enough salt. When yer moment in life came, the one your parents dreamed of since you were nothing but an embryonic peanut, you either fooked it up at University, failing your classes, or did something even bigger to really piss off mam and daidí. Can't be the usual things money make go away, you don't seem the type. Can't ever see you forcing some young lady to take your cock at a frat party or gettin' drunk and rolling over someone's nana leavin' the mini-mart with a trolly full of crisps. You've been tucked out here for something darker. Hidden from sight so you can't embarrass your aging parents with a legacy of disappointment."

Atticus took a deep breath and averted his eyes, shoulders sagging, head hanging. He took a moment to collect his thoughts before speaking. "Yeah. I suppose that's what happens when you write your dissertation on how religious hypocritical indoctrination of next wave evangelicals will be the downfall of modern America. Rich patriots, especially fastidious conservatives in the House, can't bear love a son who has a different vision of the future, even if it is merely hypothetical."

The table went quiet for a moment, everyone processing what had been said. Darnell gave Lexi a pensive look. She squeezed what was left of her bulb into her mouth. Drinking was supposed to be a time to let things out, sure, but she hadn't expected this. Who would?

"You're here to help us stay sane, sir," Keelin said, putting a hand on Atticus's shoulder. "I can't say you're not right about meself, and it wouldn't be fair if I did. Me Mam entertained a lot of men. May be true I don't know who me father is. She sold her body through a web cam, and a few times flesh to flesh, all so dirty folk could leer at their screens and make messes in their pants. But at least it's an honest living, one where she knew exactly how people were usin' her. The rest of us may not be so lucky knowin' how we're bein' fucked. But you know what else?"

"What?" he asked, picking at his fingernails. "Do tell."

"I know she loved me."

Lexi considered this. Love. Family. Complicated topics for everyone here but Darnell. Would she be a good mother? Or screw it all up like her parents had?

Keelin gave a swallow and let out a sigh. After a silent moment, Atticus reached back and took hold of her hand. The gesture was gentle in a way she hadn't expected, making her inhale. "You're lucky."

"Comes by birth," she replied, and wrapped her arms around him. "You know, you're such a cock waffle. And a terrible psychologist to boot."

"And you're a salty bitch." He raised his nearly empty bulb and pressed what was left into his mouth. "Well shit, I'm out of liquid happiness."

She squeezed him around the shoulders. "I appreciate the compliment."

Darnell shook his head and whispered to Lexi, "What a strange relationship they have."

"No shit," she replied.

"Hey guys!" Logan said, reappearing from among the crowd, their expression bright. "I may have met someone who might be able to help us with our problems."

"Help us with what?" Lexi asked, leaning forward. "And who?"

"Yeah." They raised their palms and went on. "Okay, so, they've got a job. Something big. Something where we can make at least a hundred times this shitty haul. No production deadlines. Maybe an advance to fix our shit."

"A rock?" Darnell perked up. "Please tell me I get to blow something up."

"Yes? No? Wait, maybe. I'm not so sure. It is a capture, though."

Darnell tipped his head forward and rolled his hands. "Go on, you're not making any sense."

They shook their hands. "Just come with me. The Captain is talking to them now. Easier to explain if we're all together."

Atticus patted Keelin on the hand, then sighed as if he were being forced out of a well-worn armchair. "Well then, I suppose we should see what all the fuss is about. Don't want the doctor's blood pressure spiking over nothing."

"People to impress, then," Keelin told him.

"Debts to pay," he responded.

And futures unrealized, Lexi thought.

[5] – Darnell

Captain Cho was waiting for the crew in one of the station's private communications rooms, a woman with brown skin and raven hair with her. As Darnell and the others entered, taking hold of soft hoops on the wall to secure themselves in null gravity, their conversation quieted.

The door closed and the captain took a sigh. "I can see you've been having fun." Her eyes settled on Keelin, who at this point was sweaty, her red hair a mad tangle. "The bill's going to be bad isn't it?"

Keelin flashed her teeth and gave a girlish chuckle.

Captain Cho closed her eyes and put a hand to her face before recovering. "Team, this is Sarita Anand. Sarita, the crew of the *Peridot*."

"Nice to meet you all," Sarita said, her tone pleasant. He wasn't sure why, but he'd expected an accent of some kind from the look of her, maybe Indian? But if he'd been on the phone with her, he would have sworn she was white and from Middle America. Was that thought wrong? Was it racist?

Katia went on, "Sarita would like to connect us with a man who just might be able to solve our cash flow issues. Potentially forever. I know I've made many promises to all of you, and as your captain I want to make good on those promises. That said, there will be risks and you are free to decline, but in the grand scheme of everything, this is easy money."

This statement gave Darnell a sense of disquiet. Easy money always smelled suspicious, no matter how many smiles and promises were given. He tugged on Lexi's sleeve to get her attention, but she shook her head.

"Let's go ahead and show them," Captain Cho told Sarita.

Sarita nodded and raised a tablet, tapping at its screen until the main display at the center of the room lit up. A recording of a pale, white man of late middle age appeared on the screen, his gray hair closely cropped, a set of round glasses resting high on his nose.

"Hello there. I'd like to introduce myself. My name is Car... well... maybe not. How about you call me—The Collector." The man was familiar, but Darnell couldn't say why. Familiar in a way that bothered him. *"I'd like to welcome all of you to my vault of American treasures,"* he went on, giving a gesture at the space around him. *"My collection."*

Darnell could do nothing but cock his head and blink. Lexi was just as stunned.

The Collector stood in a room with gravity, not a ship, surrounded by a museum's worth of objects. There were space capsules, from Apollo to Dragon. Cars from a dozen decades, Mustangs and Cadillacs. Pieces of buildings, brick and mortar and steel. Monuments of Civil War generals. Military uniforms in clear, hermetically sealed boxes. American flags by the dozen, some spattered with blood, some with too few stars. Modern firearms and muskets. Cast iron pieces of art, crosses and more, even the familiar Texas Star. It was a fortune of history as great as the Smithsonian's.

But where was this? And who the hell was this guy?

The Collector gave a grateful bow. *"America is not what it once was. We live in a day and age where the world has shifted, and global policies have changed. America is not first, or even second, we are somewhere else. And so, I am doing what is right, what is patriotic, preserving the past of the greatest nation that the world has ever known. Let them not forget the deeds and achievements of an exceptional people, a glorious nation."*

Music began to play within the museum, drums and brass instruments swelling into a full accompaniment. A woman sang in soprano.

Oh, say can you see, by the dawn's early light...

The Collector began to march in place, raising an invisible baton like a drum major standing before the band at a football game. Darnell felt the strings of his heart move. So many memories on the sidelines, honor given to his country even before kickoff. So many fireworks and parties on the Fourth, beers and barbecue, cold pies and soldiers given salutes as they returned from the Oil Wars.

"I aim to help others remember what makes America great," the Collector said. The music came to a stop. *"This is why I need your help. There is an item whose whereabouts I have acquired. An item which has been freely orbiting our solar system now for sixty-seven years. An item I will pay handsomely for the retrieval of. And guess what? Your flyer just happens to be large enough to retrieve it."*

In the corner of the screen another box appeared, a white, four-door convertible luxury car, all sleek features and smooth lines resolving into high resolution. Darnell felt his breath catch in his chest, as if the rest of this wasn't already a lot. Lexi took hold of his hand and squeezed till it hurt. He knew this car, it had made history, in both power and in blood.

"I can only assume that by now you are more than a little shocked to see what I have uncovered. And no, it is not the famed Tesla Roadster the great Elon Musk fired off into space in the year 2017 aboard a Falcon 9. Instead, it is its spiritual progeny. It is the achievement of the great billionaire heckler, Matteo Lindvall. I present to you, the Lindvall Slipstream, the first electric car to break two thousand miles of range on a single charge. The car, whose battery technology not only made America the most powerful nation in the world for almost half a century, but also plunged South America into war. America won again, just like we beat the Russians to the moon. We made the first true supercapacitor."

All Darnell could do was stand there and stare.

Everyone knew of Matteo Lindvall.

Born in Sweden, Matteo came to the United States on a H-1B visa after university and eventually became a nationalized US citizen. He first worked for a materials manufacturing and electrical grid transformation company, PlugON Energy Solutions, before developing his proof of concept based on his university thesis, the LindVOLT Cell. The LindVOLT Cell was a block of super capacitor materials, mainly graphene, that didn't just hold potential energy like most chemical batteries for later use. Instead, it trapped the electrons themselves within its super conductive matrix, making it the most efficient means of electrical storage to date. LindVOLT Cells held massive quantities of power for their modest size, could be charged in minutes, and due to their efficiency, produced little in way of heat waste. They were powerful, reliable, and safe to use. While Matteo was able to build a LindVOLT Cell in a laboratory, commercial scalability wasn't feasible. Many of its components were as thin as a single atom and difficult to array. That was, until his meeting with mathematician and AI expert, Justin Fairbanks. Justin joined Lindvall's team, and together they developed VERA, an advanced AI that would manage the production process of the LindVOLT Cells. Though the materials used in a LindVOLT Cell were commonly available anywhere on Earth, for fifteen years America controlled its production, and defended itself against imitations, thanks to VERA.

This invention, the LindVOLT Cell, was everywhere. Several were even on the *Peridot,* tending to backup systems and life support.

Needless to say, LindVOLT cars were an instant success, creating a waitlist that at times reached almost sixty million worldwide. The power cells were used in a thousand different industries as well, and as a result this created an unintended, disproportionate economic disparity between the United States and every other country in the world. An unfortunate side effect of this development was the sparking of the Oil Wars in South America, which had cost the lives of millions as oil barons fought to keep hold of what waning power they had left.

"Musk might have created safe electronic payments," Lexi began mumbling a line from high school history class, "the first popular electric car, and put people on Mars. But Matteo Lindvall gave America so much more power, not with the creation of his car, but its battery, that a million people died trying to hold on to the past."

And that car, the Slipstream, was still out there. It was still intact, its passengers suited in white staring off into the blackest black, simulacrums of hopeful spirits, never truly alive yet haunting the reaches of deep space.

"Who in the hell is this guy?" Darnell whispered, pointing to the Collector. "Reminds me a bit too much of my friend Austin's uncle."

"Our ticket to freedom," Logan supplied, their face bright.

Atticus raised his eyebrows. "Freedom, hmm? America. How poetic."

"Ain't this over the imitator?" Keelin mused. "The one who ripped off Elon Musk's Roadster stunt."

"One and the same," Atticus agreed. "Lindvall loved making a mockery of other billionaire's stunts. This was one of many. Might not have been his rocket that sent it up, but he put a car in space, gave it fake drivers, and played a parody cover of David Bowie's *Space Oddity*. Even the dashboard had the word KEEP CALM on the screen."

"All while knowin' he had the superior technology at the time."

"That's right."

"What a cocky dick."

"If I recall, he's quoted as saying, *'Doesn't matter who comes first, it matters only who does it best'*"

Lexi began touching her left arm with the fingertips of her right hand in a calming gesture. Darnell had seen this activity before when she was weighing out all the options of a difficult decision.

The Captain's eyes did not break from the screen. She stared in thought. Her mouth had become a hard line.

"I'm sure you have questions," the Collector went on. *"How did I find Lindvall's Slipstream? Isn't it illegal to recover these artifacts without the permission of those who first sent them into space? Isn't it possible that the UEI will prosecute if you're caught? All valid concerns, but most of them baseless when you consider one thing. Sarita, if you would be so kind, pause my playback and give them their offer."*

Sarita did so. "Alright. I am sure you have questions. The Collector, the man for which I work, wishes to offer you a hefty sum to recover Lindvall's Slipstream and return it to Luna Gateway. In order to receive your payment in full, you must exercise complete discretion. The Collector is a private man who does not wish anyone to know where he keeps his museum, especially the UEI. Do we understand?"

This was all too much for Darnell to process.

"When do we skip the foreplay, and you tell us how much encouragement we're getting?" Atticus asked, his arms crossed. "This patriotic dog and pony show is boring the hell out of me. It's a compelling fiction, I must say, but anyone can make a deep fake video of a nationalist with an offer you can't refuse."

Sarita gave him a grin. "Would two billion PAEN suffice to quell your boredom?"

Darnell felt his stomach drop as if they'd just ramped their Falkor drive up to full. For a moment he thought he might just puke. Two billion Pan American Exchange Notes? No damn way.

Keelin gave Atticus a surprised expression, her eyebrows raised.

"Sound okay?" she asked. "To prove that this is more than AI graphics and a creative mind, check your bank account."

They looked to one another, curious, then checked their hand terminals. Darnell blinked at what his screen was showing him. He saw a recent transaction for a deposit of one hundred and twenty thousand PAEN from an unknown source. This was more than he had netted since he went up the gravity well.

"Darnell," Lexi whispered.

"Butter my biscuit," he replied.

"Kaching," Keelin looked to Logan and gave them a soft punch on the shoulder. "I like your friends."

Captain Cho slipped her hand terminal back into her jumpsuit. "It seems the Collector knows how to make a girl feel good."

"I wouldn't say that," Sarita replied. "He does have deep pockets, though. So, you might want to consider getting those repairs made. I heard you guys are in quite the pickle."

"This is enough to even cover the bar tab," Keelin said, then nudged the captain with an elbow. "I'm inclined to have a few bottles sent over to me and me new friends' place after we're done 'ere. Can I order the repairs while we party?"

The captain hesitated for a moment, then nodded. Keelin started clicking away on her hand terminal. This pleased Sarita. Looked like the encouragement was theirs if they took the job or not.

"So, are we in?" she asked her crew. "Do you all want to make the biggest score of our careers before disappearing into the night?"

"So very cinematic," Atticus mused. "Much to be risked, even for us who have little to lose. Prison back home after being in null gravity for years would be agonizing."

"I don't think they send people to prison out here," Darnell spoke up. "Artifact acquisition isn't exactly legal. You hear what the authorities were planning to do with that guy who stole the Chinese satellite? We just saw him get caught."

Logan raised their hands. "You know, it's only a crime if you get caught."

Darnell's eyebrows narrowed. Could people really be bought that easy? He looked to Lexi for assistance, for a way out of this, but her eyes were glazed over in thought.

Keelin crossed her arms and drew her knees up to her elbows. "You know what they say, if it's drowning you're after, don't torment yourself with shallow water. I'm all in."

"Fine," Atticus said, nodding towards her. "I suppose I'll follow this red-headed degenerate wherever she's off to."

"So sweet you are."

"A peach."

"Of course I'm in," Logan said, pointing a finger at the paused screen. "I don't give a shit if this guy smells of a hypocritical, flag toting asshole. Money spends either way and no one is getting hurt. When this is over, I can make a real difference. I've always wanted to open a clinic."

"Let's do this," Lexi said, no hint of restraint in her tone.

Darnell's chest tightened. Everyone was so eager to rush in without thinking about the consequences. He took hold of Lexi's arm and drew her close. He didn't mean for his grip to be so tight, but from the look on her face it was. He let go.

"We would be breakin' the law," he whispered in her ear. "You saw what happened with that fella."

"So?" she said. "We will never get what we want if we keep going at this rate. This is our chance... Besides, it was all hearsay. How do we even know they plan to toss him out an airlock?"

"Are we agreed then?" Captain Cho looked to her crew one last time. "Sarita, tell the Collector we will take his assignment."

She gave a nod. "Splendid. He will be pleased. I'll meet you back aboard the *Peridot* tomorrow after all the arrangements are made."

The Captain blinked. It wasn't often Cho was taken by surprise. "You'll what?"

"Did you think you were going alone? You'll need me for this job."

"No. There's no way. My flyer, my rules. I don't know who the hell you are."

"You'll never locate the Slipstream without me." Sarita crossed her arms. "Are we agreed?" She waited for a moment before speaking again. "Two billion PAEN. Just so you don't forget. Two—billion. That's a lot of zeros, and as we all know, zeros get us the best things in life."

The Captain thought that over for what felt like an eternity, her expression like stone, then gave a reluctant nod.

"Oh! And I almost forgot." Sarita pressed a button and the video resumed.

The Collector gave the camera a hungry smile. *"Let's not forget what made America glorious once more."* He gave a wave of his arm and began to spin in circles, the music starting back up, red, white and blue confetti falling from the ceiling, but slow. *"Those vapor-headed heathens who brought us God's wrath might have forgotten, but we haven't, have we? We haven't let the soul of the greatest nation to grace God's green Earth fade away. America will rise again, with liberty and justice for all."*

The crew looked to one another and smiled, their grins wide with the lust of money, not patriotism. They had tasted the barest hint of its tainted sweetness and were hungry for more.

Darnell stared at his hand terminal, dumbstruck, a few too many zeros extending from his bank balance. Nothing about this situation felt of liberty, only a pipedream trap with a snare. This wasn't the American dream. No, this was madness.

[6] - Lexi

It wasn't hard for Lexi to see Darnell's displeasure over what had just gone down. He brooded all the way back to the *Peridot*, his eyes narrow, muscles tight. He had a lot to say about this topic, he just wasn't willing to let it all out in front of the crew and make a scene, let alone with some stranger around. Too bad for him. The crew was energized as hell, Lexi included. Every one of them was musing over things that would be there's on the other end of this. How it would improve their quality of life in such incalculable ways.

For her part, she found herself envisioning the baby room on Luna, the colors and patterns she would cover the walls in. Pinks and purples with yellow stars and unicorns. Her baby's name - Janica, Devon, Lauren, whatever it might end up being - was sketched on the wall in a flowing, three-dimensional script. She and Darnell would take turns getting up at night, feeding their little bundle of joy and rocking them to sleep, a tiny, warm body letting out soft breaths against their chest.

Could this be true? Could this really be happening?

Once they were back in their quarters with the door shut, Darnell began to massage his face and groan. "What in the hell is everyone thinking?" he began.

She took a deep breath and collected her thoughts. She had to keep the emotion out of this discussion. "Look, beau, we can't live out here forever. You know it. Space will destroy our bodies, if not our minds. This is an option to get us out. Get us what we really want before we're too wrecked to enjoy it."

"Do I even get a say? It's like this decision was made without me."

"You could have spoken up."

"Could I?" He threw up his hands. "Would that have been okay? I'd have been looked at like I was just some stupid-ass country boy."

"You're not stupid," she said, putting a hand on his shoulder.

He shrugged it off and crossed his arms. "Lexi, what we're doing is illegal. If we get caught, then as soon as we hit a safe port, the law will come down on us like a hammer. Hell, we'll be tossed out an airlock like that guy back on the station probably was. Too much trouble. Nowhere to keep us. I don't mean to bring up old events, and all, but it's not like you have the cleanest history neither."

And even though this was true, this comment cut deep. He had always been in her corner. Was he starting to see her differently now? The accident hadn't made her a criminal, had it? Maybe foolish, but not a criminal.

She sucked in a deep breath then let out her feelings. "I know, babe, but I don't see any other way."

"The other way is, we do what we're hired to do." He tossed his chin back. "We mine gold. An honest living."

She stared off into empty space and rubbed her fingertips across her lips, focusing on how it felt, the crackle of nerves, sensitive and alive. "No, Darnell, I'm done hauling gold. I'm done living for a distant dream. I want what's mine."

"What did you say?" His eyes widened.

"I said, I'm fucking done hauling gold," she raised her voice, not caring if the rest of the crew could hear her through their thin privacy door. "This is ridiculous. All of it. We're giving our lives away to make someone else rich. Sure, this is to help save humanity and all, but we all know there's some fat cat reaping the lion's share of the benefits. It's how it works. When's it going to be our time? Our turn? Huh? When are we going to get a choice about what happens in our life? I'm taking control. You want a family? Well, cheer up Charlie, this is our golden ticket."

A pained expression took hold of his face, one she had never seen. One overburdened and lost, a look of both sadness and disappointment, like a dull blade was being driven into his chest.

"Lexi..." he pleaded. "This is not the way. It's wrong, and you know it. It's wrong."

She wrapped her arms around him and held him tight, trying to get him to calm down. "Just trust me. It will be okay. Please, trust me."

After a long pause, in which Lexi questioned what might happen next, he pulled her tight as well, their bodies pressed together. "I do trust you. I just don't trust greed. I don't trust the Collector."

A chuckle escaped her chest. "No one does. I don't even believe Sarita does."

"But she *works* for him."

"So?" Lexi met his eyes, her expression softening at his naivety. "You don't run in circles like that and trust everyone involved. You can bet on it."

A knock came at the door. Lexi pushed off and slid it open.

"We're almost ready," Captain Cho said, her expression hard, all thought and business. "Everything okay in here?"

Lexi put on her best attempt at a fake smile. "Everything is just fine."

This did not appease the captain. She gave Darnell a hard look then sighed. "We'll need all hands on-deck for this one. According to Sarita, we might even need charges."

"Hooray," Darnell said, lacking his usual enthusiasm for blowing things up.

"Lexi," the captain said. "Come with me. Mr. Richardson, you might want to get some sleep."

He waved a dismissive hand as she and the captain left the room. Lexi hated leaving things unsaid. She knew Darnell was not on board with this, and there was a part of her who couldn't blame him. This was dangerous and stupid and lucrative as hell. If things went shit sideways, they were fucked. And with her record...

She knew that Darnell wasn't wrong. She just couldn't let this go. What it could mean for them was too great.

Lexi slid into her acceleration chair and began the *Peridot's* preflight checks, her eyes drifting to the half dozen pictures she had taped to the console's empty bits of real estate. There were images of her and Darnell, the crew smiling after a long haul, her sisters back home with her nieces and nephews in matching outfits. Tiny moments of happiness captured in tiny panels of amorphochromic zink paper.

Keelin had the flyer almost refueled, the repairs to the Falkor's uranium storage made. With their fresh infusion of funding, the work was a simple rush job, and now their flyer was ready to burn. Atticus and Logan brought the last of the hard goods on board: food and water, and of course, plenty of liquor. All Lexi needed was a destination to plot their course.

Sarita settled into the acceleration chair beside Lexi and smiled, flashing a set of pearlescent white teeth and wide almond eyes. "Eager to get started?"

"Eager to get it done," Lexi replied through tight lips.

"I like your attitude." She lifted a tablet and began to punch buttons on its screen. "Open up your console's network. I'll dump the navigational data over to you. It's not perfect, so we'll have to search around a bit when we get there."

Lexi did as she was instructed. Data began to transfer to *the Peridot's* main computer.

"Nice ship you guys have here," Sarita said, turning around in her seat and inspecting the bridge. "Nice ship. Looks like a lot of love has been given to take care of it. You'd be surprised how many crews trash their ships."

"Flyer," Lexi corrected her.

"What was that?"

"We call them flyers," Lexi went on. "Not ships. 'Ship' is reserved for the big ones, like the colony ships. Foundry fleet starships, you know, FICSE."

"Oh." She seemed surprised at this. "Still... Good job."

"Way we see it, when you love something, you take care of it."

Twenty-five percent of the navigational data had transferred. Lexi willed it to finish faster. She needed to get done with this and wrap up her talk with Darnell. She knew she had hurt his feelings and needed to make it right, or as right as she could.

"Everything seems disposable these days," Sarita commented. "Even relationships. People don't show hardly any care."

This comment hit Lexi's ears and made her hackles stand on end. She twisted in her chair to meet the woman's eyes. "You haven't been out in the black very long, have you?"

"Why do you say that?"

"When you live in the void," Lexi paused for a moment, turning back around to flick several switches on her panel before proceeding, "nothing is disposable. Ever. This is not some on-demand existence. You have only what you've brought with you."

"Well, you might be surprised how quickly that can change," Sarita replied. "Might not be two-day shipping, but if you have the money, you can get damn near anything you want or need. And despite what the UEI claims, there's not much oversight to this."

The data transfer's progress bar seemed to have gotten stuck at fifty percent.

"Can I ask a question?" Lexi cut her a sidelong look.

The woman shrugged. "Sure."

"Why work for the Collector?"

"Because I love America?" she mused, the corner of her right lip curling. "The land of the free, and home of the brave."

"Mmmhmm. How much is he paying you?"

"Sooo much." She tapped on her tablet several times and the transfer resumed. "But to be honest that isn't my biggest motivation."

"Then what is?"

A crooked smile crossed her face and was gone, replaced by an expression of forced neutrality. "I love the idea of America, if not always its implementation. Freedom though, that's something else. I grew up in the states, Northern California to be exact, a little town outside Sacramento. When I was eighteen, my family said we were going home. It seemed crazy to me because Cali was home. But home for them? That was Panipat, India, just north of New Delhi. I was to marry a boy named Samar, everything had all been arranged. He was handsome and rich.

They would adorn me in gold for the wedding, all traditional, even though I guess gold isn't what it once was. But you see, the thing is, I didn't really care for that idea. Being told what to do wasn't my thing. Feel me? And, well, I don't care too much for physical intimacy with men."

"Oh."

"Yeah, oh. My girlfriend and I ran away from home. Not like it was illegal or anything, I was eighteen and all. Still, haven't talked much to my family since."

"Family can be hard," Lexi said, tapping the progress bar on her display as if it might make the thing unstick. "They always think they know best. Tend to force on us what they didn't see happen in their own life. You know, their ideas of what life and happiness are."

"Preach it, sister."

"So then, your motivation for working for the Collector is just freedom? Financial freedom away from a family that doesn't get you?"

Sarita frowned, her gaze going distant. "Close enough. Sure. Having means gives you options. Right? What's family look like for you?"

"Me? Shit." Lexi took a deep breath. How much was she willing to unpack on this auspicious day? "My parents were more concerned with their friends and going to clubs than giving my sisters and I much time. Always traveling to festivals, running around in their little celebrity group, drinking all night with streamers and singers, and sleeping all day." She tapped on a photo beside a monitor of her and her sisters outside Disney World, each wearing Mickey Mouse ears, faces wide with bright smiles, each with a leg kicked up, peace signs flashing. "So long as Mom and Dad had new clothes and a party to be at, they were happy."

Sarita chuckled. "Your parents sound cool as shit."

"Wouldn't say that." Lexi swallowed. So many family trips minus her parents. Their choice. Their loss. No reason to relive it. Time to move on. "Anyways, how's the girlfriend?"

"The girlfriend? Oh, that bitch?" Sarita tossed back her head, chuffing. "Who can say? I've had six other ones since. I really know how to pick the winners. That particular one was addicted to opiates and tried to knife me one night in a Henter's Inn over twenty bucks. She needed a fix. A big scene broke out and before I knew it, we were both in cuffs. I didn't even get to enjoy my breakfast of stale bagels and dry scrambled eggs."

Lexi's eyebrows rose. "You like the crazy ones too?"

"They're the best. You never know what the hell they'll get up to. And in bed…"

Several mixed memories rose to the surface of Lexi's mind, filled with both pain and pleasure. Steamy nights with boys she had no business being associated with. Twilight races along the back highway inside a roaring Mustang. Underground junkyard parties with DJs snorting high-grade coke off retro control vinyl. Watching the sun rise three days in a row from a bass-filled park full of people, not a wink of sleep to be had. Nights hoping that no one saved those private snaps you sent out like digital candy in a drunken flurry of attention-seeking.

To be honest, it was a wonder she hadn't been arrested before the incident.

"Look, it's like I said, I work for the Collector for the money," Sarita admitted, but it felt like a dodge. "Money gives you freedom, okay? 'Merica. That's not all, though. America may be messed up at times, but it gave me the freedom to be who I am, more or less. If I had gone back home to India, I would have lived a miserable existence married to a man I wouldn't ever want to be with, and out of shame, I would have borne a whole houseful of children. It wouldn't have been fair to him or me. Not to mention that I would have lived under a stupid-ass caste system that despite the best efforts of radical social agitators, is alive and well even today. It wasn't the life for me. Bunch of bull."

The control panel chirped. Transfer complete.

"Alright." Lexi went to work. "Time to start plotting us a course."

She wondered for a moment how Darnell might consider his own sordid young adult years. Did he ever even break a rule, let alone the law? She wasn't pure enough for such a man. Then again, she knew he was just what she needed. But damn, what she wouldn't give to sweat her ass off in a crowd of strangers with chemically lifted moods connecting them to the Universe. The chase, the game, hiding away from those who just wished to ruin a good night. These kinds of moments always made her feel alive.

Several quiet seconds passed, and Sarita spoke again, "Would you take back your crazy days?"

Lexi wasn't sure how Sarita had seen the wheels turning. Was her face so plain, or was this woman telepathic? It had to be just a good guess.

"The past makes us who we are," Lexi replied, and flicked a few switches on her panel.

"I like that answer."

"May I be candid?"

Sarita cocked her head, eyes narrowing. "What do you mean?"

"Can we trust the Collector? Can we trust you? This opportunity came out of nowhere."

"Are you looking for assurances?"

"Maybe."

She thought about this for a minute then tapped her tablet. "Another twenty grand won't hurt, will it?"

Lexi's hand terminal chimed. She didn't reach for it. "You're just going to buy me off?"

"Real trust takes too long to build. I have no bridges here. Can you trust the Collector? So long as he gets what he wants, yes. Can you trust me? Well... I just want to get paid. You feel me?"

The navigational display flashed, and Lexi shook her head. Their rough course had been plotted. "Hang on, we're headed to Saturn?"

"Damn right we are." Sarita shot her with a finger gun, teeth clicking. "Transponder off. Reactor cold as can be. There's a rock with caves out there, and the Slipstream is trapped inside it. Find it. Crack it. Take the goods."

"And what if the UEI find us?"

"It'll be fine." She smiled. "Trust me." But that expression of hers did not inspire any trust, it showed too many teeth, like a used flyer salesman trying to push off wrecked goods.

"I do not think that word means what you think it means," Lexi said as she prepared the *Peridot* for egress.

"Whatever." Sarita gestured with an open hand in a wave.

Lexi clicked a switch on her panel and spoke, "Alright everyone. Grab a strap. We're about to get moving." She waited a moment, checking the status reports to be sure the air lock had been closed and everyone was on board. The system pinged the hand terminals of all crew members and came back clear. "Stratus base, this is *Peridot*. Call back."

"Stratus base," the UEI traffic controller squawked over the intercom.

"Request lock disengage."

"Confirm air lock secured on your end."

"Confirmed. All crew members aboard."

"Have you submitted a flight plan?"

Sarita swiped at her tablet then nodded. The modified flight plan appeared on Lexi's console. It had them reaching all the way out to Neptune, which was not their destination. It felt a bit dirty to lie like this.

"Sending now," Lexi said, transmitting it back to the station. What other option was there?

A moment passed and then another. She began to sweat. Maybe this had been a bad idea. The controller would see right through this, wouldn't he? Who chased rocks all the way out to Neptune?

The radio kicked off static. *"Off to crack another rock, I see."*

"Always."

"Pretty long haul."

"Got a good tip."

"Sure is a lot of reaction mass to burn. Think you can turn a profit?"

"We'll see. What's life without a little adventure?"

"Roger that. Stay safe out there, Peridot.*"*

"We will," Lexi said, and clicked off the open channel.

"Trust," Sarita whispered under her breath, and in the reflection of a dark panel, Lexi could see a wry smile forming on her face. "Trust."

[7] – Darnell

If one thing was clear about their situation, it was that they were in a big, damned hurry. When Lexi had made the call for everyone to strap in, Darnell had expected an uncomfortable burn, but nothing this hard. Everyone in place, their Falkor drive initiated, a third gen compact NTP engine capable of over a thousand kN of thrust, and they screamed off into the black at a blinding five G's of acceleration, holding steady at this clip for three hours and fifty-four minutes. Just a decade earlier, and a maneuver like this wouldn't have even been possible. What had once been science fiction was now science fact. Darnell felt as if an Olympic barbell had been laid across his chest and it was compressing bone. It was the longest burn he had ever endured, his chest and arms and muscles sore after it was over.

Saturn was now before them, but where did that put the Slipstream's location? This was an intercept. Was the car traveling that fast? Had it been accelerated over the decades beyond the initial launch? Or was there another motivation? Were they the only ones after it? Was this a competition? Each additional question made him ever more uncomfortable.

Once their burn was complete, they'd reached a cruise velocity of six hundred and thirty-five kilometers a second, but you'd never know it. The *Peridot* was now in freefall, no gravity to hold them to the bulkhead.

Another couple of years of this and he'd never be able to set foot in Texas again.

Since eating while under several times Earth's gravity was a bad idea, Darnell was hungry by now. He nodded in Lexi's direction, who was still strapped in her acceleration chair, and she read his mind, reaching into a compartment beside her and tossing him a protein bar.

"I wonder if it's true," Logan said, unbuckling, taking a stretch.

"If what's true?" Darnell tore into the chocolate flavored block and let out a sigh as it settled on his empty stomach.

"Rumor has it, there's supposed to be some sort of secret aboard the Slipstream."

"A secret?"

"Urban legend, more like," Atticus replied.

Keelin spun and scowled at the psychologist. "How you fancy that?"

"Why in God's green Earth would Matteo Lindvall hide something important in a car he tossed into deep space without any means to recover it? This went up in 2028. There was no chance of getting it back. No Space Force. No UEI."

"Had to hide them plans to the escape keys of this simulation and keep the overlords from findin' out."

Captain Cho's eyebrows raised. "I haven't thought about simulation theory in years. Are there still people who believe in that?" She opened a black bag of Exo-Bites and reached inside, popping a couple of the beige squares into her mouth.

"Oh God yes." Keelin nodded. "Got to escape the Matrix somehow. Let's not forget, some people still believe the world is flat."

"Stupidest things I've ever heard," Atticus said. "Are we sure lead paint isn't still being used in home construction?"

Logan raised a finger. "But how can you disprove it?" Their tone was sarcastic. "Tell me that."

"Have you looked out the window lately?"

This made the doctor smile.

"They do have them neural meshes coming out soon." Keelin stole one of the captain's bites from right out of her bag and bit it in half, a sheepish expression on her face as Katia rolled her eyes. "Maybe it's

Lindvall's technical plans for early prototypes in the Slipstream. Them brain implants we've all been promised."

Atticus groaned. "Doubtful."

"I'm with him," Darnell agreed. "Secrets in the Slipstream? Sounds like fake news to me."

"You might be surprised," Sarita said, her voice wry. "The Slipstream is like a time capsule. There's no telling what might have been stuffed in the glove compartment. Could be knickknacks, could be something more valuable than the car itself."

Darnell wasn't one for mysteries, but this had his interest piqued. What would he have hidden in there if he were Lindvall? Something comical or ironic? A pack of crisps or a couple protein bars for Centrum and Kósmos, the car's driver and their passenger? An atlas of celestial bodies? A few books to read on the long trip? No way of knowing.

Lexi pored over the navigational computer while polishing off her protein bar. After some time, she began to nod as if coming to a conclusion. "We're good. It will take about a week for us to cross some 4.3 AU. We'll have to pull a hard slowdown. Hope you're all up for it."

Sarita gave a nod and pushed off towards the hall. "Guess that means I better get to work."

"On what?" Darnell called after her.

"What do you think?" She disappeared through the open portal and the hatch slid shut.

He groaned and turned his attention to the captain. If God was looking to put him square in the middle of a situation that could have made him any more uncomfortable, he wouldn't know what it would be. "For real... Why is she here?"

"Because she has to be," the Captain replied.

"But can we trust her?"

"Can I trust you?" Katia's expression hardened, eyebrows crowding her face.

"You have something you need to say in front of the crew, Captain?" His back bowed up, and he could feel his face turning hot again.

She crossed her arms and narrowed her eyes. "Only that it would be nice if we didn't fuck this up. Should I be concerned about that?"

"Maybe you should."

"Hey, hey, Darnell," Logan said in a soft voice, putting a hand on his shoulder. "Let's head over to the med bay and check up on those shins of yours."

"What?" Darnell blinked at them. He turned to Lexi for assistance, but she said nothing, attention on her screens. "What are you talking about?"

"Didn't you bang them up last time you went through the airlock?" Logan went on, cocking their head to the side and offering a fake smile. "I've got some cream, well, it's more like a jelly. Anyways, it'll make them feel better." They took his hand and pulled him towards the exit. "Come on, don't be a big baby."

Lexi flicked her eyes towards the hatch in a not-so-subtle hint. He could tell she knew he was about to make a scene, and was trying to tell him that this wasn't the time nor the place. Maybe she was right.

"Fine. Whatever, Doc."

"That's it." Logan nodded to the captain. "See you later, Ma'am."

Logan led them to the end of the main hall to a room not much bigger than the quarters he shared with Lexi. Like most spaces in the *Peridot*, it was multifunctional, acting as both their medical bay and a bedroom. The space was bright and clean, stark white walls with daylight white LEDs glowing along every angle. What wasn't white, was blood red by contrast, bulkheads populated with rows of boxes stamped with medical crosses on their face. On one side of the room was a foldable examination bed with straps, white diagnostic equipment with blinking lights mounted on goosenecks. Their space was all utility. Sterile. Lacking in decoration. A contradiction to their personality.

They slid the door closed and glared at Darnell.

"What in the hell is this about?" he asked without preamble. "My shins are fine. Back hurts a little from the burn but damn..."

"You've got problems with this don't you," they said, matter of fact.

"Of course I do." He threw his hands up in exasperation. "We're breaking the damned law and it ain't right."

"Well.. that all depends on your perspective. As far as the UEI, maybe we are, but who gives them authority?"

"Don't play the debate game." He rubbed his face and shook his head. "Does an international agreement mean nothing?"

"Tell me what it means this far into deep space. Unless they can enforce it, it's not really a law."

"So, if I kill you and stuff your body in an airlock, because they can't enforce it, it ain't illegal?"

"Shut up. That's different. There's moral and ethical implications."

"Which are both in jeopardy when you do something illegal. Like stealing..."

Logan scratched at the back of their neck. The lights on their arm flashed red for an instant. "Okay, so maybe the laws out here are a little more flexible. If morals are your concern, stealing this doesn't hurt anyone. Who cares?"

"These mental gymnastics are making my head hurt somethin' fierce." He closed his eyes and rubbed them with his palms. "What happened to a simple world?"

"Here," they said, handing him a slender tube filled with a liquid NSAID pain reliever. "Should help with the muscle tension from our burn."

He took the medicine and scowled at the bitter taste. "You put this deal together, didn't you? Logan, I've known you a while and this don't seem like you."

"Meh. Opportunity seldom knocks twice." They paused for a moment, choosing their words, a finger to their lips. "Yes, I sort of put this together. I met a guy, who knew a girl, who had a friend. That sort of thing. I don't want to miss the chance to give us a better life. I don't want this just for me."

"Do you trust her? Sarita."

"Ehhh, not really. And then yes. I mean..."

Darnell raised his hands, palms up. "Look, I just want to make an honest living. What I do affects people other than just me."

And if he got caught, why would the fed let his family keep their special tax credit? That was one of the biggest reasons he was here. That credit helped his family and their ranch far more than he could working the land or sending money back.

"And that's sweet, it really is," Logan said. "Nothing wrong with that ideal. It's just, well, not the situation we're in. Stuck in an endless loop of unprofitable rock hauls isn't exactly where I wanted to be in my thirties. I have dreams of my own."

"Dreams? What kind of dreams?"

They opened a cabinet and began removing tiny bottles one at a time, reorganizing them as they spoke. "Five years back, when I was looking to get in on this business, it was hella lucrative. The wide-eyed, middle twenties person I was at the time signed up in the hopes of making a difference by first earning some quick cash. A couple years in a flyer patching up Void-Striders like yourself, then head back home. And with that money I'd have the freedom to give back. Treat people in the developing world."

His brows furrowed. "Like where?"

"Honduras." They inspected one bottle in particular, gave it a shake, then returned it to the cabinet with a frown. "Fund my own clinic. See what good I could do. *¡Qué macizo!*"

He considered this a moment, not surprised. They did always lend a hand when someone else needed it, especially those things involving their specialized skills in medicine. "Why not ever tell us?"

"Some dreams are too big to voice. Maybe I was afraid by talking about it, the whole idea might fall apart."

Darnell let out a sigh. "Well, I suppose that's a pretty noble dream. Wish you felt comfortable enough to share."

"I don't talk much about my personal life." They closed the door to the cabinet and clicked the lock. "It's easier to keep things on the surface."

"Why Honduras?"

Logan shrugged. "Fell in love with someone from Comayagua once upon a time. They turned me on to how beautiful the culture could be. Not really a place that gets much attention in the states, except by missionaries, and what with the Fifth Great Awakening, Hondurans have had their fill. Central America gets a bad rap. It's not all crime and cocaine. I mean, it has amazing beaches, its green and mountainous, good beer, warm and sunny. I know I'm making it sound like a vacation spot, but the people are great. There's such a range of emotion. Hondurans will love you easy and are offended just as quick. There's food everywhere, every street corner, every bus stop, *baleados*, *tajadas*, you name it. And... well... their lackadaisical attitude when it comes to showing up on time fits my personality quite fine. So laid back."

A thought occurred to Darnell. "Wait, hang on, isn't Honduras where that biohacker scene cropped up?"

"Maybe?" They averted their eyes and shrugged. "Just because not everyone supports the post humanist movement doesn't make it wrong. It's my body."

"I just don't see how those, *augmentations*, help you. They just seem more like novelties."

"That so?" They leaned back against the bulkhead and rubbed their chin. "Alright, dude. Goes to show how ignorant you are about this. Biohacking is not all about technological augmentations, though those are pretty amazing. It's also about being able to analyze the world around you and the one within you. Organic life is just a collection of tiny machines. Ever wonder if that steak you had for dinner was really Kobe beef? I could tell you without a chemistry set. Need to create a sensor that can detect pollutants in water? I have one connected to my right index finger, and it's biological, not mechanical. Can we cheat death through gene manipulation? Just maybe. All the results of bio-hacks and body modification. All a means of reprogramming the tiny machines that live in and make up our bodies."

This made his eyebrows raise. "You want to live forever?"

"Not forever. Nothing lives forever. But hey, what could a life accomplish if I reached the ripe old age of two hundred? Three hundred? How much more could I contribute? A hell of a lot more than fixing your banged-up shins, tell you that."

"Fair point," Darnell sighed. "So, you want to change the world?"

Logan's face split into a wide grin. "Who doesn't? Things are bad enough, let's make them better. Save the planet a person at a time if we have to. Why do you think the UEI formed FICSE in the first place? For once, it's not political fat or special interests. There's something out there that isn't human, some kind of alien intelligence far beyond our understanding, and it offered to help us. Offered to save the world."

"FICSE is fine and all, but things have always been bad." He let out a long breath, his chest aching from holding it in. He needed to relax, or this job would end in a cardiac arrest. "Life is impartial. Evil will always exist."

"So that's a good enough excuse not to try?" They cocked their head and frowned. "Didn't take you for the lazy, apathetic type."

"It's just that, changing the world sounds like too big a task. I'm one man."

"Tsk tsk tsk. Such narrow vision."

His eyes widened. "You mocking me?"

"No. Challenging you. We all have the power to make the world a better place. Ask yourself, what are you doing to realize that future?"

"So were stealing to fund it?"

"Sometimes you gotta do what you gotta do. Work with the opportunities you're given." Logan poked him on the chest with a finger. "Laws haven't caught up to reality. Ask your girlfriend."

Darnell hung his head and shook it, rubbing the spot they poked. "I'm starting to wonder if anyone on this flyer has the barest hint of morals."

"If it makes you feel better, when the cops come knocking, I'll tell them it wasn't your idea."

And, well, he was surprised to find that this statement did indeed make him feel a tiny bit better. Very tiny. Maybe he was the one in the wrong, a chicken afraid to get what he deserved in life. Would this make his family proud? Go and get what's yours. Or, if he was caught, would he become a pariah? That was a whole host of people to condemn him.

The door slid open.

"You fix him up?" Lexi was floating in the opening, her arms crossed.

Logan glanced over their pilot's shoulder down the hall. "I don't think anything can fix him."

"Good to know I'm not the only one who struggles with their work. Besides, he's pretty great how he is." Lexi waved for them to follow. "We've got a message from the Collector. Come on, let's go watch."

They gathered on the bridge and the Captain gave a gesture for Sarita to start the recording. It was unfortunate they couldn't speak to this man in real-time, but communication didn't work that way in deep space. A signal from Luna or Mars and back could take hours due to light-speed lag. Darnell hoped this message would put him at ease.

The video began, this time coming from a smaller room than the other message where patriotic posters of former world wars hung on the walls. The Collector was dressed as if he were about to hit the campaign trail, in a gray synth suit and black tie complete with an American flag lapel pin.

"I am so very, very pleased to hear you have accepted my assignment, my cause," he began. *"Together we shall preserve one of America's great artifacts. After the Pandemic, which was such a dark, dark mark in world history, America was looking for ways to rebuild its economy. To jump start and get things going again. Our great administration of the day, led by one of the most visionary men ever born, put policies in place so that opportunity abounded. It was time for a new economy. An on-demand, capitalist economy. Jobs and lives lived in the cloud, no room for socialist freeloading and infinite government debt. And what happened? Gig economics powered by platform technology thrived. But oil wasn't in high demand like it once was, and despite all our romantic nostalgia for the hard-working man who toiled beneath the Earth, hauling coal to the surface to feed his family, that life had lost its competitive edge.*

"Times had changed, and America found itself at the forefront of a ubiquitous, clean energy movement with Mr. Lindvall at the wheel, making us independent with the first electric car that wasn't just for kombucha drinking snowflakes. That Slipstream out there may not have come first, but it was the best. With its three hundred and fifty horsepower, five hundred and fifty pounds of torque. Zero to sixty in four seconds flat. It was an inspiration to anyone who had ever drafted blueprints. Let's see your toe-sucking coworker's Prius do the same. Those rolling cages are good for nothing more than for a man's purple-haired bitch to get her groceries in."

Lexi took a deep breath, as did Captain Cho and Keelin. Sarita rolled her eyes and crossed her arms. Darnell wondered if he had missed something.

He tapped his lip, wondering what in the hell a Prius was. Lexi was just a few feet to his right, he could ask her, but was too embarrassed. For some reason the word conjured a mental image of a chubby gray gerbil turning a wheel. That couldn't be right, could it? He'd owned a truck back home, one hundred percent electric, charged by the solar array on the back of the ranch, with a Lindvolt Cell at its heart, but his Ram 3500e was no golf cart. It was a workhorse. Besides, what's a snowflake? Was that an insult?

"Do you ever think there's too many rules?" the Collector went on. *"I remember back when a man could say his fuckin' mind, exercise his free speech about those thugs and rapists who cross our border. Damn did I love their food, and damn did I love their peak nose candy, but they ruined our country. They took away jobs from hard working Americans hit by the layoffs, forced us into more stimulus, more deficit spending, inflation, inflation, inflation. Should have built that wall, would have fixed everything."*

The Collector raised his hands in a pleading gesture. *"Look, look, I'm not a bad guy for thinking this. For saying it. Just unafraid. If only the platforms had blocked undocumented folks from participating in the gig economy, those jobs would have been left for the rest of us. We're overrun nowadays, near thirty percent of every city less than English speaking. Who has time to learn another language? And a K-shaped economic recovery? My ass. It was bull. There's your precious transparency.*

"I'm sure by now you're concerned that your actions are considered illegal in the eyes of the UEI, recovering an artifact. But here's the deal. Here's—the—deal. America is more important. The UEI has been watered down by international interests. They aren't putting our country at the forefront. America should be first. Always first."

America first, Darnell's thoughts echoed. *Never last.* It had to be that way. Gramps always told him so.

"Your country, not mine," Keelin mumbled, her nose wrinkling. "Devil may break your spine, fooker."

"Shh," Sarita and Logan said.

"This artifact belongs in the hands of Americans. Real Americans." The Collector tugged on his lapels and hardened his expression. *"Hard-*

working Americans with grit and God in their heart. There are countless examples of the great American spirit, many of which sit right over my shoulder, ingenuity to take the world forward, tact in international policies, and an indomitable spirit against such oppressors as Hitler and Hussein and Brazofsky. The Slipstream is just another beautiful example of this."

Darnell perked up, his thoughts spinning. There was something here he connected with.

He was a hard-working American with grit. Right? He had grown up in Texas where the Hispanic population was substantial, but he couldn't recall ever missing out on work over a single one. He'd always had enough to keep himself busy. The family ranch. Their cattle. School. Football. It all paid in one way or another. Then again, something stirred in him in listening to the Collector. Illegals had interrupted his way of life from time to time. And the UEI, even if they had indirectly afforded him a career, had put a burden on America's economy with both the colonization project and the fleets bound for the Foundry. Alien signal promising help? That shit was likely background radiation humanity had just spent seven trillion dollars chasing, a sum paid for by an additional ten percent in income tax for just about every citizen in the developed world. What's done was done, but he hoped it was not a mistake.

"America," he went on, *"a land where anyone can build the life they want. A land of dreams and opportunity. A land without limits, so long as you work your ass off and pay your taxes. So long as you come here the right way and play by the rules."*

"Is there a mute button on this monologue?" Atticus asked, rolling a hand impatiently. "My ears are bleeding at the absurdity. I could use some gauze, Logan."

"Shh," the Captain said, a finger to her lips.

"Inspiration and vision are what America needs today. A reminder of more traditional times. A devout man, a Godly man, at the head of his house leading the nuclear family under the direction of the good Lord's teachings. We've lost it and the world is suffering for this."

Darnell sighed. Was he right? Maybe the world had gone sideways. Morals had eroded. That much was clear. For most of the past century, the church hadn't been important. There were cities in the north that didn't even have places of worship. Where would people learn how to follow biblical teachings if not in church?

"God would not have brought this plague of climate change upon our world if prayer had remained in our schools. The pledge said every morning before class began. One nation, under God. God! Don't get me started on the Islamists. The socialists. The atheists. All those 'ists'. Just the Devil in sheep's clothing."

Atticus hissed and began rubbing his face, eyes closed. "Zeus help us."

Darnell glanced over at Atticus and scratched the back of his head.

He hated the Collector for what he was asking them to do, and yet, and yet...

Some of what he said between these disparate bits of ranting hit different.

Things had been good. America had been glorious. It was a land of opportunity and wealth and a shining beacon of upright living. Not so much anymore. What was the name of that religious movement again? The Fifth Great Awakening? They had made us aware of the problem, brought it back into the forefront. America had lost its way. America had lost its God. The slow decline of the world should be placed at his feet.

God is bigger than climate change.

"Anyways..." the Collector took a deep breath and fished in a pocket on his jacket for a pack of cigarettes, slipping one from a hole at the end. He lit the cancer stick and took a drag, partaking of a generation of old's vice that had been illegal for almost forty years. The gray smoke he blew from his mouth did not rise towards the top of the frame but dissipated evenly.

"I digress," he said after a while. *"Sometimes you just have to rant. Sometimes you have to get it all off your chest and not worry about whose feelings get hurt. Let's be clear, the matter at hand is the matter at hand. This acquisition will bring us another step closer to reminding the world of what we lost, and of what we can regain. Don't you worry your little hearts, we will rise again. And if you don't share my beliefs, well, who gives a fuck, I know I don't, you'll make a shit ton of cash for doing this. Go get that car. Let's remind everyone America is glorious."*

The transmission ended in a cloud of cigarette smoke.

Keelin elbowed Atticus and made a gesture, rubbing her fingers together like she was holding paper notes. She mouthed the word, money, and the psychologist relaxed.

"You heard him, ladies and gents," Sarita declared, her tone whimsical. "Let's go make that bread."

"God, I do like bread," Atticus groaned. "With butter and currants?"

"With whatever the hell you like."

Maybe some bread wouldn't be such a bad thing, Darnell thought, and felt wrong for doing so. Perhaps it was time he looked at this from a new perspective.

This job was for two good causes, right? America and Family. So maybe, just maybe, he could put aside his misgivings for a little while. Maybe...

No?

Yes?

His heart began to beat quickly, its tempo unbridled.

Was this excitement?

What the hell was wrong with him?

The Collector was making a kind of sense.

"Can it be biscuits?" he asked, hungry all of a sudden.

He could do this. Right? It wasn't the worst thing.

Lexi gave him a pained expression, then rested her hands on her stomach as she drew herself up into a ball. She looked as if she might be sick. When he leaned in to ask what was up, she pursed her lips and turned away. Something had upset her. But what?

Sarita placed a finger to her chin, considering Darnell's words. She came to a decision and smiled, her expression all teeth, no warmth. "Sure, why not biscuits? It all starts with dough."

80 | J FITZPATRICK MAULDIN

[8] - Lexi

Physical indigestion was far easier to treat than the mental variety. A couple pills downed with a glass of water, and you were good to go. But for Lexi to get her mind someplace else, that took work. Serious effort. She needed a walk, a bit of fresh air, as it were. A few minutes to let her mind wander, to process all the Collector's bullshit noise. But she was in space.

Good for nothing more than for a man's purple-headed bitch to get her groceries in, his condescending voice echoed in the back of her head. *His bitch.*

What a fucking bastard.

Walks did not happen on the *Peridot*. Their flyer was not large enough and they weren't under thrust. About all she could muster was launching herself up and down the halls. She knew the best use of her time would have been to get on the treadmill, to help keep up her muscle density and sweat her way through the anger, but she just couldn't find the motivation.

She passed the captain's quarters and paused. The deep rhythms of lo-fi trip hop reverberating the nearby bulkheads, each bass kick vibrating knickknacks, Buddhist figures, and amateur photos the captain had taken of cities around Earth. Katia had her eyes closed, back up against her turquoise striped sleeping bag, feet pressed against the bars on her treadmill. She took long sips from a tall, plastic bottle of whiskey, her shoulders rolling as she swallowed, head nodding, her mind lost in the beat.

What a great way to get your mind off of things. Listen to music, have a few drinks, space the hell out. Maybe burn one. If only that were enough for Lexi right now.

Floating unseen in the hall she felt awkward. Either she needed to go in and say hello or move on. She knew she was infringing on the captain's privacy, but she didn't move. She just watched.

When the captain had finished taking a drink, she turned back to her terminal and replayed a video from Earth, her fingertips stroking the edge of the screen. It was a message from the Cho family, a woman of Katia's age with features just like hers, though Lexi wasn't sure who she was. The video's background showed a lake with snowy mountains dressed in evergreens. Who was this girl? Katia was private when it came to family matters. Reading between the lines, Lexi had always assumed the captain came from a smaller family, two siblings maybe, a single mom, but that was it. Thanksgiving at the Cho house would be nothing like her own, which was a boiling mass of laughter and people in ugly sweaters, the air choked with a mélange of scents—turkey, dressin', baked mac and cheese, sweet biscuits, apple pie. Good memories. It was about the only time her mom and dad engaged with their kids more than they did with their precious influencers.

"Hey, Lexi!" Logan said, sticking their head out of their quarters.

Lexi gave a start. It took her a moment for her to figure out where she was. Her mind had drifted a long way away. She withdrew from the captain's doorway and turned to face the doctor.

"Want to play catch?" Logan asked, shaking a ball in the air.

"You serious?"

"It's my job to keep everyone healthy, and you like playing catch. Right?"

"Fine," she said, hoping this might do the trick. There was only one other thing she could think might help, and that was out of the question right now. Darnell had pissed her off without even opening his mouth. In fact, he had pissed her off for not opening his mouth.

What was wrong with him?

Lexi positioned herself at the end of one of the *Peridot's* hallways and drew back her right arm, preparing to throw the soft, rubber ball. She grunted and the pink mass slipped from her fingers, shooting towards the other end of the flyer like a colorful riot control device. All Logan could do in response was raise their hands to protect their face.

The ball struck Logan in the knee and rocketed in a random direction, bouncing off the walls several times before its kinetic energy was spent.

"The hell was that, Lexi?" Logan asked once they knew their face was safe from harm. Their arms flashed yellow three times, then turned green, lights under the skin acting like electric caterpillars. "I asked if you wanted to play catch, not freaking dodgeball."

"Sorry," Lexi said, lowering her head. "Guess I have a lot on my mind."

"No freaking kidding." They recovered the pink ball and tossed it from hand to hand. "Maybe you need to get laid."

From the crossway between sections, Sarita stuck her head into the hall and glanced at both of them. Logan shrugged at her and Sarita pushed off, headed for her guest quarters with tablet in hand.

It was curious how the woman never got off of that device. Sure, there was work to do, but how much? They were in freefall. This was space. All you could do at this point was kill time.

"You okay?" Logan asked. "For real. Are you okay?"

"I—" she began, but before she could speak, Darnell popped in.

"What's up, ya'll? What's up!" he said, a bit more excited than normal. "Tossing the ball?"

"Something to do," Logan said.

He pushed off for the far end of the hall and took a place beside Lexi. "I'm in. Go for it."

Logan shrugged and tossed the ball. It went a little wide, yet Darnell, an agile linebacker at heart, pushed off the bulkhead with his right foot and glided into an intercept position with ease. He tossed the pink ball back to the doctor and they returned the gesture, their game of catch falling into a rhythm.

"This is fun," Logan said after a while. "Good for the body. Good for reflexes. Can't have you people turning soft on me."

"Soft?" Darnell did a full spin, then tossed the ball at Logan like a pink missile. "I ain't never been soft."

"Grew up on cactus juice and rattlesnake meat, huh?"

He barked a laugh and caught the ball. "That was for weekends. The rest of the time we were so poor we had to eat buffalo chips and wild jackalope."

The back of Lexi's neck turned hot and her hands began to sweat.

"What has you in such a good mood?" she asked Darnell, annoyed. Why was his cheer so damned obnoxious?

"Why shouldn't I be in a good mood? Isn't that what everyone wanted? Happy Richardson, not Buzz Killington? We're about to make bank, love. Bank."

"No," she replied. "It's more than that."

Darnell squinched up his nose. He tossed the ball, and it went a bit harder than he meant to. "You okay there, Logan?"

"Got it," they said. "'Bout to show you my arm. Here's your ticket to the gun show." They leaned to the side, using one of the fabric hooks on the wall as leverage, and wound up, then threw.

Darnell snatched it out of the air and shook his hand as if the impact had stung. "Not bad. Not bad."

Lexi let out a long breath and rolled her eyes.

"I'm not the one being evasive," he said, turning his attention back to Lexi, staring her down. "What is it now?"

She let out a groan. "Just seems that you had your apprehensions about this job, and all of a sudden, everything is okay." She raised a hand and shook it. "What flipped? You're not one to waffle."

He gave a shrug and caught the ball again, then tossed it back. "I don't know. I guess I just feel a little more comfortable with our situation. Sounds like the Collector is wanting to do a little good. The world could use some inspiration, it's been a rough couple decades. They could use a little hope. And hope can be divine. Restorative."

"But what brand of hope?"

"I suppose it don't much matter. Can't say I'm not excited about the American brand, however. The Collector's right, things have gone off the rails."

"The Collector is right?" she mused, her stomach twisting again. She took a deep breath, doing whatever she could to keep the acid out of her voice. That man had ranted fifteen minutes straight over outdated, far right dogma. Zero context. Zero nuance. Pure vitriol. The fact that Darnell couldn't see this made her angry. "Do you think that? Do you really think that?"

"I don't know." The next toss ended up bouncing off a wall into Atticus's quarters. The psychologist gave a yelp from out of sight and Logan shot off to recover it. Darnell turned to Lexi. "He made some good points is all."

"Good points? That drunk uncle social media rant?"

Darnell offered a dismissive shrug as explanation. "One thing to say about my uncle Cletus, like what he says or not, honest words come from him."

"We're not talking about Thanksgiving dinner, love." Lexi moved close to him, now floating just inches away, their chests facing one another's. "We're talking about the Collector."

"I'm confused." He scowled at her. "Are you the one having second thoughts now?"

She shook her head and withdrew. The words, "No. No," quick on her lips. "It's not that. It's just..."

Or was it?

It had been okay when her moral compass was guiding them into this excursion. But now, Darnell was in, and not just in, but encouraged by this—this rhetoric that the Collector was spewing. It was so familiar. She'd heard these arguments threaded together before and in the same cadence. Who was the Collector? He has money and influence, that much was clear. People like that tend not to stay very secret. They like the attention too much. No. There was something more here.

"Not sure I believe you," he said, tone wry.

"What?" She blinked. "Believe what?"

"That you're not having second thoughts."

Her back went straight, lips forming a hard line, fists shaking at her side. "I most certainly am not, and it's bullshit you would think otherwise."

"Hey, hey," he raised his hands. "Calm down, babe."

"*Babe?*" Lexi seethed. "'*Calm down*?'" For some reason, the word *bitch* echoed again in her mind. "Don't tell me to calm down. We are getting what's ours, you heard me?"

"I guess." He didn't seem convinced. "Everything will be fine, okay? You need to stop worrying so much."

"Don't tell me how to feel."

"Okay fine. What's the matter then?"

"It's just—I'm concerned—"

She was cut off by Logan shouting, "Found it! The damn thing got stuck under Atticus's fat ass."

"Takes one to know one!" Atticus groaned from inside his quarters. "Now stay out, bitch. Bastard. Whatever the hell you are."

"Ha ha ha, ha ha."

Lexi cocked her head. The word *bitch* hit so much different when Atticus said it.

"Can I just be honest?" Darnell asked Lexi.

Her stomach tensed. "You can always be honest."

"Well... As a country we have gotten away from traditional values. Maybe this thing the Collector is doing, creating a museum of American treasures, will be a way to guide people back to better days. Make better choices. The world is the way it is because they strayed from the path, right? Sometimes all people need is a clear picture of better times. These artifacts have historical power."

"Is that what you really believe?"

"Come on, everything was fine back then. The world was safe, and we all had enough to eat. Don't recall no floods and storms like we have now."

"You guys need a moment?" Logan asked, tossing a thumb over their shoulder back off down the corridor. "I can just, you know..."

"No," Lexi took Darnell by the arm and led them into their quarters, shutting the door behind them.

"Aww damn," Darnell said, eyebrows raising, palms rubbing together like a hungry teenager eying a holiday feast. "Something good about to happen?"

"Hush," she replied.

He rushed forward, placing his forehead against hers and drew her close, his breath warm on her lips. "Seriously, love. What's wrong? You ain't acting like yourself."

Why didn't he get it? Why couldn't he understand what was bothering her. She knew he wasn't being intentionally obtuse. Yet here he was—being obtuse—making her spell it out for him. He should just know how she felt. Know what she was thinking.

"I just don't understand," she said after a moment.

"Understand what?"

"What the Collector is saying. It's wrong. I am all about making the money, and for that I'm all in, but his words... Darnell, he's a bad man, and not just in the criminal way. A bad man in his heart."

"Nah. I don't buy that. He's just proud of his country."

"There's more to it than that. He reminds me of someone. He reminds me of so many someones. You know me, I grew up with a big family. We didn't always have it easy."

"Same here."

"No. I don't think you understand." Lexi took a deep breath. "We grew up in the city, and things happened there. Things I don't want to think about again. Too many people, not enough opportunity. Mom and dad, they had their minds elsewhere, maybe trying not to think about it, but they were not much for guidance and support—or even protection. People are always out there looking to take advantage of kids, first looking like their trying to do good. I love you, but you've lived a sheltered life, a home on the literal range. Growing up on the ranch sheltered you from a lot of pain."

"You sayin' I had it easy?"

She pursed her lips and sighed. "Well, in some ways, yes," she began, trying not to sound patronizing. "Yes, you had it easy. You don't know what it's like. The world has come a long way, America has come a long way, but old sentiments die hard. Some things in the past need to stay buried for good. Or if they are remembered, they need to be a warning, not a call. Be careful looking at the past through a lens of misguided nostalgia and praise."

Neither of them said anything for a moment. The words settled in.

"You watch," Darnell broke the silence. "It'll all be okay. We're going to be part of making the world glorious once more." He gave her a kiss and squeezed her tight. Her heart softened too much. "And in turn, we get what's ours."

She said nothing in response and was angry at herself for it. Her full feelings were too volatile to let loose at this time. Was this the man she wanted to marry? Could he truly understand the path he was being led down, eyes wide open? Was he this easy to manipulate?

When Darnell let go of her, he began to undress, removing his jumpsuit to reveal his beautiful, dark-skinned body, hard lines tracing his fit form. Her heart and mind began to war with one another. It might not be the best time for them to couple, mad as she was, but then again...

"It'll be okay," he said.

It was hard to tell him no, and Lord knew, she needed it. He believed in her even when she didn't deserve to have anyone to believe in her. She had done something terrible, been careless, and people had died. Darnell had never judged her for it. He had forgiven her so that she could start to forgive herself.

The zipper of her jumpsuit came down, and she took a deep breath.

"All good things," he said, and that was that.

A cocktail of relief and guilt flooded her.

If she couldn't get fresh air, or flip a damn switch and change his mind, there was at least one thing left that would settle her stomach for a time.

She just had to tell herself it wasn't his fault.

It wasn't his fault.

[9] – Darnell

"Mr. Richardson, tell me, how have things been going the last couple of weeks?" Atticus asked, his posture leaned back, a pen in his right hand, a notepad stuck to the thigh of his crossed leg. It was such an absurd posture given that they were in null gravity. But still, it made the psychologist seem relaxed, thoughtful, putting Darnell at ease.

"Pretty good, I think. Pretty good," he replied, his mind racing with thoughts. These sessions typically made Darnell anxious, since they were not just for his benefit, but for a research project Dr. Prescott was working on. Today, however, he was in a good mood. A hopeful mood. He was excited, not anxious. "Can I be honest?"

"Of course. That's what we're after."

"I'm not just in a good mood. I am in a damn fine mood. I feel... well..."

"Energized?"

"Yeah. Energized, that's the word."

Atticus nodded and wrote a few words on his digital notepad. "And why do you think that this is?"

"Well, I mean, this whole job, this operation, excursion, whatever you wanna call it. I feel as if we've gotten a bit of clarity around the mission. And maybe, just maybe, I feel a bit more trust for the Collector."

"That so? Why?"

Darnell shrugged. "I don't know. Maybe I feel like we have some common ground."

"Common ground?" Atticus rubbed his bottom lip with his left thumb in consideration. "Tell me more."

"Maybe we want some of the same things?"

"Like traditional values?"

Darnell pointed at him. "Exactly. Traditional values."

"How are things with Lexi and you?"

This made Darnell smile, his mind drifting back to the activities of the night before. They might not be able to have kids yet, because of the birth control drugs all Void-Striders were given, null gravity dangerous for fetuses, but the practice was sublime.

"Things are great," he said. "Damned great."

"I see."

"What's that mean?"

Atticus tapped his lips with the end of the pen then made a few notes, not answering. "You mentioned traditional values a moment ago. People's ideas of something like that can vary wildly. What are they to you?"

He considered this question for a moment. It was a slippery term he had used many times in his life, and to be honest, most often he felt it described his own upbringing. The motivations of an old soul, some might say. He dug deep and did his best to explain.

"Know your duty and do your duty," he replied. "Honor another person's loved ones and family. Defend and protect those who are at a disadvantage or weaker than yourself. Don't add to others' burdens or intentionally inconvenience them. Golden rule. Family. Country. Those sorts of things."

Atticus's bottom lip twitched. "And you gleaned these common, *traditional values*, from the Collector's words?"

"Yeah. A man who talks as he does, even if he did get off track a bit, believes the same things as me, I'm sure of it."

Atticus's eyebrows raised. "Interesting."

"What is?"

"Nothing." The psychologist jotted down several words Darnell could not see.

"What does any of this have to do with your research?" he asked. "I know you're here to keep us all in good mental health, but this line of questioning, how does it help your project?"

"Does it matter?"

Darnell raised an open hand. "Maybe."

"Let's just say it's to gather your state of mind." He rolled the hand holding his pen, then pointed at his notepad. "Besides, helping you is little about me interjecting my own opinion, and more about directing the questions. May we continue?"

A thought occurred to Darnell, a constellation of scattered observations converging into insight. "Are you lonely?"

Atticus's face went slack. He took a deep breath and drew himself up, the notepad now against his chest. "Whatever do you mean?"

"I know we all get along here. Or at least get along enough. But I mean, are you lonely? I get the feeling you long for a bit of romance. Not a lot of options in deep space, mind. Not too much time at dock."

"You are the only member of the crew in an active romantic relationship," Atticus replied.

"What do you mean by active?"

"Nothing in particular."

"Look," Darnell said. "I know there aren't any other good-looking guys on this flyer who are single and all. Has to be hard."

The psychologist crossed his hands and gave Darnell a pointed look. "Relationships are not only physical."

"Fair. Do you have a special someone somewhere else?"

Atticus licked his lips and scribbled a few notes. "If I do, I'm not telling."

"Damn. And I thought we were buddies."

"We are crewmates. Professionals working together. Nothing more."

"You know that hurts, brother." Darnell patted his chest and formed a pouty frown. "Cuts deep."

"You know what else hurts?" Atticus's eyes began to glass over. He swallowed, Adam's apple bobbing, clearly trying to keep his voice level, and free of emotion. This was unexpected. "It hurts not having someone in your life who gets you. Physical or not, we all need someone who understands us. That's harder for some than others…"

The look on Atticus's face was pained. Darnell hadn't meant to upset him. This guy was hard as rocks, but even still, we all have nerves. "Look, Atticus, I didn't mean—"

"You and Lexi parade around this place, kissing on the bridge, slamming your bodies against each other at night like a couple of animals. You think you're quiet. Guess what… You're not. We share a paper-thin bulkhead." He laid a palm against the wall on the right, this slight action making him float towards the center of the room forcing him to readjust. "There's a truth to the two of you, an honesty. Not everyone is as lucky as you, Richardson. And from what I know of both of you, truth rings out again. Opposites attract. You are very different."

"Look, brother, I'm sorry."

"No." The psychologist paused to rub his eyes. "You're fine. Everything is fine. My problems are not your problems. You are too simple to be so devious. I know it's not intentionally hurtful. So why should I be hurt?"

His choice of the word *simple* made Darnell pause. "I'm not sure if I should be pissed or take that statement as a compliment."

"Compliments are hard for me."

Darnell nodded.

"Enough of that." Atticus collected himself and gave a fake smile, no teeth. "As we were."

There was no sense arguing. Whatever window into the soul Darnell had peered through was shuttered closed. "As we were."

"How do you feel about the Collector?"

"I like him," Darnell said.

"That much is clear. And does that change how you feel about this excursion?"

"It does. I know I should feel guilty, but the more I understand what this is for, the less the piracy part bothers me. We're helping to create a place where American dreams can be reborn."

"And that's exciting to you?"

"Hell yeah it's exciting. Why wouldn't it be? We're the best, damn country in the world."

"Mmm," Atticus said.

Excitement built in Darnell's chest. He began gesturing with his hands as he spoke. "Take this whole movement going on back home. The Fifth Great Awakening is bringing hundreds of thousands, if not millions back to God. Maybe it is the Almighty's wrath that brought so much hardship on the world. Maybe not. But how great would it be if these people fell on their knees and prayed for forgiveness, and then our planet were healed? If someone can do it, God sure can."

"I see," Atticus said, then wrote several more words on his notepad.

"The timing is about right. Traditional values, as we said, people let them go. They started cheating and lying to one another, asking for the government to take care of us. They let go of their freedom. Looters. Protestors. They stand against what we believe in most."

Atticus met his gaze, eyes narrowing the slightest bit as if focusing on a particular idea. "What is America to you, Mr. Richardson?"

The question hit Darnell in the chest with a weight he had not expected. To his surprise, he wasn't sure how to respond. What answer did Atticus want from him? Where was he directing him?

"Well," he began, but the words wouldn't come. This was harder to answer than he had thought. It was the land of the free, and home of the brave, that much he knew. But what was it to him? What was it to Darnell Richardson? There was far more to this than a patriotic byline. It was like asking him to explain what it meant for something to be beautiful.

"Darnell," Lexi called from the doorway, her expression hard. "Come on. Captain needs us to take care of something."

"We are in a session," Atticus groaned. "Can you come back later?"

He hoped she would.

There was something here Darnell wanted to explore. Atticus was digging deep, and Darnell wanted to know the answer. It was hard to understand oneself from introspection alone. What questions had he not asked himself?

Lexi cocked her head to the side. "And last I checked, the captain is in charge."

Darnell eyed the psychologist and gave a shrug. "Cap's orders." He could follow this thread another day, but a fight with the love of his life would not improve matters.

Still... What *did* America mean to him? Lots of people had pride for their country, even Keelin, but what made him feel as if his was more important than theirs? As if his were exceptional no matter what?

He followed Lexi down the hall, and she led him to the aft of the *Peridot* into a storage room, her body tense and rigid despite null gravity. Whereas on a normal day she flowed from hook to hook like a swimmer performing a graceful act, her every twist an expressive wonder, she now moved like a machine, efficient and lifeless.

After several minutes of silence, he decided to dig deeper.

"Are you okay?" he asked.

Lexi pointed to a set of boxes. "Filters. We're charged with changing them out."

"Isn't that Keelin's job?"

"She's busy." She reached for a storage crate and fiddled with the catches. "Captain gave it to us."

"Alright then. Still doesn't answer my question. Are you okay?"

Lexi sniffed. "Why wouldn't I be?"

"That's typically why someone asks a question. You know, to eh, find out the answer."

"I am fine."

"No, you are not. You've been prickly over something for a couple of days now. Tell me, or I'm gonna kick your ass. This about you having second thoughts?"

"I am not having second thoughts." She put her hands on her hips and tossed her head forward. "And wait, kick my ass? You would beat up a girl?"

"You know what I mean."

"Like to see you try, anyway."

He took her hands in his and looked her in the eyes. "What's wrong, love?"

She sucked on her teeth for a moment then spoke. "I—eh—fine—I feel like you switched sides too easily."

"This again?"

She let go and handed him a set of the circular filters, waving for him to follow. At the first air scrubber she paused and opened a panel in the bulkhead. He waited patiently for her to continue. "I count on you to be my guiding light."

"And you don't feel I am right now?" He scratched his beard and did his best to recall their recent conversations. He was missing something. But what was it?

"I feel like you're excited over a lie."

"What lie? That we can get all we want from stealing the Slipstream?"

"No. It's…"

He leaned in. "Yes?"

"Never mind."

"Tell me."

She slammed the panel closed after they were done and pushed off for the next access point. "You never change your mind about anything. You are a rock."

"You sure about that? I feel like I do all the time. Sometimes I want chicken for dinner, and then when it comes time, I reach for beef."

"Principles," she said, and ripped open the next panel, tossing the cover against the opposite wall with a slam. "You're principled. That's something I can count on."

He blinked at her and recovered the discarded metal cover. "Sometimes, maybe? I just want to be a good guy."

Lexi banged around inside the panel, tossing the old filter out, then jammed the new one in a bit crooked, took it out, and tried again, banging at it over and over. Once she had finally gotten it into place, she turned to face him, sweat on her brow, then frowned at a point to his left.

Keelin was over his shoulder, her hands raised and backing off. "Awkward," she said, and pushed off, retreating back down the hall.

"You're being foolish right now," he turned on Lexi, and from the crushed expression on her face he could tell that his words had cut deep. This was a sentiment that cut both ways. He hated speaking in anger. "I didn't mean. I just."

She rolled her eyes and took a deep breath, then turned away, her hurt expression replaced with one of annoyance. "Look, let's just drop it. I'm okay. It's just the stress."

"Are you sure?"

"Yeah. Don't worry about it. Everything is okay."

"I don't think I trust this, ma'am."

She smiled at him, weak, but it was genuine. "I don't want to fight with you."

"Me neither."

"Then let's not fight."

Keelin stuck her head back out into the hall. "Hungry? About to get dinner goin'."

"Yeah," Lexi said, taking Darnell's hand. "Let's eat."

He squeezed her fingers and sighed, wondering why it was so hard for her to just say what was really on her mind. He hoped it would resolve itself on its own, but had a feeling it wouldn't.

The enigma that was woman, was one subject which never ceased to baffle him. But it was a subject worth study. And study it he would.

[10] – Lexi

It had been nearly a year since Lexi last laid eyes on Saturn, and it was breathtaking even at a distance. The sun cast its light on one side of the calico globe, while the other was shrouded in darkness, swirling storms of gas and heat giving it form, blue aurorae flickering atop its northern pole, seven bands of white rings surrounding its equator.

From a young age, she had always enjoyed stargazing even if it had been difficult in the city. It was for this that she appreciated the stars and planets were far easier to see out here without all the obstructions of light pollution and atmosphere. And so, whenever she needed time to relax, time to focus on something other than her problems and just let herself drift in a river of thought, she'd slip in her ear pods, choose some deep rhythms, lay back in one of the *Peridot's* two observatories, and gaze out into the void.

Tonight was one of those nights. Darnell was asleep. The crew was playing cards, watching the stream, drinking, or just talking. For the most part, all was quiet. A picture of perfect solitude.

In these moments, she often played a game with herself to see how many constellations she could count without the need for charts. Of the eighty-eight constellations recognizable from Earth's surface, she could find between forty and forty-three with the naked eye out here in the black. For whatever reason, that was her limit. It annoyed the crap out of her that she couldn't beat it.

Her score tonight? Twenty-five. Pathetic.

Her head was not in the game.

At a distance of 1 AU, she could easily see Saturn without instruments. The sight of their general target, a complicated planetary system within an even larger star system, gave her a mix of emotions, a rush of excitement and heavy trepidation. She had checked to see if the UEI had any registered flight plans for flyers which might cross paths with their trajectory, orbits being tricky around the ringed world. None came up. Then again, they were flying without a proper flight plan, and their transponder was disabled. This was only the second time she had done that, and last time didn't turn out so well.

"Maybe Darnell is right," she whispered. "I'm being foolish." It wouldn't be the last time. She loved the man and no matter how she felt about their current employer, she couldn't let that affect her relationship with Darnell.

Lexi's hand terminal began to chime.

Her heart leaped into her throat as she read the alert. She pulled her ear pods out and pushed back into the belly of the flyer, heading for the bridge.

"Get up, everybody," she said, floating down the main hall, banging on the doors as she went. It took only a few seconds to get everyone's attention in a habitation module just a hair over twenty meters in length. "Get up. Get up. Get up."

The captain appeared first, sticking her head out of her quarters to look toward the bridge. Katia's eyes were wild and bleary, a half empty plastic bottle of whiskey still in hand. "What is it, Miss Carver?"

"We're being tracked. Painted by a targeting laser."

She narrowed her eyes and leaned forward, squinting. "We're what?"

Lexi settled into her acceleration chair and started flicking switches. If she could figure out where the targeting laser originated, maybe they would have enough time to deal with whatever threat came next. She'd evaded the police before in her youth, taking them on a chase and hiding her boyfriend's Mustang under a bridge when a midnight drag race had gone wrong. He'd run like a bitch and left her on her own, but she had saved the car, and by doing so, kept his naked ass out of jail.

"We okay?" Darnell asked, appearing beside her. "What is it, babe?"

"We're fine for now. I just don't know for how long. Someone is tracking us. I'm using the photoactive alignment cells to get a fix on where from. I know these instruments aren't exactly meant for this, they're for navigation, but they should give us a rough heading."

"What can I do to help?"

She smiled up at him, her teeth pulling at her bottom lip. He was always so eager. "You being here is enough."

"How sweet," Atticus said, then tossed a scarf over his shoulder where it hung in the air. He licked his lips and rubbed his face. "A perfectly good game of cards interrupted, and I was about to take Fire Crotch here to the cleaners."

Keelin rolled her eyes at the psychologist. "Timin' and luck sometimes line up in such a way that you can catch a break."

"This isn't over."

"Try me, Shrinky."

"Give me network access," Sarita said, settling into Logan's acceleration chair before the doctor could make a move. She got a dirty look for her trouble. Void-striders were territorial over their spots. "I had a feeling this might happen."

The captain barred her teeth in frustration and groaned, "You what?"

"It's the UEI. Without a flight plan, they are trying to figure out what we are up to. Piracy has been a serious issue out here lately."

Lexi did not like surprises. And while she was smart enough, and talented enough to roll with the punches most days, this was not her happy place. Something was wrong. It all felt wrong.

"You kidding me?" Darnell piped up. "Space pirates in the 2090's?"

The Collector's contact whirled on him. "Don't be naive. What the hell do you think we're doing? Pirates are nothing more than privateers. Contractors without a flag."

He raised a finger and pointed at her. "I am not some damned space pirate."

"Go ahead and keep telling yourself that, cowboy." She gestured towards his head, spinning her hand around in a circle. "Before this is all over, I'll buy your captain here a tricorn hat."

Out of nowhere, Atticus gave a nervous chuckle. "Finally, an opportunity to show off my fifteen years of fencing classes. I can swash buckle with the best."

"Foil or saber?" Sarita's eyebrows raised, her attention fixed back on her tablet, fingers flicking across its surface. "I bet you prefer saber."

"What do you take me for, madam?" He laid a hand against his chest, shocked. "An unskilled neanderthal? A brute? Hardly. Foil is the only true weapon. One of finesse."

"A beginner's toy."

"I'll have you know I was nationally ranked in the NCAA. I played in college. Saber is just a game of hacking with little strategy and all offense. I prefer nuance."

The captain shook her head and rubbed her eyes, trying to force away her buzz. "No time for a competition of pedantic wits, Atticus," she muttered, her words labored. "Let Sarita do her work and keep that silver tongue behind your teeth."

Logan passed the captain a flat-packed foil package of EZ-Over. It was an oral medicine designed to help the body break down alcohol in the bloodstream. She smiled at them and ripped it open at one end, sucking the contents down before giving a sigh of relief. This was a moment for clear heads.

"I can do more than one thing at a time," Sarita replied, and popped a stick of gum in her mouth.

"Right now," the captain said, "there's only one thing I want, and that's for us to escape UEI notice."

"I don't see that happening. They've got a solid lock on us. Then again..." She tapped a fingernail against her temple. "Maybe we can keep them from figuring out who or what we are."

Lexi sighed. They were in the open. Exposed.

"No matter what this laser does, they'll see our Falkor flame when we do our slow down burn," Lexi said.

The captain's expression compressed. "Shit."

Darnell frowned.

The communications light began to blink.

"They're attempting to signal us," Lexi said.

"Shut off auto-handshakes," Sarita told her. "Quick. You don't want the array pinging them back."

Lexi flicked several switches on her control panel and killed the power to the hi- and lo-gain antennas. She wasn't confident she could keep it from responding on its own, so shutting down the whole system was the best bet. This meant that they were flying even blinder.

"Was there a signal before you shut it down?" the captain asked.

Lexi nodded. "Standard UEI protocols, request for flight plan."

Sarita took a deep breath and began to chew at her bottom lip in thought. "Have you attempted to reflect their beam in any way by redirecting the solar arrays?"

Lexi shook her head. "No."

"Okay. So we're a fast moving projectile screaming towards Saturn. It sure would be nice if we could seem as if we're not a flyer. I don't think they have been locked on long enough to do a full holographic scan."

"What are you thinking, Sarita?"

She blew a bubble with her chewing gum. It let out a snap as it popped. "Keelin, do you have any insulating foam aboard?"

"The spray kind?" the engineer asked, confused. "Got some closed cell foam we use for sealing things up, fillin' holes in rocks if need be."

"Perfect. How much?"

"Good bit." She scratched her chin. "Fifty-gallon drum at least. Hope we don't have to do that much patchin'. What are you on about?"

"Can you rig it up to expand on one side of the, eh, flyer?"

Lexi's eyes widened as realization dawned. "Okay. Okay. I see what you're thinking. This is a good idea. Make a bubbly block of foam and it might look like we're just a rock out here."

"Small chance they saw us burn away from Jupiter," Sarita went on. "And at this distance, they can't tell their ass from a can of paint."

Keelin pushed off and waved at Darnell. "Come on, big guy. I need your muscles."

He gave a grunt and squeezed Lexi's shoulder before following after Keelin. "I did play linebacker."

Lexi took a deep breath as Darnell and Keelin left the bridge to suit up. Space walks this far out were always dangerous. Should she have objected? What choice did they have? If they did nothing at all, they were boned.

"I'll have to correct our trajectory after the foam expands," Lexi said, thinking it all through.

Sarita nodded. "Don't do it till the foam has expanded and we're sure the laser isn't tracking us."

"Agreed."

The captain leaned in to inspect the main display, the smell of her breath thick with alcohol even if the drugs were sobering her up. "How far off course will it put us?"

"No way of knowing. Shouldn't be too bad. Newton said it best, for every action there's an equal and opposite reaction. My hope is we have minimal spin as a result."

"Sarita," the captain said. "Did you know this was going to happen? Tell me. Be honest."

The Collector's contact gave a shrug as she fixed her hair, undoing it and tying it back again. A bubble of chewing gum popped on her lips. She did not respond to the question.

"We have a lot to talk about when this crisis is over," the captain told her.

"Talk all you want later," Sarita replied, her tone a bit too cavalier. "For the moment, we have work to do. I am doing my best to trace route the networks and make sure they can't track us through any other means. Networked systems tend to be data rich and keep heavy caches. When the antennas go back up there's no telling what information will bleed back out."

Within a few moments Darnell and Keelin were suited up and ready to go, their bodies appearing in what looked to be slow motion in the external camera view on Lexi's right display. Darnell carried a drum he could barely put his arms around, wobbling back and forth, the slack of their tether lines whipping out into space. Keelin walked in front of him, a hose in her hands connected to the drum.

"Cross to the starboard side," Lexi ordered, panning the camera around.

Keelin's channel crackled. *"On it."*

The laser was still tracking them. If they took too much longer it would get a solid scan of their shape and know *what* they were, if not *who*.

Darnell took a step and one of his magnetic boots came in contact with an uneven surface and didn't stick. He twisted as he tried to compensate, forcing his other foot free of their flyer. Under normal circumstances he could have used corrective jets to push him back towards the *Peridot*, but his hands were occupied holding the drum of foam. Both his tether and assist controls were on the backs of his hands.

"Oh, shit," he growled over his channel. *"I'm drifting out."*

Keelin sprang into action, trying to reel him back in with the spray foam's hose. When she saw the hose start to strain where it coupled with the drum, she let go.

"If I pull too hard," she said, *"it'll explode and send us both spinning out into the black."*

The distance between Darnell and their flyer widened. Twenty, thirty, forty, fifty feet. Out and out and out.

Lexi's heart stopped. Her mind reeled with a thousand nightmares. She had to do something. She would not let him be lost.

"Hands off the controls," Sarita said, not removing her eyes from her work. "We don't want to draw attention to us until the foam is in place."

"But I can do a corrective burn. I can bring the *Peridot* up to him."

"The Irish Rose will get him. Put some trust in her."

"He's my fiancé." Which wasn't entirely true. The title, Boyfriend, however, carried too little weight at a time like this. "I have to protect him."

Sarita rolled her eyes. "Then put a lot of trust in her." She reached out and pressed a button on the panel before her, opening a communications channel to the two of them. "And by the way, don't lose that drum. I'd like to not end up in prison when we hit orbit."

"So cold," Atticus said. "I bet you are real fun in a relationship."

"What can I say?" She smacked on her gum. "Some people prefer winter over summer."

"Not trying to freak out here," Darnell said, his words deliberate and measured. *"But you guys are starting to get kind of small."*

Keelin stomped her way down to the back of the flyer, magnetic boots clicking, Darnell shrinking to a speck on the screen. She took hold of his tether where it met *the Peridot* and began reeling him back in.

Lexi held her breath, hoping and praying that the line was rated for both Darnell and the drum's mass. That wasn't her area of expertise. Her trust was in Keelin.

"Got him," she said, and Darnell's image swelled once more in the monitor. *"No need to fear the wind if your haystacks are tied down."*

He hit the hull with flat feet and stuck in place, his magnetic boots reengaging, their flyer letting out a bang. *"I'd prefer not to take that ride again. Dial in my slack, Keelin?"*

"Already on it, buck-a-roo."

"Look!" Sarita commented. "He saved the barrel. Delightful. Now get to work."

It took every fiber in Lexi not to slap that bitch with the back of her hand.

Maybe this isn't worth it, she thought. *Maybe it's time to make a scene and end the game.*

They hadn't done anything illegal, not yet. All they had done was leave a station without a transponder active and submitted a bad flight plan, these were mistakes easily explained.

The captain glared at Lexi in the reflection of a black screen as if she could read her mind. Lexi swallowed and kept her mouth shut. This was for her future. Their future. A family. A house. Financial freedom.

It didn't take long for Keelin and Darnell to deploy the foam, forming it into a widening collection of knots and bumps and crannies that clung to the *Peridot* in a heap fifteen meters high and thirty meters wide. Once the work was done, they climbed around it and came back inside. Their flyer let out a bang after the airlock cycled. Shins had been the victim.

Several silent moments passed.

"Think they fell for the ruse?" Captain Cho asked Lexi.

She checked the sensors once more, reviewing fluctuations in temperature along the flyer's hull. The foam they had deployed, while hopefully enough to give the scanning laser's owner false data, was not thick enough to block all transmission of heat from a 100+W tracking laser.

There were no more abnormal readings.

"I think they've moved on," Lexi said, letting out a sigh.

Sarita spun in her chair and gave the captain a toothy grin, her arms spread wide in a gesture of ta-daa. "We got this shit."

Cho's eyes narrowed. "I'm starting to wonder why we picked up *this shit* to begin with. What was all that about?"

"There was always a risk. The UEI have assets all over the system."

"To circle back around to your comment earlier. Piracy has been an issue out here?"

"Oh sure."

"Then why haven't we heard so much about it? We are one of KTS Materials' most active crews."

"Who would want to scare off their precious Void-Striders?" Sarita's pouty lips turned downward in a mocking expression. "Or whatever the hell the moniker is for people like you these days. There's work that needs doing and they want to keep it up. If that info went public, the company you work for would have to pull their contract. The spice must flow, Captain."

"They lookin' for us?" Darnell said, appearing once more on the bridge in his cowboy, dragon rider painted space suit, sans the helmet. His brow was slick with sweat, his face painted with unease. Lexi reached out and steadied his shaking spacesuit gloves. They shared a look and she fought back tears. She wasn't the most emotional woman, but her man had almost been lost in space over this stupid errand.

Damn Sarita and damn this job. She would have scooped him up herself if she'd had to, to hell with being caught. She would not have let him be lost.

"I don't think they're looking anymore," Sarita reported.

Atticus stroked his chin for a moment then waved a finger at open air. "Does anyone else know the Slipstream is out here?"

"Almost certainly not."

"And how do we know this for sure?"

Sarita gave a grin, her self-possessed look returning. Lexi's bottom lip trembled.

"The Collector has his ways," Sarita said, then began smacking on her gum again.

"His ways had better get our asses paid," the captain told her. "Two days till our slow-down burn. Let's hope that UEI flyer is on the other side of Saturn by then."

"Are you still in?" Sarita leaned back and crossed her arms. "And what if it is the UEI? Hmm? What if they come after us? How are we to react?"

The captain crossed her arms. "They have to catch us first, and it's not like there's any armed ships out here. If the Slipstream is there like you say it is, we're getting our prize, have no doubt about that."

"Still on then," Sarita said, nodding as she turned back to her work, screen covered in network code.

Something in how she said this gave Lexi pause. There was a subtext she wasn't sure she liked. Sarita might just be the death of them. Their dreams had been the bait, the money, the hook.

"Just hang in there," the Collector's contact said. "Not too much longer, and all your worries will be over."

[11] – Darnell

As far as they could tell they were no longer being tracked. Their ruse had worked.

They drifted for some time, allowing whoever had been tracking them to move on, then Darnell went back out onto the hull and with the help of a plasma torch, separated the foam insulator from the *Peridot's* skin. For safe measure, as not to damage any other flyers by chance, they attached a heated charge to the vestigial chunk and burned it up once it was several kilometers away. There was a pop of bright light and a flash of heat as the foam melted back into its base components. Not the most gratifying explosion, but a good one, nonetheless.

One thing was for sure. In all of Darnell's life, he had never expected to find himself in this position. Sarita was right. He was fast becoming a pirate. A damned space pirate. And not the kind of pirate you saw in cartoons or on Halloween, filthy, rum-drinking folk in long coats with peg legs and parrots on their shoulders, but the kind that hurt people and stole things. A thief. A swindler. Would he become a murderer before this was over? There was no way around it. He was avoiding the authorities. He was on the path of becoming a criminal.

But did the ends in this case justify the means? The Collector's intentions might be good, but his methods... Why couldn't it be black and white? Right and wrong?

He had spent the last few days thinking over all that had happened. This had been a close call in more than one way. Had it been a UEI flyer that found them? And if it wasn't, what would they have done to them if an intercept course had been plotted? No calling for help out here. You were on your own.

Atticus floated across from Darnell, Lexi, and Keelin, the three of them gathered in the galley at the back of the habitation module. The door was shut, and their voices were low. Logan was keeping Sarita and the captain busy while they ate dinner.

"That woman says the Collector has his ways of knowing things," Atticus said, "but right away, we almost got caught."

"Still might be," Darnell said, tossing him a hot meal pack full of BBQ pork.

"I tend to agree." Atticus ripped the silver package open and inhaled the steam that came out, a satisfied look on his face. "Freeze dried or not, this keeps pretty well. Oh, do I miss it fresh."

Darnell gave a grunt and nodded. It was true. Texas-style BBQ, which is what he preferred, wasn't the best tasting in null gravity, unless you only wanted dry rub. Whatever this Kansas sweet sauce stuff was, it had been tasty, sure, but not like home.

"I'm going to be honest, guys," he said. "I'm feelin' pretty scared. I know I should be tough and all, but I'm shook."

"It's almost over," Keelin replied. "We finish the slow down burn, and we're at our destination. Crack the rock it's trapped in and load it up."

"Which is something that has been bothering me," Lexi said. "How is it inside a rock? Unless it was inside a ship at some point, the Slipstream should either be in freefall or ground to dust on the surface of some random moon. What are the chances a rock would not only match the Slipstream's velocity and trajectory, but also have enough gravity to pull it in without destroying it?"

"Does it matter when your makin' billions?" Keelin asked. "Feel like this is one of 'em times speakin' up could mean you find a sliver of metal crammed between your ribs."

"It just doesn't add up, that's all." Lexi squeezed the contents of a strawberry flavored juice pouch into her mouth before moving on. "I don't trust her. All I'm saying, is we need to be ready if this goes tits up."

"What do you suggest?" Atticus asked, looking directly into her eyes. "Dumping the body out in space? All my education, and I didn't take you for a sociopath."

"No, no. I mean... I don't know." She let out a sigh. "It would make me feel more comfortable if we had a contingency."

"Okay then." Keelin tipped her head. "How about this, if she don't deliver we'll toss her in the guest quarters and lock her up without anythin'. If she puts up a fuss, there's always a blanket party to be had. Don't want any free-floatin' crimson to get in me equipment, mind."

"We aren't killing her," Darnell said, his heart thundering in his chest, blood going hot. The sudden, casual talk of violence went against his core values. Love thy neighbor. Do unto others as you would have them do unto you. He pointed a finger at the engineer. "That's what's wrong with you people."

"You people?" Keelin's eyebrows raised, her pale face transitioning to the color of her hair. "What's he on about?"

"That's an UnAmerican way to act."

"Love, 'ear 'ow I talk. I ain' from America." Keelin scratched at the back of her cocked head. "You Americans think everythin' good came from the States. You ain' the only model of a good life, a good country."

He dug in on his position, leaning forward, meal pack shaking in his hand. "We're the best model."

"Debatable."

He crossed his arms and shut up. Lexi grinned at him and offered up a freeze-dried French fry. He snatched it from her fingers and chewed it with prejudice. He hated being mad just to be mad, and he wasn't sulking.

"We do need leverage," Atticus offered after a moment of contemplation. "If she crosses us, it might not be bad to hold her. However, the Collector, well, he has to know we aren't cold blooded killers. Besides, she might not be the best leverage."

"He probably doesn't give a shit about her either," Lexi put in.

"So what do we have?"

Lexi's hand terminal began to chime. She fished it from her jumpsuit and stared at it.

"What is it?" Darnell asked.

"Well, shit. Time to get back to work," she replied. "Finish up your food. I'll need everyone strapped in by 17:20. Should give enough time for it all to settle."

"So much for our scheming," Atticus mused.

Darnell crammed the rest of his sandwich down his throat before following Lexi to the bridge, leaving Keelin and Atticus alone to talk. This whole, "back room chat" had made him feel dirty. While he didn't fully trust Sarita or the Collector after their little scare, how could he expect to earn her trust if they were plotting behind her back at the same time? It went against everything he was taught growing up. You handled problems in life head-on.

"We're not going to hurt anyone, are we?" he whispered low enough only Lexi could hear.

She paused just before the bridge's pressure hatch, turning to face him. He reached out and took hold of her hands and they squeezed one another.

"I hope not," Lexi replied after a deep breath. "I really hope not."

"I can't lose you."

"And I can't lose you. Remember what we're doing this for. It's for us, and no one else."

He let go of her fingers with a sigh. It was all too much to process. Everything had turned morally gray. Not his happy place.

Lexi took her acceleration chair.

"How was dinner?" Sarita asked. Lexi did not respond. "That good?"

Darnell took his spot beside Logan, who had moved into Atticus's. Logan gave him an annoyed look and leaned in. "She took my seat."

"I can see that," he replied, voice low.

"I don't like it when people take my seat."

"Maybe ask for it back?"

Logan's spine went stiff as they raised their voice, "Hey! Sarita!" A silent moment passed. "Sarita!"

"What do you want, plug jockey?"

"Give me my damn seat back."

"No." Sarita's eyes remained focused on her tablet. The display before her flashed with a series of wavelengths and signal readouts. Darnell had no idea what any of it meant.

"How about yes?"

"How about, fuck no?"

"But it's my seat."

"How about I don't care if it's your seat? It's beside the pilot. I need it."

"Calm down everyone," Captain Cho said. "We are near the target. Chairs can be sorted out later."

"We that close?" Darnell asked.

"We're close."

His breath caught, overwhelmed in an instant with both excitement and trepidation. Good or bad, this would all be over soon. He could go back to living a life less encumbered. Less complicated. Praise God.

"If Sarita can give us a solid fix on the location, I'll make an adjustment burn," Lexi replied. "Right now, we're holding orbit just north of the B ring's inner edge. If you take a look out the starboard observation window, you can see Titan." She began panning around with the high-resolution cameras, inspecting the hundreds and thousands of satellites around Saturn, from chunks of ice to massive moons that would one day host human colonists.

"Any UEI activity?" Captain Cho asked.

Sarita nodded. "We may have evaded one ship, but there are at least another dozen actively moving around Saturn's system. Hard to say if any of their orbits will intersect with ours. Stumbling upon us is really the only way they'll catch us. We're close, though. Soon as I can get a solid fix, we'll move in." She paused for a moment, then smiled. "Speaking of a fix."

"You found it?"

"Looks like it." She narrowed her eyes at her tablet, an orbital map filling the screen. "The carrier signal was designed to closely match the background microwave radiation of the universe but with a slightly different oscillation. Unless you're looking for it, you won't find it."

"I can see the target," Lexi said, changing the angle of the cameras. "Adjusting course in one minute." She triggered a burn klaxon across the *Peridot*, alerting those not on the bridge to prepare themselves.

Darnell tugged on his harness and turned to Logan. They sighed and buckled in, relegated to an acceleration chair farther back.

Atticus and Keelin appeared a moment later and strapped in. Darnell could see a hint of something in their eyes; a wariness, a plot? What had they talked about after he and Lexi had left?

"Here we go," Lexi said, and lit the main engines.

Everyone was pressed back in their acceleration chairs. A bang echoed from the back of the flyer. Someone had forgotten to secure something heavy. Darnell only hoped it stayed in whatever room it was in.

Glittering chunks of ice rushed beneath the belly of the *Peridot*, for once giving the crew a visual sense of motion. Titan receded from view around the curve of Saturn's horizon like the setting sun. Saturn's north pole came into view at the edge of the high-resolution camera feeds, with its hexagonal storms and swirling blue aurorae. Their burn didn't last long, three G's for no more than five minutes before cutting off. The *Peridot* drifted away from the equator, Falkor cold, edging around towards the A Ring in a widening spiral, a peculiar satellite in its path.

"It's on Pan?" Keelin mused, pointing to the main display. "Ain't that what it's named? One of them weird rocks that looks like ravioli?"

Sarita shook her head. "Not Pan, but similar to it. There's more than one odd-shaped rock out here."

"I know we just ate and all," Atticus began, "but the idea of a ravioli-shaped rock suddenly has me famished. Can it be stuffed with lobster?"

"You ain't alone," Darnell replied. He always got hungry when he was nervous. Food was a good distraction. What he wouldn't give for a rack of ribs and a plate of brisket.

"Suppose we should designate it," Keelin said.

"MT-997?" Logan mused.

The engineer nodded. "Aye. It be our next meal ticket. Kaching. Kaching."

"Kaaaaching."

"Oh shit," Lexi said out of nowhere, alarmed. She flicked a series of switches in sequence and changed one of her displays.

"What?" The captain perked up. "What is it?"

"We've got a UEI flyer on our approach vector."

"Shit. Have they spotted us?"

"No targeting lasers, but I'm pretty sure they can pick us up visually if they know where to look. We're on the day side of Saturn now, and our hull, it's bright and shiny."

"Keep an eye on it for anything suspicious."

The *Peridot* approached the rocky satellite, Lexi firing the retrorockets to slow its relative approach as they neared. So far, the UEI flyer had shown no signs of seeing them. Its course remained steady.

"The Slipstream is inside the rock," Sarita told the crew, and turned to Darnell, twisting around in her chair. "You ready to break it free, cowboy?"

"How did it get inside?" he asked, raising the question from dinner.

"There are caves on the surface. It's not solid. The Slipstream drifted in."

"How deep?"

"Hard to say. Signal ping puts it a few hundred feet below."

"Fine then," he replied, turning his attention to the captain. She gave a nod. "It's going to take a lot of charges and a bit of time."

"Keelin," Katia said, and the engineer gave a grunt.

Be careful, Lexi mouthed at Darnell. He tipped an invisible hat at her and gave a wink.

Darnell and Keelin bolted for the airlock, helping one another suit up before heading into vacuum. Within just a few minutes they were out on the hull, magnetic boots clicking with each step. Both wore satchels on their backs full of explosives.

Danger? Bombs? He found himself more excited than nervous. What was wrong with him?

Lexi had parked the *Peridot* about five meters from their target, extending the lattice onto the surface to hold them in place so they could track its gentle rotation. As Darnell and Keelin made their way down the lattice onto the rock, he found their sky made of rings, then stars, then moons, then the planet itself and back again, every sixty-four seconds. He tried to keep his eyes focused on the ground so that he didn't get too sick from the spin.

"We'll take it a layer at a time," he told Keelin over comms.

She waved a white suit glove. *"Aye, then."*

Without time to set the usual safety net, Darnell and Keelin fired impact spikes into the rock and connected secondary tethers. He had no interest in repeating the incident from his last trip outside. Space could be deceptive, making you feel as if you were deep underwater, until it came time to swim and there was nothing to press against. He was not making that mistake again. They followed a trail around the outside of the rock, leaving more spikes, moving safely away from the lattice.

Darnell switched to a local comm channel with Keelin. "Mind if I ask a question?" he said while searching for the best place to position the first charges.

"Free solar system, an all," Keelin replied.

"We all have our reasons for doin' this. Not sure if I understand yours. I keep going back and forth between this being a good or a bad idea. Can't make up my damn mind. But why did you jump in with both feet? Youth and greed?"

Keelin pointed to a place on the rock where they could begin. *"A little of that, maybe."*

"But that's not all. Right?"

"Folk are complicated." She handed him a set of tools. *"We're onions, ey?"*

He accepted them, picking at the surface of the rock. Not satisfied that this was the right place to start, they went a little further on. "I know you and I don't always get along, but I've always respected you. This flyer stays safe and moving because of what you do. I appreciate that. Maybe I just want to understand why everyone's so eager to put all they've ever worked for at risk."

"Fair question." She paused, and her head hung for a moment. *"Maybe I just have an agin' mum who could use a bit of peace in her later years."*

"What do you mean?" he asked, even as he realized the answer.

"You got ears. You heard Atticus back on the station. He weren't wrong. Mum did some things to keep a roof over our head, and I ain' ashamed of it, but her body ain't what it was. Young things can turn dollars easy. Get them wrinkles and sags and next thing you know you're living on social insurance and protection payments."

"On what?"

"The government's tit, cowboy. State welfare."

"Oh," he said, and thought about that. He had been foolish to think greed was the only motivating factor. Not a single one of them wanted to retire to a private island or become an interplanetary jet setter. They just wanted a better life. A home, a cause, a bit of dignity, and a legacy.

"Mum made some bad choices," she said after a moment. *"Got caught up with some rough men, there. I aim to bring an end to that if I can."* Keelin chuckled. *"Besides, ain' you a bit curious what's in the glove compartment?"*

Darnell found himself nodding. "Strange as it might be, yes, yes I am." They settled into a new spot, and he picked at the surface. This place looked good. It was far enough away from the lattice, in a small recess of the rock, and was facing away from the ship. He shaped a charge into place. "Look, I'm sorry about earlier. I was just—"

"I'm gonna stop you right there, Richardson. I don't do sappy. I ain' no flower, even if I may look an' smell as pretty as one."

"Just the same."

"Aye." She paused and took a deep breath, her spacesuit heaving. *"Ready to blow the first charges?"*

They took hold of one another's hands and pushed off, the safety line hooked to one of their impact spikes going taut. The line swung them back to the surface like a tetherball some distance away, the rock offering protection from the blast. The idea had been Keelin's, and given the recent near-accident, the swing made Darnell nauseous.

Once they had landed on the other side Darnell raised his right hand and opened a narrow beam channel back to the *Peridot*. "Detonation in 3... 2... 1..."

The explosion's vibrations traveled through the surface of the asteroid and a spray of white shot up from just over the rock's horizon. The carbon-fiber lattice the flyer was anchored with flexed for an instant before returning to its rigid shape.

"Let's see how deep it went and go again," Darnell said, before Keelin and he reversed their tethered hop.

"You okay out there?" Lexi asked over the open channel.

"Just fine, love," Keelin replied. *"Your boy here is quite the dancer."*

"Don't I know it. Do me a favor and don't steal him away."

"Too pure a boy for me. Might just stain me soul with a bleach spot if he gets too near."

"I'll take that as a compliment," Darnell added.

"Can we hurry this up?" Sarita asked, her tone insistent. *"It's not like the UEI have gone anywhere. Pretty sure they're still poking around."*

After a quick depth check with a handheld laser, Darnell began setting the next round of explosives. He had to be quick, but not go too deep.

A flash of light came from over his shoulder. He pivoted his body to look. Another flyer much like theirs was on a course heading straight for them.

"Speaking of the UEI," he groaned, finger extending. "I do believe we've got ourselves a little company."

[12] – Lexi

"Signal incoming," Lexi reported, her heart thundering in her chest.

Captain Cho licked her lips and leaned forward. "Who are they? What kind of flyer?"

"Looks to be a UEI science vessel. They're fitted with all kinds of sensitive particle tracking equipment. Plasma spectrometer, cosmic dust analyzer, manometers, magnetospheric imaging. There's likely plenty more. My guess is that they're here to study Saturn."

"Scary police are walking around in the dark with their flashlights," Sarita said off-handed. "I'm sooo terrified."

"Shut up."

"Have they said what they want from us?" Captain Cho asked.

"To know why our transponder is off," Lexi replied.

The captain took a deep breath, smoothed her hands down her jumpsuit, and smiled. "Open an audio channel."

Lexi flicked a switch on her panel. "Yes, ma'am."

"This is Captain Cho of the rock hauler *Peridot*. Reply."

A moment passed. Nothing. Then the line began to crackle.

"Good afternoon, this is Captain Gordan of the Corona," a baritone voice echoed over the bridge's speakers. *"We just picked you up one of our regular passes and noticed your transponder wasn't functioning. Almost didn't spot you, but those charges lit up our instruments. We want*

to check in and lend any assistance needed. Not a lot of help out here, and our vectors aren't all that diverged."

"Good day, Captain Gordan."

Lexi was surprised Cho had used their actual name, but what could be done for it? Not like the UEI flyer couldn't just look out the window and see it painted along the side of the hull.

"Pleasure to meet you. Rock haulers you say? That's hard work we all need done."

"That it is."

"Lonely work though."

"Same as yours, I'm sure," Captain Cho said, her face taking on an expression of vacancy. "Five years yet before the station is assembled. Bit of a wait."

"That's our mission. Still looking for the best position and learning what we can about the old god. That transponder though…"

"I appreciate the concern. We are just fine. Once our engineer works her way back inside, we'll have her take a look at it. According to our pilot's readout, it's working fine."

Lexi tapped the transponder's status indicator bulb on her left, its light off. Despite what others might think, Darnell included, she hated lying. Thankfully, she didn't have to this time. Lying got complicated fast.

"I won't candy coat this," Gordan said, his tense but cordial tone turning serious. "We've seen a lot of illicit activity out here lately. What with all the probes the Chinese and Europeans shot out here and left to rot. There is a substantial black market for those right now, and I am sure you know the laws. Unless you are officially representing the country that sent them out, these are artifacts of SOL and are to be left alone."

"That so?" Captain Cho said, eyes focused on Sarita. The girl shook her head, appearing more annoyed than anything.

"What are you out here for?"

"Same as always. Digging up rare metals, turning them back in at Stratus."

"Long way to come for a haul to Stratus."

"We've been tracking a rock that might be a small treasure trove. Thought it would be worth the risk."

"Oh ya? I hate to break it to you, but these satellites are junk. This isn't Pan, is it?"

"No, it isn't. I'm not even sure it has a designation. In case you're curious, though, we gave it one, MT-997."

Lexi silently willed Captain Gordon to move on, to leave them alone. Being found now wouldn't do. Wouldn't be good for any of them.

"MT-997?" He sounded confused. "I'm not seeing it on our orbital charts. We'll have to add it to the model. It's like it appeared out of nowhere."

"Like I said, just another rock we named. Another meal ticket. Far too many to catalog in one day."

Gordan let out a sigh. "Ain't that the truth. There's always another. Look, we want to get you guys shipshape as quick as possible. Our contract with KTS Materials requires us to offer assistance when needed. While your demolitionists do their work, we'll come over and take a look at that transponder. Might just save your life if something goes wrong."

The captain's hands balled into fists and she swallowed. "While we appreciate that, Captain, it won't be necessary."

"Be our pleasure to help. Our legal requirement."

How much longer would it be until Darnell and Keelin uncovered the Slipstream? Minutes? Seconds? They had stopped blasting for the time being, but if they waited too long to start again, it might seem suspicious. They needed a backup plan.

Lexi began plotting a course away from MT-997. Maybe they could nab the Slipstream and still run? Soon as the rock was broken and the jig was up, all they would have to do was toss it in the hold and burn baby burn. If they were quick enough, they might just get away with it.

The captain continued her conversation with Gordan. Lexi tuned them out for a moment.

She leaned to the side and whispered to Sarita, "Where are we turning this in?"

The woman pursed her lips. "Excuse me?"

"After we get the Slipstream, where are we going with it?

"An undisclosed location."

"Might be useful to know where. Then I can get us out, get our courses."

"What sort of stupid thing are you thinking of doing?"

"Snatch and burn."

Sarita shook her head. "No. Let your captain work her magic, she's onto something."

Lexi ignored the Collector's pawn and started prepping anyways. What authority did this woman even have? At the end of the day, she was at their mercy, not the other way around. This was their flyer, not hers.

Lexi entered a rough burn into navigation, seven G's applied in a hard, ninety degree angle perpendicular against Saturn's equator, set to hurl them straight past the oncoming UEI flyer to take them over the northern hemisphere. This would take them within just a few hundred feet of the approaching vessel, potentially catching these unwitting people in their drive flame. She didn't want to hurt anyone. Never again.

"How long has it been since you've been at dock?" Cho asked the other flyer's captain, Lexi ears tuning back in like a radio, the math tumbling out of her mind as she struggled to concentrate on Plan B.

"Damn," Gordan lamented. *"Almost six months?"*

"How is your reaction mass holding up? Had to make a lot of corrective burns?"

A pause on the line.

Lexi readied to make the call. She was the pilot. Orders or not, this was her domain, this was under her control. Just a couple button presses and they were out of there. Cho would get over it if they didn't get caught. Darnell and Keelin just needed to hurry the hell up.

But what if the UEI have weapons? No. That was a silly thought. Who went armed out here?

"Are you okay, Captain?" Cho asked after too much time had passed.

"Yeah, we've made a lot of unscheduled burns, unfortunately," Gordan said, resigned. *"You know how it is, think you've got the right vector for your operation, and it doesn't quite work out. Why do you ask?"*

"I would hate for you to waste Delta-V helping us with a situation that isn't an emergency. That extra reaction mass might just save you in a pinch later. Perhaps give you the chance to scout an additional ring before you have to head back. That's another couple years of data for the lab."

The line was quiet for a moment. The rock flashed in Lexi's display, another set of charges set off, Darnell and Keelin were working their way back to the deepening hole to set more charges.

Hurry. Hurry.

If the *Corona's* crew came aboard at this point, there would be nothing to find but a transponder that had been switched off. However, the *Peridot* would have to abandon this errand. No billions for them. No dreams realized.

The *Corona* was now two thousand relative kilometers away and closing at a rate of five km/s. They had very little time left to decide whether to turn and burn to match the *Peridot's* orbit and board. Lexi could have sworn she saw their attitude jets fire in her scopes. Was it just her eyes? Her fears made visually manifest? The escape course had been set. Her finger hovered over the safety, shaking, her neck and forehead sweating.

Darnell, hurry up and get back inside, she thought. *Hurry the hell up.*

"I know that look," Sarita mumbled. "This is a bad time to make an impulsive move."

"I can do it. I can get us through."

"Look, where we're going they can still track your tags. The transponder might be off but there aren't that many rock haulers out there. Captain Cho called us out by name, for Christ's sake. They'll identify the ship for sure."

She had a point, though Lexi did not want to admit it.

"Stealth is key," Sarita said. "Hold the course. Trust me."

"Trust you?" Lexi gave her a hard look, eyes narrowing. "Trust… you?"

The captain put a fist to her chin and sighed. It was clear her mind was working overtime, playing a mental game of chess against the other captain. Lexi wasn't sure if she was winning.

"*We're just cogs out here, aren't we?*" Gordan asked, his voice hardening.

Captain Cho gave a weak grin. "In a much, much bigger machine. A species size machine."

"It's true." A pause. "Damn, I hope this machine can fix things. Everything is fucked landside. Got family on the west coast that had to move inland, tides and fires are running rampant. A house that's been in my family since the pioneer days burned down two weeks ago. Historical landmark. Heirlooms. All gone."

Captain Cho said nothing in response, letting silence do the heavy lifting. No one on the bridge dared even breathe.

"Look," Gordon finally spoke up. "Tell me you're not up to anything shady."

"We're not up to anything shady," the captain repeated, her voice deadpan.

Lexi stared at the visual scopes. Jets fired on the Corona. They were turning. Turning.

She was about to signal Darnell, to tell him and Keelin to hurry their asses up, when Sarita put a hand on her shoulder and shook her head.

The intercom crackled and Gordon spoke, "Alright. Fine. You're going in the flight log as being here, but it was determined that there was not enough cause to investigate in light of conserving Delta-V. Keep your nose clean, Captain Cho. Get that transponder fixed."

"Fly safe, friend."

The channel went dead. A flash came from the rock. The Corona zipped overhead on their way to make yet another revolution around Saturn.

"Richardson," Captain Cho called over the ship-to-suit comms channel. "Hurry your ass up. We have till they swing back around to get out of here, or we're screwed. I don't think I can pull that off twice."

"Aye aye," he replied. "Almost there."

Logan put a hand on the captain's shoulder and squeezed. Cho nodded and Logan pushed off, going with Atticus to the aft of the ship.

"Clever subversion, Captain," Sarita said. "You are a wonderful liar."

"I hardly lied."

"Come now. Omission is a lie unto itself."

"Do you always have to be such a bitch?"

Sarita scoffed at her. "And do you? I've heard how you ride these Void-Striders."

"I only 'ride them' because I know what they can really do. I only ride them because I give a damn about their well-being."

Lexi's finger over the engine's safety relaxed. There would be no heroic burn today.

The monitors flashed again. Another explosion on the surface of the asteroid. The knot in Lexi's chest loosened. Was her hesitancy under pressure foolishness or maturity? She wanted to believe it was the latter.

"That oughta do it," Keelin called back.

"Headed in," Darnell replied. *"Can I just say I'm ready to see this done?"*

"Say whatever you like and pour me a drink, love."

Captain Cho was leaning over Lexi's shoulder, chewing at her nails. Sarita, for her part, was a mask of collected calm. All this expression did was make Lexi angry. How could that bitch be this calm? They'd almost gotten caught.

The relative angle of the *Peridot* made it impossible to see down into the hole Darnell and Keelin had made. They vanished over the lip of the void, communications signals crackling as the rock itself interfered.

"Activating spotlights," Darnell called back. *"It's a cave under here, just like Sarita said. Doesn't go far. If we had rotated a little more, we might have skipped blasting entirely."*

Keelin cleared her throat. *"Does it go back any further, Richardson?"*

"Dead end over here."

"Same here."

"Where is it?" Cho blurted. "What is its condition?"

"Captain..." Darnell paused as if considering his words carefully. *"I hate to inform you, but, well... the rock is empty."*

"I am not in the mood for jokes," she replied, her face turning red. "What is the Slipstream's condition?"

"Condition? That's an easy one. There's nothing in here. The rock is hollow. Hell, I don't think it's even real." Darnell took a moment to inspect the rock more thoroughly. *"No, it's not real. It has latticework and structure. This rock was man-made."*

"A fake?" Logan squeaked, having just reappeared on the bridge with drinks in hand, the psychologist beside them. They'd been ready to toast success.

Atticus floated beside the doctor, his mouth wide, eyes blinking. "I—this..." For once he had nothing to say.

Lexi unbuckled from her acceleration chair and pushed off toward Sarita. She was ready to beat the shit out of their guide. They'd been led into some sort of trap, put their lives and futures at risk for what? This was bullshit. Bullshit.

"Hey, hey, everything is fine," Sarita finally said, raising her hands in a pleading gesture. "Just fine. Come on back in, ladies. Oh, and nab that transponder while you're at it. Should be straight ahead and to the left, if I am orienting correctly. Hard to tell over these tiny ass screens."

"What the hell is this all about?" Darnell mumbled over comms. *"Will someone tell me?"*

"Getting paid, son," she replied. "It's about getting paid."

[13] – Darnell

"You better start talking," the captain told Sarita.

The hacker had been forcibly pulled from her acceleration chair, her electronics taken away. Sarita now floated in a corner of the bridge, her shoulders shrunk between a bundle of network cables and portable instrumentation, the crew staring her down like a pack of hungry wolves. She raised her hands in supplication and offered up a fake grin, her self-possessed look replaced with actual fear.

Darnell was covered in sweat and his forehead was as hot as a cast iron skillet ready to fry eggs. He wasn't one to fly off the handle, but this had brought him to the edge. They'd traveled all this way, and for what? What game was the Collector playing? This wasn't integrity. This wasn't a somewhat foolhardy move to do something ultimately great. He should have listened to his first instincts. They were working for a criminal who wanted them to also become criminals.

Even worse, they had been betrayed.

"I can explain," Sarita replied. "I can explain."

"If I were you, I would be very careful what you say next," Atticus said, her arms crossed, one hand raised, inspecting his nails. "The way I see it, the *Peridot* has about sixty kilograms too much mass."

"Okay, okay," she pleaded. "Here's the deal. The Collector needed to know you could be trusted. The Slipstream itself is out in the open. Once you got a fix on its location, there would be nothing to stop you from taking it for yourselves. Not even the UEI. Plus, you had to be willing to go into the situation and stand up to the authorities."

"What?" the captain's face went slack. "You're telling me this was a test? A stupid, goddamn test?"

"I swear, that's all it was. This part, anyway. It was all that James, I mean, shit, the Collector... It was all he could think to do. If you weren't up for a little trouble, you might turn tail. If you weren't trustworthy, you could capture the Slipstream and make a run for it, tossing me out into space."

"Hang on a second..." Lexi raised a hand. "You said James. You can't mean James Carlisle? The Collector is James, freakin' Carlisle? I knew that man looked familiar. I fucking knew it."

"Who's that?" Keelin asked. "Looked like just another blustery right winger to me."

"Yes, fine," Sarita conceded. "The Collector is James Carlisle. He altered his appearance in the videos so that you might not recognize him."

"Oh, Lord." Atticus pinched the bridge of his nose. "Great. Just great. Of all the people for me to get mixed up with, it had to be him."

Darnell knew *of* James Carlisle. He was the figurehead of the Fifth Great Awakening, a movement which had gained considerable traction back in his hometown, despite its hellfire-and-brimstone approach to Christianity. He himself had a deep-rooted faith, one instilled by his God-fearing grandfather, but Carlisle's doctrine went a bit too far for his taste. Carlisle fueled the fires that climate change was the wrath of God, and that repentance, and donation to his movement, were the road to salvation. To Carlisle and his followers, science had nothing to do with the Earth's troubles. To them, climate change was a spiritual war, not a physical one.

"This doesn't make sense," Logan spoke up. "The reason I was able to connect with you is because you happened to know some of the most fringe people in my circle. Body hackers and political doxxers, pretty much anti-government anarchists, and you happen to be working for the most extreme conservative on the public stage?"

Sarita crossed her arms and took a deep breath.

"This isn't about money, is it?" the captain asked, having seen something in Sarita's expression, pieces put together over time. Cho had a way of reading people, a high degree of emotional intelligence that Darnell couldn't comprehend.

The hacker hung her head. "Not entirely."

"What is it about then? Tell us. Come clean or get off my flyer."

Sarita considered this for a while, staring off into blank space as if recalling, then filing a host of memories.

"He has my wife," she whispered.

"Bullshit," Keelin spat, finger pointing. "Too convenient."

"I'm telling the truth." Sarita's eyes began to gleam with moisture. "Open my tablet, the code is six seven three two."

Darnell reached for Sarita's confiscated tablet and entered the code. He located a folder with personal photos and began to swipe through them. There were dozens of screen-captures of memes, selfies with filters, and snapshots of the inside of a dirty spacecraft. He kept scrolling and found a series of images with Sarita and a pretty, blue-eyed blonde girl in professional work clothes.

The gallery of pictures began with them having drinks and dinner on what appeared to be Luna, continuing in reverse chronological order. There were random captures of time spent with one another like Lexi and he might take on date night—the two women coming up the gravity well from Earth to ST1, a vacation on a beach with white sand and crystal-clear water. Video of a carousel ride at a state fair. Cotton candy bundles so big both their heads were dwarfed. And then there was Sarita, dressed in white, the woman in question with her, her soon-to-be-wife dressed in a black suit and tie, a gathering of friends in a botanical garden sitting on wooden chairs before them, an arch adorned in flowers at their side. Time stamps. Days. Weeks. Months. Years apart. Private moments kissing in the rain. Silly faces and tongues stuck out. Laughter. Love. Contentedness. The story of a relationship in picture form.

"She's telling the truth," Darnell said after some time.

Katia scowled. "How can you tell?"

"Besides the way she's acting, ma'am? This last picture. Take a look."

She narrowed her eyes at the screen, taking in the image he had paused on, then looked to Sarita.

Her wife was on a space station, maybe a base, with gray industrial looking halls, empty but for a few letters painted on the walls in red that could not be identified at this angle. She stood uncomfortably close to two large men in suits, a forced smile on her face, a silver necklace with an S at its end around her neck. Sarita clutched a necklace just like it in her fingers, its slender chain floating before her.

While a cursory glance at this photo did not tell the whole story, there were spots of blood on the carpet if you looked close enough, and a slender cut running down her right cheek. Her hair was a mess, unlike the rest of the images, and there were dark bags under her eyes. One of the guards had a pale teardrop tattoo under one eye, the other guard's knuckles so rough they looked as if he'd used a cheese grater to toughen them up.

"If these are fake, there sure as hell was a lot of work involved," Darnell went on. "Yeah, we got generative AI and all that, but there are subtle signs when that goes wrong. There are hundreds of pictures, different places, same face. The most recent date stamp is only four months ago. It's clear Sarita loves whoever this woman is."

"Sarah," she mumbled, closing her fist so hard around the necklace Darnell suspected it might draw blood. "Her name is Sarah."

"Let me see," the captain reached out her hand and Darnell turned over the tablet. A moment passed and Cho's anger began to deflate. "Well shit..."

"I didn't mean to get her wrapped up in this. I have a special set of IT skills. For the most part, I have used them ethically. Most of my adult life, I've worked in cyber security and network administration. I've also worked as a consultant performing penetration tests on government networks. My first life had been lucrative, and we wanted to give it a go on Luna. Plenty of work to be done on the moon colony for people with my skills. That's when James found me. I should have known something was wrong."

"Why did the preacher need a hacker?" Atticus cut in, his expression as bored as ever. Darnell wondered if anything ever really made the man mad, or was he just that good at hiding it? Would a psychologist really bottle it all up? Seemed unhealthy.

"How do you think we found the Slipstream?" She pressed her palms to her cheeks and closed her eyes. Beads of water floated beside her face. "Someone in the Chinese government found it a while back and tagged it for recovery. No one in their fleet has had the time to go get it. A flyer is schedule to scoop it up in about six months. This is our only window to capture it."

"So, let me get this straight," Atticus started, then paused, taking a deep breath. "You and your wife travel to Luna to start a new life. Yes? When you go looking for work, James Carlisle, figurehead of the Fifth Great Awakening, offers you a job to get information from the Chinese. You likely see it as doing no harm, and whatever work comes your way is good, yes? After you acquire this information, however, he knows that this request could cause a scandal if it ever got out. The leader of the Holy Word of Calvary Church paid a black hat to locate Matteo Lindvall's Slipstream in order to illegally recover it and add to his personal cache. I still don't fully understand what he thinks he will gain by acquiring this particular item, but he does have quite the American artifact collection. Thus this appellation, his handle, 'The Collector,' is accurate. And you and your wife are just caught in the middle."

"He's fearful that you might squeal at a later date," the captain finished for Atticus. "He wants the capture behind him before letting you go. A woman in love can provide much leverage."

"So long as we complete the job, he'll give her back," she said, her words pleading. "All we have to do is recover the Slipstream. You'll get paid. I promise. I wasn't trying to hurt anyone. All I want is my Sarah back."

"But why do I doubt that?" Logan mused. "This is all so slippery."

There were so many unanswered questions. Why was the Slipstream so important? Why would a religious figure who, despite being a bit extreme, that had brought so many to God, want to hurt others? How would any of this push forward his agenda? Was it the secret, the object in the glove box? Would he even keep his word if the job was completed?

Darnell wanted to believe he would. But taking a hostage? Was that what a Godly man did?

"I think it's pretty clear what we need to do," Darnell said, his back going straight.

Everyone turned to look at him, surprise on their faces. Keelin squinted.

"What?" the captain said. "What are you saying?"

"To hell with the money," he went on. "I see someone in danger, two someone's actually, and we have the opportunity to save them."

"It doesn't change that this is a crime," Keelin said. "You ain' been too keen on bein' a gurrier."

"No, it doesn't change the legal status of all this, but I can't in good conscience let someone get hurt. If it wasn't us, the Collector would have just forced Sarita to find someone else. Might as well be the *Peridot's* crew."

Lexi's face brightened, a smirk curling her lip. She pulled back, turning neutral once more. "Leave it up to a cowboy to want to save the day."

"Might still hurt her anyways," Atticus mused. "People like him are not to be trusted. Hippocrates."

"Might just," Darnell replied. "But I get the feelin' if he doesn't get what he wants, it's not just a might."

"It's not," Sarita said.

"Are we sure about this?" the captain asked. "We are going into much stickier territory than I had first considered. This is no longer just a quick stealth job. If we get caught, all of us are going down. Carlisle is an influential public figure, with allies and enemies. All I can say is, I recommend you make a plea deal if we get caught so you don't end up on the wrong side of an airlock."

"What's the difference who catches us?" Lexi asked. "The UEI won't be much kinder than Carlisle."

Keelin started chuckling at the absurdity of it all, making a manic, frustrated sound. "Might be foolish, but I still want me money, risk of the rope or no. I gots things to do. Far as I can tell, doin' the right thing might just still pay."

"It will," Sarita whispered.

Atticus rolled his eyes at her and worked his way towards the exit. "I've had enough hypocrisy for one evening. You do whatever you want to do, I'll be waiting to hear your ill-fated answer."

Sarita was silent. Her body curled up in a ball. She was no longer crying, but her expression was heavy despite null gravity, her black hair wild and tangled.

"Will you help me then?" she asked after a while.

The captain crossed her arms and looked to her crew. No one twitched. "Can he be trusted to let her go if we get what he wants?"

"Again, he can be trusted to hurt her if he doesn't."

"Christ on a cracker, Sarita." Cho rubbed her face for a moment. "Okay. Unless anyone has an objection, we go ahead with the plan. Recover the Slipstream and deliver it to the Collector."

"And what if he flips on us?" Lexi asked. "What then?"

"We're creative," Logan said, their voice far more chipper than it should have been at a time like this. "We'll figure it out."

"Great plan, very specific," Darnell said, raising an eyebrow. "Remind me not to hire you as my life coach."

They stuck their tongue out at him, and as they did their arms flashed red.

"Tell us everything you know," the captain told Sarita. "We'll need to find us some leverage of our own."

This was it. This was the right thing to do. Didn't matter if theft was involved at this point, Darnell saw no other way to make things right then to help her, even if she was a criminal. Jesus made friends with criminals, right? Thieves and whores and tax collectors.

There was hope yet.

All he had to do was survive this test.

There was hope yet.

[14] – Lexi

Lexi adjusted course, pointing the *Peridot* in a new direction. They corkscrewed out from Saturn in a Hohmann transfer orbit, a maneuver which still remained the most energy efficient method to escape a gravity well. She was happy to see that the UEI flyer did not come near them again, their new trajectory out of alignment with that of the science vessel's.

Although the Slipstream itself was not in orbit around Saturn, it wasn't far away in a solar scale. Sarita had tracked its signal to a position three AU to their stern. Two weeks is all it would take to capture the Slipstream. Then it was back to Luna to do some hard negotiating. Could they save the girl and still get their prize? Lexi felt bad for even thinking it, but she still wanted the life she wanted. She deserved the opportunity to raise a happy, healthy family away from the many dangers planet-side.

The bridge was quiet the evening after Sarita's revelation, most everyone having turned in early, including the hacker herself. The only ones awake were those who couldn't sleep, including Darnell who thumbed through a book, and Atticus, who watched network TV streamed in from Earth. Sarita had been locked in her quarters without any electronic equipment. Her hostage story didn't seem like a lie, but it was hard to say for sure. Better to be careful than end up dead.

Lexi remained seated in her acceleration chair, harness only partially clicked into place to keep her from free floating. She played a matching game on her hand terminal to pass the time, something mindless with lots of color and chimes and sugary music, with a title she couldn't remember.

Atticus hummed to himself as he watched an old sitcom from the late 1990s. From what little she had gleaned, the show was about a tight-knit group of casual lovers who lived in a coffee shop and enjoyed jumping into fountains with their clothes on. Lexi had never seen the appeal of shows like this. Whether she wanted to admit it or not, teenage dramas were her guilty pleasure. Stories of puppy love and backstabbing friends caught in webs of adolescent lies were like eating candy.

Out of the corner of her eye, she noticed that Darnell had closed his book and was eyeing her screen.

"You okay?" she asked, and then pressed down her thumb, clearing out an entire column of pink crystals in her game before time ran out. Her screen flashed, *You Go!* And another level began.

"I just..." Darnell started, then paused, his expression one of deep thought. "It's hard for me to wrap my head around all of it."

"What part?" Atticus groaned. "It's all quite simple."

"We talking about Carlisle?" Lexi asked.

Darnell sniffed. "No, not Carlisle. Well... Maybe Carlisle. Part of it. Can't believe he'd take hostage over somethin'..."

Atticus pursed his lips. "You might try forming a complete thought before opening your mouth."

"Why you gotta be so rude?"

Atticus's television stream cycled through a series of commercials, all of them either food or beauty products. The jingle for Exo-Bites began, and even though the damn things tasted like cardboard, the catchy pop song they used to sell it made her feel a might peckish.

Lexi turned away from her game to glare at the psychologist. "You are the worst therapist I've ever known, and I've been to seven." She tipped her head at Darnell. "Go on, beau. Let your thoughts out, even if they're messy. It's okay. This is a safe space."

Darnell pulled a pouch from his jumpsuit and took a sip of water before continuing. "It's a lot to take in. I still can't reconcile it. What he's done and might do to Sarita's wife. And then my feelings... I can't stop thinking about something. Is it so bad to remember what America was?

What made it so great? I get that Carlisle's means are extreme, dangerous even, but was this country not founded on freedom and God? Freedom of worship? Seems that all people want to do these days is trash our nation. We are the greatest country in history."

Lexi lowered her hand terminal and sighed, her game pausing. "Yes, we are, and no we aren't."

"What do you mean? It ain't complicated. We're either the best, or we ain't. I for one still think we're the best."

"Say what you want, it's complicated, love."

"How's it complicated?"

Was it really time to have a discussion like this? She needed to dump all serious thought from her mind, not go down the twisty path of amoral American history.

"Do you not remember what happened in the early 2020's? Should have at least learned it in history class."

"Learned what?" he asked, attention focused off to the side as he sifted through his memories like a set of dusty bins.

Atticus pinched the bridge of his nose. "You know what, Lexi, you're right. By damn it, you're right. I need to be better to my clients. I'll be nice. Please, don't hold this bit of knowledge against him. He lived in a red state all his life, sans Austin. History was likely not a major focus. Or should I say, unpopular history, you know, the parts we don't like to talk about."

"I know there was a virus," Darnell said, raising an excited finger. Lexi was afraid to hear what might come next, but she had given him the license to speak his mind even if it was wrong. Or wrong in her opinion, at least. "There was a virus and that the president made it go away and saved the world. It was a time for America to get back to its roots, get back to the things that made it glorious to begin with. We cast off the racism and all that for good. Brought law and order back to the people. The Slipstream is from just after that era of prosperity, so why not use it to celebrate those days of glory? It's Carlisle's way of doing things I take issue with, not his objective."

"So much of that is wrong." The psychologist shook his head and tsked. "Wrong, wrong, wrong."

"What in the hell do you mean—*wrong?*"

"Yes, we had a pandemic, one of many," he went on. "And yes, a vaccine came about, COVID went away, XR5 went away, and so did BRIGHTS. This was not because of, or in spite of, the administration at the time. There was a need that had to be filled and the American people, as well as countless others around the world, worked as one to find a solution. Hanging the success of a country on a single leader is narrow minded. But what you so fondly recall, or rather what you were told, is just more American exceptionalism. America was not some ever-shining beacon of greatness, back then or now.

"So, we're the greatest country, but we have the highest incarceration rates? We're the greatest country, but we have the least healthy population? We're the greatest country, but we have the greatest number of children in poverty? Truth is, we have our challenges like everyone else. We're all on the same living spaceship. Just because you put the word American before it, doesn't patently make it better."

The room felt a bit colder for a moment. Atticus had never been afraid to share his opinions, but this, Lexi had a feeling this particular thread was attached to the family tapestry outlining why he was out here. She knew he had deep-seated political beliefs and that they were diametrically opposed to his parents'. But were they really so extreme? Humanity had bigger problems.

Darnell's eyes narrowed. He shook his book in the air at Atticus. "Are you saying you hate America?"

"Hate?" The psychologist laughed. "No. No. No. Not at all. Let us not forget my parents are politicians, and despite their shortcomings, I don't hate them either. You have to love someone to hate them. America has done good and bad things just like any country, even leaders I care little for were able to broker lasting peace in regions we never thought possible. But you have to take the good with the bad and hold people accountable.

"It's naïve to believe that progress doesn't have a cost, that there won't be pain, or that even well-intentioned people can't fall short. Not to mention, the divisiveness and lack of nuance a two-party system engenders. I can't love LGBT people and oppose abortion? I can't support the decriminalization of drugs, yet oppose heavy-handed gun laws? I believe that much of our social unrest was, and is, the result of so many different groups feeling as if they weren't being heard, all because of the backwards policies of those afraid of change. Not enough nuance, not enough granularity. There might only be two parties, but there's a far wider spectrum of beliefs. When the people don't feel heard, however, that's a dangerous thing."

"People like Carlisle?" Darnell asked. "Far as backward policies, that is?"

Lexi closed her game and slipped her hand terminal into her jumpsuit. "People like Carlisle ignore the sins of the past by putting the focus only on the best and brightest parts of history."

"And why is that so bad?" He whirled on her. "Why focus on the negative all the time?"

She unbuckled from her acceleration chair and floated up beside him. "History tends to repeat itself."

"Take a look at your skin," Atticus said, pointing a finger at Darnell.

"What about it?" He looked at his bare arm, confused. His skin was dark, just like Lexi's. So what? He was of African descent. "My skin has never kept me from anything I wanted in life. Look where we are."

"But what did it take to get here?" she asked. "Not just for you, but all of us. It took blood, sweat, tears, and time. It didn't happen overnight."

"And it's still a struggle in many places around the world," Atticus added. "Equity isn't easily won. It's a destination we'll likely never reach in perfection, and yet we should aspire for it."

"What are you saying then?" Darnell asked.

The psychologist's expression turned sad. "I'm saying that the Collector, and those like him, subscribe to a certain version of history in which America is blameless. This idea that we are the only ones who really matter on that pale blue dot known as Earth. That it is up to us to bring order to the rest of the world, at any cost. That because we are the biggest, and the best, it is our God-given responsibility to see it done. That if we don't fall face first on the ground, prostrate every day of our lives, God, who is supposedly *the most loving being in all of creation*, will continue to punish us with famine and plague."

"Like I said before, sir," Darnell replied, "I don't subscribe to that idea, well, not entirely. Sure, I've entertained it. Seems about right, timin' an all, hardships when the world went away from God, but I guess I just know too much now. I guess I'm not saying God ain't trying to teach us something, he always is, but I know deep down we're the ones who trashed the planet. This ain't no plague. But is it not America's responsibility to be the leaders? To show the way?"

"To show the way for who?" Atticus asked.

"The rest of the world."

"And what if our way is wrong?" He rebutted. "Can we admit it? Is it okay to fail and do it another way?"

Lexi stared at the floor as she rubbed her left arm with her fingertips. "The danger with Carlisle and his supporter's line of thinking is that blind nationalists will do whatever they please so long as it is in alignment with their cause. There's no room for new ideas. So long as America is first, the ends justify the means."

Atticus nodded. "Which is why a more global view was adopted as the century marched on and things got worse. Wildfires. Sea waters began to rise. The reefs turned white and died. The UEI and FICSE never could have happened politically without a massive paradigm shift in thinking. Still there are holdouts, those who would not believe a bit of it. That was until there was no other choice, then it became a religious war cry. In their eyes, this is the end of days."

"I know, the Great Awakening," Darnell whispered.

"A trite denomination," Atticus groaned. "People are screaming through the vacuum in artificial environments propelled by nuclear candles. And yet, some believe that our planet's struggles have a purely spiritual cause, despite empirical evidence to the contrary."

"I—well," Darnell stammered. "I try not to judge others for their beliefs, but what I do know, is God is in control in the end. Everything will be okay. This alien structure humanity is burning towards, this Foundry alien offering help, that could be God as well. Right? Looking over us, giving us a way out of this flood."

"Like the three boats?" Lexi suggested.

Atticus cocked his head, looking confused. "I've not heard this one."

She went on, "So, a man was stuck on the roof of his house during a flood, and he prayed that God would save him. Three boats show up to rescue him, one after another. He turns them all away because he's waiting on God to save him. A beam of holy light or an angel or something. In the end, he dies of exposure and ends up at the Pearly Gates. He asks God, 'Why didn't you save me?' And God replies, 'I sent three boats, what else could you ask for?'"

Darnell pointed at her and smiled. "Right on the money, love."

"Look, Richardson, I like you," Atticus continued. "You're a good person. I do not discount the need for spirituality, the need to connect to something higher and bigger than yourself. God and gods are mere symbols to move and awaken the mind, a means to look beyond oneself.

"We all need it, even godless heathens like myself. What bothers me, is when people of power use religion as a tool to manipulate others. It's not the personal relationship with God, or nature, or whatever you believe in. It's the doctrine, the dogma. It's a fierce weapon that can be used to push any agenda forward, no matter if it is right or wrong, best for everyone or just a few. It's a justification."

Darnell's cheeks reddened. "So you're saying my religious beliefs are an excuse?"

"Maybe not to you, but to some. One who believes God *leads* them to do something, can be just as dangerous as the person who says, 'the Devil made me do it.'"

"What are you trying to say? Get to the point doctor."

"My point is." Atticus paused for a moment. "Carlisle, the Collector, he smells of those who would manipulate just like this. Old money. People who remain hidden to control the sheepish public with whatever means they have at their disposal. There's change back home. Another wave of intellectual enlightenment. He seeks to undo that progress, or at the very least, to perpetuate a fantasy in which he can keep telling himself, and his followers, that the world should be what it once was, devoid of any progress. And he's willing to take a hostage to see this done. Think about that."

"But wasn't the world a better place back then?" Darnell looked to Lexi and back to Atticus, hoping for agreement. She couldn't give him that. While part of her wanted to agree, just to make him feel better, more at ease, the truth was that his view was narrow. "Forget about Carlisle for a minute."

"We'll have to agree to disagree on that, love," she told him.

His expression sagged in resignation. "I just don't get it."

"The world has always been a harsh place, good and bad," Atticus said, his attention focused on fingering his soft, blue scarf. "It wasn't perfect then, and it isn't perfect now. We tend to remember only the good of the past, while we allow the negative in our present to overshadow that which is great."

Darnell rubbed his eyebrows. "But that past all seems so wonderful. No floods, four seasons, snow at Christmas time and presents under the tree. All the good things. People dressed nice on Easter, huntin' for eggs and eating candy. Choirs singing the gospel, clapping and dancing, hands raised. The government not having to offer financial aid to those in need, the church stepping up for others. Nuclear families, husband, wife, children. Drug free. Safe streets. Gangs a thing of only nightmares, not reality."

"I'm sorry," Atticus said, blinking. "Do we need to go down to the corner drugstore so you can have a float with your best girl? What alternate universe are you living in? I swear you're describing a Norman Rockwell painting. How about some baseball and chewing gum, son? Hate to tell you, but the folk on that ranch you grew up on, they lied."

Lexi had always known Darnell was sheltered, that his upbringing was tantamount to paradise. He lived the western dream, riding horses on the range, wrangling cattle, enjoying the simple pleasures of the land, far removed from the bustling city life of Dallas. He was a country boy who'd rather wake up at 4 AM and watch the sun rise with a cup of black coffee in hand with the wind as conversation than to drop molly and sweat it out in a crowded dance club. He was pure, and though that could be frustrating at times, it also made her feel like she didn't deserve him.

"The world was a good place," Darnell mumbled as if he were trying to convince himself as much as them. "A good place. It doesn't have to be just about people hurting each other all the time. I won't be swayed by your bitterness."

Atticus paused his TV show and leaned forward, head in his hands. The bridge went silent but for the soft hum of electronics and air recyclers. "I just get tired of hypocritical people in positions of power always getting away with hurting others to push an agenda forward. Power should not make you blameless, or above reproach. If you do something wrong, you should be punished no matter your status."

"With great power comes great responsibility?" Darnell ventured.

"Precisely."

"We can agree on that one."

Lexi flexed her back and stretched out her arms. A groan of relief came up all the way from her toes. It always felt good to stretch, even if your body hadn't had any real weight pressed down on it in months. "Atticus, are you going to be up for a bit? Mind being on watch?"

He waved a dismissive hand. "So long as you turn the coffee maker on as you pass the galley. I'm gonna finish this season of *Friends*."

"Can do." She took hold of Darnell's hand and led him back towards their quarters. "Have a good night."

"That's the plan," he said, unpausing his show.

Lexi led them back into their quarters and closed the door.

"Get comfy," she said, staring at Darnell with a hint of mischief in her eyes.

He made no complaints and stripped out of his clothes, revealing his well-muscled, statuesque body. Despite all the disagreements, she had come to the conclusion that God must be real, because every time she looked at him like this she saw something divine.

"You still love me, in spite of my beliefs?" he asked. "We're just so different."

She considered that for a moment, holding back a smile. "Beliefs tend to change over time, beau. Hearts don't, and I know your heart. That's all that really matters."

He was about to say something else, but she put a finger to his lips. Enough of that.

They slipped into their sleeping sack, adjusting positions in their cramped quarters to offer skin to skin leverage. Null gravity wasn't one to give favors when playing bareback games.

She loved how he smelled during sex, his musk, the taste of salt on his skin. The harder they went, the more her body ached for him to make her full. She wanted so bad for him to leave a piece of himself inside of her, and he would, but it would all be for naught. No spark. No life. Until they found a place on Luna or went home, the UEI-mandated birth controls would render this beautiful moment of creation, and any others, into nothing more than erotic recreation and release.

She told herself it would be enough. For now.

Afterwards, they cleaned up their mess and he fell right to sleep. A typical end to a fitful session, sweaty and snoring.

She floated beside him, unable to close her eyes. Her mind reached out beyond the walls of their flyer into the future, a hand on her bare belly rubbing as she dreamed. She was on the cusp of great events.

What would come tomorrow? Freedom, heroism, or a painful end? She wasn't sure. All she knew, was that there was no other person she wanted at her side when fate made its decision known. They might have different views, different beliefs, but she saw this as a strength not weakness, because what they had in common mattered so much more.

[15] – DARNELL

Despite a wonderful end to a troubling evening, Darnell found himself tossing and turning all night, which was no easy feat in null gravity. As he turned around in their sleeping bag, Lexi pursued him, arms grasping, drawing him close whenever he drifted away. He just couldn't get comfortable no matter what he did. Several loose thoughts in his head acted like rocks under a pillow out on the trail. No matter how you turned, your head came to rest against them, hard points of stone pressing against your skull ensuring sleep came only with exhaustion.

He told himself to close his eyes, even if sleep didn't come. As gramps always said, you should get what rest you could. This worked for about an hour, but when sweet oblivion never arrived, he decided to revise the plan.

There was no point fighting it. He was up.

As he slid from the sleeping bag, Lexi held onto him. Even in slumber, she wasn't interested in letting him go. He peeled her hands away and gave her a kiss on the forehead, then zipped her back in as she let out of a soft groan of displeasure.

He had intended to head off to the galley and nab a meal pack, but when he saw an unopened bag of Exo-Bites stuffed in an open wall duffel, he decided to stay put. Chocolate peanut butter-flavored wasn't too bad. It would do in a pinch.

Popping in his earbuds, he began to munch while scrolling through his hand terminal's timeline. Even out here he got to see his nieces and nephews grow up. Jan, his brother Demarcus's youngest, was playing violin at a recital, getting a little too into the music for her teacher. She was dancing to the rhythm of *Ode to Joy* by Beethoven while bobbing and weaving herself around the stage of a high school auditorium. Her passion made him smile. Kevin, his sister Alexis's oldest, had won a school robotics competition just hours before he made the game winning touchdown which would take his team to state. Brains and brawn.

"Runs in the family," he mumbled.

Darnell left his mark on their feed from deep space, a few likes and quick video replies. In about two hours they'd see these responses appear in their notifications, light speed lag creating its own form of time travel. Being an uncle was pretty cool, but he knew it wasn't the same as being a father.

He scrolled down though his feed and stopped. A friend of his from high school had shared a video of a rally in Dallas from the previous weekend. Thousands had gathered around Belo Garden downtown, homemade signs in hand, pleading for the residents of that sinful city to turn back to God before it was too late.

The crowd chanted.

The fire in our air, is the fire of Hell come to take us. Cool us down, oh Lord, we seek your forgiveness. Purge the wickedness from our hearts and set us free. Let your glory be known.

Carlisle was nowhere to be seen. It only made sense. He was off world, having set his machine in motion, crowds gathered without his direct influence. Ideas were often bigger than people. They could take on a life of their own.

"At least no one is looting," someone said in the comments. "A classy protest! God Bless America!"

"The right to assembly is a third amendment right!" Another said. "This is what our founding fathers died for."

Darnell didn't think that was right, but he kept reading.

The Feed stirred at his actions.

Uncle Cletus was even in the comments, but for the sake of keeping the peace in his family, Darnell scrolled on without reading. Whatever it was his uncle had said, he knew it would likely be wildly inappropriate and ignorant, driven by impulse, not logic.

College football season was about six weeks away. Texas and Oklahoma State would be kicking off the first game. He hated not watching them live from the *Peridot,* but could still have the flyer's computer record the feed. Might not be the most interesting matchup to start with, since Texas's kicker, Bradley, injured himself pre-season, and Oklahoma State's quarterback, Williams, couldn't throw worth a damn as a sophomore, but it was football and that was a welcome distraction. The world might be falling apart, but the Big 12 had games to play.

His feed, the Feed, soon became a slog of social media filler, videos of people doing coordinated dances, inspirational moments from celebrities speaking at graduation ceremonies, as well as recipe videos of tasty, southern-fried treats.

Another Exo-Bite went in his mouth and crunched between his right molars. At least they had a bit of texture, if not much flavor. He liked peanut butter well enough, but he sure had a craving for some hot chicken. He set a piece before him where it floated, then opened his mouth wide and ate it like a whale scooping up krill. As he chewed, he bounced his way into the bathroom, still scrolling, and operated the vacuum powered urination tube with one hand, eyes ever fixed on his hand terminal.

More videos began to appear. Rallies sparked by Carlisle's cause were happening all over the continental United States. In many cities, the protesters were being met by counter protesters. In Florida, a group of men calling themselves "The Honor Guard" had begun showing up to events strapped with military grade weapons common at almost any gun store. Claiming he had been defending a group in prayer before Tampa city hall, a young man in his early twenties was facing first degree murder charges for killing a counter protester. As the story went, someone had thrown a foam block at the marching Great Awakening crowd, and the boy had thought it was a brick and opened fire.

It pained Darnell to see people caught up in the middle of this. Violence wasn't the answer. Then again, was that kid just trying to protect them? What about the right to bear arms? Damn. Why couldn't they just sit down at the same table and talk? Sure, it made him angry some days that the world was headed to hell in a handbasket, but screaming about it, what did that do? He wasn't sure. He was taught growing up that when the screaming started, the argument was over. None of this was right.

Rumors abounded that martial law would be imposed soon. Many argued that the only way to get these dissidents under control was to bring in the military. This made sense to a degree, but seemed a little extreme. Was there any precedence for this? Does that level of law-and-order spell, dictatorship, rather than, democratic republic?

The Feed was fully awake. It went on and on, offering, suggesting, calculating.

He read of men in black clothes taking the Fifth Great Awakening followers away in the night and threatening to kill their families if they didn't stop. He read that billionaire Adrian Blask, CEO of Blask & Denton Pharma, was working on bio-machines that controlled peoples' minds through hormones and Wi-Fi. There were Illuminati pulling the strings as the five most powerful families controlled the path of the world again and again, generation after generation. The aliens of the Foundry were subverting democracy to steal infants and genetically manipulate them into trans-dimensional psychic warriors. Socialism was destroying America, public safety nets should be removed, twenty percent unemployment in the US was acceptable. Plenty of work was available, these people were just lazy, unmotivated.

Darnell's blood pressure rose.

The Feed carried him onward.

An image appeared with an outside link to a news source he wasn't familiar with. *March 15, 2092, Leader of the Fifth Great Awakening movement given Vatican blessing.* It went on to explain about how Pope Francis had begun a movement in the early parts of the century to mobilize members of the Catholic Church and other faiths to unify and take better care of the planet, to care for our common home. Carlisle was praised by the current Pope, Pope Angelo Flavio, for inspiring many to make changes in their personal lives that would lead to net zero carbon emissions. Both agreed that God gives us the tools to affect change if we only humble ourselves before His will. Hard to disagree.

Another link, farther off the beaten path. Followers of the Fifth Great Awakening part of a chapter from Oxford, Mississippi, coordinated a force of six hundred contractors to put boots on the ground in Honduras. They worked for a solid year to build seven schools and three hospitals. Darnell pursed his lips at this. Logan might find it interesting. He forwarded them the link to look at later.

Colorful text and familiar GIFs led him to another news site he hadn't seen before, something called the Freedom Warriors. So many like this had cropped up lately. The article had to do with sex trafficking and how Carlisle worked side by side with the Missing Girls Foundation. With the aid of his followers, he'd personally rescued hundreds from a farm in the middle of nowhere Georgia. Within the article, front and center, was an image of countless girls under the age of fifteen leaving a rotted, red barn in a weed choked forest, police leading them to a bus, girls hugging one another, sending a mix of emotions through Darnell he couldn't fully understand. There was anger and rage. Relief. Hope.

But before he could metabolize his feelings, process these ideas, the Feed drew him someplace else. A group of faith-based scientists adjacent to the Fifth Great Awakening's cause were working tirelessly to develop technologies that would remove carbon from the atmosphere and reverse climate change. Giant tubes shot into the sky like smokestacks on a factory, able to filter carbon from the atmosphere using electrical charges. The scientists referred to this as re-terraforming. It was interesting. Maybe something like this is what the Foundry, if the aliens were to be believed, would help humanity create.

So much information in such a tiny sliver of glass. His hand terminal was a portal to what seemed an infinite number of realities, connected across vast gulfs of nothing through the cloud, the hidden motivations of the Feed dragging him along an invisible conveyor belt of existential dread.

He hit a fork in the road, two links before him. On the left, a story about Carlisle's organization giving ten thousand dollars a day to struggling families who agreed to pray with him. On the right, Carlisle's support for a militant leader in East Africa who was determined to stamp out the drug trade with violence.

His thumb wandered between both, unable to make a decision. One part of him wanted to believe that the man had done more good than harm, another did not. How could you say you walk with God and yet, hold someone against their will to get what you want? How?

Lexi had disagreed with him and his beliefs, about all this, about how America had been a better place once, and that the bad should just be left in the past. Not that it didn't happen. Not that there wasn't injustice, or that people didn't get hurt, but focusing on the past and ignoring the future did no one any good.

He glanced up from his device in her direction, the Feed discontented that he had looked away, his hands shaking.

I know your heart, she had said. And if he was being honest with himself, he knew Carlisle's as well. Its color was that of poison and tar. Sticky and deadly. Not a man of God. A man playing the part, a demon in sheep's clothing.

Darnell's device chirped. A notification. The Feed calling him back. He wanted to follow every link, fact-check every post, but it was all too much. Who could he trust? Who could he believe? Atticus had once told him that these platforms were designed to keep him engaged so they could expose him to advertising, no matter the content. And that was exactly what the Feed had done, even if he was millions of miles away. Exo-bite ads. Exo-bites in his mouth. Three items bookmarked for later purchase, and he hadn't even realized it.

Four hours had passed, and he was no sleepier, his brain brimming with a cocktail of dopamine and cortisol. He didn't know what to believe anymore. What was real? That seemed to vary, based on who you asked and what they wanted. It frustrated the hell out of him how malleable ideas were.

Lexi moaned and rolled around in the sleeping bag. She cracked her eyes open and peered at him.

"You up already?" She began to slide out and get dressed.

He gave her his best fake smile. "Yeah. Just wanted to get an early start."

"Sounds good." She kissed him on the forehead. "Want me to make some coffee?"

"Please."

She booped him on the nose with a fingertip and pushed off. "Coming right up, Mr. Richardson."

He raised his hand terminal again, staring at the links for a moment, then shook his head and locked the screen. Enough for today. What was happening back home had no bearing on what was happening on this flyer. He prayed he made the right choices, would make the right choices. The holy spirit spoke to him, he thought. At least he hoped that's what it was.

When the time came, he knew he would do what was right. Not only did Lexi know his heart, he knew it too, but most importantly, so did God almighty.

[16] – LEXI

Coffee just wasn't the same in null gravity which bothered the hell out of almost everyone in their crew. Without the weight of the world pulling down on the grinds, it brewed differently, came out tasting more acidic and far less fragrant. Each cup had to be enjoyed from a pouch or bulb to keep it from oozing its way around the flyer and ending up in sensitive equipment. Lexi had always preferred her coffee from a French press, boiling water poured over grinds at the bottom of a glass pitcher left to sit and steep. She loved the smell as it brewed, the sound, the action of pressing down bits of black before pouring a cup of the dark, divine liquid.

Too bad that would make the biggest mess in null gravity.

Their coffee maker, as it were, was a box mounted into the wall of their galley with two water pumps that kept the mixture of near boiling water flowing at all times. The constant whirr of the machine ensured it maintained an even temperature, pockets of super-heated liquid equally distributed.

"It will never be espresso," Logan said, floating up beside her and coffee machine.

Lexi let out a sigh and nodded. "The crema of a well pulled espresso would make life hell for Keelin, if we could even get it to form."

"Fifteen to twenty-one seconds, let it pour from the filter like the mouse's tail and it will leave a layer of rusty foam both bitter and sweet." They placed fingers to their lips then kissed the air as if saying *bon appetit*.

"You a barista in a former life?"

"For a couple generations, pretty sure everyone was a barista in a former life."

The coffee maker beeped. The brewing module was full, its cycle complete. Lexi pressed a single serving plastic bulb against a spout and smiled as it filled, her mouth watering at the prospect of its taste.

Keelin poked her head into the galley, her orange-red hair a tangled mess of curls. "Mind drawing me one while you're at it?"

"Damn. This pot is dead before it hardly got started."

"It's the way of thin's."

"No tea?"

"Not today, sunshine. Could use somethin' a wee stronger. Got to clear me system of all the wrong I've done to it." She pushed off and vanished down the hall, shouting back, "Thanks, deary!"

Logan smiled, her arms glowing red beneath the skin. "So you're pouring me one next, yeah?"

"Guess I better start a second pot."

Lexi emptied the coffee maker, pulling bulbs for half the crew before making her way to the bridge. She was amazed to find that the forward end of the flyer was louder than normal, everyone on board present, each glued to their respective devices. Or in the case of Atticus, watching TV on a wall panel, a bottle resting in the crook of his arm. She checked the time just to be sure it was early, rather than late. Time was weird in the void, fluid and nebulous, but it was morning for most of them.

Darnell looked bleary eyed and stared off into nothing, as if he hadn't slept well the night before, maybe not even at all. It took several nudges to snap him out of it.

"Oh, hey," he said, then took the warm bulb of coffee from her. "Mmm. Thanks, love."

"My pleasure." She gave a bow, then distributed the rest of the coffee. "You okay?" She slid up beside him whispering, head resting on his shoulder.

"Yeah." He grinned. "I'm good. This'll help. Just didn't sleep well."

The intro to one of Atticus's shows started up and screamed at everyone on the bridge. Lexi fought to ignore it.

"Atticus, turn that shit down!" Logan growled.

"Why?"

"Just go watch it in your quarters if you're going to blare it like that."

"Pfft," Atticus sputtered. He pointed a finger at them. "You remind me of—of my dad, trying to take a nap on the c—couch in the living room when everyone was watching TV, then get—getting mad he couldn't sleep with all the noise."

Every word of his was a slur.

"This ain' no livin' room," Keelin added. "Put your pods in or get back in your hole."

"Cunt."

Keelin gasped at the word, a hand on her chest mocking surprise.

Darnell narrowed his eyes and sipped his coffee. "What's his problem this morning?" He kept his voice quiet enough that only Lexi could hear him.

"I'm not sure."

"Bit early to be drinkin', yeah?"

"Yeah."

"Shit," Sarita said, banging her head against her tablet several times.

"What is it?" the captain asked.

"Carlisle," she said, twisting around in her chair. "He wants an update."

"Show us."

"The message is just for me. It's not, well, it's not..."

"It's not a theatrical production like the rest of his crap?" Logan ventured. "Ooo, I like this."

The captain brushed her chin with her knuckles in thought. "Me too. Put it on the main screen."

Sarita's body sagged. "Fine." She swiped her screen towards the display and a video window appeared.

"Time for Uncle Cletus," Darnell mumbled, then took another sip of coffee. Lexi knew just what he meant.

Carlisle appeared, dressed in the same suit as always, but this time his eyes were red and twitchy, the round glasses he had previously worn having been tossed away. Had those merely been an affectation? A way to make him appear approachable? His hair was wild and unkempt, like someone who hadn't slept in days.

"Sarita? Are you there?" Carlisle began, his voice sharp as a knife. "Why haven't I gotten an update? This is some bullshit. If you don't want to find an empty room when you get back, you'd best let me know where we're at. She is fine, for now, and I'd like to keep it that way. It hasn't been easy holding my guards back from, let's say, entertaining her. She's a pretty woman and it's not like there's much action up here for men like them."

Lexi had to give the man credit. For being such a bastard, he sure hid it well. The man was a two-faced religious icon. If Lexi had the opportunity, she'd drive a knife into his throat all the way to the hilt just so he'd shut up.

"I'm kidding," he back peddled, palms raised before him. "Oh, of course, I'm kidding. I will keep her safe till you return with the Slipstream. What would God think of me if I didn't protect the weak and helpless? But we need this artifact, and we need it now. There are others to gather. More to make the collection complete. More to paint my vision of greatness." He scratched at his neck with the backs of his nails and barred his teeth. "God and America first."

Sarita paused the video. The room was silent. Even Atticus had turned off his show. Until now everyone had just taken Sarita's word on Sarah. This message, it was confirmation.

"Play the end of it," the captain ordered.

"I'd rather not."

Cho's voice took on an edge, "Play it."

With a click, the video resumed. "I will give you two days to respond, to update me on your job and what is happening, then I might have to take certain preemptive actions. Have you ever bent back a fingernail before? Reached for something too quick and caught its corner? Flesh turning white from the pressure under thick layers of keratin? Hurts don't it? Hurts like a bitch. A fucking bitch. I can only wonder how bad having them pulled back would feel, you know, with a pair of pliers." Carlisle rubbed his chin then shook his head. "No. No. I must walk in the light. God be with me. You know how serious this is. Do not take me for a fool. Call. Me. Back."

The screen went blank.

"Will he really torture her?" Keelin ventured, her face pale.

Sarita shrugged. "I don't think he has the stomach. But then again, he did look pretty high. It's hard to say what he'll do."

"Yeah," Logan said. "My professional opinion via tele doc, is that he looked to have been breaking in a few bricks of Bogota Bullion."

Atticus tossed back his bottle and took a long drink, then glared at everyone in turn. He raised a hand as if to speak, then lost his train of thought.

"Lexi," the captain said. "Let's stack on a bit more velocity. If we can shave a little time off, it might help. It's worth the reaction mass."

She nodded and slipped into her acceleration chair. "Good idea. Everyone, buckle up." They did as they were instructed with the exception of Atticus, who needed Keelin's help. It took far too long for her to wrestle the bottle from his hands and stow it in a cabinet for safety.

Lexi wondered what the hell was his deal today. He never got drunk in the mornings. Never. He could be reprobate at times, but he showed up every day for work, clear-headed and ready to go.

"What do I do?" Sarita muttered under her breath. "What do I tell him? I have to respond somehow. Something has to be said."

Lexi did her best to calm herself, but her anger was burning hotter every day over this asshole. She regretted ever encouraging the rest of the crew that this was a good idea.

"Let the fucker stew," she said while preparing the *Peridot* for another burn. "Let him guess what's going on. Communication can be shoddy in the void."

"It can," Sarita agreed. "Maybe a few words that get cut off suddenly as a reply?" She typed several sentences into her tablet and reviewed them. "Darnell?"

"Yes, ma'am?" He twisted around in his chair.

"Mind praying for Sarah?"

"Not at all." He gave Sarita a warm smile. "I already am."

"Thank you."

"You'll get her back. You'll get her back."

"I want to believe."

Lexi grinned as she spoke up, "Then believe."

[17] – Darnell

Three metallic knocks pierced Darnell's fog of exhaustion. He fought to rouse himself, hungover from another night of scrolling through his feed, lost in a sea of information without context. Everything ran together. So many questions, no answers. Oceans of emotion, rolling waves of hate and passion with no vessel to cross it.

"You up?" a voice called.

He blinked and shook his head, letting out a groan, reached for Lexi and found their sleeping bag empty. He'd been so spaced out he hadn't noticed her leave for the bridge.

"I'm trying," he mumbled, and his eyes began to clear. Logan was at the door with a plastic bulb of coffee in hand.

"Pot's on in the back," they said. "Why don't you run a cold rag over your eyes and get a cup. We're here. Time to get busy."

He nodded and Logan went on their way. He had not slept well in days, merely laying still while drifting in and out of REM sleep, never staying under long enough to get any real rest. But he was well aware that some days you run on sleep, and some days you run on caffeine and grit.

Darnell took Logan's advice and ran a cool rag over his face, got dressed, then snagged a quick bite from the galley, boiled eggs and pre-cooked bacon with a bulb of coffee, black.

This was the big day. The day they would capture the Slipstream.

He shoved his food down his throat and pulled another bulb of coffee from the pot, taking a fresh serving with him up to the bridge where everyone had gathered.

"That it?" Darnell asked Sarita, pointing a finger at the main display. "Doesn't look like anything more than a background blip."

"That's it alright," she replied. "What's our distance looking like?"

"A little under ten thousand kilometers," Lexi reported, then began to maneuver the flyer around for a slowdown burn.

It wasn't that much of a turn, but still enough to make Darnell grab a strap on the bulkhead above him to steady himself, coffee sloshing around inside his bulb.

"Should be easy," the captain said. "Standard grab and burn. We all set in the cargo bay? I know it wasn't exactly made for this sort of operation."

Keelin nodded. "Aye, aye. All set, ma'am. We'll pull her in an' tie 'er down. By the time we're done, she might as well be welded to the hull."

"Very good." The captain gave an unusual grin. She was in good cheer. "Logan, be on standby just in case someone busts up their shins when they go out."

Logan narrowed their eyes and rubbed a hand down their arm, skin glowing red in response. "Tis my job."

From the corner of the bridge, Atticus stared off into space, clasping and interlacing his fingers against one another at a cool, methodical pace.

"You okay, buddy?" Darnell asked, then took a sip of his coffee. The psychologist didn't respond, and so he bumped him with an elbow. "You in there?"

"Hmm?" Atticus said. "Oh, yes. Just fine. A little lost in thought."

"Don't get too lost, buddy."

"Perish the thought." Atticus reached into his jumpsuit and fished out his hand terminal, fiddling with it for a moment.

Darnell frowned and shook his head. Lexi gave him a wink, and this made him perk up a little.

"I'm having issues with the comm array," Sarita reported. "We have the fix just fine, but only because its course is predictable. Not like a car in hard vacuum has any Delta-V to speak of. But the waves, they... they keep going in and out. Started up about a half hour ago."

"What's going on?" Lexi flicked several switches. "Let me take a look."

Keelin drew up her mop of red hair and sprang into action, pushing off towards the aft of their flyer. "I'll go have a peek at the hardware. An old broom knows dirty corners best. Everythin' passed inspection two days ago. Could be the buffers, I'd say."

Lexi nodded. "Would make things easier when we head back."

"You break it on the way to Saturn, Lexi?" Logan said, a wry tone in their voice.

"I did not," she spat back. "All I did was shut it off."

"Temperamental flyer. Got to rub that baby the right way."

Darnell took a deep breath. It was almost over. The Slipstream would be in their cargo hold and Carlisle would get what he wanted. He wished that part didn't make him feel so dirty. Good guys didn't hold someone's spouse hostage just to push their agenda forward, and he didn't like working for the bad guys. Was there a way to bring Carlisle to account for this? Could they tell the authorities and see justice done without getting both Sarita's wife killed and their own asses thrown in jail? It didn't seem possible. They had to play ball. They had to do something illegal in order to set things right.

Was he one of the good guys?

But the notion of good guy, bad guy, Lexi and Atticus would both remind him, were subjective ideas, based on your perspective. They were childhood fantasies. Every bad guy is a hero in his own mind. Everyone a freedom fighter or terrorist. A patriot or a traitor. A hero or a villain. Carlisle wasn't immune to this way of thinking. Darnell had no doubt that he believed himself to be the hero of his own story.

"Just a little more," Lexi mumbled just loud enough Darnell could hear. She eyed him and offered a tired grin. "We're almost done."

He gave a nod, hand tipping an invisible cowboy hat.

"Captain?" Keelin called over the intercom.

"Go ahead."

"Comms seem to be fine, clearin' the buffers now, will take a few minutes. There was some kind of overflow error and it started savin' all kinds of junk data in triplicate. Just about caused the system to crash on us from hitting its storage limit."

"Is this error dangerous?"

"No, but it would've made the array inoperable for a tick."

"A buffer caching error," Sarita said, turning to Lexi, Sarah's necklace gripped in her fingers, thumb rubbing its surface of the S thoughtfully. "That's weird. Has it done this before?"

She shook her head. "Not that I can recall."

"Clear it out and we'll do a factory reset from the backup," the captain told Keelin. "We don't need any issues on the next leg of our trip."

A light began to flash on Lexi's console. She cocked her head and stared at it, confused with what she saw. "Either we're getting another error, or there's a hotspot on the hull."

"A hotspot?"

"Yeah. It's small."

"Could it be another targeting laser?" the captain asked.

"That's what the 'ol girl is telling me. Doesn't make sense, though. I would check the local transponder frequencies, but Keelin's got the array busy."

"Could someone be following us?" Sarita asked, her voice shaky. "Total transparency here. Being followed is not part of the plan."

Darnell slipped his empty coffee bulb into a compartment and scratched at his stubble. "Anyone else know about the snatch?"

"As I said before, just the Chinese and Carlisle, and the Chinese aren't supposed to be here for months. We should be alone."

"This timing feels a little too convenient," the captain commented, eyeing everyone in the room.

"I've got them on the high-resolution cameras," Lexi said. The main display lit up. "You can't see much, but there's a flicker."

"Scan them back, get a map of their hull."

"This isn't right," Logan said. "Maybe we should just go."

"No way," Sarita growled. "No freaking way. We are not leaving without that Slipstream. Sarah's life depends on it."

"Keelin!" the captain called. "How's the comm array coming?"

"Two or three more minutes, ma'am."

"Oh, shit," Lexi mumbled.

"What is it?" Darnell asked, leaning in to see.

A three-dimensional scan of an approaching flyer began to appear in the corner of the main display. It had an unusual shape, not a cone like the *Peridot* and other rock haulers, or a series of cans strung in a line like the colony transports. It had hard edges sticking out at oblique angles, asymmetrical stretches of hull a dozen meters each, appearing as if it were hastily thrown together from scrap. Due to its odd shape, radar scans did very little. This did not make things simple for the targeting laser, either. If not for faint sunlight, this craft would have been invisible.

"What the hell is that?" the captain hissed. "It's not from the UEI."

"Is it even a flyer?" Logan asked. "Looks like trash to me. Manmade, but trash."

"Are the buffers cleared, Keelin?"

"Almost," she replied. *"Almost."*

"I told you there were pirates out here," Sarita shuddered. "And not *our* kind of pirates. The *board your ship and slit your throat* kind."

"How did they even know we were here?" the captain asked, her face scrunching up as her thoughts went internal. "Are we to assume—"

The *Peridot* rocked as several alarms began to scream bloody murder. Emergency lights washed the room in flashes of red interrupted by white. Terror struck at them as they had all been drilled to death what this was during their training. Decompression alert. A hole had been punched in their hull somewhere near the aft-end of the flyer and their precious air was leaking out into space.

"We're being pushed off course," Lexi said. "I think we've been shot."

"Shot?" Darnell's eyes went wide as he fumbled to get out of his acceleration chair. Who the hell put guns on a flyer? It went against every non-aggression pact signed in the past fifty years. Space was dangerous enough without putting guns on pressurized ships.

"Darnell! Keelin!" the captain shouted, reaching under her seat and taking hold of a pair of patch kits. "Let's go."

Darnell spun to leave, taking one of the kits.

Lexi squeezed his hand before he went. "Be careful, beau."

He gave her a weak smile and nodded. "Fly us straight."

"Trying."

The pressure door of the bridge closed and went red, keeping those inside safe. Decompression forced the flyer to turn like a slow top, making it more of a challenge to get around. When he failed to secure himself, he found the *Peridot* spinning around him, turning his stomach on end.

Darnell and the captain split up and followed the sound of the alarms... Air pressure was plummeting, the standard of one atmosphere already at only eighty percent, according to the colored safety badge on his jumpsuit's sleeve. Darnell took a breathing mask off the wall, slipping it over his face and pressed the self-sizing button. A soft plastic seal secured itself across his forehead, cheeks, and chin, and he began to breathe from a small tank on its side. He didn't need to be passing out or have his blood turn to sludge when the air got too thin to breathe.

Seventy percent of normal air pressure. Dropping fast.

The breach wasn't in his and Lexi's quarters. It wasn't in the galley. Logan's space was clear, as well as the server room.

Where was the breech?

Sixty percent of normal air pressure.

The flyer was turning cold. Ice was crystalizing on the hairs of his arm. He shivered and brushed them off, casting a spray of glitter. Pressure doors closed behind him, sealing him off along with the damage. He hoped the hostile vessel didn't take another shot at them. Had this one been an accident? Who could tell? The array was down.

Fifty percent of normal air pressure. People would start passing out if they didn't have masks.

Something hissed. It was close.

Forty percent.

Where in the hell had these people come from? Was this more from Carlisle?

Thirty percent.

That didn't feel right. This couldn't be Carlisle. This wasn't his style.

The air was turning thin. From his training he knew that if pressure went below ten percent, it would reach what was called the Armstrong limit, and if that happened, no amount of breathable oxygen would be enough to sustain life for long. The breathing mask would help, but only so far. Atmospheric pressure was necessary to sustain carbon-based life.

He rummaged around in a storage room, floated past a series of wall-mounted Lindvolt cells, and found a string of scattered Exo-Bites drifting towards an exterior bulkhead on the other side of a locking rack.

Just as Darnell was about to force himself around the shelving into a press of metal beams not much wider than he, the *Peridot* rocked again. Inches from his toes a hole the size of a baseball appeared in the hull, giving him a porthole view of hard vacuum bathed in red emergency lights. His eyes widened at how close it had been. A tenth of a degree difference and it would have knocked the hat right off his head, just after splitting him from crotch to skull.

Twenty percent pressure.

In the storage room there were now two leaks. One was easy to access, the other, not so much. There was no way he could get to both before pressure got too low. If he went for the nearest of the two, the one by his feet, he could seal it in time. But what if the other was bigger? He might fix one just to find himself dying from the other.

He danced back and forth for a moment, looking around the room for answers, his breathing mask fogging up. He had to make a decision. Which one was more critical?

Exo-bites floated past his blurred vision, two solid streams made of the cube-shaped, crunchy snack. One headed through the shelving, the other towards his feet. He watched them twirl for a moment, transfixed, then saw his answer.

Darnell reached for a storage duffel on the wall and tossed it at the baseball size hole but didn't wait to see if it helped plug it. First taking a deep breath, he squeezed himself and the patch kit around the shelving to the back side of the storage room. For the first time in his life, he wished he'd been born a beanpole like his cousin Jerry. The beams dug into his back and stomach. For a moment he worried this squeeze might just rip off one of his nipples.

"Come on, come on, come on," he told himself. "Suck it in."

His body gave way and he burst out onto the other side, struggling with the kit for a moment, its mass turned sideways and catching against the metal. The hole he'd plugged with the duffel hissed, but the cloth sack held.

More Exo-bites bounced off Darnell's breathing mask and he swatted them away like they were swarming mosquitos. Along the wall on his left and the outer perpendicular surface, were two holes the size of a football, each one far bigger than the other.

"Found it," he called over the intercom, voice raspy. "Working on it now."

The patch kit came open and he removed the carbon fiber sheets, anchoring them around the hole with a rivet gun. Once they were in place, he began working the outside edges with a foam adhesive, securing the panel. It was a dirty patch job, one that Keelin would give him hell over later, but air in the lungs was better than air in the vacuum, no matter how it got done.

A new alarm went off.

His safety badge had turned black. Ten percent atmosphere remained.

"Come on," he said, working his way around the hole. He was not the fastest at this and that might just cost him his life. "Come on. Come on."

He scanned the first patch with the kit's portable test laser, ensuring the seal was solid before moving on to the second. His skin began to burn, not just from cold, but something else. His joints ached.

This was just the start. The hostile flyer would fire again, and he'd be chasing yet another hole, and another, and another. What were they going to do? The *Peridot* didn't carry any weapons at all. Their mission was to break rocks, not heads.

The second patch went into place, was tested, and he let out a sigh. The emergency alarms ceased. Darnell fell back and his body went limp.

Keelin appeared an instant later, breathing mask covering her face, red hair a tangle in its straps. She kicked the duffle away and patched the smaller hole with practiced ease.

The walls of the storage room hissed as pressure was pumped back in.

"You ain' dead yet, are ya?" she asked.

Darnell squeezed back around the storage rack. "I was starting to wonder."

She reached out a hand and pulled him through the press of beams. "I got ya friend, what a whale of a time there. But we need to get up to the bridge, post haste. Captain found somethin' real."

His hands trembled, fingers sore. "She found something during our emergency?"

"Aye, she did."

"Like what?"

"Somethin' a mite bit incriminating."

[18] – Lexi

Lexi was relieved to hear the alarms die off. Now that holes were patched, the *Peridot* was repressurizing in the rear sections. As soon as internal pressure was within twenty percent of normal, she would be able to unlock the doors to the bridge.

She looked at her monitor and immediately slapped her palm down on the burn alarm, a roar signaling the crew she was about to make a maneuver.

"I think they're taking another shot," Lexi said, counted to two, and swung the *Peridot* to port. Her stomach dropped for an instant as they shifted to the side, and she heard those on the bridge beside her suck in a breath. "Should be able to stay ahead of this. Whatever they are using, isn't nearly as fast as they'd like it to be. Light travels faster. I see the flash, we move."

Sarita smiled through gritted teeth at Lexi. "Great idea, fly girl. I think I've been working for the wrong team."

"Everyone makes mistakes."

The pressure alert board went green, and the bridge doors behind Lexi swooshed open.

"No more holes," the captain said, eyeing everyone still on the bridge. From the reflection on the main display, Lexi could see her attention linger on Atticus. "I don't hear the *Peridot* screaming at us anymore."

"No ma'am. We're fine. Keeping ahead of their improvised weapon."

"Good."

Logan spotted Darnell and Keelin returning, unbuckled from her acceleration chair and began to check the big guy over. Lexi's heart dropped for an instant. He was sweaty and pale.

"Before you freak out," Logan blurted. "He'll be fine. Just a little, well, hypoxic."

"A little hypoxic!" Lexi screeched. "How can you be a little hypoxic?"

"I'm okay, love," Darnell said, waving a hand. "Our flyer is still in one piece, more or less."

"Shite job patchin' though," Keelin spat. "Looked like an eight-year-old hopped up on juice and candy took hold of Mum's hot glue gun. I'm havin' classes again when this is over."

"Atticus," the captain said. "Do me a favor."

"Yes?" the psychologist said, rolling his eyes. "What?"

"Show me your hands," she said, her tone hard as steel. "Now. Put them where everyone can see."

Lexi blinked and spun around, her jaw slack. The rest of the crew had equally flummoxed expressions.

"Here," he said, raising his hands away from his jump suit. "What, you think I have a gun? A knife or something?"

Lexi blinked. What the hell was the captain onto? This wasn't right.

"You left the terminal in your quarters unlocked," Cho went on. "I went through your recent messages on a hunch. After we left Saturn, I know you contacted someone. Who you contacted, I can't say, just that you told them of the location and gave them the Slipstream's transponder information."

"Atticus," Keelin mumbled, her expression crestfallen. "Captain, you sure? I know you said we found something', but this can't be. Atticus... You—No—"

"Fine," the psychologist let out an exasperated groan and crossed his arms. "There's no reason to hide it."

As she sucked in a breath, Lexi's chest caught. After all these years working close with each and everyone in this room, Atticus especially, she couldn't believe what she was hearing. She knew anger was the appropriate response in the moment, but she couldn't yet summon it.

Her mind demanded she spend more time in denial before hitting the betrayal and disappointment phase. Anger could only come after that.

There was no way he could have done this. No way he would have. He was an ass, but a loyal ass.

"Why?" the captain asked, before wiping her lips with a free hand. "After all this time. Why?"

He turned away from them, crossed his legs and put his hands on his knee. "I knew someone who might want the Slipstream and would be willing to pay even more than Carlisle."

"So, it's about the money? That's all this is. Greed?"

"No," he lowered his head and closed his eyes. "I couldn't bear how that manipulative, false prophet was out to ruin the world for his own ends. That hypocritical bastard preaches the love of God and shows none himself. When he double crossed us for some stupid-ass test and we found out what he did to Sarita's wife... That was it. So yes, I did it. To hell with Carlisle and the horse he rode in on. He's a little bitch that deserves everything that comes to him!"

"Atticus," the captain growled. "Who's flying that piece of junk on our starboard?"

"How would I know?" He raised his head and threw up his hands. "I had a reputable dark web contact, and now their people are here to claim the prize."

"Pretty clear they intend on killing us."

Atticus ran a hand over his bald head and looked down. "I didn't mean to get anyone hurt. I just didn't want to see him win. People like him always win."

"How does any of this matter now?" Sarita asked, unbuckling from her chair, voice raised. "If they take the Slipstream, not only will they kill us, but Carlisle will kill Sarah."

"A miscalculation on my part."

"Miscalculation! That's all you've got to say about it?"

Lexi saw a flash of light from her visual lock on the other vessel. "Hold on," she said, and without truly giving anyone the chance to do so, she fired the control jets in a random direction to avoid the incoming projectile.

As a result, Sarita went shooting across the bridge, shoulder first, body slamming against the far bulkhead like a hammer. As she came to a stop, her neck snapped, head slinging against a ninety-degree edge of space-grade aluminum. Droplets of blood formed around her temple, suspended in null gravity like beads of water in oil, tiny orbs of crimson oozing out in a string. Lexi gasped. The woman hadn't been ready, hadn't been secured.

"Sarita!" Logan sprang forward. "Atticus, unbuckle your narcissistic ass and come help me."

Lexi had tried to warn them, but there wasn't enough time. She was just trying to keep them from being shot. Keep them from explosive decompression.

God, dear God. This was her fault.

"We aren't done with him," the captain said, her voice angry and uneasy. "Take care of Sarita and lock him up." But even as the words came from her mouth, she seemed uncertain about them.

Logan took hold of Sarita and began to apply pressure to her temple with a torn jumpsuit sleeve. "You'll have plenty of time when this is all over. I need hands, and his are useless anywhere else."

"Appreciate the compliment," Atticus said, positioning himself to assist.

"Is she okay?" Lexi's heart sank. No, no, no... Her impulsiveness had hurt someone again. It was a reaction, that's all. But did it matter? No, no, no... She'd screwed up. She'd screwed up. "I didn't—"

"She hit pretty hard," Logan replied, "can't say till I get a good look. Just get us out of here alive. Give us more lead-time next burn."

"Need help?" Darnell asked and Logan waved him away.

Lexi watched as Logan led the unconscious Sarita off the bridge with Atticus's help. She was critically injured and it was her fault. Deimos all over again.

Darnell put a hand on her shoulder and squeezed. He said nothing, but the message in his eyes was clear.

"Atticus has been a fook," Keelin said. "But that doesn't change what's going on now. Way I see it, we have two objectives that need doing."

"Get the Slipstream and stay alive," Darnell whispered.

The captain crossed her arms and rubbed her chin. "You're right." She took a deep, clarifying breath and turned her attention to the problem at hand. "Are communications back up?"

"Aye," Keelin reported.

"Can we open a channel and talk to them, even if it's likely a waste of time?"

Keelin pressed several buttons on the control panel beside her, waited, then shook her head. "No handshake from the other flyer's array. They're running dark as night."

"Seems about right."

"They have a gun," Darnell said. "Not sure what it is, but even a dumb projectile can be dangerous."

"Working on that," Lexi said. "Keeping us out of the way. Um... trying, at least."

He nodded. "Ya'll know me, I ain't no proponent of killing no one, but I think I like living more than dying."

The captain narrowed her eyes. "Sounds like you might have an idea."

"Might not have weapons that we can return fire, but there is one thing we do have aboard this flyer in abundance."

Keelin spun on him and gave a slow, devious smile. "Aye, buckaroo. Feelin' like letting that pyro loose?"

"If setting bombs off in vacuum without any fire still makes me a pyro..."

"Rock-busting charges," the captain ventured. "Holy shit. We have more than enough to render that thing into a drifting hunk of trash. But how can we get them there?"

Darnell looked to Lexi, their eyes locking for a hot second before turning back to the captain. She knew what he was about to say, and it was the stupidest, bravest thing he had considered doing in all his life.

"I plan on delivering it in person, right to their door."

"Yipee ki yay," Keelin said, and in response Darnell grinned.

What a beautiful, beautiful, stupid man.

But if anyone could do it, he was it.

[19] – Darnell

There was no time to argue. The *Peridot* and the pirate vessel were nearing the Slipstream. The closer they came to one another, the more dangerous the improvised weapon on the hostile flyer became. Lexi had done well dodging their weapons fire ever since they first attacked, but she couldn't keep it up forever. The warning muzzle flash of their weapons could be obscured at any second.

Darnell hurried to the supply room and recovered a container of black paint gel used for marking shipping containers in null. He hung the powered flight assist module he would use to cross the gulf between flyers next to his personal spacesuit and went to work. The white of his equipment was highly reflective and could easily be spotted by the other flyer. They would know something was up and there was no telling what action they might take. It pained him to make the dragon cowboy Lexi had painted on his suit disappear but staying invisible was more important in the moment. He could get another design when this was over.

While he went to work, Keelin put together an improvised tether made of a coil of carbon nanotubes a kilometer in length with a magnetic claw on its end. This space-age grappling hook would act like a lasso if he overshot their target.

He took a heat gun to his equipment to quick-dry the paint, which hadn't applied like any paint he'd ever seen. With all the black, the suit was now so dark it appeared as if it had been edited out of existence entirely.

"It'll be hot," Keelin told him. "That there is Vantablack, soaks up all the photons. Heat radiation be dangerous."

"How long will the suit keep me cool? I don't want to end up like a smoked brisket."

She shrugged. "You've got air for days, but with that there black, you might be looking at four hours at most. Imagine wearin' a shirt dark as a black hole in the height of Summer in Phoenix. The suit'll radiate some of it back off into the void, but not forever."

Darnell switched off the heat gun, running his hand over the suit and down into its crevices to be sure it was dry. His fingers came back warm and clean. "Alright. Time to suit up."

"You got this, friend," Keelin said, helping him put on the bulky suit and powered assist. A task not easily done alone.

He smiled at her and buzzed Lexi on the bridge. "No chance you can come down here and wish me well? Give me a kiss for luck?"

"No, beau," Lexi said over the intercom. *"I wish I could see you off in person. I've got to keep our position fluid in case they fire again. Keelin can kiss you for luck."*

The engineer's eyebrows raised. "No offense, but he ain' me type."

Darnell pursed his lips at her. "What's that supposed to mean?"

"Cowboys ain't me kind of trouble."

"I hate not saying a proper goodbye." He slipped into the legs of his vacuum suit. "Feels weird."

"This is not goodbye!" Lexi shouted into the intercom, speakers crackling at her intensity. She paused for a moment before continuing. *"Sorry. I will not say goodbye. You're going to make it back alive. Far as I'm concerned, we have unfinished business. Part of it involves a ring. The other part, a tiny us."*

"Guess I can't die knowing I have unfinished business." He slid his arms into the suit's open slots. "I'm a man of my word. I keep good on my obligations."

"I'd hate to chase you down in the afterlife."

"I love you, Miss Carver."

"I love you too," Lexi whispered, and for a moment it was almost as if the *Peridot* held its breath. All that could be heard was the soft thump of machines at its core.

Keelin handed him his helmet and he slipped it over his head, twisting it with her guidance until it snapped. A whirr filled the inside of his suit as it pressurized. Information appeared in the heads-up display following the curve of the helmet's visor. He patted the pouch on his chest, which was packed with plastic explosives and triggers, more than enough to send the approaching flyer spinning off into the void.

Although there was no gravity, mass and inertia were still a factor. When Keelin clipped the powered flight assist module to the back of the suit, Darnell found it immediately more difficult to move under his own power. Mass was mass, no matter what gravity decided to do with it.

He turned to watch Keelin retreat through the inner airlock. She blew him a kiss for luck. "May you get all your wishes but one, and you'll always have somethin' to live for."

The airlock door swooshed shut, blocking her from view. Darnell waved at the tiny window, then waited for the air to evacuate the space. He said a silent prayer, hoping God could hear him so far away. There was no way he could do this alone. No way in hell.

"Here we go," he mumbled before pushing off into the black.

[20] – Lexi

Lexi watched the high-resolution cameras like a hawk, doing her best to keep track of Darnell and his progress. The trouble was, as dark as the suit had become after its Vantablack treatment, all she had to go on was the occasional dip in starlight when he reached just the right angle. She knew where he was almost down to the inch from his telemetry beam, but a bit of mathematical data wasn't enough to put her at ease. She needed visual confirmation. He had exited the airlock without incident and made a burn towards the pirate vessel using the powered assist module. It seemed such a frail little craft to cross such a vast, dead ocean.

It would take two hours for him to reach the target, almost half the recommended safe time given the suit's Vantablack treatment. Six thousand kilometers to go, and a man in a suit traveling at a relative velocity of almost a kilometer per second. He had become a bullet.

At their current trajectory Darnell would resolve this hostile situation with the Slipstream and *Peridot* less than a hundred kilometers distant from the explosion. She hoped the resulting debris wouldn't cause any issues. She hoped the debris wouldn't shred her love in two.

A flash of light came from the pirate vessel and Lexi made a corrective burn. The *Peridot* rocked a few seconds later, the projectile having grazed one of the instrument fins on the starboard side.

"How did they hit us?" the captain asked.

"They are getting closer. I'll have to make wider burns. The change in the angle of attack needs to be higher."

Logan appeared on the bridge a moment later, taking hold of a soft wall hook to brace themself, expression drawn. "Sarita is stable for now."

"Will she be okay?"

"I can't say. She has a pretty serious concussion. That bulkhead did her brain no favors."

The captain repeated Lexi's question, "Will she be okay?"

Logan sighed. "Being honest, she's mostly lucid. Atticus is keeping her busy for the moment, but she'll need to rest. Only time can tell when it comes to concussions. Her brain was tossed against the inside of her skull pretty damn hard, and that spongy thing doesn't like it."

"It's my fault," Lexi mumbled. "I—"

"No," the captain cut her off. "No. We're not playing that game. The question is, how are we going to deal with Atticus?"

"He has to be punished," Keelin said, returning to the bridge. "But I can understand why he did it."

"Doesn't excuse it."

"No, ma'am. That it don't."

Another flash of light came from the hostiles. Lexi sounded the alarm, counted to three, then initiated a corrective burn, the ship rattling.

"The UEI has to get a handle on this," the captain commented, fingers digging into the arms of her chair as their acceleration slowed.

They sat in silence on the bridge, watching Darnell approach the target. What was there to say? What was there to do? Their hopes rested in his hands. If he couldn't plant the bomb, everything was over.

For his part, Darnell said little over the comm channel. He'd gone internal.

"Come on, baby," Lexi whispered to herself, these words her own version of prayer. "Come on. Come on."

The gap closed.

Darnell drifted towards the pirate vessel.

[21] – Darnell

It didn't take long for Darnell to realize that holding your breath not only made you woozy, but eventually caused severe chest pains. He had to put his mind somewhere, anywhere, and controlling his breathing was all he could think to do. Never in his life had he been this far out from anything terrestrial; the flyer, a rock, a moon or a station, with nothing but his suit to rely on. The idea was overtaking him. The void was a mental weight pressing on his chest. All he had to orient himself was a destination on his HUD in a field of infinite black, nothing more. And so, he held his breath and focused his mind on the picture the holographic scan had given them.

"This isn't helping," he told himself. "You best pray on it, son. You ain't alone out here. You're not the only living soul for thousands of miles. God is here too. The Universe is alive."

His breathing resumed, slow and steady. Meditation wasn't just for Shaolin Monks, Gurus, or white wine yoga students. What was prayer but another form of meditation? A way to get your mind on something both outside, and yet deep within oneself.

Darnell prayed. Nothing fancy, nothing specific from the great book, but a prayer of his own making, an honest dialogue with himself and the great almighty. He had always prayed honestly. Why say things that weren't in your heart? Did the creator of the Universe not already know your thoughts? God was after humility, not doctrine. He longed for thine heart to be true.

As Darnell fell into his prayers, his mind began to wander. He was on Luna, standing in the corner of a dark room illuminated by glowing pink string lights. Lexi was at his side, staring with him over the edge of a stomach-high plastic gate wrapped in synthetic cloth. Yellow stars and teddy bears as tall as children were painted on the walls, the spaces between them a mélange of colorful unicorns, sprinkle-covered donuts, and geometric shapes.

He couldn't quite resolve what the child sleeping in the crib looked like, but he knew that they were beautiful, and that he loved them with all his heart. Lexi put her arms around him. He leaned into her.

"You're almost there," she said, and he let out a sigh. "Time to burn."

"You're right," he said. "You're always right. Nothing but time to burn."

They were safe on Luna, their child sleeping. The world was at peace. The future was secure and certain.

All was well.

"No, Darnell. Listen to me. You're almost there... You need to burn."

He pressed his palms against the glass of his helmet, and he shook his head. The vision of Luna retreated as he came back to reality. He was hurtling through the void, not on the moon.

"Do I need to get my ass out of this flyer and slap you?" Lexi growled over the communications channel. *"Wake up, Darnell! Snap out of it!"*

"What," he said. "What is it?"

"If you don't do your slowdown burn now, you'll overshoot the flyer."

"Right, right." He entered the commands on the back of his palm and triggered the assist module's automated burn sequence. It reoriented his position in space based on star fixes and began applying Delta-V, bursts of hydrazine thrust adjusting his position. A moment later, Darnell was unable to see what he was approaching, the thrusters mounted on his back now facing the hostile flyer.

"Good work," Lexi said. *"Get Keelin's tether ready. Won't be long before they see your burn and wonder what's up. If I were them, I'd be suspicious and get the hell out of Dodge."*

"Okay."

He removed the spool from his waist, then checked and rechecked that it was properly secured. His HUD reported that the distance between him and the hostile flyer was closing. The numbers first counted down fast, then went slower and slower. Distance narrowed. Trajectory solid.

A hundred kilometers. He readied the tether.

Fifty kilometers. He wondered how fast the grapple would travel. Even if it was long enough, could it catch up?

Ten kilometers. What if it didn't find a solid surface to grab on to?

Five kilometers.

An alarm sounded.

The hostile flyer's drive lit up like the sun as they began to initiate a burn toward the *Peridot*. They streaked ahead of him, his trajectory utterly shot. If he didn't take action, and quick, he'd be out here alone.

"Fire the tether!" Lexi screamed over comms. *"Fire it now!"*

Darnell depressed the trigger hoping this would work. There was no way he could catch up with them. They were getting away. Had he been too slow and missed their opportunity?

The drive flame of the hostile flyer blossomed in Darnell's visor, blinding him. He pulled down his sunshade.

"Did you fire?" Lexi asked, frantic. *"Darnell. Are you okay? Darnell!"*

"I think I missed," he said. "I think—oh—"

The tether's line was slack, then instantly went taut, and Darnell found himself folded backward, jerked forward at an impossible speed by the line attached to the waist of his suit. His insides turned to jelly as the suit's instruments went wild. Keelin's little device had worked, maybe too well. He'd hitched a ride on the hostile flyer and was being dragged along.

"Darnell!"

The pirates continued to accelerate. Even with the rigid structure of the assist module, his suit was not meant for this kind of maneuver, let alone the weight distribution. Every bit of pressure focused on the point where the tether was secured, not evenly distributed like in his acceleration chair aboard the *Peridot*. He worried his spine might just snap.

"Darnell!"

His eyes pressed into the back of his skull, making his head throb, tears oozing from the corners of his eyelids. His chest tightened. Teeth grinding against one another like a belt sander.

Pressure. Pressure. Pressure.

Space spinning, perception twisted up into a ball.

Vision blurry.

Throat dry.

So much pain.

It wouldn't end.

It felt like he was being pressed between two sheets of steel.

It kept going.

On. And on.

Body trembling, wordless screams.

And on. And on.

His arms and hands and bones tingled, then cried out in agony.

Alarms shouted in his suit, blood pressure through the roof. He was about to stroke. To pass out. A vessel poised to burst in his brain.

How much more could his body take? Should he cut the tether?

Several agonizing seconds passed, bones creaking, tissues swelling. The G-force of their burn was tearing him apart. He was stuck on a roller coaster ride he didn't ask for.

A pause in acceleration came. A moment of blessed peace. His speed normalized and the pressure on his spine began to subside. He took a deep breath, testing his lungs to see if they still worked, his heart rate close to maximum.

"Darnell! Come back!"

"I'm here. I'm here," he wheezed. "I roped the damned thing. I can't believe it. I roped it!"

"We can see that. Are you okay?"

"Think so."

He began initiating the tether's recall motor and pulled himself towards the hostile flyer. He wasn't sure how he'd get around their drive flame, but thankfully, he didn't have to worry for long. After a few more seconds, they cut their engines and went back into freefall. It was nice not to get his ass cooked by heat and radiation. For that matter, he had no idea how it had missed him during the burn. All he could think was that they had been cutting at an angle.

"Holy shit," he said into comms. "Nice work, Keelin. Feels like I've been beaten within an inch of my life, but the line held up. The crazy thing held up."

"Never had no doubts," Keelin replied.

God bless was he sore.

The asymmetrical lump of metal which made up the hostile flyer began to resolve into view. As deep as they were in the solar system, sunlight was at a premium, and the human eye wasn't the most sensitive instrument in this application. He struggled to see any details beyond a silhouette. The tether retracted, and Darnell soon found himself on the outside of their hull.

"Does it matter where I put the bombs?" he called back while securing his magnetic boots, making sure they would stick to its collection of unusual angles. As cobbled together as this pirate flyer was, there was no guarantee it was even magnetic. When his boots clicked into place, he let out an audible sigh, as he worked towards what he believed was the rear of the craft, lifting one foot at a time.

"I don't think it matters," the captain replied. *"I suppose near the drive would be useful. Still, decompression of any kind will be crippling."*

"Right."

Spines of obsidian metal and irregular shapes jutted out all along the hull. He navigated around them, careful not to touch anything he didn't have to. Sometimes he found it easier to climb over the triangular shaped hull sections with the magnets of his hands and knees rather than walk upright.

Click. Scuff. Click. Scuff.

A thought occurred to him. There might not be any air in space to translate sound, but the hostile's hull could very well be a resonator. He, for one, could feel the vibrations of his movements. And so he knew they could likely hear them as well.

He approached the drive section at the rear of the vessel and found that his communication lifeline to the *Peridot* was winking in and out. Too many obstructions for the laser's line of sight.

"Give—if its—are you?" someone called over the channel.

"I'm here," he said.

The line went dead, and he found himself hoping he'd get it back once he pushed off again.

With the drive cone in view, he stopped and went to work. The yield on this package had to be enough to wreck it from here. He bent over and began applying blocks of plastic explosive, spreading the soft material over a wider space than usual to increase the surface area of the explosion. It wouldn't take much to puncture the hull and cause trouble for those inside.

Sweat was running into his eyes. His visor was turning foggy, streaks of moisture connecting a field of beads. "God this suit is getting hot."

A glint of light flashed off to his right and his heart skipped a beat. He shoved a detonator into the explosives he'd set and stood up, then began backing away.

On the other side of the drive cone, a dark form in the shape of a person approached, something heavy in their hands. Darnell didn't wait to see what it was. He started clicking his way back around to the other side of the hostile flyer. The easiest way to escape would be to push off into space, but without line of sight for his communications and telemetry, the star mapping on his assist module might not work as intended.

Before he could take more than a few steps, something heavy slammed against his suit, its impact like a hammer. He went tumbling across the hull, his magnetic boots having failed, his suit skidding and scrambling for purchase. Bits of the flyer's unusual design and structure rushed at him like a blind stampede. He bounced and twisted and tumbled off into space, then reached for the tether at his waist and fired it at the hostile flyer, pulling himself back to it.

"Anyone out there?" he called in a panic over his comm channel. All he needed was a connection to the *Peridot* and he'd hurl himself off into space away from his attacker, away from this monstrosity of a flyer.

No response came. The telemetry link had been re-established, but that was all. The crew was silent. There was no time to troubleshoot. Everything on this screaming lump of metal was trying to kill him.

The charges were in place, he just needed to get back. Darnell twisted and saw his attacker gaining, a white space suit bounding towards him in silent leaps.

"I can't even scream at you!" Darnell said, throwing his hands up in exasperation. "Forget this shit."

He unfastened the tether and hurled it at his attacker hard as he could. It was clear that the person was not expecting this move when it struck them in the chest, stunning them for an instant. This was his moment to escape.

Darnell took a deep breath and disengaged his magnetic boots. He pushed off from the hostile flyer and burned away, hisses of thrust making it shrink into the distance. The telemetry link to the *Peridot* flickered and went dead. Something long and hollow mounted to the hull rotated in his direction.

The improvised weapon.

"Not today, *desperadoes*." He depressed a button on the back of his vacuum suit's glove, and flashes of light began to appear in sequence along the rear of the hostile flyer. Debris scattered everywhere, coming in glittering waves, sections of its drive cones and hull twisting at the force. The flyer cracked in two, its oxygen evacuating in a spray of white, lives snuffed out in an instant as the change in pressure sucked the very air from their bodies. He'd seen many an explosion in his time, yet this was the first that ever left him with mixed feelings.

How guilty should he feel? This was self-defense.

His suit started to beep. Temperature alarm. The Vantablack's superior light absorption traits were starting to overtake the suit's climate control systems. Before long he'd start to cook in his own juices, but at least his friends were safe for now.

Where was the *Peridot*? No communications. No telemetry. All he could find nearby was their target.

"I'm on my own for now," he whispered, then took a deep breath of the suit's warm, moist air. "Where are you, my wayward Slipstream? I'm coming. I'm coming."

He rolled away from the scattering debris of the pirate flyer and burned towards their target, alone.

[22] – Lexi

The indicator light showing the comms link between Darnell and *the Peridot* winked out. He'd moved out of line of sight to the other side of the hostile flyer. He was on his own setting the explosives, God willing. Lexi chewed at her nails as she readied to move in. Her fingers stung and she took a look, finding blood at the corner of her right thumb, teeth having gnawed too deep into the quick.

The distance between them and the Slipstream was narrowing, but not fast enough. So was the distance between them and the pirate vessel. With Sarita's injury, it was a bad idea to push any harder. Even two or three G's could cause irreparable damage to her brain. And still, there wasn't much time. Darnell's suit had less than an hour before he would begin to cook alive.

Lexi's bleeding thumb hovered over the Falkor activation switch. How fast could she push it?

Shouting came from over her shoulder, and she twisted in her acceleration chair. Atticus shot onto the bridge, backing up as if retreating from an attack, hands raised in defense.

Sarita was hot on his heels, her face a mask of rage, body trembling.

"You fucking asshole," she screamed. "You did this, you did this!"

"I did," he said, tone laced with an uncommon degree of regret. "And I'm sorry. It was a lapse in judgement."

"Lapse in judgement? My wife is going to fucking die because of your lapse in judgement and you're *sorry* about it? Forgive me if that doesn't make me feel better. I'm *sorry* that your guts are about to be on the outside of your body."

"Hey! Hey!" the captain said, holding Sarita back. "Let's just calm down here."

She whirled on her. "Calm down? Calm down? Is the most important person in your life about to die because some self-righteous Nancy decided to take the law into his own hands?"

"Carlisle is going to do what Carlisle wants," Atticus fired back, the psychologist turning angry for once. "If he's going to hurt her, he's going to hurt her. That's not on me."

Lexi took a deep breath, and against her better judgement, unbuckled from her acceleration chair. If she didn't deescalate this situation, someone was going to get hurt. "Alright, hey, everyone's emotions are high right now." She raised her hands in a gesture of calm and positioned herself between Sarita and Atticus. "Let's all take a deep breath. One problem at a time."

"Bastard," Sarita shouted, and a glint of silver flashed in her right hand. She made a move for Atticus. Lexi twisted out of reflex.

Silver whispered across skin.

Shock.

Disbelief.

It all happened so fast.

A stream of crimson scattered across the bridge, beads of blood spraying in rhythmic lines of dots and dashes like morse code forming an organic SOS. Lexi's arm ignited with pain, her body screaming *emergency*. She'd been cut before, sure, who hadn't? This was different.

She stared at the blood, the red slash along her arm, and said nothing. It didn't feel real. Cuts that wide, that deep, they couldn't be real.

"Oh my God," Sarita blurted, the scalpel tumbling out of her fingers, its mass spinning away. She drew her hands up to cover her mouth. "What have I done? Lexi. My God."

"Logan!" the captain shouted. "Logan!"

Lexi licked her lips. The world around her was becoming hazy, darkness creeping in at the edges as if someone were dimming the lights in a vignette. The bridge was cold, shivers skipping down her spine like electric shards of ice. Her stomach flipped and what was left of her last meal ejected out of her.

"Lexi!" Logan cried, medical kit in hand. They took hold of her arm and went to work. "Oh geez, this is deep. Captain, hold her arm still for me."

"Oh God. Oh God," Sarita continued, her bandaged head shaking. "What have I done? What the fuck have I done?"

"The scalpel severed the radial artery." Logan guided the captain on where to press down on Lexi's arm to slow the bleeding. "The hell were you thinking, Sarita?"

Details were sketchy, but Lexi watched as Atticus eased around the disconsolate hacker and recovered the scalpel, locking it in a wall panel for safety. His expression was slack, his eyes wide.

Was that a look of regret?

Lexi watched the corporeal nature of the room waver in and out. She twisted her head towards her console and blinked several times, an eternity between each closure. The telemetry light on her control panel was green. Darnell's suit had reconnected to the *Peridot's* array. She reached towards it with her good arm and tried to say something, let them know that he was okay, but no words came out.

Darnell, she thought. *I need you.*

She was in a darkening room. She was lying at the bottom of a deep well looking up.

Logan's voice cut through the haze, tone hard as iron. "Lexi, stay with us. Do you hear me?" They put a hand on her face, fingers soft on her cheeks, drawing her eyes ahead. "Focus on me. Stay with me..."

But it was so hard. Lexi was tired, so God damned tired. A nap wouldn't hurt, would it? A little rest and refresh.

Everything in life was so hard, an uphill battle both ways. Was she asking for too much out of life? All she wanted was the American dream. A home to call her own, a kitchen where her and Darnell could make meals together, bake cupcakes and cookies, a couch to pile up and snuggle and make forts out of cushions. A wall to hang photos, a crib for their baby. A perfect little photograph, for a life she didn't deserve, a life she had stolen from three others because of her impatience.

She closed her eyes and let the world fade away. Just a few minutes of rest and she'd be right as rain, or—maybe she wouldn't.

Maybe a justice of its own would be done.

Maybe, just maybe, this would be her final rest.

[23] – Darnell

"*Peridot*, call back," Darnell said into his comms. "*Peridot*?"

There was no response. The telemetry signal was good again, but the line was dead. No one would answer.

He drifted ahead, attention fixed on the Slipstream, the nearest solid object of any description for thousands of kilometers. Seemed fitting for him to capture the car himself.

Debris from the hostile flyer glittered from time to time in the distant light of the sun, but so far, he'd been lucky enough that none of it had decided to find him.

"I hope everything is okay," he mumbled, but wasn't convinced.

The fog within the suit thickened, sweat pouring off of him in sheets. He drank an electrolyte-rich mixture through a tube and found it squeezed from his pores moments later, like he was a wet sponge being wrung out. He'd be not much more than a steamed chicken if this kept up.

Ninety-nine degrees. Eighty five percent humidity. Climbing.

"Lexi?" he called again. "Come on now, beau. Call back. You out there?"

Nothing.

"Shit, what's going on?"

In the absence of information, nightmare scenarios played out in his imagination. *The Peridot* had been hit by the enemy weapon and were decompressing. Atticus had found a gun and gone mad. The captain had decided to use this here cowboy as a decoy, then turned tail and ran. No. None of these were possible. It would be something far worse, maybe a reactor leak dosing everyone on board with lethal radiation, or a headshot from an errant piece of debris. Something catastrophic.

"Richardson," he told himself. "Listen to me, son. Stay positive. God is in control. All is well. You've been through worse."

But had he truly? Lexi was right. His upbringing had been tame.

Light flickered ahead. He squinted at his HUD and still couldn't read what it said. He drew his arm out of the suit's sleeve into the chest section and fished his fingers up over the helmet collar, rubbing the moisture off the inside of his visor with a tiny square of microfiber.

The Slipstream was less than a kilometer ahead.

He slid his arm back into place and initiated a short burn. The car swelled into view, a luminous shimmer against a field of black with white dots. Sunlight caught the car's trunk just right, and the words LINDVALL appeared in silver. This was it. Their prize. This was *the* Slipstream. The visionary Matteo Lindvall's personal vehicle, hurled into space by a chemical spear nearly seventy years earlier. It was real, and somehow it was still here. A key to so many things. A rescue. A better life? Perhaps. A madman's trinket? Almost certainly.

The assist module took over, navigating him towards the drifting object which was easy to spot by comparison to the hostile flyer. Stark white. Four doors. Convertible. All sleek features and curves. A pair of human shapes in brilliant white space suits up front. Driver and passenger. Centrum and Kósmos. Eternal travelers adrift on the oceans of nothing.

It was the strangest thing Darnell had seen in all his life, a high-performance electric car, responsible for sparking a revolution in the automotive industry, as well as that of a season of American economic dominance, and here it was, all alone just like he was in the vacuum of space. It was preserved like an artifact in a museum, kept safe within a hermetically sealed box made of mystery and emptiness.

Darnell's vacuum suit's emergency alarms were beginning to blare. The temperature inside was reaching a hundred and five. He wasn't going to make it if he didn't do something quick to get rid of this heat.

He reached out and took hold of the lip behind the back seats where the sunroof compartment was located and pulled himself in. There was no way he could fit all the way into the car with the massive assist module mounted to his back, and so he clipped himself to a headrest with a safety line, then let go of his only means to get around in space, kicking the module off into nothing. Though it felt strange to let go of the device, it wasn't as if he could fly to Stratus Base with it.

A thought occurred to him as he worked himself into place along the bench seat in back. The reason his suit could not properly evacuate the heat it collected from the sun, was that there was no atmosphere to facilitate convection. But there was more than one way to transfer heat. A cast iron skillet didn't burn your hand just because the bottom was hot, it burned your hand because the heat of the stove was conducted into the handle through the base. He just needed to conduct the suit's heat elsewhere, spread it out a bit, and he had an idea just how to do that. He just had to sit down and find a good position. It might cause damage to the artifact itself, but dying didn't do him or the Collector any favors.

Darnell found a spot in the middle of the back bench between Centrum and Kósmos and buckled himself in with the lap belt. He pushed against the seat, placing his lower back flat against the black accented, white leather seats.

"Peridot?" he called again, heart rate increasing. Something had happened, he knew it, something bad. What, though, he wasn't sure. His gut told him this was not the normal variety of bad. "Trust. I need to trust. Calm down. Communication issues happen all the time. Right? Sure. They do. It's okay. This is normal."

Centrum and Kósmos gazed into the black before him, a focused driver and their faithful companion, travelers with more miles crossed than anyone else in history. They were deep in the middle of a silent conversation for which Darnell was not privy, one that had been going on for decades. As he watched them, he fiddled with the radiator on the suit, redirecting it into the seat. He knew that this would likely ruin the leather, melting it upon contact, but it was the only option he could think of. A series of clicks vibrated up the suit as the radiator pulsed, switching its modes. A moment later, the temperature within the suit stabilized at one hundred degrees.

This was no dry heat, sure, but at least it was stable. He'd bought a little time.

Desperate to put his mind elsewhere, he began inspecting the interior of the car. The center screen of the car's sleek dash read: KEEP CALM, no doubt another poke at Elon Musk's Roadster stunt, in which his car had said DON'T PANIC, a reference to some old book. For Lindvall's part, he knew that the words KEEP CALM were a throwback to British posters hung during World War 2 meant to inspire during the German bombings.

And yet... And yet all this... There was one thing that caught his eye and made him laugh. Laugh a bit too much given his dire situation. Between the screen and one of the vents was mounted a tiny version of the car; its body made of dicast zinc-aluminum alloy. There was no question that this was the Hot Wheels special edition of the Slipstream. A one of a kind original.

Darnell considered reaching over the seat and taking the tiny car, adding it to his own collection aboard the *Peridot*. It would be a unique piece, for sure. But would the Collector finding it missing say something? Could this cost Sara's life?

He left the collectible where it was.

No sense making things worse.

Upon inspection, he came to realize that all the sentiments about this legendary car were true. The Slipstream was the very model of a modern luxury vehicle, sleek with smooth curves and lines, pure white exterior, and hand-stitched white leather seats with black panels for contrast. The buttons and switches within were made of metal, no plastic in sight, arrayed like the controls of an advanced space craft, not just some cheap automobile with touch screens. Despite it having been out here for so many years, a soft glow of LED light came from hidden recesses within the doors, giving them a pinkish outline. The Lindvolt Cell powering this vehicle was still good.

But was that a shock?

As the temperature lowered slightly, Darnell felt the need to lean forward and keep trying to strike up a conversation with his passengers. No sense remaining quiet in this hurtling stretch of luxury. Besides, he had to keep himself busy or his anxiety was going to take over and no one needed that. It was such a strange dichotomy that he could be sitting in the greatest expanse of all creation, and yet, feel so claustrophobic.

KEEP CALM.

A borrowed mantra.

KEEP CALM.

"Does it get lonely out here?" Darnell asked, turning to Centrum first, then Kósmos, while keeping the radiators on the seat. "I'm sure it does. You two been here for a while."

They said nothing, but he kept it up. Processing out loud was one of his coping mechanisms.

"I'm sure you're wondering what we're doin' out here after it's been so long," he went on, putting his elbows on the shoulders of the front seats. "You're a prized possession, an artifact of humanity. I bet that's kind of weird to hear, sure would be for an old top like me. Sixty-seven years you've been truckin' along. How ya feelin, son?"

He gave Centrum a smile, who in turn did nothing. Was the driver being rude? Or was the antique man a stoic?

"The strong silent type. I see how it is. I understand. Came from a time when Stigs were Stigs. Can't ever see your real face, no matter where the episode went, hmm?"

They sat still among the great gulf of stars. Without any near reference points in view, relative velocity meant nothing. Humans didn't evolve for this kind of life, and yet circumstance and hubris had thrust them into it.

Given this rare opportunity of quiet, he allowed his mind to drift, to travel the many pathways in his head. His thoughts had been heavy over the past few weeks. Maybe it was time to work through some of those. He did have a captive audience.

"So, Mr. Centrum, here's the thing," Darnell went on. "The world has changed so much since you burned into the void on the tip of a rocket. Good things have happened, bad things have happened. But us? The people coming to find me and take you along for another ride, we're just folk caught up in events. A man named Carlisle wants to tell a story a good many people want to hear, a story of a perfect America, one without sordid narratives of mistakes or missteps. He wants to tell the story of an America above reproach, a hardline religious doctrine, and of a path to return things to what he believes was a golden age of glory before we opened our borders and embraced change."

An America before cultural growth, Darnell thought. Before global humanism.

He closed his eyes and sighed, then rubbed the visor of his helmet out of habit forgetting he couldn't touch his face.

"While I'd like to see our country in the forefront again, always leading the way for humankind into the stars, settin' an example to be kinder and better to others, pretty sure Carlisle would find it easier to just kill off those who disagree with him. Suppose it's easier to work with people who already believe what you do than to change minds. Easier to stand in an echo chamber shoutin' the same words over and over until they become truth. Standin' on the outside, makes me see that pretty much any belief is brainwashing in its own way, a kind of tribalism. I reckon none of us want to be left out, do we? We want to belong. We want to be safe. And so, we build a strong culture with its own practices and conventions that we then swallow blindly to stay part of the group. We trust it without question, and yet, so much is truly unknown. Tell you what, Mr. Centrum, all this makes me wonder how a person sets their moral compass at all."

His attention was drawn over to the glove compartment before Kósmos and a lump rose in his throat. An idea began to form.

"Been wonderin' long and hard about a good many things," he went on, his breathing labored, words cutting off. "Things like, ain't we all the product of our environment? Feels a lot like chance that any of us—any of us turn out okay. I could have become Carlisle if given the right upbringing, couldn't I? And ya know what? That part scares the hell out of me. I think of myself as a good guy, a God-fearing man, and like I've had to justify so much of this job in my heart, so has that monster. He was willing—willing to take someone hostage just so he could have your car to push his agenda, to tell this maleficent story to a group of people strung out on emotion and misinformation. We're all good—and we're all bad—ain't we?"

Darnell's right-hand shook in anger. He pressed it palm down against his leg to steady it. Light flickered from up front. The glove compartment. The glove compartment called to him. What was—

An overpowering wave of nausea swept over him, heat blotting out any thoughts in the moment. He tried to take a drink from the tube inside his suit but found the reserves empty. And while his skin was slick with moisture, he felt as if he weren't sweating anymore. That was a bad sign.

"We do—we do what we have to do sometimes," he said, his words slow and heavy, "but I hope I never—" he paused for a moment, taking several ragged breaths, "Never have to do it again. Those folk on that pirate vessel are dead because of me. They are dead—dead because of Atticus and Carlisle. I became the sword, but they were the storm, the will—the will behind the need. Should a sword—a sword even if it was not its choice, regret fulfilling its—its purpose? Sure, I like blowin' up rocks, but that ain't the same as people. Those were lives. Families maybe. Friendships brought—brought to an end. Human potential snuffed out. There's a reason I didn't ever—ever think of joining the military..."

Centrum's visor flickered and went dark again. Was the mannequin attempting to communicate? Darnell couldn't be sure. He checked his comms for a response from *the Peridot*, pinged them again, and got nothing.

He was so thirsty...

The suit was so hot.

It was getting impossible to breathe, as if he were slowly being lowered into the atmosphere of Venus, its thousands of pounds of hellish, toxic pressure resting upon his chest.

Darnell lowered his head, hands coming together. "God almighty, I—I'm—so sorry for what I had to do to them people. Please, Lord, forgive me—forgive me for everything. All I wanted was to stand by the woman I love, and maybe, your—your will be done, have the chance to start a family. I don't—don't need much in life. Just love and legacy. Is it vanity that I want—want children? Hubris? To know that my life doesn't end when this body gives up? Is that—is that so wrong? Is it?"

Darnell's eyes began to water, not from the moisture in his suit but from the final drops in his body. The suit's health alarm was screaming, his core temperature far above safe, human levels. Hyperthermia would overcome him soon, and he would close his eyes for good. He wanted out of this situation, but there was nowhere to go.

How in the hell had he ended up here? He'd been raised right, yeah? He'd made good decisions. But when everyone was tempted, he'd been quiet. He'd been weak. He hadn't wanted to put anyone out and so he hadn't spoken his mind. This had all been stupid. Foolish. But what could he have done to make things right? He loved the people on the *Peridot*. He wanted only the best for them. He would lay down his life for them. He'd killed for them.... Oh God. He'd killed...

"I don't deserve good things," he whispered while hanging his head, the back of his helmet exposed like someone ready to be executed. "Do I?"

Snot dripped off the end of his nose down onto his faceplate, forcing him to take a sniff.

"Darnell?" his comms crackled. *"Darnell?"* Was it Captain Cho? Or had he lost his mind?

His back went straight. A smile took hold of his face. "You're alive! Thank God."

"Yes, we're all alive—at least for now."

"What—what do you mean, for—for now?"

"Look, Richardson, Lexi is hurt." The captain paused for a moment. *"Logan is taking care of her, but things went sideways fast after you left."*

His hands began to shake. The suit started tightening around his body. He had to get out, right now. Everything was too close. "How far—far away—are you?"

"We're almost there. Hold on for just another moment and prepare to get back. We know your suit has to be having issues keeping up by now. We'll get you inside and worry about the Slipstream after you're secure."

"Copy," he replied, then eyed the glove compartment once more. "Last chance."

"What was that, Darnell?"

"Nothing, ma'am."

Desperate to keep himself busy while they closed the gap, he reached around Kósmos and pulled on the glove compartment's handle. The mannequin wobbled, its helmet clicking against the side of his own. To his surprise, no blueprints tumbled out of the opening. No Easter egg snacks. No advanced neural chips.

There was just a plain, white envelope.

He fumbled with its edges, fingers of his suit unwieldy, and removed its contents, reading it while he waited to be rescued. It was getting hard to focus on anything hot as he was, his visor covered in moisture. His face was on fire. His heart was racing.

He read.

Then read again.

And again.

Darnell came to a decision.

He slipped the envelope into his suit, before stuffing a package the size of a lunchbox under the passenger seat.

"Goodbye, Centrum. Goodbye, Kósmos," he said as he unbuckled, then gave them each a squeeze on the shoulder. "Every great journey comes to—to an end. Every great cowboy rides—rides off into the sunset."

He turned to see the Peridot approach from out of the black and pushed off towards it, leaving the Slipstream behind. The air lock to his flyer irised open and invited him in. Soon as he had passed the emergency doors, Keelin compressed the chamber and came rushing inside, removing his helmet from its collar.

Steam rose from Darnell's skin, the difference of temperature from the inside of his baking suit and the ship a welcome, icy wind.

The captain appeared a moment later with something to drink. She forced him to take slow sips as Keelin freed him of the Vantablack vacuum suit, its surface so hot she had to use gloves to handle the pieces.

"That was close," the captain said. "Damned close."

"Is Lexi okay?"

"She's okay for now, but she's hurt real bad."

"How hurt?"

"Well… Sarita cut her in a fight that shouldn't have happened. It's deep. She was after Atticus, and Lexi got in the middle, scalpel clipped her radial artery."

His body trembled. Did he hear that right? "Sarita did this?"

"Yes. She's been tied up and is confined to a corner of the bridge. The situation is under control."

"Get me out of this damn thing." He started to wriggle inside the suit, trying to worm his way out, elbows banging against the bulkhead.

"Workin' on it, cowboy," Keelin said, steadying him. "She ain't goin' nowhere. In this life or the next."

The final piece of the suit was removed, and he felt was if he could finally breathe again. He needed to go to Lexi, but there was something to take care of first. Too many assholes doing stupid things.

Was it the right thing? Had he made the right decision? He considered this as he shakily finished off his drink, gaze fixed out the window on the Slipstream. He let the empty pouch go and put a hand to the window, light from the Peridot's floods reflecting off the helmets of the car's passengers.

"You okay?" Keelin asked, putting a hand on his shoulder. "I know your heart, friend. But the tough times have passed."

He gave her a weak smile and raised the disconnected glove of his vacuum suit. "Maybe so. Maybe not. But I got one last thing I have to do."

His eyes closed.

He took and deep breath and swallowed.

He depressed the trigger.

A light flashed on the other side of the airlock window as the Slipstream shattered into a thousand tiny pieces. Scintillating bits of paneling and glass and metal chassis scattered in the void, forming an uneven cloud of devastation. In the distant light of Sol, the debris was more like glitter cast into a dark room by a mischievous child, than the chunks of a relic of bygone days.

It was done.

The choice was made.

The Slipstream was no more.

God forgive this thought; but fuck that fucking Carlisle.

Darnell took a deep breath and felt a melancholy sense of peace settle into him. The Lord's good works came in many forms. He had made the right choice.

Keelin's hands shot up to cover her mouth. The captain's face went blank, her limbs rigid.

"Darnell!" Keelin shouted after a moment of disbelief. "What the fook did ya do that for?"

The trigger glove floated away as he turned to face his crewmates.

"Atticus was right about one thing," he said, his words deliberate. "Carlisle can't be allowed to have his prize, and so now, he just won't."

[24] – Lexi

Lexi woke sometime later in Logan's quarters, the doctor floating to her left, Atticus on her right. Her injured arm screamed in pain, but it was no longer bleeding. She was nauseated, but even that feeling was beginning to subside. Drugs were being pushed into her, an I.V. pack fastened to her chest pumping into her uninjured arm.

"That was close," Logan said, seeing she had woken up. "You've got some serious damage, deep enough you'll likely have nerve issues, but you'll live. It wasn't completely severed, so I was able to suture the artery and close you back up. Not an easy task in null gravity, let me tell you. We'll be vacuuming blood out of consoles for months."

"That bitch," Lexi hissed, her anger weak. "That bitch." And she meant it one hundred and fifty percent. She'd started to like the woman, relate to her in a way, and now...

"Yeah," Atticus echoed. "That bitch."

Her eyes drifted over to him and narrowed, a fresh kind of anger bubbling in her belly. "This is what I get for trying to save your effeminate ass."

"I appreciate that, I really do."

"Yeah, well, fuck you."

He let out a long sigh and scratched at the back of his neck. "Yes. Fuck me."

The pressure door to Logan's quarters slid open, and a haggard-looking Captain Cho appeared. "Lexi," she said, her tired expression relaxing the slightest bit as she braced against the door frame. "So glad to see you're alive and awake."

"Wouldn't let her go," Logan said, patting the captain on the shoulder. "Besides, got to earn my way on this stupid flyer somehow. Patching up shins only gets you so far in life. Not the big kaching and all, but it's a living."

"Yeah." The captain chewed on her bottom lip. "Speaking of earning our way." She paused as if considering her words. "Look, so long as Lexi's up for it, let's have a powwow on the bridge. Situation's changed, yet again."

"Float me there?" Lexi asked Logan, and they nodded, taking hold of her shoulders to help guide her out. God, her arm hurt like hell.

Once on the bridge, she saw Darnell had returned and was in one piece. Without regard for her injury, she pushed off a nearby wall, slipped free from Logan's care, and cannonballed into Darnell. He tossed his arms around her and she yelped at the sudden shock of pain that ran up her arm.

"Sorry," he mumbled.

But she didn't care. The love of her life was alive and well. He was safe in her arms. Nothing else mattered.

"You okay?" he asked, putting his forehead against hers, their noses less than an inch apart. "Does it hurt?"

"Like hell. I'll be okay."

The room fell silent as the captain recounted the events from start to finish, from their taking of the job, to Carlisle's loyalty test, to Atticus's betrayal and the most shocking of all—Darnell's decision to destroy the Slipstream. They floated in their respective locations, stunned at his choice. To be honest, Lexi couldn't blame him for what he'd done, even if it might unravel their dreams.

"This job went to hell from day one," the captain said after giving everyone time to metabolize the details. "It would be easy to start pointing fingers, and truth is, Carlisle is the biggest target, but all of us have had a hand in this. I didn't get consensus from everyone when we set out, especially Darnell. And as your captain, it's my job to take care of you. That's what my family does. My desire to free us from this rat race overrode my better judgement. I should have looked harder at this opportunity before jumping in with both feet, and for that, I am sorry."

"I threw gas on that fire," Keelin said, crossing her arms and shaking her head. She turned a hand over to inspect her fingertips. "Me fingerprints are 'ere."

"And I made first contact," Logan added. "My hands certainly aren't clean, even before being on the *Peridot*. I've done some questionable things for money, legally questionable at least. Thought this would be a victimless crime. Boy was I wrong."

Lexi reached out with her good hand and took hold of Darnell's. He eased up beside her and hung his head. It was clear as day that guilt weighed heavy on his shoulders. The dead pirates. His and her dreams. Sarita's wife at risk. He carried all of it on his back.

"I'm sorry you got drawn into this," Sarita said, raising a hand and rubbing her cheek. Her eyes had become moist, her focus distant. "I'm so sorry. And Lexi…"

"Stop," she growled back. "Not now."

Sarita withdrew.

"I just didn't want him to have it," Atticus explained, his voice not much more than a whisper, fingers picking at the end of his scarf. "The money sounded great, okay, but the idea of what that asshole would use this for, I started having doubts. When Carlisle crossed us, it went too far. He thinks himself above the law. Whatever he can get away with, he will get away with."

"Which has to stop," Darnell said, growling his words. He pointed a finger towards the back of the ship. "And that's why I trashed the Slipstream."

"But it was our bargaining chip," the captain exhaled, fingers pinching the bridge of her nose. "Now, not only are we left empty handed, but despite the incident on the bridge, we still care Sarita's wife is in mortal danger. Richardson, I know you're a man of principle. Why put someone at risk like that?"

His face twisted as a kaleidoscope of emotion washed over him. "Way I figure, she was always at risk, even if we showed up with the goods. I—"

"But now he'll kill her for sure," Sarita cut him off. "He'll kill her and find it funny."

Darnell raised his hands. "Hold up. Hold up. Before everyone gets too riled up, I think we have something worth just as much as the Slipstream." He reached in his jumpsuit and produced an envelope.

"What's this?" Lexi asked. "That paper. It's old."

"Yeah," he said, removing the letter from the envelope, the sound arresting everyone's attention like a sword being drawn from a scabbard. "Very old."

"Be careful," the captain urged. "What is it?"

He smiled. "A relic of its own kind."

Darnell read aloud.

'My dear great-grandchildren,

Hi. I hope that I have gotten the chance to know you. My greatest pride in life has come from being a parent to your parents' parents.

I wanted you to know, the world can be hard at times, cruel even. Some of us will see things that others do not. Existential threats. Opportunities. When the Universe has given the vision to look over the horizon, you can often be seen as a bit crazy, maybe even mad. When you truly fight to shift the paradigm, to change how a fundamental piece of humankind is viewed, you will almost always meet resistance. Humans do not like change. Change is uncertain, unknown, and yet we all know it is the only constant in the universe.

The world is ours to make, and as we make it better, it should be made better for all, not just for one. To move forward as a species, to save us from our eventual extinction, we must work as a single entity, one body and one mind. Life matters, it is worth it. Don't spend your days sleepwalking, doing what you think others want, go make things better. Give the people something to believe in that is bigger than country, than creed, than religion. Life is the higher calling. You will fail, but if you're not failing, you're not learning, and without learning we will go into the night never again to see dawn.

Be the light in the dark, find a way to a brighter future. You have it in you. You've always had it in you.

All my love,
Matteo Lindvall'

Darnell carefully folded the letter and slipped it back into the envelope. He held it to his chest in reverence.

No one said a word. Lindvall's great secret hadn't been hidden technology or corporate dirt; it had been words of vision for his great grandchildren. Words to inspire them through the dark days ahead.

"I may have been cooking alive in a space suit and hallucinating," Darnell said after some time, "but it made me think. We all screwed up, yeah? We're all at fault for coming to this point, but it don't have to stay there. We have leverage. We have a prize. It's high time we made friends with one of the most influential families on Earth."

The captain's eyes widened. "You don't mean…"

He nodded. "Lindvall's vision of the future didn't include people like Carlisle, far as I can tell. I think he really wanted to make the world a better place. He was an enigmatic troll at times, but there's no doubt his inventions, once they were available to everyone, made things better for us.

"I say it's time to draw a line in the sand and say no more. I think it starts with more than just turning Carlisle into the authorities. It takes the whole mess of us forgiving one another for where we've gone wrong."

Lexi's face scrunched up. She shook her head and glared at Sarita. The pain in her arm had returned. Was it time that Logan could give her a shot to help? "Forgiveness is hard."

He reached for the hand of her good arm. "Let us forgive one another, for only then will we live in peace."

She knew he was right but wasn't sure this was her day to offer forgiveness. The agony of her injury made it impossible to focus on much more than anger. The pain gave her flashbacks to her childhood, the time she broke her arm at ten on the stoop outside playing with friends. She'd had to force her hungover mother to take her to the hospital down the street, and when she couldn't be roused, almost grabbed her closest sister and took herself. Once the x-rays revealed the arm was broken, her mom had asked her to forgive her, but it was too late. Her mother hadn't cared when it was just her words. Soon as other people were involved, that was the only time she was repentant. And her father? There was no telling where he had gotten off to.

Had she ever forgiven them for that? No. They didn't deserve it.

"Should we forgive Carlisle then?" Keelin asked. "Not trying to throw salt on a wound or nothin'. The Irish forgive their great men when they are safely buried."

Darnell chuckled under his breath. "After he's brought to justice, I do believe we can forgive."

"What about..." Lexi leaned over and whispered in his ear. "What about our dream? This could land us in just as much trouble as him."

"Have faith," he said, taking hold of the hand on her good arm and squeezing. "I'm not letting our dream go. We will have our home, our family."

The conviction in his eyes melted her heart, not a glimmer of doubt to be seen. Maybe he was right. For once, maybe she should have faith in something. Even if it wasn't God, or some higher power, she could always have faith in people.

"All that work just to blow it up," Logan said. "But is it weird that I feel a little better? Anyone else feel better?"

Everyone on the bridge looked to one another and nodded the least little bit. This cut the tension and made the space feel larger than it was, the bridge had somehow become a great hall full of possibility. The Slipstream's destruction had lifted a thousand tons off of their shoulders. This feeling might only be temporary, but she'd take it.

"Forgiveness," Atticus mused. "Such a difficult thing for us humans."

"Should we give it a go, then?" Keelin asked, eyebrows raised at him in a curious gesture. "Forgiveness that is? Lettin' go?"

"How do we even start?"

Silence.

"We start here," Captain Cho spoke up after some time. "Unless anyone has anything to add. I, for one, am ready to lighten my burdens. And in a way, I already am. We know what to do." A pause. "Lexi, if you would, connect us with the Luna relay. Have them patch us through to the Lindvall family steward. Let's take Carlisle down."

Atticus eyed Sarita and smiled. The woman let out a sigh and curled up into a ball, turning her attention to the bulkhead.

Lexi eased into her acceleration chair with Darnell's assistance, careful not to touch her injury. She flipped several switches with her good arm and aimed their antennas back towards Luna.

Lost in her work thoughts drifted, and she began wondering what color they'd paint the living room of their apartments if all went well. Something drab and standard? Or bright and eclectic? A color that would have to go if they ever sold their place and moved somewhere else? She wondered what Darnell would look like twenty years from now with gray in his beard, a few extra pounds around the middle. Wondered what it would feel like to wish their little one the best as they went to school for the first time. These were precious, fragile, dangerous thoughts, and she didn't give a damn. She was going to allow herself permission to have them. If she deserved them or not, they were hers. She would give her children the life her parents had not given her. She would show them the love she had been denied. She had the perfect partner for that.

As she calibrated the angle and ran a diagnostic test, Darnell settled in beside her, his attention focused on a tiny, die-cast Lindvall Slipstream in his fingers—another Hot Wheels car for his collection.

Where did that come from?

"Ready Miss Carver?" the captain asked.

"Yes, ma'am." She pointed at the screen. "Array is back up and running. Channel open."

The captain nodded, then leaned forward in her chair, arms resting on her legs. "This is the rock hauler *Peridot* calling out to the Lindvall family. We have a story we'd like to share with you. One that, well... You might not believe, but sure as hell need to hear."

[25] – Darnell

"Come on, answer," Darnell grumbled as he free floated alone in his and Lexi's quarters, relentlessly checking the notification center of the wall display for a return message like a junkie with an itch. "Come on. We know you're out there."

He rubbed his eyes with fingertips and groaned. Everything was hazy, a world of physical and mental exhaustion overtaking his cognitive functions. If he could have one wish in this moment, one answered prayer, it would be to freeze time and allow him to unplug his brain from reality long enough to rest. Long enough to contextualize all that had happened.

It had been seven hours since they had sent the message to Lindvall's estate, and no reply, not even as much as a read receipt. Even with light speed lag, they should have gotten something in response. Lexi and Sarita had confirmed multiple times this was the proper number and frequency, and being that the signal had come from space, not the ground, someone should answer. But there was no luck.

He rummaged through a wall duffel and found a sheet of sticky glue balls, removing one and putting it to the bottom of the battered Slipstream Hot Wheels he'd plucked off Centrum's dash. It was scuffed and worn, some of the paint missing from having spent the past seventy-seven years exposed to hard vacuum and cosmic dust. Collecting Hot Wheels hadn't been an easy hobby in the wider solar system, so any opportunity to add to that collection, especially with such an important artifact as this, was welcome. This might just be the prize jewel of his collection. Certainly was one of a kind. Was it theft that he swiped it from the car's dash? Did any of that matter now?

"Vroom, vroom." He clasped the car between his fingers and pretended like it was driving on an invisible road, then laughed at himself and let out a sigh.

He stuck the Slipstream into place above their sleep bag, adding it to the line of existing cars beside a red and silver open wheel with a cab that looked like a World War II German army helmet.

His collection, as it was, started at most valuable on the left to leads valuable on the right, the Slipstream first, then the Red Baron, a custom blue Volkswagen Beetle, blue Rodger Dodger, and a white enamel Camaro. The rest were less valuable yet no less sentimental. He had a cherry red Ford Shelby Cobra, a '76 Greenwood Corvette, a '17 Ford GT, and on and on and on. All this from a guy who hadn't hardly driven at all, other than a truck on his family's ranch.

Once autonomous vehicles had become ubiquitous and cheap, almost no one but the rich got behind the wheel. Peasants like himself had hailed a cloud lift and been taken wherever they needed to go for pennies on the dollar, riding in an empty vehicle a hundred others had used that day. He'd ridden more horses than driven cars, yet the nostalgia, the romance of sitting in the driver's seat controlling a machine of such power as an extension of your will, an embodiment of freedom, was unique. It must be what Lexi felt piloting the *Peridot*.

Darnell pushed back to admire his little collection. It hadn't hurt anyone. It hadn't started a religious or political movement. It just sat there on the bulkhead looking pretty, acting as a time portal for his private thoughts.

A burn alarm echoed throughout the *Peridot*, Darnell's eyes widening. He leaped straight into action, not pausing, strapping himself into an emergency harness on the back wall as he braced for acceleration. They had drilled for this, there was no time for thought. After the five-point harness clicked into place he closed his eyes and wrapped his hands around the shoulder straps resting against his chest.

"*Hold on,*" Lexi called over the intercom.

The *Peridot* shook as the Falkor drive ignited, a swift, rising whine that could be felt through the bulkhead. The conductive noise of the engines was louder here than on the bridge, their quarters closer to the aft end of the ship, less distance for vibrations to disburse. His spine ground against the hard metal behind the padding of his jump seat with a sudden and intense force, its cushion made for only emergency use, not comfort. With his recent dealings over the pirates, his body was in pain.

As the heavy acceleration settled upon his chest, he twisted his head and peered at one of the wall displays, reading off their flyer's acceleration. He could not think of any reason why they needed to burn, not now. They were in the middle of nowhere and were still waiting for a response to proceed.

But Lexi was burning at six G's. Six G's.

Something was wrong.

"What's the situation?" Darnell croaked into comms. "What's going on?"

"We're being tracked," Captain Cho replied.

"Again! More pirates?"

"No—not pirates this time." Her breathing was labored under the weight of the roaring drive. *"Wuh—worse. The Chinese have realized their prize is missing."*

"Shit," he mumbled.

Darnell was no expert when it came to the consumption of reaction mass and Delta V, orbital mechanics and intra-solar navigation, but what he did know was that they were already running the burn tables pretty narrow. Now, Lexi was torching their reserves. If they didn't cut thrust soon, pursuit or not, they'd have no way to safely arrive at any destination. Whatever course they'd locked in would be their course for all eternity, till they were captured by a gravity well in a distant solar system or crashed into a rock and turned to dust.

"Are they still gaining?" the captain asked.

Lexi let out a string of curses under her breath. *"Shit they are determined."*

"How did they find us?"

"Debris signature," Sarita added. "Only way. There was no active transmitter. When the signal died, they started scanning for it in space. Found the debris, then found us."

This was his fault. He'd screwed up. He hadn't followed the plan, and now not only did they have the Collector after them, but the Chinese.

"Thirty thousand kilometers," Lexi said. "Still narrowing."

"Increase by another G."

His body tensed. This was not the position he wanted to be while enduring nearly six G's of acceleration. How long till he passed out? Till the blood vessels in his head burst? What if one of them had an aneurism?

His spine crackled against the bulkhead, his cheeks pressing back against his face. The Slipstream Hot Wheels came loose and fired across his quarters like a bullet, landing inches above his head with a bang, sticking to the wall like a magnet under their acceleration's titanic force.

"I thought we had another six months," the captain said.

It seems they had been watching all along.

"Lexi," Darnell said. "This hurts. The—safety—harness. Not meant for burns—this—hard."

"If I cut thrust, how fast do you think you can get up here?"

"Less than a minute."

"Do it," the captain ordered. "Be quick, Richardson."

The roaring drive went silent, and the pressure on his sore body vanished. Darnell unbuckled from the harness. After being under heavy G forces for only a few moments, he was already sore and weak. He reached for the door and pulled himself through, reorienting and tossing himself up the hall. Captain Cho and Logan grabbed his hands when he entered the bridge and tossed him towards his acceleration chair.

"Twenty thousand kilometers," Lexi reported. "Damn those fuckers are moving fast. Hard to gauge their relative velocity, but they have to be hitting almost two hundred KPS."

Darnell slid into place and clipped into the five-point harness. As soon as the final buckle clicked, Lexi reengaged the Falkor, tossing everyone back into their cushions. The weight of acceleration returned but was far easier, far more comfortable to manage with the proper equipment.

"Can—we outrun them?" the captain asked, breathing hard.

"Maybe," Lexi said, but it was clear she was not certain. "We have less mass than them, I think. We're—not carrying a load." She took a deep breath. "But this won't bode well for us reaching Luna safely."

Darnell groaned, "How far we off?"

"We were down to a fifteen percent margin of error—before this maneuver—but now? Maybe five percent and dropping. Do I keep burning?"

"Are they still closing?" the captain asked.

"Under ten thousand, but it's slowing. We're catching up to their velocity."

Cho grunted. "Keep burning." From the reflection in a dark display monitor, Darnell could see that in spite of this heavy maneuver, the captain was somehow making use of her personal terminal. How were her fingers not breaking under all this weight? What was she looking at, and at such a critical time?

"When do I stop?"

"When the distance between us widens."

"But what about reaction mass? We won't have enough to get us to Luna."

"What choice we got?" Keelin mused. "I don't fancy a visit from the People's Republic."

"I'll take responsibility for the reaction mass," Captain Cho said. "Keep it going."

Lexi frowned at this idea, her expression difficult to interpret under so much acceleration. Her skin, as was all theirs, was being stretched out like Silly Putty.

"Should have saved the transmitter," Sarita grumbled. "Should have at least recovered—the—box before—setting off your charges."

Darnell chose not to reply. He'd messed up and he knew it but didn't have the energy to argue. Not with her. She had nearly killed Lexi. God may forgive, but at this moment, he wasn't going to.

Atticus shouted back at Sarita, "Why not try shutting up?"

"Nine thousand kilometers," Lexi reported. "Eight thousand nine hundred."

The weight on Darnell's chest was becoming unbearable. He wanted to scream, if only he could draw in enough air to make it happen. Lexi ramped the drive up higher, and higher. It might have hurt when he lassoed the pirate vessel, but that was quick. It was over. This wouldn't stop.

7.1 G's

How long would they have to keep this up?

7.2

He felt blood vessels burst around his eyes and lips.

7.3

The skin on his face felt as if it might rip clean off.

7.4

Every breath became an asthmatic challenge.

7.5

"Distance widening," Lexi reported. "Ten thousand six hundred, seven hundred."

"Keep up our thrust but pull it down to a single G," Cho ordered.

The effect was immediate, the easing of pressure enough to bring a temporary state of euphoria, stars cast before his eyes. A wave of discomfort swelled over his spine and into his head, then broke atop his skull and washed back down into his belly. He scrambled for a storage pouch mounted on the side of his acceleration chair and shook open a plastic bag. There was no hesitation as he emptied his stomach's contents and heaved again and again.

"Fuck," Lexi said, slamming her control panel with her good hand. "Fuck. Fuck. Fuck."

"What is it?" Logan asked, lifting their hand terminal. "Are they still gaining?"

"No. We're ahead by quite a margin. I don't think they can catch us now, or at least I don't think they have the balls to do it. It's the fuel tables. We don't have enough reaction mass for the necessary burns to slow down from this velocity and enter an insertion orbit around Luna. We're underwater by twenty percent."

Darnell hated being right. This left them very few options, most of which involved phoning for help and hoping it came in time. It's not like it was back in the road trip heydays on Earth, where you could just get off at the next exit, fill up your tank, grab a few snacks and go. In this case, the next exit was several AU away from them, and you still had to catch it.

"Don't see what much else could be done," Keelin said. "Chinese flyer gave us little options."

"The transmitter," Sarita growled. "All we had to do was keep the transmitter running."

"Shut your fookin' hole, bitch. What's done is done. Question is, what we gonna do?"

"What indeed," Atticus mused.

"An' shut yours too." The engineer pointed a finger at him. "If you fancy, cram a cock in it to help."

He put a hand over his mouth in shock. "Language."

"We really are a shitty team," Logan said, shaking their head.

It was hard to argue at the moment.

"I'm sorry everyone," Darnell finally said. "I didn't..."

Lexi reached out and took his hand, wincing as she brushed her bandage against an arm rest on accident.

Everyone sat in silence for a time, listening as the roaring drive vibrated the hull. Most often the *Peridot* traveled in freefall, so having a sensation of normal gravity, even if the orientation was wrong, was strange. It wouldn't remain for long. They were screwed and it was his fault.

Captain Cho began to nod thoughtfully, then broke the silence, "I guess it's time to call in favors."

"What are you talking about?" Darnell asked. "If we contact the UEI, they won't take kindly to everything that's happened."

"No, not the UEI. At least, not directly. But we can get help from them." She rubbed her nose and sniffed. "I'm not the only captain in the Cho family. My sister Tao is captain of the CNES colony ship *La Révolution*, a Mars settlement hauler. They carry more than enough fuel for us to make up our difference, and if my estimations are right, we can adjust our course with little cost and intercept them."

"French space program or not, the UEI will be all over that."

"This could be a good thing," Sarita chimed up, her face turning bright. "We can resubmit a valid flight plan when we reach *La Révolution*. If you and your sister are as tight as you imply, she can make your arrival disappear. Most cases, the UEI won't dig that deep. When we hit Luna, they'll see we last made contact with the colony ship and wave us in."

"Fuel and a lie." The captain rubbed her face. "This is going to cost me."

"Cost ya what?" Keelin asked.

"Don't you worry about that," she said. "All in, right? You need my help. I need your help. We stick together and see this through. If Lindvall's Estate isn't stepping in, we've got to do this on our own."

"We've always been on our own," Lexi said.

And Darnell couldn't have agreed more.

[26] – Lexi

It had been quite some time since Lexi had seen a colony ship up close. Compared to the *Peridot,* the vessel was a giant fifty times more massive than their rock hauler. Its mission: to ferry colonists from low Earth orbit to Mars and back again. Colonization had changed drastically in Lexi's lifetime. In her childhood, the exclusive interplanetary vehicle was Space X's Starship, a fifty-meter-tall gray canister more reminiscent of a bullet than an advanced reusable flyer. While Starship had done well carrying groups of no more than a hundred, they were not the best for long-haul missions. No gravity. Limited space. Chemical propulsion. With the demand for quicker colonization to meet the goals of the UEI, they needed something bigger.

And so entered the United Exploration Initiative's Excelsior class transport vehicle, which was a scaled down version of the FICSE mission special issue, which featured much more powerful fusion drives and were nearly twice as big. At a length of just over one hundred and fifty meters, they appeared as a lumpy white spear tossed down the center of two flat hoops, one end dotted with a sphere, the other set on fire. As the hub made its slow spin, so did its habitat wheels, twisting through the void in a never-ending corkscrew to create a constant 1 G of artificial gravity for the safety and comfort of its passengers.

A part of her looked upon its spoked form and wondered what her life would have been like if she'd become one of those pilots, had had a ship that large under her charge to navigate through the void. The kid in her approved of this dream.

La Révolution burned slow to match velocity with the *Peridot*, its mass propelled by a cluster of Falkor cones at the aft, the command sphere at its forward end scintillating against a backdrop of darkness. As it was currently traveling from Mars, not to it, the two hundred or so passengers that would typically inhabit the wheel were absent, and so the spinning windows of the habitat were dark, temporary quarters empty.

Fewer people around to question why a rock hauler had decided to dock with a colony ship. This was for the best.

Lexi brought the *Peridot* around to the docking clamps on the rotating hub of the spine. Thrusters fired in a continuous pattern, and *La Révolution* went from corkscrewing through the void to standing still, the spin of the two vessels matched. An expandable clamp extended from the colony ship, bringing them in the rest of the way, connecting to the outer coupling of the *Peridot* and drawing them against its hull.

The *Peridot* gave a shudder and the yellow indicators on Lexi's overhead turned green. They were secure.

"*Vive La Révolution,*" she declared, then unbuckled herself from her acceleration chair careful not to touch her bandage.

"We goin' to be welcome here?" Keelin asked the captain. "Comm chatter was hushed comin' in."

Katia paused in unbuckling her harness for a moment, fingers caressing cold metal in an absent gesture. "Hard to say. Not a lot of options, though. Been a few years since I've seen my sister. A few months since we've spoken."

"That so?" Darnell helped Lexi over to the hatch, following Atticus, Logan, and the others. "Y'all good?"

"Just an old argument hanging over us."

They floated to the aft of the *Peridot* and over to *La Révolution,* the dock open but without anyone in sight. A bang came from over Lexi's shoulder, and she saw Darnell twisting around in the air, his eyes closed, hands clasping his right shin, air sucking between his teeth. She reached out with her good arm and pulled him through the lock, feeling guilty for wanting to laugh... but this was funny.

A group of four appeared just ahead of them in the expandable docking chamber. They did not wave or offer any greeting, opting to wait for the new arrivals in silence, blocking the end of the accordion shaped hall with their bodies. From the expression on their faces no one seemed happy to see the *Peridot's* crew.

"I got a bad feeling about this," Sarita whispered.

Lexi ground her teeth.

"Pretty sure I've seen more smiles at a funeral," Atticus groaned.

Logan took a deep breath and her right arm flickered blue. They rolled their sleeves down to cover it up.

"What do we do if this here goes cattywampus?" Darnell continued to rub his battered shin. "Damn that stupid bulkhead."

"It won't," the captain assured them. "Everything will be fine."

"Hello, sister," a woman said as they made their final approach, raising a hand to forestall any further progress. She stared the captain down with narrowed eyes, her arms crossed in such a way they appeared like armor. This had to be Captain Tao Cho. She stood with three others, each dressed in jumpsuits of the Tricolour, the blue, white, and red of the French flag. "Love to drop in at the oddest times, don't you?"

"I don't get to choose when the universe throws a curve ball," Katia replied.

One of *La Révolution's* crew members, a woman of middle age with bright blue eyes came forward. "What is this all about?" she asked, finger pointing at the group, her graying bob of hair framing her face like the snakes of medusa. "This is highly irregular."

"What can we say?" Logan mused. "Space is dangerous. Shit happens."

"And what kind of shit is this?" a thick man on the left asked, his baby smooth jaw hard set as if he were chewing on a bundle of nails like bubble gum.

"May we speak in private?" Katia asked, leaning towards her sister.

Tao sighed and waved her sister over. The two of them floated to a place beyond the blockade of *La Révolution's* crew and their conversation continued, rapid and hushed. They did not shake hands nor hug like most families; even dysfunctional ones like Lexi's could at least pretend to play nice around one another. They kept their distance. Everyone else remained where they were, afraid to move an inch.

"Heard any good jokes lately?" Atticus ventured, breaking the awkward silence.

"Shut up," the woman in front told him.

"Want to hear one I came across the other day? Memes and all." Atticus removed his hand terminal then affected a gesture, adjusting invisible eyeglasses. "Do you know what you call a pretentious mime?"

"What?" Darnell asked, curious.

Atticus turned to him. "A dick in a box."

This made Lexi curl her lips in on themselves to stuff down her chuckles. This was the least appropriate time to be telling jokes like this, but that made it even funnier. *La Révolution's* crew was not amused.

"I don't care what she said!" Katia shouted; her arms raised. She glanced back in the direction of the group, then back to her sister, her hands gesturing apologies.

Darnell leaned in close to Lexi. "What do we do if they don't help?"

She had no answer to that question.

"A Roman walks into a bar," Atticus went on, hand terminal raised. "He holds up two fingers and says to the bartender, I'll take five beers."

No response. Not his best. Even Sarita almost seemed embarrassed for the psychologist.

"Well," he shook his head. "You're no fun. Should we speak of anthropology then? Theology?"

Lexi wished that she were a fly on the wall, able to hear the conversation between the two sisters. The discussion was a tense negotiation. From their postures this reminded her of the time she fought with Candice, her youngest sister, over a stupid stuffed animal their Uncle Darius had put in her Easter basket. He'd gotten gifts for each of the Carver girls, but Baba, a gray, furry rabbit with floppy ears and a multi-colored vest, was hers. Candice had gotten one as well, Uncle Darius attempting to be fair, but the drug store he'd dropped by had had only one like Baba, and she loved Baba.

Candice had lost her ever-loving mind and began to scream over it. Her rabbit was ugly, sure, and she had wanted Lexi's. But Lexi did not want to give it up. She'd immediately bonded with this stuffed animal who fast became her confidant, the one person in their family who could hear her lonely thoughts when she lay down at night, whether it was real or not. The one who could make her feel like it might be okay to dream of better days.

It was silly sure, just a stuffed animal, but it had made for a few tough years between her and her sister. Baba gave her comfort in a way Candice had wanted, too. A way she had needed.

"Fine. Fine," Captain Cho said after several tense minutes, reaching into a pocket and removing something oval shaped no larger than the palm of her hand. She brushed its smooth, ivory surface, a look of longing on her face, before turning it over to her sister. Tao smiled at the object, slipped it into her pocket, then rested a free hand on her sister's shoulder.

Lexi blinked at them, attempting to figure out what it was she had seen exchanged. Was it a coin? A disc? Impossible to say. Was this all the argument had been over? A trinket? Was there power and history in that tiny object?

Katia and Tao returned a moment later.

"We're going to offer them assistance," Tao declared. "They got into a bit of a rough situation on their last capture and according to UEI regulation 6.1.24, we may offer them fuel and repairs so long as they do not put our ship in mortal danger."

"*Capitaine*, this does not feel right," the man said, his voice pleading.

"You will do as I command. They are fellow Void-Striders, out here working to build a better future for humanity. We will give them aid."

He turned around and pushed off, grumbling to himself as he left.

"One last chance," Katia said, drawing her crew in close so the others could not hear. "Tao said you guys could be part of the next colony run. Become Mars citizens and no one would ever notice. She can handle the papers. We can make it all go away."

"No," Keelin spoke up first. "Ma'am, I say we see this to the end."

"It's the right thing to do," Darnell added. "Backin' out on Sarita and Sarah, even if she did lie and hurt us, it ain' right."

"Thank you," Sarita whispered, head lowering.

Darnell sighed in response.

The rest of the group gave their consent through silence, Lexi included. This was the way, even if she wanted very much to clock that fucking bitch in the nose for what she'd done. Carlisle was the true enemy. He had to go down.

Katia rubbed her face and nodded. "Alright then. Keelin, Darnell, get to work. Danielle here will help you get the *Peridot* fueled. They've also got a spare spacesuit we can use to replace Darnell's Vantablack paint job. No artwork, but it's part of the standard form factor and we can service it. Logan, keep an eye on the troublemakers."

"Hey now," Atticus said. "By the laws of the universe, I've already committed one betrayal. It can't happen twice."

"And you'll get the chance to pay me back for that one, you just wait."

His face went deadpan. "I'm so thrilled."

Darnell squeezed Lexi's good hand and took off with Keelin and the rest of the group, leaving her alone with the captain.

The exchange with her sister was burning up Lexi's imagination. She had to know the truth. "Mind if I ask you a question, Captain?"

"Someone has to ask," Katia replied, spinning to face her. "Maybe that's why I left you behind with me. Maybe I needed to tell someone I trust."

This made Lexi's heart swell. She didn't quite know how the captain saw her. Sure, she had given her a job, but that was on tenuous terms, given Lexi's history.

"What did you give your sister?"

There was a pause as the captain considered her words. "A brooch."

"A what? Like the pin you clip to a dress?"

She nodded.

"Okay. What is so important about it?"

Katia looked off to the side and took a deep breath before scrubbing her nose with the back of her hand. "It's an old disagreement between Tao and I. The brooch is a family heirloom."

"How old is it?"

"Very, very old." She smiled, and her attention wandered off to distant memories. "My great, great, great, great... well, you get it. Grandmother, Mei Chen, was born in Hong Kong in 1835, more than two hundred fifty years ago. When she was twenty, her heart was full, having had two beautiful children, twins no less, by her hard-working husband, Ping. One summer, he caught a fever and within a month he had passed, leaving her widowed in a shack off Kowloon Bay. She had loved Ping dearly, so to keep his memory alive, she had his likeness carved into an ivory brooch. The very same ivory brooch I gave my sister. I promise you now, it's not some 3D printed trinket, or made of plastic, it's carved from actual elephant tusk, sourced from India.

"By the time the children were eight, Mei made the choice to leave. She had no more family but for her children. Her parents had passed a few years before meeting Ping. Since Hong Kong was a British colony at the time, she decided to make a go of it in London by way of a merchant ship. She didn't have much more than a steamer chest, the twins, and the memory of her husband to her name. Arriving in London they thrived as a family. She met another man, also Chinese, by the name of Li, and had a third child by age thirty. Her youngest grew up with the same adventurous spirit as her mother, and decided to move to America, seeing opportunity even amidst struggle and persecution. And so, Mei gave her the brooch to remember them before she boarded the ship to the new world. The two of them never spoke again."

Katia paused for a moment, looking down at her empty hand, a finger tracing a line across her palm. "You see, it has been passed down in my family from mother to daughter. When my mother passed, it was to go to the oldest daughter, me. But Tao felt it was time to put the brooch's journey to rest. She wanted to take it to Mars and place it upon the explorer's memorial at Olympus Mons. And now, well, she can."

Lexi nodded at this. She had once been to the memorial, a massive obelisk in Apollo Park set beneath a clear dome, surrounded by a green space at the city center. It was one of those images she would never forget, a sense of awe having overcome her with the power and history behind it. It was a testament to every life lost in the pursuit of exploration and humanity's renewed hope, its seven faces festooned in trinkets and heirlooms of a thousand explorers and their many bloodlines, a memorial to the best of humanity.

"You couldn't let go, could you?" Lexi asked.

"No." She lowered her head. "I couldn't, but now I guess what's done is done. It's all I had left of Mom. She passed about ten years back, massive brain aneurism that came out of nowhere. Then there was a fire at my childhood home during the funeral. No foul play or anything, just screwed up luck and bad wiring. It still hurts some days. I miss her. I hope she would be proud of who I am and what I've become."

The captain may not have been a touchy-feely sort, but Lexi didn't care in that moment. She wrapped her arms around Captain Katia Cho, uninvited, squeezing her tight. Katia did not resist. Her head came to rest on Lexi's shoulder as the two held one another for what seemed forever.

"I see no way that she couldn't be proud," Lexi whispered in her captain's ear. "She looks to you from the other side with a smile on her face. You've done good things for yourself. You've done good things for others."

"Thank you, friend." The captain sniffed and shuddered. "Thank you."

[27] – Darnell

The crew of *La Révolution* was helpful, if less than amicable. They followed the orders of their captain without any additional niceties, showing Darnell and Keelin what they needed without a fuss, though hovering over them what felt inches away as they made for engineering. Darnell made a point to appear non-threatening, keeping his body language submissive, his back bent and hands down, his expression soft and uncertain. Once Danielle's companions were satisfied Darnell meant her no harm, they scurried off, mumbling under their breath in French as they vanished to their own tasks. Darnell couldn't blame them for this caution. The whole situation was suspect. He would have acted just the same.

It was fortunate that both the colony ship and the *Peridot* used the same type of reaction mass in their nuclear thermal propulsion drives. The process to transfer excess fuel from *La Révolution* to the *Peridot* would be slow, a flow of cryogenic hydrogen cooled to near absolute zero and compressed to nearly three hundred times that of Earth's atmospheric pressure moved between tanks. It was a tricky, dangerous operation topping off the tanks. Many a ship had gone boom under similar circumstances.

Danielle had brought them into a crowded space near the aft of the ship's spine, a dark room with pipes covered in warning labels, monitors displaying a dozen different angles of the outside of the colony ship. The bottom right screen showed the *Peridot* stuck to the outer hull, its mass spinning along with the much larger craft in black and white.

"I'll make the connections, you can monitor them from here and on your ship," Danielle said, pressing controls on a wall panel. A pair of WALDO gloves appeared from a compartment, much like those Keelin used at Stratus Base to unload their cargo hold. *La Révolution's* engineer slipped them over her fingers and began to work a cargo arm on the outside of the ship.

"Beats goin' for a stroll," Keelin said.

The engineer nodded. "Soon as I have a connection in place, we'll run a few tests to be sure it's solid. No one wants liquid hydrogen leaking into open space."

"Stay here?" Keelin asked Darnell.

He nodded. "Yeah. You head back and open the port on our flyer. I'll help Danielle if she needs it."

The engineer chuffed at that. Keelin squeezed out of the room and headed back.

"I just want to say, 'preciate the help," Darnell said, addressing Danielle. "This is mighty neighborly."

Danielle stared at him, her eyes narrowed. "So, let me get this straight, you went out to bust a rock and made the wrong burns? Went through too much fuel? Sounds like you have a poor pilot."

The back of his neck turned hot at the comment out of reflex, but he knew she was right given what she had been told. This was not personal. "A whole lot of unexpected things can happen on a long trip."

"So they say." She lifted the cargo arm and moved it into position, a thick, flexible tube held in its robotic grip. A silent moment passed, nothing but the clicking sound of the WALDO filling the cramped space. "Why are you out here? Why really?"

"To bust rocks," he told her, matter-of-factly. "Make it easier for the folk you ferry to get on." Which was true, right?

"So that's the story you're sticking with, huh?"

"It's the truth, ain't it? We're all out here trying to make sure humanity keeps going. Trying to make sure the species survives."

"Hmm." Using the robotic arm as an extension of her hands, she lowered the snaking fuel line towards the *Peridot*, careful not to tangle it.

"Then tell me this, why do you have several obvious patch jobs on your hull? I can see something popped a few holes in you."

Darnell felt his body tense, his lip twitch. He'd hoped it wasn't obvious. He knew his patches had been messy, but that was from the inside. "Like I said, a whole lot of unexpected things can happen."

"How are we looking, Darnell?" Katia asked, popping her head into the engineering room.

He waved to the display. "Making the final connection, ma'am, about to get it started."

"Good. When you've got the transfer going, meet me in room G-7 on habitat ring 1. We're going to have a meeting. Tao has extended her hospitality, and we'll take her up on it while we're here. Would you mind keeping an eye on the pressure, Danielle?"

The woman gave a shrug at the *Peridot's* captain. "Tao asked that I help any way I can. So, no, it's fine."

"Good. And thank you."

Darnell's radio crackled. *"Bring it in the rest of the way,"* it was Keelin's voice.

"Copy that," Danielle twisted her fingers and the arm moved closer to the *Peridot*. A port had opened near the aft of the ship where a collection of white spheres were mounted. "I see the clamps. I am going to bring it in easy." She twisted her hands and the mechanical arm responded in kind, the fuel line whipping around in the void like a lazy snake.

La Révolution's transfer line made contact with the coupler of the *Peridot* near the ring of the Falkor drive, the ends drawn to one another like magnets. A speaker on the wall made a sharp click as they made contact. Danielle withdrew the manipulating arm and slipped off the WALDO gloves.

"Perfect," she said. "Have your engineer check the connection on her end. I'm showing green down the board."

"Keelin?" he asked.

"Aye. All good. Start it up."

Danielle did as she was instructed, pressure within the line increasing, its limp material going rigid. "We're holding at a two bar per minute increase. No leaks. Looking good. I got it covered. Go to your captain."

"Yes, ma'am," he said, tipping an imaginary hat, and for whatever reason, it made the older woman blush.

Following the wall directionals, Darnell made his way to the elevator and descended onto habitat ring 1. As the elevator came closer to the relative bottom of its shaft, gravity began to reassert itself due to the ring's spin. While in one sense it felt good to be under weight again, in another, it made him weak and sick. His legs were wobbly, balance tenuous. By the time the doors opened once more, he was holding onto the wall to keep himself steady.

Lexi appeared beside him, put her hands on his arms, and smiled. "Bit of a shock, isn't it?"

"And we used to handle this shit all day with no complaints."

"Atrophy," she whispered.

And that word gave him chills. It was only spoken in hushed tones among Void-Striders. This was the price they paid. No matter what they did as far as countermeasures, working out or eating right, gravity was necessary for humans to remain healthy. We did not evolve for this life.

Room G-7 was just down the smooth, curved hall. There were so many doors and rooms here. More than even on Stratus Base. This colony ship was a paradise. And to think, the FCISE versions of this ship, currently in route to the Foundry facilities, were even larger with more than four hundred people living aboard. Darnell supposed they needed space to stretch out given the forty-year round-trip they'd embarked on.

The captain, along with the rest of the crew, waited for them at a large, round table with a spread of preserved meats, cheese, crackers, and of all things, wine. Freaking wine. Lexi led them around to the opposite side of the table from Sarita. It was obvious that she was doing whatever she could to put distance between them. He couldn't blame her, given what had happened. And so, Logan acted as a buffer between the two reprobates, Atticus on their left, the hacker on their right. The captain stood at the head of the round table, a red logo of the ship's insignia before her.

Atticus reached for a bottle and poured a measure of red wine into a stemless glass. After all this time in null gravity, it was strange to see the liquid did not go everywhere, remaining in place as the good Lord intended. He closed his eyes and placed his nose against the lip of the glass, taking a deep breath.

"Plan on snortin' up your booze?" Keelin prodded as she came skipping back into the room, then reached for some crackers before stacking them with slices of meat and cheese.

The psychologist did not open his eyes. He gave a sigh and took a sip. "For a time I wanted to be a sommelier. To taste wine and talk to people and help to create culinary experiences."

"I thought you enjoyed whiskey," Darnell ventured, taking his seat.

"That too." He paused and licked his lips. "I can't say for sure, but if my senses are right, this came from the southern region of France. The Bordeaux region. Full bodied, notes of currants, plumbs. An aroma of wet gravel and pepper."

Keelin poked out her lip, appearing impressed for once. "What a refined palate we have."

The captain shook her head. "It's from California. Napa Valley to be exact."

"Oh." Atticus peered into his glass, eyebrows furrowed in consternation as if his drink had betrayed him. "Perhaps this is why I never became a sommelier."

Keelin snatched the bottle up by the neck and tossed it back, taking several good swallows before passing it to Logan. "Good shit."

"Indeed," Atticus agreed.

"You can thank Tao later for the amenities," the captain said. "While we refuel, I want you to take some rest under gravity as well."

No one complained at this order, although everyone knew they'd be sore for days after this furlough.

Darnell reached for a healthy serving of crackers and cheese, squares of gouda and white cheddar, stacking them with hard salami and prosciutto. The flavors were overwhelming, crispy, savory, and creamy. Acquired taste or not, this sure as hell beat munching on Exo-bites.

Keelin removed her hand terminal and nodded. "Ten percent," she said.

Good. Transfer was coming along.

After giving them some time to eat, the captain stood, an open can of soda in hand. "Still no word from Lindvall's estate," she declared, tone flat and unsurprised. "Far as I'm concerned, this makes it official. We're on our own. It's time we come up with a real plan. Here's the situation, we need to put in a flight plan from *La Révolution*. We'll need to answer a few questions. Why are we headed to Luna? Rock haulers don't commonly make that trip. What will the UEI believe?"

Sarita raised her hand. "Carlisle was going to say we were visitors, come to pay tribute to the Fifth Great Awakening's Chapter on Luna. That we wanted to know more, wanted to be part of it. But to be honest, I'm less concerned with the UEI at this point and more concerned about the Chinese. While the same flyer won't likely follow us there, others will be looking. The closer to Earth we get, the more traffic there will be. The more traffic, the more danger."

"'Aight," Darnell said, plucking a tiny pickle from the side of the tray. "So, we get past the Chinese, what then? Sure we can come up with some creative solution. But we ain't got no Slipstream, ain't got no Lindvall. Sorry, I miscalculated."

"I've been thinking about that." Sarita produced her tablet and waved everyone closer so that they could see. A wireframe map appeared of Luna Base: the space port and industrial district in the west, the *Gardens of the Moon* and its three domes in the east. "See that building on the southern end of Dome 3? That's where Carlisle keeps his trove. Being that the moon isn't exactly hospitable, the security on the airlock here, well, it's nonexistent. If we have a way to get to that entrance without anyone knowing it, we could easily sneak in the back. Sarah is most likely being held there. I'm confident that we can rescue her without much fuss. He has a few enforcers, yes, but they aren't the brightest. They won't be expecting this."

"Enforcers?" Logan asked, one eyebrow raised. "Are they like, armed?"

Sarita shrugged.

No matter how they sliced it, this was going to be dangerous. Not only would there be Carlisle's muscle to deal with, but station security. For the first time in years, Darnell wished very much that he had his Ruger. He didn't want to have to shoot anyone, but he sure as hell didn't want to die, not now.

Keelin frowned. "Don't be seein' how base personnel will allow a bunch of crazy Void-Striders they don't know pop out a lock for a stroll. Even if they do, I'm bettin' Mr. Holy Soldier Man will have folk watchin' the docks."

"Where will he be expecting to make the trade?" Lexi asked.

"The Slipstream would have to be moved between shifts at the docks," Sarita said, tapping several buttons on her tablet. "He'll want to make contact first, look us in the eye and feel out the situation, then get his people in place to move it from our cargo bay to the collection."

The captain nodded. "That's our chance for misdirection. While he's meeting with Sarita and I, the rest of you have the chance to free Sarah."

"Meeting with us?" She shrunk down in her chair. "I want to be with those who are saving Sarah."

"He'll be expecting you. There's no way around this one."

She gripped her left arm with her right hand and sighed. "You're right."

"So, we nab the girl," Logan said. "And what then? We just tuck tail and run?"

"We get justice," Sarita replied. "I've taken video of his collection. Soon as Sarah is clear, I release it to the authorities. We burn clear of Luna and look at our options. We'll be broke, but we'll be safe and free."

"Why does broke make me cringe?" Keelin asked, her lip curling. "Bit of a swing in events, don't you think?"

"We have some money put back," she added. "It's not anything like what Carlisle was going to give you, but enough that you can go back to your lives without interrupting them much, I hope."

"We ain't in it for the money." Darnell crossed his arms. "There's things worth more than a stack of PAEN."

"Speak for yourself," Keelin barked, her tone halfway to a laugh. "I was lookin' for a big, shiny, kaching, kaching. Doin' right is gonna break me piggy bank."

The captain mulled this over for a moment, pacing around the room, fingers rubbing her chin. "After we get her free and send the surprise to the authorities, can you ensure we have a clear flight plan back to Jupiter? Makes the most sense for us to go back to our previous routes."

"Yes." Sarita nodded. "Can't say what the Chinese will do, that's a wild card, but at some point, they have to let it go. We get out, you can all go back to your lives. Sarah and I will go back to ours. We'll never meet again."

"Aren't we forgetting one challenge?" Atticus said, voice raising. "I do believe there's a back door we need access to, and without anyone seeing us coming. This flyer landing won't be missed. Big bright candle, big hunk of steel. Do we plan on just winging it like a bunch of teenagers breaking into their friends' house?"

Darnell looked to the captain and smiled, his expression turning dark. The entire mission was playing out in his head, one scenario after the next. Of the many ideas he entertained, though, only one succeeded. "I have an idea, Cap. It'll work, I think, but Atticus almost certainly won't like it."

To no one's surprise, this thought pleased the captain. "Something Atticus won't like? Got a feeling that this idea, even half-formed, is a great one. What are you thinking about, cowboy?"

"Let's just say, it involves a long drop and a lot of prayer."

The psychologist's face crashed into his hands and he groaned, "Shiiit."

And this made the captain chuckle.

[28] – Lexi

It took twenty-two days for the *Peridot* to travel from *La Révolution's* position near Mars to Luna's orbit. A lot happened in that time.

After their planning and strategy session, Captain Cho insisted they stay aboard *La Révolution* an additional two days to get in a few regular meals, not to mention some extra rest under the closest thing to real gravity outside of Earth. Lexi was grateful for this respite; it made her feel like more than just a dried-out barnacle stuck to the bottom of humanity's lifeboat. She'd been given the opportunity, deserving or not, to lay her head upon Darnell's chest. Given the opportunity to feel his weight beneath her. It was too bad they were both so beaten up by the events surrounding the Slipstream's destruction that they didn't have the energy, nor the desire, to do anything more exciting than lay around like slugs. This was okay. Their love was far more than sexual.

During their short furlough, Captain Cho spent most of her time with her sister. While the first day might have been awkward, by the time they prepared for departure, something had changed. Katia and Tao hugged in full view of both crews, embracing one another with more than a few tears in their eyes. Lexi was happy for them, but this left her with a mélange of emotions towards her own siblings she couldn't resolve. They had had plenty of stale arguments that might never get settled, and yet, Katia and Tao had found a way. Maybe blood was indeed thicker than water.

The crew of the *Peridot* gave their thanks and said their goodbyes, receiving little in return from the French Void-Striders. This was not shocking. Lexi only hoped none of her crew mates had said anything stupid that might later reach the authorities.

Back aboard the *Peridot* and buckled into her acceleration chair, she felt refreshed and prepared. Good or bad, she was ready for what was to come.

"Here's the flight plan," Sarita said as she ping her over the network from her tablet. "This will keep the UEI from looking too close at us."

Lexi sucked on her teeth then sighed. "I know what it's for."

"Look, Lexi," Sarita began, but Lexi cut her off with a raised hand.

"That will be all, Sarita. Take a seat in back. This is Logan's spot."

The woman did not protest as she once would have, retreating to the back of the bridge to find an empty acceleration chair. Logan settled in beside Lexi and fought back a grin.

"Oh, how the tables have turned," they said, buckling up.

The triumph Lexi felt in that moment was sublime. She was trying to be amicable, but damn it was hard. "Getting your arm cut open over some bullshit can drain the fucks right out of you."

"Yes, yes it can. How's the pain?"

"Getting better."

"Good. Soon as we get up to cruise speed, I'll take a look at it, make sure it's healing up nice."

"Everyone buckle up," Captain Cho declared as she entered the bridge. "Time for us to get moving."

Harnesses clicked into place. Lexi pulled her straps of webbing tight, the gentle pressure against her stomach, chest, and shoulders reassuring like a bear hug. She reached her good hand behind her and Darnell clasped it, the two touching fingers for a moment.

"Everyone ready?" she asked, then began ramping up the Falkor drive.

The *Peridot* crackled and vibrated, pressing them back into their chairs at just under two G's of acceleration. It would be a long burn, if not a hard one; sixteen hours at this rate to reach cruise velocity. After the emergency maneuver a few days earlier, however, this was child's play. Several of them used this time to take a nap, Keelin and Atticus included. Captain Cho managed to play a game on her hand terminal. Lexi and

Darnell watched several old movies. At the halfway mark, they cut their burn for lunch and bio breaks before initiating the drive once more.

"And there we are," Lexi said a few hours later, shutting it all down to leave them in freefall. "One hundred fifty km/s. Hurts getting up that high, but sure is nice to clear half the inner planets in less than a month. Can you imagine what it was like taking half a year to get anywhere?"

"Perish the thought," Atticus said. "Wasn't good for Columbus's crew, even worse for us."

Keelin slapped him on the shoulder. "Less scurvy, though?"

"Suck on it, limey."

"That's for them Brits, not me."

"He's getting impatient," Sarita reported, having finally found herself in a position to check the waiting messages on her tablet. "Carlisle is wanting proof, and we don't have anything to show for it."

Keelin flashed a grin. "And you're the hacker, little missy? Come back 'ere, got me an idea to deal with him."

"Oh yeah?"

"Trust."

Darnell watched them go, his attention lingering on the empty hatch.

"Everything okay?" Lexi asked him, voice low.

"Yeah." He shook his head, unsure. "Everything is fine, it's just…"

"Just what?"

"Well," he began, then paused for a moment, considering his words. "You told me not so long ago not to judge anyone's path, and I haven't. Tried not to at least. The whole, walk a day in someone else's shoes. Just gets me thinking about how we got roped into this to begin with. Hard to tell who's the good guys, and who's the bad guys. We're all just one bad decision away from ruin, taking the left road instead of the right. The path is narrow, ain't it? Real goddamn narrow."

She reached out and squeezed his hand. "Narrow as a razor, love. Even those who do the most good, often do bad sometimes, even if it's unintended."

"I can see that." He paused for another moment, hand rubbing at his beard. It had grown a little longer than normal, a few sprigs of gray showing themselves. This didn't bother her in the least. It made him look confident, resolute, distinguished. "You think God can sort it out? Or is his judgment indiscriminate?"

"Carlisle had best hope it's indiscriminate, that's about the only way he's making it out with his soul intact. But sure, I believe God looks at hearts and intentions, not just actions."

Darnell drew in a long breath while massaging his face. He floated in place for a while, knees drawn up. "We're doing the right thing."

"We are," Lexi agreed.

"Tada!" Keelin declared, reappearing on the bridge with Sarita at her side. She raised her hand terminal and tossed a picture through the network onto the main display. The Slipstream appeared, sitting in their cargo bay where chunks of raw metal usually lay, its white body bright and shiny, Centrum and Kósmos behind the wheel peering off into nothing.

"Holy crap, did you render that in like two seconds?" Logan asked, squinting at the screen. "Pretty damn convincing, dude. We did blow it up, right?"

"Unfortunately," the captain replied.

Keelin shook her head and tossed a toy car the size of her palm at the doctor. Logan caught it and laughed.

"Shut the fuck up," they said, pointing a finger at the screen, their arms blossoming with red lights. "You 3D printed the damn car!"

"Had been playin' around early on the trip and did it for fun. After that, all that needed doin' was to take a picture, forced perspective an' all. Looks giant on the frame. Took a few small calculations for scale. Not much way to tell that's no real car in an FG-67 unihold."

Logan poked out their lip, impressed. "Didn't know you enjoyed photography."

"Used to do macro for giggles."

"Think he'll buy it?" Lexi asked. "It's a little blurry, isn't it? The lighting isn't the best."

"He'll buy it," Sarita said. "Pretty sure he'll buy it."

"Good an idea as any," Captain Cho told her. "Send it on."

"Done."

"Now we wait. Luna, here we come."

An hour out from Luna's orbit, with the first of the slowdown burns complete, their sensors and communications began to light up. Signal bleed between dozens of ships and flyers represented by every major country began to crowd radio frequencies. It was hard to keep track of who was who, and who was where, but Sarita began breaking them down into groups.

"They're looking for us," she said. "At least, that's what the chatter implies."

"Has anyone spotted us yet?" The captain scrolled through the data Sarita had sent over from her terminal.

Sarita shrugged. "I can't say. Best I can tell, they have fifteen flyers in or around orbit, with at least one parked near the Earth-Sun L1 Lagrange point. All of them are broadcasting their mission intentions on sub-channels."

"A science mission, I would venture."

"Of course. There's nothing else they could be up to."

"Nothing at all." The captain ran a hand through her hair, letting loose her ponytail and retying it. "I bet they're pissed."

"Why get pissed over the Slipstream, though?" Darnell asked.

"Matter of principle. We destroyed their prize. The People's Republic doesn't want to be embarrassed. Would America be any different?"

"Good point."

"They're on us," Lexi said, flicking several switches on her control panel. The hull was starting to heat up along their aft end.

"What?"

"Several targeting lasers have started painting us. This is not typical navigational activity. No one is that concerned about collisions at these ranges."

"They're going to ID us," Sarita said. "Near as they are, there's no way we'll make Luna's orbit before they get to us."

The captain rubbed her chin. "Can we do anything to throw them off?"

"I have an idea. There's a weakness in their overall network. Trouble is, after I use this exploit, they'll know it was me. I've been in there before. It's how I got the initial data. A combination of a million slaved IOT devices attacking network weak spots while another virus crawls its way through a back door that has some broken hashing algorithms. Now, it will take some time for them to trace it back to us, a day or so, but they will find us. Still, should leave them confused for a while, chasing down ghosts and false positives. Since they use a distributed sensor network, making use of all flyers within a sixty light second radius, that's a lot of lag to deal with, which is good for us. I give this a fifty percent chance it'll work, fifty percent it won't."

The captain nodded. "I'll take those odds. We have to make it past this blockade, or all is lost."

"Deploying virus," Sarita said, tapping buttons on her tablet. "You should start to see a shift in their activities within a few minutes."

"Get ready," Lexi said. "Time to do the final burn."

Earth blossomed on the port side of the *Peridot* through the high-res cameras, the pale blue dot looking like anything but. From here, it was a massive globe of water and life so fragile yet so resilient. Lexi hoped that even if humans found a way to thrive outside of her that Mother Earth would not be lost in this transition. There might be no going back for herself, but the children of humanity deserved a future which involved more than pressurized chambers and steel walls.

"They're turning away," the captain said. "Lexi, can you confirm?"

"Confirmed." She took a deep breath. "Don't know where they're looking, but it's not at us."

"They're looking everywhere but," Sarita said. "Best I could do."

"It'll work." The captain tugged on her harness, tightening the straps. "We stick to the plan. Lexi, Logan, Sarita and I will remain here. Soon as we break through the blockade and hit orbit, we make for the docks and contact Carlisle. As for the rest of you."

"This is the part I won't like, isn't it?" Atticus ventured, his face drawn.

"This is the part you won't like," she echoed. "Darnell, Keelin, you guys have everything ready?"

"We do," Darnell said, matter-of-factly. "Ready to take a walk."

"Lexi, bring us down close."

She realigned the *Peridot*, swinging them around and angling the Falkor drive to point towards the surface at a steep angle. "Burning to bring us in thirty-five kilometers from the surface."

"Luna tower is goin' to freak the hell out," Keelin said. "I can't wait to hear about the buzz."

This was a risky maneuver and Lexi knew it. She just had to make sure this wasn't Deimos all over again. Running this close to the lunar surface did not leave much room for errors. She'd gone through the precise burn and their sequence in simulations a hundred times over the past three weeks. Everything checked out. It was time to prove her worth.

"Here we go," she said, and their drive roared to life.

It was time to skim their tiny ass over the surface of the moon and drop folk down on Luna base like bombs.

[29] – Darnell

The *Peridot* swung around the moon at a breakneck ten thousand kilometers per hour, skimming close enough to the surface it felt as if they could reach out and touch it. Darnell, Keelin, and Atticus stood on the edge of the flyer's open airlock in vacuum suits, watching as dawn was drawn towards them, fingers of sunlight reaching for the ancient craters rolling below. They were transitioning from the dark side of the moon into light, waiting for their perfect moment.

The three of them were a tangle of suits, tied together with a webbing of straps, a single assist module pressed against their collective backs.

"This is stupid," Atticus said over their suit-to-suit comms, his body leaning forward. *"Textbook psychosis. And I would know. Hallucinations. Illusions. Derealization. Definite déjà vu. Have I started smelling colors yet? I've got clammy hands. Do you hear me, clammy hands!"*

Darnell patted him on the back with a gloved hand. As thick as the vacuum suits were, he doubted the man even felt it. "It's dangerous, not stupid. We can do this."

"No. No we can't. We'll be a smear of dust on the lunar surface. This is some stupid cowboy shit."

"Been over the numbers enough times," Keelin said. *"I reckon we can do it."*

"Please, let me back inside," Atticus pleaded, twisting where he stood, the visor of his suit facing the *Peridot*. *"Let me back inside."*

"This is the price, son," Darnell said. "And we all have to pay a price. Just take a deep breath and hold on tight."

"Almost there," Lexi said over comms. *"Go time in ten. Nine. Eight."*

"We're all going to die," Atticus said. *"We're all going to die."*

"Seven. Six. Five. Four."

Keelin cackled; her mad face visible through the visor. *"Die? Maybe. Be a hell of a ride first. Bettin' this ain' never been done."*

"Three. Two..."

The *Peridot's* Falkor drive flashed for several seconds, the three of them gripping the airlock's hold points for dear life as momentum shifted. Their orbital velocity slowed. Eight thousand kph. Seven thousand. Six thousand.

"That's it, Darnell," Captain Cho said over comms, *"four thousand kph. Go. Go. Go."*

Darnell kicked off from the *Peridot*, dragging his friends with him, the three of them dropping away from the flyer. He depressed a button on his right glove and the lines holding them to the assist module went taut, drawing them into a shoulder-to-shoulder lump.

"Yippee ki ay!" Darnell shouted.

Atticus growled into the channel, *"Motherfucker."*

The *Peridot* slid away, the gulf between them and their vehicle widening fast. Once the flyer was at a safe distance, Lexi gave her the spurs and they sped off, returning to orbital velocity. Darnell, Keelin, and one screaming Atticus Prescott fell. The surface of the moon, just thirty kilometers beneath, swelled to encompass all they could see.

Darnell began to work the jets on the assist module and arrest their deadly orbital velocity and descent. They were coming down quick, his stomach dropping with the fall, not from a change in acceleration, but a visual shift. Earth rose upon the horizon, a sphere of blue and white with spots of green, storms swirling over thousands of miles and billions of people.

"Slowing us down," he said, kicking on the attitude jets of the assist module. It was all they had, and before it was over, they'd run its fuel tanks dry.

Their forward momentum began to slow as the surface drew near. In the distance, lights began to blossom, a scintillating expanse covering the moon's powdery surface. Luna Base. He had to bring them down fast enough to reach their target, but slow enough that it didn't kill them.

Keelin read out their numbers, calling for him to make various maneuvers, the tiny jets of the assist module hissing as gas was released into the void. Atticus had gone silent. The psychologist was either dead or passed out from shock.

"Ten kilometers from the surface," Keelin called, and Darnell peered down, feeling the bottoms of his feet tingle as close as it was. *"Shave off some more velocity. Six seconds, lateral thrust."*

"Tanks are running low. I've got maybe a couple of seconds left." The lunar surface was getting too big, too fast. The horizon spread out so far it had almost vanished into the black backdrop of space. His heart thundered in his chest, feeling as if it might just burst through his suit. Sweat rolled down the back of his neck.

"We're still coming in too hard. Fire the jets. Fire—"

"Oh shit," Darnell mumbled, and the powdery surface of the unforgiving moon rushed up to greet them like a giant slap.

The impact was like hitting a stone wall. Darnell's face slammed against the inside of his suit's visor, his throat catching on the metal collar. Their tangled mess skipped once, spinning ass over teakettle, then came down again, this time flat on their backs.

Grunts and groans came over the comms, his view filled with gray dust, then black, then gray dust. He had to arrest their spin or there was no telling how long it would take for them to stop.

With what fuel was left, he fumbled with the switches and fired all the nozzles at one go, intent on holding till the tanks went dry. White gas spread out around them, a cloud of hydrazine dissipating in the void. Vision blurred. Eyes began to water. What way was up? What way was down? Gray rock. Black sky. Rock. Fingers tingling. Spine screaming.

Their tumble slowed as they skidded across the surface, rolling without bouncing away. After a few seconds they came to a stop in a deep recess, the light of the sun casting severe shadows, their awkward landing leaving a trail of dust in their wake.

Darnell laid there for a moment, staring at the sky, trying to determine if he'd broken his back in the fall. This was a hundred times worse than when he'd got bucked off Trigger all those years ago when she'd seen a rattler. They'd come in too hot and skipped for miles. Every inch of his body ached, and yet, his suit was pressurized. Praise be to God. A quality vacuum suit was one thing a Void-Strider sure as hell didn't cut corners on, and this UEI replacement was quality.

"Is anyone alive?" he called, reaching out to his left and right. Their bodies were there, and so he hoped their minds were as well.

"Psychosis," Atticus mumbled after a long moment. *"The color gray is giving me pain."*

Something tapped Darnell's leg. Keelin groaned, *"I'm here, friend. Shite. Don't think nothin' but me pride is broken."*

"Pretty sure we can live with that."

"Speak for yourself."

They helped one another stand while removing the tethers that bound them together. The assist module was out of fuel, and so they left it where they'd come to rest and began walking in the direction of Luna Base, the three of them stiff and achy, but breathing.

"Peridot to ground crew," Lexi called over comms. *"Are you okay? Did you make it?"*

"Rough landing, but we're alive," Darnell reported back. "Headed in."

"Copy. We're swinging out of line of sight. Stay safe, love."

"You too."

While Keelin's calculations had been off by a little, they were close enough that they'd landed only a few miles from the airlock Sarita had pointed out. Given the fall, Darnell found himself thankful Luna's gravity was only a fraction of Earth's. After experiencing a full G on *La Révolution's* habitation wheel, it was nice not to feel as if he was carrying an extra copy of himself over that distance. The three of them hopped and skipped over the powdery surface, traveling light, nothing more than Keelin with her bag of tools. Luna Base swelled up ahead, its domes rising spaceward. Flashes of light glittered in the dark skies above, showing that the moon's orbital lanes were busy with traffic.

The airlock came into view, and they crept up on it. As best they could tell, they were the only ones outside the base. It was far too easy to get back inside. No code, no key, just a button. The air around them cycled and within a few seconds the safety lights turned green, allowing them to step within.

"To say security is lax would be an understatement," Atticus mused. *"Any ol' ruffian can just walk in the back door?"*

"If they have a flyer," Keelin replied. *"An' a means to get up the gravity well. Don' think too many criminals have that."*

"Except for us," Darnell said, sticking his head out into the hallway, looking left, then right. The space was empty, the curved passage quiet, its heavy carpet absorbing nearly all sound, making it near acoustically dead. He dusted himself off, then stepped out of the airlock, unclicking his helmet and holding it under his arm. Keelin and Atticus followed suit.

"This way," Keelin said, pointing to the right. "Section F-26. That's where Sarita said they should be keepin' Sarah."

"Okay," Darnell said, taking point. "You guys keep an eye on our rear. Act natural, I reckon. We're just some rock haulers who got asked to fix something outside the Base."

"That's fine for the rent a cops," Atticus said. "What about the criminals with guns?"

"Cross that bridge."

"Cross that bridge?" He squeezed the middle of his nose. "Cross that bridge..."

It was surprising just how quiet the outer dome of Luna Base was. Though habitation was mostly confined to the inner city, *The Gardens of the Moon*, plenty of businesses had offices out here with staff that numbered in the hundreds. It was no wonder that Carlisle had chosen this particular spot. How close were they to the collection?

"Here we are," Darnell said as they approached a T in the path. "F-26."

At the base of the T lay an antechamber with an outer and inner lock, a clear redundancy in case the base decompressed. While the outer opened at their approach, the inner did not. It required a six-digit code or authentication scan from a hand terminal.

"Door's locked, just as Sarita said." Darnell twisted, looking for their way in. And then there it was, as promised, a hatch to the right of them half a meter from the floor, not much taller than an air vent. Sarita hadn't crossed them. She had told the truth. This was going to work. "You know what this means?"

"No," Atticus said. "I don't think so. No. No. No."

"Cho was mighty adamant about you earning your way out of the debt you owe us. Strip down out of your suit and into the maintenance duct you go. It's made for people. At least I think so."

"What if I told you that I have an aversion to tight spaces? A phobia, if you will."

Keelin shrugged. "I'd say, you best get over it."

"May it go on record, that according to the DSM, this is not the way to properly treat such a condition."

"Noted."

The psychologist slipped out of his vacuum suit and piled it up in the alcove, out of sight from the hallway while Keelin opened the maintenance access port with a pistol-gripped driver. Even with all the thick carpeting, the space was quiet enough that the driver's noise was jarring.

"Can we keep it down?" Darnell asked. "They may not see us here in this nook, but they sure as hell can hear us."

She paused and stared at him. "What you expect that I do? Tell it to shush?"

"I don't know, wrap it in a cloth or something."

"Won't do no good. Vibrations will still make noise."

The first of the four bolts fell into Keelin's palm.

Atticus took a moment and peered out into the hallway. "Might want to forget the noise and hurry up. Appears we've got visitors on the way."

"Oh shit," Darnell said, taking a glance for himself. At the end of the hall two men in white and red uniforms approached, utility belts around their waists, tasers mounted in holsters at their sides. "Station guards."

"Almost there," Keelin said, removing the last of the bolts. "Okay. Atticus, hop in boi."

He glared at her. "What? What about the guards?"

"Not your concern. I'll seal you in."

"So I just crawl through and open it from the inside."

"Easy as it gets."

"Shit." He bent over and squeezed into the hole in the wall, crawling quick as he could. Soon as his feet were inside, Keelin replaced the panel, twisting the bolts back into place by hand so it would stay in place.

"What do we do?" Darnell mused. "We need a distraction."

With Atticus secure, Keelin stood and nodded, hanging on to her power tool like a gun. "You leave that to me."

"Do you plan on shooting them with an impact wrench?"

"Serious?" She gave him a withering glare. "I've talked me way in an' out of plenty. Let me do the heavy lifting."

"'Aight. All yours."

"Follow me lead," she said, and they stepped out of the antechamber into the hall.

The guards came to a halt and peered curiously at them in their dirty vacuum suits, sans the helmets. They stood tall with hands resting at their sides, fingers twitching to take hold of their tasers.

"What's going on here?" the one on the left said, a large, bald man of middle-years who carried himself with the confidence of someone who had done this job for a long time. "We've had reports of some noise. Can we help you?"

She raised a finger to speak but was interrupted.

"Wait. Keelin...? Is that you?" the younger of the two guards asked, head cocking. He was a slender man in his twenties with a silver coif of hair swept to the side, his jaw smooth as a baby's bottom. Darnell recognized him, if vaguely. He wasn't sure where from, but he recognized him. "You okay? You look surprised to see me."

"You know each other?" the big man asked, his eyebrows raised.

"Yeah, man. We met a few weeks back on my trip out to Stratus. Hell, that was a good time, right?"

"La—Landon?" Keelin began, stepping closer to him, the grip on her tool loosening slightly. She flashed her pearly whites in defense. "How are ya? Been a minute since Stratus. What a night, am I right? Where's, em, Jennifer?"

"Clara," he said, letting out a sigh. "Her name is Clara."

"Aye, so silly of me. Cracking ass on her."

No wonder the boy looked familiar. Landon had been one of the two Keelin had snuck off with after having drinks with the crew. He wasn't a miner like them, but security of some kind that had taken a trip to the outer planets and back. Not UEI, but a contractor judging by his uniform.

"What are you doing here?" he asked.

Darnell gave Keelin a look. They needed a distraction, something to keep their eyes off Atticus's actions and get them to move on. Getting busted now wouldn't do. Everyone would be screwed. She took a deep breath and flashed another smile. He sure hoped she knew what she was doing.

"What am I doin' here?" Keelin spun around, staring at the walls as if confused. "You don't know, do ya?"

"Know what?"

"Landon, lad. There's somethin' wrong with, the, em," she pointed down the hall, "the turbo encabulators on this end of the base. Could be bad for everyone, and I've been asked to handle it."

Darnell blinked at her, trying his best to keep his face neutral. Turbo what? That sounded like the most made-up shit he'd ever heard. What was she doing? Was she trying to techno speak her way out of this?

There was nothing to do but keep his mouth shut and let her work.

The security guards exchanged a look. Landon's eyebrows furrowed. "You? Why you? You're a Void-Strider, a rock hauler, not Base maintenance."

"Aye, but I do favors for me friends from time to time, got experience in this." She took a step towards Landon and leaned in, a hand beside her mouth doing a poor job blocking her voice but somehow still acting conspiratorial. "You see, friend, there's a problem supplyin' inverse reactive current to the unilateral phase detractors, when they are also capable of automatically synchronizing cardinal grammeters. Follow? This has to be corrected. The malleable logarithmic casing was installed in such a way that the two spurving bearings are in a direct line with the panametric fan. The latter consists simply of six hydrocoptic marzlevanes, so fitted to the ambifacient lunar waneshaft that side fumblin' was effectively prevented. At least, that be the intention. Make sense?"

Landon rubbed his right arm and gave an uneasy grin, glancing for a moment at the older guard who looked just as confused. "Um. Yeah, I know all about the—"

"Panendermic semi-boloid slots?" she suggested, leaning towards him.

"Yeah. Those. The slots."

"This can be a dangerous mix when vacuum hits fluorescent skor motion in conjunction. Major inusoidal repleneration."

"Geez, this is pretty serious," the other guard said, his expression slack. "Like, people could get killed, right? I've heard of this."

"Half the base could be spaced if I don't handle it," Keelin insisted. "I need to get on now. If you would, let me get on."

"Of course," Landon said. "I'm so sorry. I didn't mean."

Keelin grabbed him by the face and planted a solid kiss on his lips. "Call on me later, would you?"

His face flushed with red. "Uhh, uhh, okay. You'll be on Luna for a minute?"

"Long enough for you."

"Okay," he swallowed and turned to leave. "Let me know if you need anything to fix the, boloid slots, or whatever."

"Ambifacient lunar waneshaft," Keelin corrected, and it sounded rather convincing with the word Lunar in it.

"That."

The guards turned the corner and left them alone.

"What the heck was that all about?" Darnell asked, blinking.

She shook her head. "An engineerin' craic, a gag. They'll figure it out quick enough. Don't take Landon for a stupid boy. Foolish maybe, a bit too thirsty, but not stupid. We got to keep movin'"

The door behind them swooshed open and Atticus stood on the other side, sleepy eyes focused on his nails as if bored.

"This way, ladies," he said, waving them inside with a flourish and a bow.

"Consider your debt paid," Darnell said, patting him on the shoulder. "You done good, brother. You done good."

"So long as we don't get shot now," Keelin said, aiming her impact driver ahead like a pistol. "This is where things get dicey."

Darnell went first, leading them into Carlisle's personal section of Luna base, mumbling, "Into the den of thieves we go."

"The den of thieves," Atticus groaned in response. "Whoopee."

[30] – Lexi

"*Peridot* to ground crew," Lexi called over comms from the pilot's seat. "Are you okay?" She'd been so busy watching the instruments, it had been hard to keep track of their telemetry signal. It was still broadcasting, so she took that as a good sign.

After dropping off the ground crew, she'd pitched the *Peridot* back till its drive was pointed at the surface, then pushed them straight up into a higher orbit. The busy hub of human activity, Luna Base, slipped away as they whipped around the moon.

All that remained aboard the flyer was Lexi, Sarita, Logan, and Captain Cho. It felt weird for everything to be so quiet, to not hear Atticus and Keelin at each other's throats every two seconds, but she knew that wouldn't last. They'd be reunited soon enough, running away from this hunk of cheese like any other rock. Or so she kept telling herself...

"*Rough landing, but we're alive,*" Darnell said, his voice hoarse over comms. "*Headed in.*"

"Copy. We're swinging out of line of sight. Stay safe, love."

"*You too.*"

Their plan was in motion. There was no turning back now.

Based on where the party had landed, she estimated they had about three hours before they could cross the Lunar plains and reach the target. That would be plenty of time for the *Peridot* to reapproach Luna Base.

They dove towards the dark side of the moon, everything outside their flyer going black as the sun was eclipsed. Comms went dead.

"This should time out well," Captain Cho said. "What's the status on Carlisle?"

"He's waiting for us," Sarita reported.

"What about the Chinese?"

"There's lots of comm traffic. Can't say what it all is, though."

Logan raised their arms in sudden alarm, both of them turning bright red beneath the skin. "Holy shit."

"What? What is it?"

"Did you feel that? I mean—" They paused and shook their head. "Never mind me. A massive wave of EM radiation just passed over us. That was the craziest thing. Maybe it was a solar flare?"

"No solar flares," Lexi said, checking the official geomagnetic weather forecasts again just to be sure. "Not due for any substantial events for another month or two."

"Can your implants tell you the frequency range?" Sarita asked, her tone curious.

Logan nodded. "Yeah, sure. Around two hundred and fifty gigahertz? Why do you ask?"

"Hang on, those are radio astronomy frequencies," the captain said, blinking.

"They found us," Sarita whispered. "Not sure how they're identifying us, but they found us."

"The Chinese?"

Lexi felt hot all of a sudden, as if their environmental controls had gone on the fritz. She rolled her jumpsuit sleeves up and zipped the front down as far as she could without being completely indecent. The webbing of her five-point harness felt restricting, but she didn't dare get out of her acceleration chair.

"Radio astronomy?" Logan asked. "How do you know that's the Chinese? Could be anyone."

Captain Cho began pressing buttons on her console. "Science vessels. They may not have weapons, but that doesn't mean we aren't in danger. How many are we looking at?"

"Painting the surrounding area with LADAR," Lexi said. There was no way she'd get the readings they needed in time. There was a lot of space out there, and she didn't even know which sector to start in.

"Do you know the approximate direction the sweeps came from?" Sarita asked Logan. "I've got an idea, if we can narrow it down."

"Yeah." They pointed. "Two places, to my right, near the back of the flyer. The other, to my left in front of us. This way somewhere."

Lexi nodded and began to aim the LADAR scans in the general directions Logan had gestured.

"I'm pulling apart the frequencies," Sarita said. "They've been unable to purge my virus and somehow I'm still in their network. It's the Chinese government alright."

"Getting pings back," Lexi said. "Two. Three. Six flyers."

"What in the hell?" Captain Cho exclaimed.

"No. Twelve. All ahead of us. They've got the path blocked. What do they intend on doing to us? Ram us? Use an improvised weapon like the pirate vessel?"

"I'm scanning their databases on flyer types," Sarita said. "Okay. It looks like these particular ones are multi-purpose, science vessels first, but they're also fitted for orbital cleanup."

"Fitted for what?"

"This is bad," Captain Cho said. "Real bad."

Sarita nodded. "They deploy massive catch nets to scour Earth's orbit of space debris. Dead satellites and rocket stages, things like that. Takes four flyers moving in formation, each one holding a corner of the net, that they then bring in."

The captain drew in a sharp breath. "Okay, so they're deploying nets in front of us. It's the only thing that makes sense. We really did piss them off, didn't we? They know we're the ones they're after because of the virus. Now, they plan on getting back and making it look like an accident. A KTS Materials Tambora class rock hauler finds itself turned to Swiss cheese when it hits their trash net at twenty thousand kilometers an hour."

"Oh shit," Lexi said, and began trying to map out their relative coordinates. "There's a lot of space out here, are we sure they can be so accurate? How big can those nets even be?"

"Real big," Sarita said. "From the technical specs I found on their network, at full deployment we're looking at about fifty square miles of net. With twelve flyers out there, well, there are at least three of these nets. Might even be more."

"How far out are they?" Captain Cho asked. "How much time do we have?"

"A few minutes," Lexi said. "Hard to say with all the jockeying. They aren't staying still. Can't tell what direction they're orbiting the moon, either."

"Can we get around it?"

"Maybe, but it's going to be a rough burn, and a good chance we won't make our rendezvous on time."

That would leave Darnell and the rest of them hanging. Without a distraction, Carlisle's people would be sure to overwhelm them. Darnell, Keelin, and Atticus had no real weapons, other than a few power tools. Forget bringing a knife to a gunfight, this was even worse. What had they been thinking going unarmed?

"Then we'll have to go through it," Cho said.

"Go through it?" Lexi twisted around in her acceleration chair and gave the captain a look. "Are you serious?"

"Let's do all we can to determine their paths, then map it out. Fifty square miles of net might seem like a lot, but we're in space. And as they say, there's a lot of space out in space."

"If they catch us with even the smallest thread of carbon fiber, we'll be sliced in two."

"It's a risk we'll have to take. Our friends on the ground are counting on it."

Lexi's hands shook. Her throat went dry. "I'm not sure I can do this. There are too many factors. Those flyers will be too close. Hell, nets aside, we could even run right into one of them. It will be Mars all over, like De—"

"Listen to me, Lexi," Captain Cho said, cutting her off. "You might have made a mistake once, but I trust in your abilities. If we don't get down onto the surface before they find Sarah, all will be lost. We have to meet with Carlisle."

Lexi took a deep breath. Beads of sweat ran down her forehead. Everyone was counting on her to pull them through this. What happened over Deimos was a different situation. She had been trying to save time, and it had *cost* her crew their lives. Today, however, she was fighting *for* their lives. In this moment, she had a clear enemy to escape. A noose was closing around their necks, she just had to avoid the drop. It was all in or all out.

"See if you can triangulate their positions using ground pings," she told Sarita, making her choice. "I've linked the survey radars to your tablet."

"Okay."

"Logan, I'm opening access to your terminal. Every wave of EM that hits you, do your best to map where it's coming from. Point in that direction. I'll use the LADAR to get hard fixes."

"I can do that," Logan replied.

Lexi licked her cracked lips. "We've got about three minutes to figure out their trajectories before we'll have to pick a direction and burn."

"3D map coming online," Captain Cho said. "I'll fill in the nets." She began to draw in their shared holographic space, attaching wireframes to the approaching flyers to illustrate their locations and plot a safe course.

"I've got a fix on three out of twelve," Sarita reported. "Adding their trajectories. Can't seem to get a lock on the others."

"Two of their pairs are easy to track, since they move in groups of four. We'll give them the same relative velocity and angle."

Sarita nodded.

"There went another wave," Logan said, raising their arms. "To the front and right. This many degrees." They pressed a location on their terminal and the model updated again.

"One minute, thirty seconds," Lexi reported. "We're cutting it close."

The model was filling in nice. It showed three sets of flyers as they had expected, dragging massive nets and traveling towards one another on converging trajectories. One formation of four approached the *Peridot* at an oblique angle to the starboard, another on the port side, while a third rose from the surface of Luna cutting out towards a higher orbit. Given that they were all on the dark side of the moon, there was nothing but sensors for feedback. High-resolution cameras were worthless without light.

"Warming up the Falkor drive," Lexi said. "This might be rough. Make sure you're secure."

Her fellow crew members pulled down on their harness straps, tightening themselves into their acceleration chairs.

Seconds ticked away. The model updated again. Lexi readjusted the LADAR scans, locking onto each of the flyers in sequence to update their range finding. The net on their starboard side, the closest of them, began to increase their velocity. Given the small amount of data, it was hard to tell by how much. She could see a path through the nets, a burst of acceleration down the middle, then a twist to the port side, and another burn.

"Twenty seconds to contact," she said, then sucked in a breath. "Wait, the fuck is that?"

"What's what?" Cho blurted.

"I just crossed something with LADAR. I think there's another set of flyers. A fourth net."

"I see it," Sarita said. "Oh shit, it's close. It'll be on us in just a few seconds, coming in from above."

Lexi didn't wait for any orders. She was the pilot. She took hold of the stick and lit the drive, tossing them back into their acceleration chairs, a weight like a tightening vice pressing down on their chests. The wireframe model of the approaching Chinese flyers began to twist and turn as she reoriented the *Peridot*.

"Hidden flyers are coming in on the starboard side, fast." Sarita added them to the model. "Fuck me."

The *Peridot* threw them sideways as Lexi turned the drive towards the approaching net, hoping to cut through it. The wire model showed the formation of enemy flyers overtaking their position, then nothing. Had the net missed them? Were they okay? She almost relaxed, then heard a scraping noise along the surface of their outer hull. Alarms went off. Fuel began leaking from two external tanks, liquid hydrogen spiraling at their aft. The redundant communications array went offline. Four of their sixteen Lindvolt cells fell to zero volts. There was a hull breach in the galley.

"Good job, Carver!" Captain Cho whooped, no sarcasm, no rebuke. She was genuine in this and that felt good. It felt encouraging. "Punch us through the rest. We're not dead."

Lexi nodded. They weren't dead, despite all the damage. They weren't dead. Their drive flame had been hot enough to burn a hole through the approaching net like a blow torch. All they'd been tickled with were the edges of its threads, and those had been more than enough.

More nets were ahead.

The flyer lurched for a moment, Falkor drive sputtering. "Fuel tanks," Lexi said.

"Can I have engineering access?" Sarita asked.

Lexi let out a breath and nodded. "It's yours."

"Rerouting fuel lines. I am going to purge the damaged tanks if that's okay with you guys."

"Do it," the captain ordered.

The *Peridot* jostled as fuel was expelled from the damaged tanks, sending them into a spin for a moment before Lexi was able to arrest it. This left her with far less reaction mass than they had started with, but hopefully enough to make one orbit and land safely. Before anyone could speak, she kicked up the Falkor, the main lines under pressure once more. The flyer shot forward and went into a roll as she threaded them through the eye of the needle.

Ahead, two of the nets converged. Lexi pushed down, diving the *Peridot* towards the Lunar surface, then came from the left side at a sharp angle to one of the nets, flying parallel to its surface. LADAR pinged back, showing that the flyers pulling the second net were accelerating, closing the distance fast, attempting to slam the net against them. She bared her teeth and pushed the Falkor drive as hard as it would go, accelerating the *Peridot* at eight G's, drive cone flashing white hot, sparks firing out in its wake. The world became hazy. Her nose and the bottom part of her face felt wet.

"We're clear of that one," Sarita reported, her voice rough. "Last net coming down."

Lexi cut the drive and twisted them around. She was not prone to motion sickness, riding the Tilt-A-Whirl at the county fair had proven that many times over, but this was pushing her to the limit. "I'm on it."

She wasn't the only one struggling. Logan couldn't keep the contents of their stomach down, and they began to puke. There wasn't enough time for them to reach for a bag. When they made the next hard turn, the floating chunks of Logan's vomit splattered against the far wall by Keelin's empty station and stuck in place.

"Almost there," Lexi growled, flipping the *Peridot* into another turn. The controls were sluggish for a moment, the hydrazine maneuvering thrusters sputtering. She pressed the joystick to the left three times, but they didn't turn any quicker. They twisted in circles. "I can't reposition us. I'm having issues, not enough pressure in the line."

"Must be damage from the first net," Captain Cho said. "How far are we from the edge of the last net's path?"

"A few miles. It's closing in."

Lexi fought against the *Peridot's* weight and momentum, their spin becoming worse by the moment. It was hard to tell which thrusters had enough pressure, and the instruments were useless. If only Keelin was here. She could fix it in under a minute, even in a flat spin. Lexi tried to troubleshoot the busted lines and shut them down, rerouting to auxiliary feeds. It might even be possible to use the water tanks, if necessary, but these were all manual operations that involved her leaving her acceleration chair. Not an option.

Captain Cho raised a hand and pointed. "I have an idea. Sarita, can you pressurize the airlock with your engineering access?"

She pressed a few buttons and began to nod. "Yes!"

"Do it. If Lexi can't get control back quick enough, get ready to evacuate the docking airlock. As close as we are to the edge of the net, it might give us enough of a push to move us clear."

Three more quick bursts. Lexi was able to slow their spin by a few revolutions per minute but couldn't get the drive cone pointed in the right direction to get them out. Plan B it was.

"Twenty seconds to impact," Logan said. "We need to do something quick, guys."

"Are we pressurized?" Captain Cho asked Sarita.

Sarita grit her teeth as she willed the airlock cycle to go faster. "Almost. Almost."

Two more quick bursts. Lexi managed to turn the *Peridot* so their airlock was perpendicular to the center of the approaching net.

"Ten seconds to impact," Logan said, closing their eyes. "Oh shit. Oh shit."

"Pressurized!" Sarita declared. "Are we in line?"

"About as in line as we can be with this busted bitch," Lexi growled. "Blowing it now."

The *Peridot* made a violent jerk as air exploded from the lock. They began to spin once more, but it had worked, at least in part, lurching them sideways toward the edge of the net. The final hostile formation drifted closer. Lexi wasn't sure if they'd make it before the net caught them, a fine mesh of carbon fiber slicing the *Peridot* to bits as it struck with a relative velocity of ten thousand KPH.

Lexi closed her eyes like Logan, unable to do much more than hope.

The chaos of the *Peridot's* situation fell away.

She could see her and Darnell holding a smiling bundle of joy, young and healthy, looking out the window of their apartments on the surface of Luna, the green Gardens of the Moon below. They'd made it. They'd found the mother lode and it had given them a new life, the start of their family. Once Sarah had been rescued, and Carlisle brought to justice, they were free to be as they were. They'd done the right thing. They'd saved a family of two, even if one of them was a bitch.

A letter from her parents lay on the bedside table. Even they were proud in their way, asking if they could visit, meet the local influencers.

They'd grow old and gray here, maybe. Watch their child grow up and be better than they were. Be a shepherd to those who would leave the bounds of Earth for a fragile, dangerous life.

"We're clear," Captain Cho whispered, her tone fragile as if speaking might make it untrue. "We made it. We actually made it."

Lexi opened her eyes. "What?" She rubbed her face with the back of her hand. It came back covered in dried blood from where her nose had been pouring. "I can't believe it."

"We're free of the nets. We're free!"

"We made it," Lexi hissed. "Holy shit we—"

Captain Cho smiled and reached over to squeeze her on the shoulder. "I never had a doubt. Think you can put this girl down, busted up as she is?"

After a series of maneuvers like that, anything was possible. "Yes, I believe I can. Need some help with a few things in back first. Sarita? Logan?"

"On it," Sarita began unclipping from her acceleration chair. "Let's get down there and get this over with."

"Think we'll be safe?" Logan asked. "From the People's Republic, that is?"

Captain Cho nodded. "They won't be as brazen to come after us on the surface. They won't risk that kind of embarrassment. What just happened could be called an accident. Attacking us in the open can't. We're safe for now, at least from them."

Safe for now.

[31] – Darnell

There was no doubt in any of their minds they'd come to the right place. The narrow halls of section F-26 were lined from front to back with paintings of American history. On the left side they were covered with oil portraits of the presidents, from George Washington to Higgins Daniel; on the right, great events in history, the crossing of the Delaware, the founding fathers signing the Declaration, and so many more. Darnell might not have been a historical art expert, but from where he stood, they looked like originals, not prints.

Darnell, Keelin, and Atticus each clutched a tool of some kind. A wrench, an impact driver, a welding torch, ready to fight if need be. Not that it would matter much if Carlisle's men showed up with guns. They'd stowed their vacuum suits, hiding them in a nook inside a wall never to be seen again. This left each of them feeling exposed, naked. It was easier to get around this way, even though it did feel like giving up some protection, no matter how minimal it was. Darnell searched the halls for security cameras, but Keelin assured him again and again that none were active. She'd accessed the secure power connections once they were on the other side of the pressure hatch and shut them down. They had at least thirty minutes before an alert might summon maintenance to come and take a look. And while this didn't mean there were no cameras, it did mean there was nothing official. Nothing attached to the station.

A small comfort.

As they worked their way towards the doorways at the far end, Atticus counted the presidential portraits, a perplexed look forming on his face. Something about them had caught his attention.

"Looks like you're trying to read buffalo chips like tea leaves," Darnell said, stepping up beside him, arms crossed. "What's up?"

"Can't say I'm shocked." Atticus let out a sigh. "We just elected the 59th president of the United States, and yet, I see only fifty paintings."

Darnell cocked his head, considering this. "Think he just doesn't have the whole set? Could be on his list, yeah? Take a lot to get hold of those kind of knickknacks."

"No," he replied. "That doesn't feel right. This seems, well, intentional. Look, Kennedy is missing. So is Obama. Biden. Green. Clinton. A couple others I can't recall offhand, despite Mom and Dad making me learn them all from memory, but I am pretty sure I know why."

Keelin eyed the two of them. "What's that mean? Don't know them names."

Atticus paused, running his fingers down the gilded wooden frame of the current President, Roland Daniel, a republican from South Carolina. The piece was a spot-on rendering of the man in oil, capturing both his rugged looks and that signature, rakish grin that had put him in office. "Carlisle is editing history. Preserving only the bits he likes."

"Shaping a narrative?" Darnell ventured.

Atticus nodded. "Stories are powerful, they dictate our subjective reality. He who controls the narrative, controls the people."

This is what Lexi and Atticus had warned him about in that heavy conversation what seemed a lifetime ago. America had much to be celebrated, but you had to take the good with the bad, not cover it up. History was messy, and any time we hide our sins to save face, we do ourselves an injustice, opening the door for that same history to repeat itself.

A crash came from up ahead, and the three of them crouched in an instant, squeezing themselves up against a nook in the wall of the long hallway.

"This is stupid as shit," someone said through the doorway up ahead.

Darnell swallowed as he eased his way forward, Keelin and Atticus following, each careful not to make any noise. This was no easy feat for the engineer with a bag of tools slung over her shoulder.

Voices came from inside a large, open room. It was a storage space from the looks of it, boxes and crates marked with shipping symbols and QR codes, and high ceilings with industrial lighting. It was impossible to see the faces of those within, given the angle, but the *Peridot's* crew members crouched on either side of the door, ready to jump anyone who came through.

"He wants us to just sit around all day, keeping an eye on that bitch," one of the voices said, its tone high, almost squeaky. "We should just go ahead and kill her. Stuff her out an airlock. Come on. No one will know."

"Why not shove her in the organic recyclers the garden uses to keep the soil happy?" Another voice, deep in such a way it made your chest rumble. "That goo in there will eat the flesh right off of her."

"I like the way you think, buddy."

"We can't though," he paused, "we need leverage over these idiots until the deal is done. Soon as Carlisle, Danny, and John finish meeting with that flyer's crew, we'll take them all for a walk in the back domes and finish the job."

"All this over a damn car."

"An important damn car."

Atticus's eyes widened. He tossed a thumb over his shoulder in the direction they had come as if to flee. Darnell shook his head. They were committed now, for good or bad. He made a hand gesture like that of a gun, then shrugged his shoulders. Keelin carefully set down her tool bag, not making a sound, then began to crawl through the door and behind a set of storage crates. She disappeared out of their line of sight.

"What do we do?" Atticus whispered.

Darnell put a finger to his lips.

"Richardson, they can't hear us from here."

From within his jumpsuit pocket, Darnell's hand terminal vibrated. He reached for it more out of habit than anything, wondering if it was a message from the *Peridot*, but it was Keelin. She'd snuck around the outside of the room, taken a picture and texted it to him. As they had assumed, there were only two men, standing alone in its open center by a series of shipping crates. One was short and wiry, dark hair and glasses, the other broad shouldered and tall, baby faced and bald. Both were dressed in crimson jumpsuits with black mermaids printed on the back between the shoulder blades, with what looked like utility belts around their waists.

"Weapons?" he texted Keelin, hoping she could tell.

She replied with a shrugging emoji. A moment passed and she added, *"Crack them over the head."*

Sounded like as good a plan as any.

"Glory be to God that this shit worked out," the man with the higher pitched voice said. "Glory be to God in the highest."

The two burst out laughing, their enjoyment so fierce it was as if they might split in two.

"Cut the shit, bruh," the one with the deeper voice, the big man, said after a moment. "That hurts. That really hurts."

"You making fun of my religion?"

"No, bruh. You can believe whatever stupid shit you want. And for their sake, I hope these idiot Void-Striders believe in something, otherwise we're about to send their asses straight to hell. I might feel a touch guilty for that."

"I'll pray for them."

"You do that. And look, since we're not planning on keeping the girl anyways, want a go before I put a bullet in her?"

"I don't know." The man with the higher voice took a moment before he sighed. "Maybe? Shit, it has been a while since I dipped my wick in something sweet. Was it that waitress? Damn, I can't remember."

"Ask for forgiveness, not permission. She's got a sweet ass on her, though. And this time, you won't have to buy her dinner."

"Damn, you sure? Don't want to catch the clap or nothing."

"If you won't take a go, I will. Hell, think I will anyway. Sloppy seconds can be mighty tasty. Don't you agree?"

Darnell's blood began to boil. They had to do something and fast, there was no way he was letting those men—

But before he could finish his thought, a loud crash echoed through the warehouse. Even in low gravity, it was easy to tell something incredibly heavy had fallen a short distance.

"Oh God! Shit, man, shit!" the one with the high-pitched voice cried out in pain. "Oh shit!"

"Who's there?" the other shouted. "Who the fuck is there?"

Darnell raised his weapon and charged into the room. Unexpectedly, Atticus followed.

"Who's fuckin' there!" the deep voiced man bellowed. "Show yourself!"

Now that they were inside the space, it was easy to see the two men, one laying on the ground clutching his thigh, a dark-gray box covering half his body. Keelin had pushed the crate onto the man hoping to take him out, but it had instead pinned him to the floor, the heavy materials coming to rest on his leg making it impossible for him to stand.

"Shit, shit, shit," the injured man hissed. "It hurts."

The broad-shouldered man reached into his jumpsuit and drew a pistol from a chest holster. He began to aim the menacing weapon around the room. "Come out, come out. Make this easy on yourself."

Darnell peered at the right side of the room and caught a flash of movement. Keelin was working her way around the other side between rows of silver and black shipping crates and storage containers. He took a deep breath, knowing just what to do. She needed a distraction. It only seemed fair.

"Wanna go, asshole?" he shouted from cover, tapping his wrench against the metal crate in front of him to draw attention. "No one takes a young lady's virtue without her consent on my watch."

"The fuck is this cowboy shit?"

"It's your goddamn fall," Atticus screamed from the other side, affecting a touch of a fake Texas twang. "Don't mess with us boys from the frontier."

Darnell gave him an appraising look. The guy was growing a pair.

The big man left his injured friend behind and advanced on Darnell, his barrel raised. He pulled the trigger, and the shot struck the edge of the crate. Darnell hit the deck and began to crawl, scrambling after a moment to get into a crouching run. Atticus split off and went the other way.

Two more shots struck the wall just over Darnell's head, sparks casting down on him. Where the hell was Keelin?

He was thankful for all the crates. They made it hard for Carlisle's men to get a clear line of sight. He kept on the go, unsure when to make his move. Maybe he could goad the man into wasting all his bullets. But how many were in his clip? Did the guy have more clips? He knew a little about firearms, sure, but he didn't recognize the gun that had been drawn. How many shots did it have? Eight? Ten? Fifty?

Bullets pelted around Darnell, ricocheting off the metal walls of the base. It was a miracle of God he hadn't been hit.

More crates began to crash onto the floor on the other side of the room. The shooting paused for a moment, and Darnell ventured a look. The big man had spun around.

"I don't play fuckin' games," the attacker said. "When I find you, I'll make it hurt. You okay, Steve?"

"I can't move," the skinny man pinned under the crate whined. "It's so bad. God damn it. It's so bad."

Darnell raised the wrench in his hand and stared at it. This had been stupid. It was his only weapon, a length of alloy steel the size of his forearm. They should have found a few guns. Called the authorities. Something more than this.

A scream like a battle cry came over Darnell's left shoulder. He spun to see a tiny woman leaping from the top of a stack of containers, her red hair trailing behind her like a banner in the low G environment. She fell onto the broad-shouldered man like a hammer, impact driver brandished in her right hand. Before he had a chance to react, she struck him across the chest, missing his head but knocking him off balance. He tumbled back, and Darnell took the opportunity to dash out from behind his hiding spot.

As the broad-shouldered man fell in low gravity, slow motion, he spun and squeezed off another round. Blood sprayed from the left leg of Keelin's jumpsuit. She squeaked as she crashed onto the floor, curling up into a ball, skidding till she came to rest against a row of boxes. She didn't move.

Atticus appeared on the other side of the opening, a look of fury on his normally unconcerned face like a feral, rabid animal. He thundered towards the man who had shot his friend and hit him across the face with the tank of his welding torch.

Once.

Twice.

Three times.

The big man let out a yelp and struggled against Atticus, blood spraying from his nose in a mist. He grabbed the psychologist by the jumpsuit and head-butted him. Atticus stumbled back a step.

The man with the injured leg cried out, twisting where he lay pinned under the crate, his face a mask of agony. He reached into his jumpsuit and drew a long-barreled pistol of his own, then pointed it at Atticus, who was in the open and exposed. Darnell was too far away to stop him, so he did all that he could. He tightened the grip on the wrench in his right hand, drew back, and tossed it hard as he could at the man on the ground. In the low gravity of the moon, the wrench became more of a projectile than it might on Earth. It spun end over end like a chakram, smashing the man in the face.

The pistol discharged, shot going wide.

Atticus continued to struggle with the big man, unable to gain any leverage over him despite having hit him in the face repeatedly with several pounds of titanium. In that moment, Darnell found himself torn between checking on Keelin and helping Atticus. She still hadn't moved from where she fell, blood soaking her pants leg.

The smaller of the two was down for the count. Darnell rushed over and pried the weapon from his hand, pointing it at the big man.

"Atticus, back," he shouted, taking a step towards the scuffle.

"No," the big man growled, taking hold of Atticus around the neck with the front of his arm. "Put the gun down or I'm going to break this asshole's neck."

"Fuck this bastard," Atticus hissed, and slammed his fist into the big man's groin. The man folded up like origami, retching. Atticus slid from his grip and rushed to Keelin's side. "You okay? Don't do this to me, you damned cunt."

She let out a groan and squeezed his hand. "Ain' out yet."

Darnell nodded and kept the barrel of his weapon fixed on the big man. She was alive, thank God. "Don't move."

The remaining thug recovered himself and raised his hands. He let out a long groan before speaking. "What do you plan on doing to me? You don't have the eyes of a killer."

"Don't push a kind man," Darnell replied, "there's nothing more dangerous in all the universe."

"Richardson," Keelin barked, then tossed a bundle of zip ties in Darnell's direction.

"Here," Darnell said, tossing them along. "Tie yourself up."

The man caught the bundle and scowled. "Carlisle is going to skin the three of you fuckers like a cat. I know who you are and he doesn't suffer transgressions. You're some of those doomed Void-Striders. If you had just stuck to the fucking plan, he might have let you live."

"What about the girl?" Keelin hissed, Atticus helping her stand. "What about her?"

"Who's to say," the big man began tightening the zip ties on his ankles before putting them on his wrist, biting the end with his teeth. "Won't take long to find out. A few minutes and he'll be back. Why not hang out with me until then and find out?"

"We'll pass," Darnell said. "As for you, this crate here looks big enough to hold your asses still for a while."

Atticus checked the tightness of the plastic ties, pulling till they stopped clicking. He led the man by the arm into one of the crates. It was a wonder he didn't fight back. The one on the floor whimpered in his half-conscious state. He was coming around.

"Let's gag 'em first," Keelin said, producing a few strips of cloth. "Don't need them cryin' for help."

Once Carlisle's men were secure, they made for another door at the back of the room. Keelin limped all the while, an arm over Atticus's shoulder, a makeshift bandage tied around her leg. She'd insisted on doing it herself, until Logan could finish the job and patch her up after they escaped. Darnell decided to keep the guns and any extra clips. He still wasn't sure what make they were, but that didn't matter. Guns were guns.

"How bad is it?" Atticus asked Keelin, her bandage already soaking red.

She shrugged. "I'll live. Just a graze, but it hurts like a raw lady gash stuffed full of salty bangers."

"What deliciously descriptive powers you have, my delicate flower of a friend."

"I get it honest."

"So sorry, Keelin," Darnell said, tossing her bag of tools over his shoulder. "We'll get you patched up right. God get us through this."

Atticus sighed. "You think he can hear prayers from space?"

"I sure as hell hope so."

They opened the door and entered a ten by fifteen room with dim, recessed lighting, a distinct odor of old takeout and stale beer lingering in the air. On the right side sat a modern desk with a high-end terminal of some kind, one used for advanced communication or decryption. On the left, a metallic chair was bolted to the floor facing a blank wall. Sitting in the silver chair sat a petite woman with dark hair that fell halfway down her back, her mouth gagged with a rubber ball and strap, arms bound behind her back with nylon cord.

Darnell approached the woman, setting the tools down and stepping into sight, his hands raised.

"Howdy," he said, and the dark, almond eyes of her round face went wide. There was no telling what they had done to her, how she would react. Best take it easy. "Don't worry, ma'am. I ain't gonna hurt you. Just a country boy at heart here to help get you out. I'm going to ungag you, is that okay? I don't need no one screaming. Carlisle's men might still be around."

She took a breath and nodded, a sweep of brown hair obstructing her vision as she turned her head. He reached around the back of her neck and unstrapped the leather ball gag, her skin red under its strips. It fell out of her mouth, and he set it on the floor. She took several long, deep breaths and popped her jaw.

"You're Sarah, right?"

"Yes," she said, her voice small like a cowering mouse. "I'm Sarah. Who are you?"

"Doesn't matter. Sarita sent us. We're here to rescue you."

"Sarita?" She leaned forward in the chair, expression shocked. "She's alive?"

Darnell reached in his pocket and removed a knife. He flipped it open and began sawing at the nylon cord. "She is. It's a hell of a long story, but if we can get out of here unnoticed, you'll be safe."

"You sure? Carlisle's a bastard. A smart, connected bastard. He'll find us. He'll kill us."

"Let's see the fooker try," Keelin said, spitting blood on the floor then offering a smile, her bright-white teeth framed in red.

Sarah blinked at Keelin then turned back to Darnell. "Thank you. All of you."

He tipped his head as if he had on a ten-gallon hat. "Ma'am."

The last of the cords snapped as Sarah's hands came unbound. She stood, her balance a little unsteady, then stretched. "I've been in that chair for so long. Days. There's a quick way out, through the back. It'll take us to the Gardens. I doubt he'll risk pulling guns out in the open."

"Okay," Darnell said. "We'll follow you."

The four of them stepped back into the storage room, moving quick as they could with an injured Keelin in their midst. They just had to get out into the public around prying eyes. This seemed easy enough, sure, but as soon as they stepped around the tallest stack of crates, everyone froze.

A middle-aged man dressed in a crimson jumpsuit stood on the other side of their battle zone, massive headphones cocked over his ears at an angle. In his left hand he held a pink donut with sprinkles, frozen inches before his mouth, face frozen in shock. They stared at one another for a moment, unable to make a move.

Before Darnell could twitch, before he could take a step or reach out, the man spun on his heels and headed for the far end of the room.

"He's going to alert Carlisle," Darnell growled. "Sarah, help Keelin walk. Atticus, get them out of here. Take this." He tossed the spare pistol to Atticus, who fumbled but caught it.

"Don't have to tell me twice."

Darnell cocked his stolen gun and took off after the fleeing man, hoping to God he wouldn't have to use it. He sure didn't want to shoot someone in the back, but desperate times may call for desperate measures.

[32] – Lexi

The *Peridot* came to rest on a landing pad at Luna Base, its Falkor drive popping and crackling as it came down, gas leaking from half a dozen broken lines along its back. To say landing wasn't easy would have been an understatement. Not only had it been over a year since Lexi had touched down on solid ground, but with the damage the Chinese nets had done to their flyer, half the attitude jets didn't work. Several times the busted reverse thrusters had forced her to make a full revolution to line the flyer up. Logan and Sarita had done their best to patch things up, but they weren't Keelin.

Docking clamps took hold of the flyer and a pressurized connection was made with Luna Base. When she finally let go of the controls her hands were cramped, fingers stiff like delicate machines that had run out of oil, their parts worn out from grinding against one another during heavy use. The muscles of her injured arm throbbed along its length from all the strain, bringing back flashes of the sharp pain that Sarita's scalpel had summoned. It would be some time before it fully healed, though thankfully it no longer bled.

They crawled out of their acceleration chairs and down to the exit, each room now sitting at a right angle to what their vision told them it should be.

"Let me do the talking," Sarita said before they entered the base. "If I'm correct, all we need to do is stall. Darnell and the others can extract Sarah to a crowded area. Carlisle can't make a move in the open. He's too public a figure, even on the moon where he has a lot of power."

Captain Cho nodded. "Agreed. Have we heard from the rest of the team?"

"No." Lexi raised her terminal, the joints of her hand popping, and sent a message. It took everything in her not to start freaking out. This was a time to keep it cool. "Darnell is receiving, so is Keelin, but no response. They could be in the middle of a situation."

"Let's hope it's not too bad."

Logan pulled the sleeves of their jumpsuit down, covering up their glowing arms. "Lots of stimuli here. There's a thousand active wireless networks."

"It's the largest human settlement outside of Earth," Sarita declared. "Over ten thousand people live here now."

"A spit in the bucket compared to home," Lexi said, waving to the exit. "Why not go say hello?"

"Can't leave him waiting."

They walked through the dock and into the spaceport's main concourse, a lightly populated, wide-open area with impossibly high glass ceilings made of geometrically shaped windowpanes, triangles and squares, hexagons and pentagons which together formed a mosaic of abstract art. The view on the other side of the five-foot thick glass was that of Earth rise, the Atlantic Ocean in daylight, a mist of clouds forming a storm cell at its center as large as the Gulf of Mexico. They'd renovated since Lexi's last visit, adding lines of soft blue and white lighting to the inner walls, bright directional signage, and even a few pieces of institutional art, colorful metalwork and sculptures. She could smell food cooking, a noodle bar and a taco joint nearby, pork and chicken sizzling on pans. Her stomach growled in spite of their situation.

A few wealthy families strolled around the main level, working their way towards the Gardens, luggage and children in tow. This was indeed a good place to raise a family. Safe from conflict and violence, a quarter million miles away from 99.9% of all humanity's troubles. No riots. No Fifth Great Awakening protests. If only you could afford it.

Personnel in blue jumpsuits scurried around the main level in motorized carts full of tools and equipment. One of the cart's drivers spotted them, made a sharp turn and headed their way.

"Welcome to Luna Base," a man said, pulling up to their dock and remaining seated. "I am Flyer Tech Sam Givins." He raised a tablet towards the *Peridot,* which was in clear view on the other side of the glass windows. "Holy crap, folks, you've been through it. Looks like you'll be needing repair services. Your flyer, the banged up Tambora class parked in 17, it's confirmed to be an active contractor of Kentara Mass Holdings, LLC, dba KTS Materials. Is this correct?"

"Yes," Captain Cho declared, taking a step forward. "We work for KTS."

"How did you guys get so banged up?"

Lexi swallowed. She hadn't considered spaceport workers asking sensitive questions.

"Ran into a Chinese garbage net on the dark side of the moon," Cho supplied.

"Chinese garbage net? Scows aren't supposed to be out right now. Are you okay?"

"We made it through just fine."

"If you like, I can help you press charges. They're not legally permitted to operate those ships in low lunar orbit, even if they do have claim to territory on the moon. Low orbit is international, ya know? Had a friend who dealt with that a few weeks back. Different issue, same folks. They don't always play nice with the UEI, sovereignty and all. We were able to get his claim pushed through with the Central Authority real quick. All I got to do is make a few calls. Big settlement on the way. I'm happy to help."

Three men approached on foot from the right side of the concourse, passing under glowing signs for THE GARDENS OF THE MOON. Lexi couldn't make out their features, but by the way they walked, she somehow knew it was Carlisle and his men. Too purposeful to be otherwise.

"It's fine," the captain told the tech, smiling. "Do me a favor and work us up repair estimates. Insurance will cover it. I'm sure it was not intentional."

"Are you positive?" Tech Givins narrowed his eyes at her.

"We're positive."

"Alright then." He flipped his cart's motor on and backed up, a series of beeps alerting anyone standing behind him to move out of the way. "I'll get the crew and shake her down."

"Thank you, Tech."

He gave a wave, his cart speeding off towards a maintenance entrance with an electric whine.

"Logan," Captain Cho said, stepping towards the doctor and slipping something into their hand. "Take this."

"What is it?" They stared at a thumb-sized memory stick of dark plastic and gold sitting on their palm. They closed their hand and slid it into a jumpsuit pocket before anyone could see.

"Evidence. Sarita helped me put it together with messages she received from Carlisle. If this goes south, you take it to the authorities. No matter what happens to us, he has to go down."

"I don't want to leave you guys alone," they said. "What if you need me?" They swung their portable medical kit around and patted it.

"It's okay. We'll be fine. There's more at stake here than just us."

Logan let out a long sigh. "Should I feel guilty this is a relief? I don't do well when things get ugly, at least, not this kind of ugly."

"No need to feel guilty," Lexi said, feeling a touch envious of their position.

"Go," the captain nodded, and Logan did just that, walking away from them and threading themself into the growing press of arrivals till they vanished.

The three men spotted Sarita among the *Peridot's* crew and headed over, a smile blossoming on the face of the tall man at the center. He was well-dressed in a tailored, royal blue suit, had skin as pale as sand, cropped gray hair with bits of black, round glasses, and a build like a linebacker aged out of his position. There was no doubt who this was. It was the man from the videos, the news feeds, the leader of the Fifth Great Awakening himself, James Carlisle, the Collector in the flesh.

"Hello Sarita," he said, stopping a few steps away, his men, his bodyguards, flanking him. "It is good to see you made it back to Luna base alive and well. Is that a bruise on your head?"

"Small acceleration accident," she offered, two fingers touching the wound. "Nothing serious."

"Good to hear. I would hate for this to have been a dangerous trip for you." He paused, then brought a hand up to his mouth in mock surprise. "Where are my manners? I am… The Collector."

"You're James Carlisle," Captain Cho blurted out. "What? No sense playing stupid games. I knew your face was familiar the first time I saw it. If you wanted that to stay a secret, you should have tried to conceal that fact a bit better."

"You know of me," he said, amused. "Then you must be a follower of the great works our organization has undertaken. The Lord calls those of the Fifth Great Awakening to do good the world over. Just last week we built three Christian schools in an impoverished region of Western Africa, saved fifteen minors from a group of sex traffickers in Georgia, and turned the midterm elections around in three blue states, gaining us a Republican majority in Congress."

"I vote independent," Captain Cho replied, crossing her arms.

"A wasted vote. You know that that's how *they* win. Divided we fall, is that not right?"

"James," Sarita took a step forward, "we didn't come to talk politics. We came to do what we came to do."

He nodded, a heavy look of resignation in his expression. "Of course, of course. Whether you support my cause or not, your efforts deserve a reward. Come, we must talk terms." He turned and started to walk away, his guards holding still.

"Terms?" Captain Cho hardened her expression and kept her feet planted. "The terms have already been set. We are here to transact, nothing more."

"Have they?" Carlisle rubbed his chin. "We will go over them again soon as we are not in such a… well… public venue. Don't want prying eyes and curious ears to learn the sordid details of our negotiations. Wouldn't be fair for you. KTS ship captain sent to jail for life over stolen artifacts?"

"You wouldn't dare," she said, voice taking on a dangerous edge.

"Let's talk, I'd rather you not find out."

"Katia, we should talk," Sarita said, gesturing towards Carlisle. "It's the prudent thing to do."

"Prudent?" Captain Cho shook her head.

Lexi's hands began to sweat. It was hard to tell in the moment if this was anger, or another act of the captain. She was cool under pressure, a talented persuader. Letting Carlisle believe he was in control, that they were surprised at this change in events, was a smart move.

They began to walk away, and the crew of the *Peridot* followed. Lexi eyed the people in the concourse, her right hand gripping her left arm. The only protection they had in this situation was being out in the open. As soon as they were behind closed doors, there was no telling what the brutes Carlisle brought with him would do.

As everyone passed under the directional signage at the far end of the concourse, the aroma of cooking intensifying, Carlisle paused and raised his hand terminal. He stared at the screen, perplexed, then whirled to stare at Sarita.

"This meeting is over," Carlisle growled, then spun on his heels and began to walk away, not at a run, but moving with a new purpose. His guards followed suit.

Lexi knew from the look on his face that their other group had been discovered. Darnell, Keelin, and Atticus were in danger. Had they found Sarah?

"What was that about?" Sarita asked.

"They got caught," Lexi said, and checked her hand terminal. "No messages, but that's the only thing it could mean. We've got to help them somehow."

"Agreed," Captain Cho said, and they began to jog in the direction Carlisle had gone. She raised her hand terminal and spoke into it. "Send message to Logan. *You know what to do. Wait ten minutes, then go find the authorities. We'll keep him busy till then.* Send."

"How?" Sarita asked, her expression panicked. "If they get to Sarah first."

"I know. I know."

"We'll make it," Lexi said, patting Sarita on the back. There was no time for hard feelings right now. "We'll make it."

[33] – Darnell

The moon granted some unexpected advantages. Low gravity made it easy for every body type and size to move quickly. Which is why Darnell had been shocked that the donut-eating man was as nimble as he was, with a waistline easily at forty-five inches. He'd taken off at a dead sprint through the side door, drawn Darnell down a set of hallways, and into a massive warehouse in just a few seconds. While Darnell considered himself to be in pretty good shape by comparison, null gravity fatigue or not, this was something else.

It was impossible to stay on top of the man and send a message at the same time. His hand terminal buzzed a couple of times in his jumpsuit pocket, but he dared not remove it in fear he might drop it. He kept the stolen pistol raised ahead, gripping it with both hands. Gramps had been clear, you always used two hands. People who shot one-handed were more interested in wasting ammo and looking cool than hitting targets.

Donut man burst into another open warehouse, this one larger than the last. Darnell followed after. He paused on the other side for a moment and gasped.

He was there.

This was the warehouse.

This was *the* collection.

There was even an empty spot the exact size of a Lindvall Slipstream already marked out on the floor.

In all honesty, even without the time to take it in, the collection was impressive. American artifacts were lined up in neat rows, clothes from famous Hollywood films placed in hermetically sealed glass boxes, curios full of silver trinkets engraved with names, copper bells and tattered sail cloth from famous ships, flags of a dozen eras folded in neat rows under glass. Then there were the Civil War cannons, flintlock rifles from the American revolution, military uniforms from the Confederacy to World War II, Neil Armstrong's space suit, and of all things, a pioneer's wooden wagon. Was this Uncle Sam's mini storage? A remote location to shove all those things that junk up the house?

The man paused a few rows down and raised his hand terminal. Darnell didn't wait. He squeezed off a shot, not intending to hit him, but to scare him. The tactic worked well enough, and the man jumped into cover, startled.

He advanced on the man, running between a series of open crates filled with paintings. Before he could reach the corner of the aisle the man reappeared, a bolt action rifle in hand. Darnell scrambled back, slowing himself. The rifle discharged, and on his right, splinters sprayed from a wooden crate at the edge of his peripheral vision. How in the hell had that idiot missed a shot like that? Divine intervention...

"Should have shot him when I had the chance," Darnell muttered to himself and bolted for an aisle opposite the other man. He took cover behind a shoulder-high, steel cotton gin, the words LUMMUS embossed on the side.

This was his moment to try and send Lexi a message, but as he fumbled with his hand terminal, he dropped it on the floor, where despite the advantages of low gravity, the screen landed on an upright bolt and shattered.

"Shit," he mumbled. "Just my damn luck."

Darnell took a deep breath and started to work his way around, attempting to listen for movement. He had to stop this man before he alerted Carlisle. Although truth be told he probably already had. From two aisles over, something glass shattered on the floor. Darnell made his way in that direction, listening closely.

As he slid his way around rusty stills and wooden chairs, the man reappeared inches from his face. How had he gotten so close, and so fast? The noise had been on the other side of the warehouse. Right?

The butt of the man's rifle came down and struck Darnell in the chest, slamming him back onto his ass, pistol tumbling from his grip to skitter under a pallet. The man raised his rifle to shoot him in the chest, but he was not having any of it. He took hold of the barrel with both hands and shoved it to the right, the weapon discharging beside his ear with a deafening bang. Darnell could hardly hear as he shook his head, attempting to clear the ringing from his ears, feet scrambling to get him back up.

Holding to the rifle for dear life, the man attempted to leverage Darnell's grip free, but all he did was help him stand. The barrel remained pointed over Darnell's shoulder at the artifacts. Darnell knew he had to change the power dynamic. Had to get an advantage or a lucky shot might be the last thing he saw. And so, he pushed towards the man, lifting the barrel of the rifle like it were the half of a spear, the man's feet leaving the ground. He knew the man would not let go, and so he slammed the barrel down, careful not to put it in front of his chest, and he heard the crack of bone upon impact. Donut man had not been paying attention to his footing and had come back down at an awkward angle producing a yelp.

The side of the barrel slapped Darnell in the face several times. He worked to wrench it free, the two of them grunting at one another as they struggled for their lives.

"Let go," the man growled. "Let go!"

Darnell gritted his teeth. "You first."

"This is so damn stupid. He'll kill you anyway. He'll kill you."

"So people keep telling me."

With his free hand, Darnell reached for the bottom of the rifle and fumbled with its clip. He was able to press his arm against the man and remove it. That left only the bullet in the chamber. Or did it?

He let go of the rifle and the man stumbled back. The barrel rose again on Darnell and the man pulled the trigger.

Nothing happened.

"Empty chamber, sir," Darnell said.

"Shit." The man tossed the rifle down and took off at a limping run towards the emergency exit, but it was no use. With his ankle twisted he'd lost most of his agility.

Before giving chase, Darnell scrambled over to the pallet, reaching underneath to take hold of the pistol he'd lost. When his fingers touched cold steel, he let out a sigh, then took off after.

About the time the man hit the exit, he tripped over his own feet and fell face first, letting out a yelp as his nose cracked against the door frame and began to spew blood.

Darnell stood over him; gun pointed at his chest. A hand terminal lay on the ground, the words "Message Sent" written across its cracked screen.

"Bend me over with a broomstick," the man mumbled.

Carlisle and his men were coming for them, but how many reinforcements did they have?

He had no clue.

[34] – Lexi

Lexi repeatedly checked her hand terminal as they hurried after Carlisle and his men. They hadn't quite broken out into a full run, but their jog was more than enough to work up a sweat. The spaceport's concourse soon gave way to a tunnel filled with lines of LED lights blinking blue, white, and purple in sequence. Crowds of residents began to thicken. The gardens were ahead.

"He's trying to lose us," she said, and Captain Cho let out a grunt. "Sarita, how well do you know your way around?"

"Well enough, I suppose."

"They're turning," the captain said, nodding in their direction, her hands in her jumpsuit pockets attempting to look casual. "Let's move quicker."

No messages had come through from Darnell or the rest of the crew. Lexi prayed it hadn't gone bad.

They passed a series of security guards. There were no guns on their hips, just batons, tasers, handcuffs, and radios. One of them looked familiar, though Lexi couldn't place where from. There was certainly a security presence on Luna, but they didn't resemble a police force by any means. They seemed far more relaxed, perhaps even a bit less restricted. Luna Base was a UEI colony, which meant it was multinational, free from specific government control than its own, but still...

Restaurants blurred past on either side, food court-style plastic seating in fenced off sections full of colonists of all varieties scooping up noodles or sawing away at meat delivered fresh from Earth. It was a cross-section of human culture and nationalities: white collar, blue collar, growing families, and those who were on their own. From the outside looking in, everyone seemed to treat one another the same. No one table was dominated by a particular subsection, be it socio-economic or racial. Was this the future they had ahead? Was humanity headed for a day beyond divisions? Was the survival of the species a unifying enough cause to cast all that aside?

She refocused on the back of Carlisle's head through the crowd.

"Just seeing what I want to see," she mumbled and shook her head.

Captain Cho gave her a glance. "What was that?"

"Nothing."

"There," Sarita pointed at a tunnel past the food court, "that leads into the Gardens. He can easily lose us in there."

"But we know where he's going, yes?"

"I sure hope so. Who's to say he hasn't moved the collection?"

As they jogged through the tunnel, it opened up into a massive dome of glass and steel so high a city skyscraper could have fit beneath. Her boots crunched as she stepped onto a gravel path, its edges hemmed with moss-covered stones.

Lexi found it hard to contain her awe, even in the thick of this dire situation. She was standing on the moon, a place that until about the past one hundred years had been nothing more to humanity than a dream, a white ball tracking across blue and black skies, its surface dead as any asteroid they'd ever captured. And now? She stood in a forest, a forest of thick, green, deciduous plants dense enough she could hardly see more than a few feet down the trail. To her left and right, babbling brooks burbled, a slow flow of water tumbling over smooth rocks, casting a fine mist into the air. This made the air cool, clean and fresh, nothing like that of the *Peridot,* or any flyer or station for that matter. For an instant, she was transported back down the well, back to the woods behind her grandparents' house in West Virginia.

It was beautiful.

The work it took to build and maintain this...

But it was beautiful.

Carlisle and his men took off at a run down the trails, curving around to the right, dashing over wooden footbridges. They were now well away from any bystanders or prying eyes.

"Can't let him get away," Sarita said, taking off after him.

Captain Cho picked up the pace. "Wait for us. Stay together. No telling what trap could be ahead of us in this... this..."

"Garden," Lexi supplied, eyes tracking up the length of the tall trees to the curved windows of towering apartments looking down at them along the outside edge of the dome. "It truly is a Garden on the Moon."

And she would never get to live here. That dream had been taken away the moment Carlisle betrayed them.

"I feel like we're a bunch of mice chasing a lion," Lexi went on, drawing herself back into reality. "What do we do when we catch these hunters?"

Captain Cho considered her question before answering. "Hope that the lions behind us will eat the ones before us."

The trails of the Gardens wound around, raising up and down, sometimes with steps, sometimes as slopes. From time to time, the thick trees gave way to small patches of grass where groups of colonists gathered, colorful blankets laid out for picnics under starlight. When they caught sight of Carlisle again, he had slowed his stride.

At a fork in the trail, one of Carlisle's bodyguards turned around, reaching into his jacket to remove a pistol. He raised it towards them, then stuffed it back into his suit as a pair of security guards walked past. Lexi swallowed her relief, then wondered if they would be best served grabbing the attention of security now.

"Don't do it," Captain Cho said. "You'll just get those boys killed. They need to prepare, bring their full force."

The path curved again, becoming darker as the underbrush and tree canopy overhead thickened. Lexi could still see the back of Carlisle's head, but one of the guards was missing.

"Where did he go?" she whispered, then noticed another had vanished.

Captain Cho raised a hand for them to stop. "This isn't good."

"I see Carlisle, but—"

Something hard and cold pressed against Lexi's lower spine. She reflexively raised her hands.

"Keep quiet and you won't end up bleeding out on the trail," one of the guards said from behind her. Out of the corner of her eye, she could see Captain Cho was in a similar situation. The bodyguards had somehow circled back around and snuck up on them.

Carlisle stopped and turned to face them, a small device in his hand. He clicked on it with a thumb, and the guards reappeared beside him. He clicked again, and they vanished. What in the hell had he gotten his hands on?

"Military grade holographic projector," he supplied, stepping close enough to Captain Cho that their noses were mere inches apart. "Doesn't work for shit in bright, well-lit environments, but in the dark it does swimmingly."

And they were indeed somewhere dark and secluded, nothing but trees surrounding them, birds tweeting overhead.

Sarita shrunk down into herself, placing her hands in her pockets. She let out a sigh. Lexi wondered briefly if she had betrayed them? No. Not this time.

"Beautiful, isn't it?" Carlisle mused as he spun around, taking in the garden. "All because of people like me. Great things happen when a vision bigger than yourself is cast. When the message is right, it resonates within the hearts of those who need it most, sending ripples out into the universe. We stand on the moon in a forest of green, a place never meant for life to thrive, and yet, here it is. The true gift of God making us in his image is the power of imagination and creation—the spark of life. The trick, however, is knowing what vision shall resonate, what will create the ripples that touch each heart in turn."

"What do you plan on doing to us?" Captain Cho demanded.

"To be frank, I haven't decided yet." He gave a wave, and his guards urged everyone forward. "Let's see how much of a mess your people have made of things. I'm shocked they were able to get in. What ship did they arrive on? I've been watching all traffic in and out and saw nothing. You're a clever bunch, and clever people, well... they have a way of finding themselves dead around me."

Lexi gave the man behind her a glare and reluctantly stepped forward. If she had even the smallest opening, she was going to burn these people down. Here's hoping Logan was okay. The cavalry would come, right? All the authorities needed was the evidence. Surely Carlisle wasn't so well connected that he owned *everyone* on Luna Base.

Surely...

"Darnell," she whispered as they made their way through the trails of the Gardens of the Moon and entered the business district. "Are you okay?"

[35] – Darnell

The man Darnell had been chasing now sat against the wall of the Collector's warehouse, massaging his ankle and wincing. Darnell wasn't sure what to do with him, he had nothing on hand to tie him up or restrain him, and if he left the man alone, he'd just limp off and cause more trouble. Being a criminal was hard work, even if you had good intentions at heart.

"He's coming for you," the injured man said. "He's coming."

"Shut up." Darnell wiped his sweaty forehead with the back of his arm. "Just shut up."

"First time being on this side of things, isn't it? Skirting the edges of the law." The man chortled. "You look like a damned goody goody. Never stole so much as a stick of gum in your life."

"Stealing is wrong."

"Keep telling yourself that." The man coughed, the sound dry and scratchy. "We all steal. Ownership is relative."

Darnell considered his options. Did this work like the movies? Could he just hit the man across the face with the butt of his pistol and knock him cold? He doubted it. More likely he'd just give him a concussion and lifelong injuries. But why should he care? Just a few minutes ago he'd been willing to shoot him dead, and now he was worried if the man would be left with a disability. God help him. This was not the line a work for someone like him.

Time was running out. Lexi and the others had to be meeting with Carlisle by now. Maybe they were able to distract him long enough so Atticus and the rest could get away.

"Put the gun down," a voice said from behind him, and his stomach dropped. As focused on his prisoner as he was, he'd not been paying attention to the other entrance. Stupid mistake. Stupid. "I said, put it down."

He slowly turned and saw a familiar, middle-aged man pointing a pistol at him. Two guards were flanking the man, their own pistols pointed at the backs of Lexi, Captain Cho, and Sarita. Darnell sighed and crouched down, setting his weapon on the floor.

It was immediately clear what had happened.

They'd played the game and lost.

How high would the cost of failure be?

"At least you didn't get the girl," Darnell said, proud that Atticus, Keelin, and Sarah were not present.

Carlisle smiled, a self-assured look that made Darnell's stomach twist. "I have resources, Mr. Richardson. They're headed this way right now."

And true to his word, a downcast group from the *Peridot* appeared through the far door, an injured Keelin and Sarah, Sarita's wife, among them. Four more guards appeared for a total of seven armed guards plus Carlisle, including donut man who was struggling to his feet. Any aggressive move taken would be met with deadly resistance. There was no way out of this.

"Have you not figured it out by now?" he went on. "You can't cheat me. I have people every place, eyes everywhere. I did not amass my wealth by accident. It took the careful investment of many years. I was once like you and the rest of your crew here."

"We're nothing like you," Darnell spat.

"But I *was* like you," Carlisle replied, unfazed. "I came from a family of no riches, but we had stability. Safety. Security. That's more than many can claim at the late hour of our century. I can see you are shocked by my knowledge, but Mr. Richardson, I do my research. I know about the ranch. I know about the tax breaks the Fed gives your Gramps and the rest of your family for your work with the UEI. They can't make it without those, you know it. I know it. What a sad state of affairs we're in, salt of the Earth, hardworking, and still can't easily make both ends meet in the middle."

Darnell's mouth went dry.

"Here's the thing," Carlisle went on, scratching at his temple with the barrel of his pistol. "I caught a few lucky breaks in my early years. Found some success in business arbitrage, that is, the importing and exporting of virtual goods, as well as some emerging stock flips. Before I knew it, I was able to start investing back into more traditional asset classes. At one point I was purchasing more than fifty properties a day in countries all around the world. How did I get better? Earn more? I read. I learned. I traveled. But as my riches amassed, one thing soon became clear as crystal to me...

"Though this new wealth gave me power, luxury, and options, there were many things wrong with the world that money itself could not change. Some resources are fixed. Wealth is a construct, an idea, a mindset. Influence can be purchased with this nebulous idea, but that influence can be just as immaterial, just as transitory. So many years I had remained in the shadows with my private yachts, my six islands, no real family but plenty of wives, and then I met a preacher on the road. Cliché, I know." Carlisle gazed off into nothing, a wistful expression on his face. "The preacher told me that with great wealth, came great responsibility. He told me that the talents Christ spoke of in the parable of the book of Matthew were meant to be invested for the glory of God, not for thyself. That despite my hundreds of billions of dollars, I was just an overpaid servant of the Devil."

Carlisle lowered his weapon and sighed. He looked tired and far older than he had just moments earlier. What was he trying to do here? Was he trying to justify himself, or convince Darnell?

"He was right," he said, voice sad. "The preacher was right. I lived by the dollar. Served the dollar. Fought for the dollar. In every conceivable way, I reached for every single one I could put my hands on, and when I couldn't find enough, I fabricated them out of nothing. Banking is such an interesting thing, my friend, money isn't real. Just another idea we all believe in. A societal hallucination over value. And so, coming to this great revelation, what did I do? I did the only thing that was appropriate. I fell onto my knees and repented, then and there, my face to the floorboards of a dusty old church in Middle America. I gave my life, my money, my soul, over to God. I could see clearly that our species had fallen into disarray. We had left Him far behind.

"God had given us this wonderous, abundant world, a place of endless beauty and splendor, our own Garden of Eden, and we had exploited it. I had exploited it. Explorative drilling. Unsustainable business expansion. Plastic everything. Toxic landfills. Dying species. All because of our malleable morals and a lack of responsibility. Everyone wanted something easy, something for free. Riches for the sake of riches. But you see, everything has a cost. And that cost must be paid."

"The Fifth Great Awakening," Darnell whispered, the words now holding far more meaning for him than ever before.

"Yes," Carlisle said, smiling. "I myself did not name it that. But once the idea was born, it took on a life of its own, making ripples upon the waters of existence. God revealed it to others, and on and on it went. If I were to be given the knowledge to build an empire of wealth, then that wealth had to be used as a force for good." He waved at the space around them, the many American treasures they stood surrounded by, the weight of history oppressive. "And so, I stand here ready to inspire, to give others something greater to believe in than self-anesthetization and death. I want to take people back to a simpler age socially as we move forward into the stars. The Foundry expedition will not save humanity, those who have set out to make contact with that alien machine will die. Only demons and devils live outside of our solar system. And so, we must lift one another up into the embrace of the good Lord. This is our redemption. SOL is our holy land."

Darnell licked his lips and drew them into a hard line. "God the father."

"Yes. The father. Do you see, now, Mr. Richardson? We are not so different."

How did it all go so wrong? How could people like this man twist the message of the Bible, God's own word, in so many terrible ways? How could he justify this madness? Everything in Darnell screamed that this was wrong. Call it Holy Spirit, intuition, your humanity... they all told him that this man's actions were pure evil.

"No." Darnell shook his head. "I'm nothing like you. I don't care how much money it puts in my wallet, I ain't gonna kill people to get it."

"What if the money it put there could help you change the world?" Carlisle began to pace, side to side. "If you had infinite resources, what would you do? How would you steer this great ship differently? Humanity is headed to ruin, be it spiritually or physically. Something has to change."

"You're right, something does have to change." Darnell stared Carlisle dead in the eyes. "But this is not the way. Your heart might have once been clean, purified by the blood of the lamb, but not now. You have forsaken the path and you have a heart of sin black as night. You have killed in His name, and that... That is true blasphemy."

Carlisle's face went red, the pistol at his side shaking. "You dare talk to me like this."

"Everything here is stolen," Darnell said, gesturing with his chin. "Given the company you hold, you can't tell me that any of it was procured honestly. God knows a man's heart. His actions reflect his soul."

This was not what Carlisle wanted to hear, even if it was the damned truth. He raised the weapon to the side of his face, gesturing with it, about to speak, then someone burst into the room.

"Sir!" a panting man hissed. "It's the—" But before he could go on, the man's legs gave out and he collapsed into a heap on the floor.

"What in the hell?" Carlisle raised his weapon and pointed it in that direction.

"UEI Security Forces!" a voice shouted from out in the hall. "We've got you surrounded!"

Carlisle and his men wasted no time looking for cover, leaving the crew of the *Peridot* standing in the center of the main aisle, exposed.

"Go home, Sergeant," Carlisle called as he vanished from sight. "This does not concern you."

The security officer waited for a moment to respond as his men shuffled through the doors and into place. "When I have reports of gunfire in the business district and evidence of criminal activity," the sergeant said, "it becomes my concern."

"Evidence?" Carlisle turned to look at Sarita. He whispered, "Wonder where that came from?"

The balance of power in the room was shifting.

Even though the UEI had not yet fired a shot, they did indeed have Carlisle's men, and the *Peridot's* crew, surrounded. By Darnell's count, ten UEI Security guards stood by the two entrances of the warehouse, five on each side, each armed with more than mere crowd suppression equipment. They wore the same orange uniforms Keelin's friend had, plus body armor, chest plates and helmets, and were armed with short barrel rifles. All it would take was one itchy trigger finger and this place would become a bloodbath.

Darnell gave Lexi a pleading look. What could they do? None of them had a weapon of any description. And even if they did, their position was about as poor as it could be, right in the middle of everyone. They could do nothing more than hope the security forces de-escalated this situation. How did they find out to begin with? Where was Logan?

"Put down the weapons, Carlisle," the sergeant shouted, his tone hard as steel. "Let's do this peacefully."

"You break into my private residence," Carlisle said, his face hardening. "My private place of business, unannounced, and you say let's do this peaceful? How much do I pay you again? How much does the UEI benefit from me?"

"This isn't the place," he replied. "Last chance, put down the weapons. We'll talk about all this privately."

Darnell watched Carlisle exchange glances with one of the bodyguards. The man's lip twitched, and he reached into his jacket and removed his hand terminal.

"Get ready to get down," Darnell mouthed to Lexi, and she let out a slow breath, reaching back with a free hand to Captain Cho who reached for Keelin, who reached for Atticus, who reached Sarita. Sarita twisted her head in Sarah's direction, and she received the subtle message as well. What else was there to do? When the shooting started, get out of sight and see who lives.

"For God's sake, James," the sergeant tried again. "After all we've been through, don't let this be the end."

"It won't," Carlisle said, and the room suddenly filled with a cold mist.

Darnell and the crew of the *Peridot* hit the deck, laying themselves flat against the metal floor. Flashes of light blossomed above them in the ever-thickening fog of what could only be the fire suppression system; gunshots coming in rapid succession. Breathing became difficult. Whatever this gas was, it was intended to replace oxygen to smother any fires, keeping them from spreading. Fire was not all it could smother though.

Darnell took a deep breath at floor level, then started to crawl away through the chaos. Gunshots trailed overhead. It was a miracle they didn't tear through every bit of the collection. Lexi and Captain Cho made their way over to Darnell, Sarita having vanished in the fog. Chances were she had gone to grab Sarah.

"What do we do?" Darnell asked them. "See if the dust settles?"

"I've got a bad feeling this isn't going to end in favor of the UEI," Captain Cho said.

Lexi reached out and took hold of Darnell's hand. "We need weapons. Something to fight back with."

"From where?" Darnell stuck his head up for a moment, attempting to orient himself in the fog.

A shout came from a place on their left, voice sounding familiar.

"This way," he said, then lowered himself to the deck and took another deep breath.

By now the fog was as thick as any he'd ever seen in Dallas, and he could remember one particular event where dozens had died in a massive pileup on the interstate. They could hardly see three feet in front of themselves. The sound of gunfire was muffled by the fog, the muzzle flashes diffused like explosions underwater.

Men began to cry out, likely a few having been hit. Who was winning? Who could say?

"I'm not feeling well," Lexi said, her crawl slowing. "It's hard to breathe. Hard... to..."

"Here," he pushed her in the direction of a fogless corner in the room. The three of them took deep breaths then turned to the left. A body of a UEI security guard was on the floor, no blood, no wounds of any kind. The man had passed out, leaving his weapon lying beside him. Darnell wasted no time and took his rifle, then checked for more weapons. A pistol was on his belt. He passed it to Captain Cho.

Lexi removed the body armor and put her ear to the man's chest. "Still breathing. He's knocked out, but alive. Much like we'll be when this fog closes in."

The fighting began to die down, the UEI forces succumbing to the fire suppression systems. Carlisle and his men must have had a way to counter the effects.

The thickest portion of the fog began to fold in on them, and Darnell, Lexi, and Captain Cho gave each other a look. They could feasibly run for the door, but either side might shoot them if they did. They were stuck, nowhere to—

A whir of fans began overhead. The fog began to clear, thinning by the second. Air became easier to breathe, oxygen rushing back in. A few more shots rang out, but it was clear from the lack of noise that many of those involved in this battle had already been rendered unconscious.

They kept low and crawled towards the front entrance, hoping to see a clear line to the exit. The way, however, was blocked by the bodies of guards. It would be hard to make a run for it over that human obstacle course. Lexi slid up next to one of them and grabbed a fallen rifle.

"Soon as we kill you all," Carlisle called from somewhere out of sight near the center of the room. "I'm taking the prize for myself. You hear me? I had planned on still sharing some of the spoils."

"Good luck with that there," Keelin shouted from the opposite corner of the warehouse. It was good to hear she was still alive. "That fookin' Slipstream's no more than stardust now."

"What?" he shouted, his voice taking on an unstable edge. "What are you talking about? I saw pictures. I saw evidence."

Lexi and Captain Cho gave each other a look, then began to spread out. If there was no easy way to run, they'd have to fight.

"That's right," Darnell growled. "I blew the damn thing up. An asshole like you doesn't deserve it. Just like you don't deserve *this*."

He raised his weapon and shot one of the glass cases containing Hollywood paraphernalia. Even in that moment, it pained him to do so, but he needed to distract Carlisle. He needed to give his fiancée and the captain an opportunity to even the odds. Could he pull the trigger on another human next time? Could he kill to protect himself? He'd soon find out.

"No!" Carlisle screamed like a petulant child. "No! No! No! Do you know what it took to get that? It was from the Wizard of Oz. THE Wizard of Oz! One of the greatest films of all time."

"How about this?" Darnell pointed the gun and squeezed again, shattering a gilded, porcelain vase with John Adam's face rendered on the side. "What a satisfying sound that was," he shouted, tone mocking.

"Bastard! That's history! American history! That piece came straight from the White House!"

Darnell cringed at the idea. Shit, he really needed to stop.

One of Carlisle's guards came around the corner of the aisle and this time Darnell did not hesitate. He pulled the trigger three times, catching his target in the chest and knocking them back into a glass display case. Several other shots rang out to his left and right on the other side of the warehouse.

He held his weapon eye level, steady, scanning the room along the sight. Where was Carlisle?

"Do I need to destroy anything else?" Darnell mused, trying to get him to speak, to reveal his position. It didn't work.

"Take that!" Keelin shouted from behind a row of furniture. A good sign, but where were the rest?

Darnell eased himself around the corner of the next aisle, scanning side to side, and as he came back around Carlisle appeared one row up. The man took aim and fired, forcing him back. The shot missed his face by inches and sent a shock of cold through his body, down his spine and into his toes. He scrambled back, keeping his weapon ahead, but failed to notice Carlisle had scaled the storage crates on the aisle beside him and jumped down. Low gravity made it easy for even a man of Carlisle's age to accomplish this. He crashed down on Darnell, taking him by surprise, the butt of his weapon hitting like a sledgehammer.

It struck Darnell across the chin, sending him to the ground, the back of his head slamming against cold steel. He tasted copper, smelled burning hair. He attempted to draw himself up, but Carlisle struck again, sending him into a roll.

"You think I got where I am without getting my hands dirty?" Carlisle said. "Sometimes I have to be the monster. But God forgives all sins, big and small."

Darnell raised a hand to block his next blow, but his vision was hazy, his reflexes sluggish. His head struck steel once more, and another cold chill shot through his body like lightning at the impact.

The Collector stood over Darnell, the warehouse's lights casting the man into a silhouette. He pointed the barrel of his weapon at Darnell's face, his shadowed form taking on a smug sense of triumph.

"I used to look up to you," Darnell mumbled, blood dribbling from the side of his mouth, the back of his head throbbing.

"Looks like you still do," Carlisle said, pulling back the trigger. "And now, you always will."

[36] – Lexi

The security guards from Luna Base had yet to stir. They laid on the floor near-motionless, but for the slight raising of their chests. They weren't dead, and Lexi sure could have used their help. This was not what she was trained for in any kind of way. She wasn't handy with a gun and had never been in a fight involving more than fists and fingernails, let alone low gravity and hired muscle. Nevertheless, she and Captain Cho put up a good front as they worked their way around the outside of the room, weapons raised in front of them, mimicking what they had seen in movies more than anything else.

"I'll cover your back," Captain Cho said, turning around.

Lexi nodded. "Okay."

It seemed logical, though it was likely asinine.

The rows of artifacts made for uneven cover. Some spots were as good to hide behind as a wall; others, were like stalls at an open-air market. Something beside Lexi flashed as a shot landed off to her right, but before she could turn, Captain Cho fired back.

"I got them," she said, breathing out the words. "That was close."

They had to come around behind Darnell. He was keeping Carlisle busy by destroying artifacts. This was their chance to tip the scales. As they advanced on the next aisle, she could see a large man through the scattered artifacts. He raised his pistol and fired twice. The shots missed Lexi, but one hit Captain Cho, sending her twisting around onto the floor. Lexi fired in his direction, but the man vanished from sight.

She crawled to Captain Cho, checking her over. Her face was a mask of pain, her jumpsuit sleeve soaked with red.

"Oh God," she said, setting down the gun and raising her hands to her mouth. "I don't know what to do. Logan would. I don't."

Captain Cho coughed. "My shoulder. It hurts. Hurts so fucking bad. This is what it feels like to get shot? One star, would not recommend."

Lexi looked for anything to bind the wound and slow the bleeding. Nothing was within reach. Her jumpsuit sleeve wouldn't even come loose when she tried to rip it, having been double-stitched and made of a hearty synthetic material.

"What do I do?"

"What we have to." Captain Cho raised her good arm, pointed her gun, and pulled the trigger. Someone had been sneaking around on the other side when Lexi wasn't looking. A mistake that could have been far worse than an injured shoulder.

Before Lexi could do much to process the new development, she heard a grunt she recognized. Not just any grunt, no, it was Darnell. Somehow, she knew he was hurt. She scanned the room looking for more of the bodyguards but didn't see any. It had to be Carlisle.

She squeezed Captain Cho's hand, who nodded in return.

"Go to him," Katia said.

"Okay."

Lexi took a deep breath, squatted down, then leaped straight up. It seemed a good idea at the time, to make use of low gravity and get a clear look at everything that was going on in the room, but as she began to fall back to the floor slower than she had expected, she saw the error in this. Two of the bodyguards were still up and active. They turned and fired in her direction, but both missed.

Scary or not, she did get what she was after. Darnell was two aisles over in an alcove of antique, turn-of-the-19th century equipment. Carlisle was lording over him, weapon raised. She didn't have time to run around the equipment, she had to act now. Lexi dug in with the ball of her foot, and squatted down again, this time ready to launch herself up and forward. She went careening over the aisle, almost overshooting her target. As she landed, several feet past the spot she was aiming for, she stumbled for an instant, then twisted around and fired.

Carlisle's eyes went wide. He rolled to the side, hopping out of the way. Darnell lay motionless on the floor. Lexi's anger doubled. She regained her balance and walked towards Carlisle, weapon raised.

Carlisle took a shot and missed. She took a shot at him and missed. Actors made it look so easy when it was scripted. Neither of them were professional soldiers, and there was too much chaos to distract them. His weapon clicked. So did hers. This couldn't be coincidence, could it?

He came running at her, anger on his face, confident he could overpower her. They threw punches at one another, but Lexi was faster, younger. He swept his leg out and nearly tripped her, but she recovered, taking a step back. Having a tussle in low gravity was awkward, like two flies struggling in a pool of honey, nothing to leverage themselves against and no standard downward pull to steady you. The only difference here was that the punches came just as hard and fast.

His right hand was like a hammer, Carlisle caught her across the face and began to throttle her. She went flying back against a steel cotton gin, metal ringing as her back struck. A stainless-steel rod lay on its edge, a tool of some kind. She took hold, swinging out at Carlisle, catching him on the nose. He put a palm against his bleeding face and tried kicking at her, his legs long enough to keep her unbalanced swings out of reach. She decided to change her strategy and instead clubbed him on the shin, eliciting a shout. She hated to admit it, but that cry made her heart thunder in her chest with victory.

"Bitch," Carlisle growled, then threw himself at her like a feral animal, teeth barred. He'd timed the moment just right, and she fell back onto the ground. Despite the low gravity, he had leverage on her she could not overcome being bigger, stronger that her. He punched her in the face once, twice, three times, then grabbed her by the lapels of her jumpsuit and slammed her onto the floor.

The rod tumbled from her grip.

Everything went hazy for a moment.

She felt nauseous.

Tasted copper.

Smelled something burning.

Pain became a cloud of black crowding towards the middle.

"No," she whimpered. "No."

Out of the corner of her eye, she spotted the metal rod she'd been holding moments earlier. She reached for it, fingertips grasping at its smooth end, Carlisle raining a hateful onslaught of fists down upon her, his tempo unrelenting. Her trembling fingers wrapped around the rod.

With all she had left, she swung her newfound weapon, cracking him on the back of the head. Carlisle's skull made a crunching noise as the impact vibrated back through her grip, forcing her to drop the rod. He let out a squeak and his body went limp, every muscle switching off, eyes rolling back. Her lips trembled as relief flooded into her. He'd been stopped.

She slid out from under him, body so shaky she could hardly move.

Darnell stumbled back onto his feet.

"You're okay," she said as he came over.

He nodded. "You look like hell, love."

She smiled and it felt wet. Must have been real attractive to see a mouth full of bloody teeth.

Darnell gave her a squeeze around the shoulders, and she winced, not in pain from her injuries, but from the gun he held in one hand.

"This needs to end," Darnell said, letting go. He stood over Carlisle for a moment, then rolled him over with the toe of his right foot, waiting patient for the man to regain consciousness.

"What are you doing?" Lexi asked, watching as he pointed the pistol at Carlisle's face.

The Collector, the man who had started this whole fucked up adventure, blinked up at Darnell, dazed, but not fully comprehending.

"I should pull the trigger," Darnell growled. "Paint the floor with your godforsaken, evil mind."

"Go ahead," Carlisle mumbled, a weak hand raised. "Pull the trigger. Do it. Do it!"

Darnell's hand shook, a war taking place behind his moistening eyes. All the wrong Carlisle had done could be paid for, right here and now, justice done with no chance of a return. But this was not who Darnell was. Lexi knew that if he pulled the trigger, he'd regret it for the rest of his life. It was one thing to kill someone in a firefight, it was another to execute them.

"You're too weak to do what needs doing," Carlisle said. "You have squandered your God-given talents."

"No," Darnell responded, lowering the weapon. "I made my choice to follow the narrow path."

Carlisle growled and reached for his gun. Lexi wasn't having it. She kicked him in the teeth as hard as she could with the steel tip of her boot and sent him sprawling back on the floor, a spray of blood lingering in the air as he fell.

She had to say it felt good after what he had done to her face.

"Can someone get me something to tie this fucker up?" she asked, and Atticus limped over, a bundle of cord in hand.

"Some might find this kinky," he chuckled, red dribbling from his lips. "Pain and pleasure seem to be a thing for this man."

As Atticus moved to tie up Carlisle, an alarm began and the doors leading into the warehouse closed shut. Everyone froze.

The loudspeaker squawked: *"This is UEI Security Forces, drop your weapons or we'll be forced to pump the warehouse full of knockout gas. I repeat, drop your weapons!"*

Lexi heard the clatter of guns a few aisles over. It seemed they hadn't gotten all of Carlisle's bodyguards. They dropped their weapons where they stood, hands going up. She kept an eye on Carlisle to be sure he didn't make a move during this shift in power, but all the fight had left the corrupt man.

The doors to the warehouse opened a moment later and security guards cuffed each of them but for Keelin and Captain Cho, who were allowed to remain where they were while medical personnel were brought in.

This was it. This was the moment of truth. They'd done the right thing, so she thought, but what would it cost them? Their dreams? Almost certainly.

Or could it be something even worse?

[37] – Darnell

There was hardly a place on Darnell's body that didn't hurt in one way or another. He'd been beaten within an inch of his life by Carlisle, but thankfully, it was all over. Once the dust had settled in the warehouse, and everyone had been taken into custody, them included, Logan had been allowed to join their group. They tended the wounds of those who were less injured like he, Lexi, and Atticus. Captain Cho and Keelin had been taken to the hospital. While no one's injuries were life threatening, theirs could cause long-term damage.

There was some pride, however, in how it all turned out. Even though they were in holding, Sarita and Sarah were reunited, and Carlisle was locked up. Lexi and Darnell watched them all evening, smiling as they held one another and talked in hushed tones from the corner of the holding cell. There was no telling what Carlisle's men had done to her, and yet, she had survived. Two lovers had been reunited. The sight was beautiful. It almost made it all worth it.

"I'm happy for her," Lexi said, nodding towards Sarita, one hand rested on her injured arm. "But she's still a bitch."

Darnell grinned at that. "We all have our path, don't we?"

The UEI Security Forces were not sure what to do with the *Peridot's* crew. They had been interrogated over the events of the last few months, using the evidence Logan had turned over as a guide. Two camps had begun to emerge among the UEI ranks. One, who believed it was all a misunderstanding, and that Carlisle must have been forced into this situation. Two, who knew the slimy bastard had been up to something all along. It didn't much matter for the crew of the Peridot which outcome was decided upon. They had broken more than a few laws, each of which had punishments far greater than a few days in holding.

After being patched up, Darnell was taken from the room and moved into a private interrogation space. Lexi urged them not to take him away, but the security forces promised he'd be returned in a few minutes. He wasn't so sure.

"I love you," he told her. "Be back in a few."

The sergeant who had led the raid, Kevin Driscoll, took a seat across from Darnell in a small room with a metal table. Darnell sat, resting his handcuffed wrists before him. While he was used to cramped spaces, having served on a flyer for so many years, this interrogation room made him uncomfortable. The walls were hardly three strides end to end, and the light was far too bright, making him squint. His chair was off balance, as if one of the legs had been sawed short. And it was hot, really, really hot.

"Mr. Richardson," Sergeant Driscoll began, gesturing through the feed on a tablet. "Do you understand all the charges against you?"

"I ain't too sure," Darnell replied, rocking on his uneven chair, making it click against the floor. "I could use me a lawyer to explain them, if you wouldn't mind."

The sergeant waved a hand. "Your counsel is on the way. But in the meantime, we're gonna have a chat."

"Do I have to speak, sir?"

"No... You have the right to remain silent."

"I opt for that right, sir."

"Good God," the sergeant sat down the tablet and pinched the bridge of his nose, then let out a groan.

"Indeed He is," Darnell paused, "sir. God is good to all His children."

"Is this funny to you? Six people are dead. One of them is a boy who had only been working with me for about six months. Shot down by one of those thugs Carlisle, I'm sorry, *the Collector,* had hired. Now, I'm not surprised in the least someone of his means had a private security force. His people always did make me nervous. Still, if you hadn't started all this, that kid might still be alive. His name was Jason Anderson. He was getting married in two months, had a bright future on Luna. Haven't had the heart to call his family yet."

Darnell's chest seized. He knew that some had died, but he had assumed all of them were Carlisle's men. How did this translate to him? He didn't pull the trigger on anyone who wasn't working for Carlisle. Was he still an accessory to murder?

He really needed that lawyer.

"So just to walk through this for the fifteenth time," the sergeant began. "Your little crew here fell on some tough times in the outer planets, boo hoo hoo. You aren't the only one, buddy. Found yourself working hard for very little and so when this opportunity to steal an American artifact was given to you, everyone thought it would be a great idea to take the job. No one out there, no way to get caught. You narrowly escaped UEI involvement and were betrayed by Carlisle. Once you discovered what he really wanted, and that he had Sarah Conyers as a hostage, you decided to do the right thing. Up until that point, you were acting as thieves. Criminals. Does that sound about right?"

Darnell pursed his lips, pinching them with a thumb and forefinger. "Memory is fuzzy without my lawyer, sir."

"God damn." He tossed the tablet down on the table, its surface letting out a metallic ring. "You ain't sure about shit, are you?"

"Just a simple boy from the country, sir."

"Simple my ass." The sergeant collected himself and forced a smile. "Okay. So, somehow, others get word of this little capture in progress. An undisclosed group of pirates, as you call them, show up at the scene of the crime about the same time you do. They have an improvised weapon of some kind. In self-defense, you attach a mining charge to their hull and decompress their ship."

Darnell swallowed and the officer saw this discomfort. It had been self-defense, he knew it, and yet, he still felt like a murderer.

He did what he had to.

"It *was* self-defense, yes?" the sergeant pressed. "Or did you just not like the idea of someone else getting to the prize first? A bit of deadly competition?"

A silence settled over the room. Darnell wasn't going to give him the courtesy of a sir this time.

"Then, as if we can't get more complicated, there's the Chinese government. They intended to steal this from America. I might be UEI now, but I'm damn sure an American, and this pisses me the hell off. Bad enough a crew of society's blue-collar underbelly decided to do something like this, but what the Chinese did, and just over our heads on Luna... that's inexcusable. Don't you think so? Hmm?"

"I'm not allowed to have an opinion at this time, sir."

"Sure you are. Doesn't it just piss you off?"

"It's all over space junk, sir."

"Space junk?" The sergeant let out a laugh. "Space junk? Lindvall's personal Slipstream is just space junk? Space junk worth more PAEN on the black market than you can make splitting rocks in a hundred lifetimes."

"People in my family live to be long in the tooth, sir."

"I sure as hell hope they do." He shook his head. "Because you're going away for a long time. Not only are the crimes you committed before reaching Luna punishable with a minimum of fifty years in prison, that stunt you pulled on this station, *my station*, that got Anderson killed, will put you away for at least another fifty more. You better be glad we're as close as we are to Earth, otherwise I'd stuff your ass in an airlock and press the button myse—"

"Sir," another officer stuck his head into the room. "Sorry to interrupt, but Richardson's counsel is here."

"His what?" The sergeant shot up, surprise on his face. "How in the—"

A sharply dressed dark-eyed man in his forties entered the room, wearing a tailored, royal blue suit, crisp white shirt and black tie, with a crimson and cream scarf stuffed in his jacket pocket. He clicked as he took a step forward, drawing attention to his well-worn, and likely borrowed, magnetic boots, an incongruous detail against that of the rest of his fine attire. As he ran a hand through his cropped gray hair, recomposing himself from a brisk walk, he smiled at the sergeant, the sort of practiced smile politicians and public relations officials gave. It wasn't genuine, or warm, but it made Darnell relax a bit.

"I apologize for taking so long," he said, his voice mild and measured. "I caught the fastest shuttle I could. Takes some time to cross a quarter of a million miles, does it not?"

"You're my lawyer?" Darnell asked the new arrival, incredulous. He raised his cuffed hands. "Any way we can get these off? They're chafing my wrists worse than if I'd been ridin' all day without chaps."

"Who are you?" The sergeant crossed his arms, eyes narrowing. "We only sent for counsel a few hours ago."

"My apologies," the man said, then nodded his head. "Devon Wainwright, head counsel and custodian for the Lindvall family."

Darnell's eyes went wide. The message must have gotten through. They had assumed they either did not receive it or didn't think it was worth their attention, but this man's presence was evidence to the contrary.

"Please, Mr. Richardson is my client. Isn't that right Mr. Richardson?"

He nodded emphatically. Gramps didn't raise no fool. "Yes, sir."

"I beg of you, remove my client's restraints. He will not make any fuss, I assure you."

The sergeant let out a long sigh and unlocked Darnell's cuffs. He swore the man's face was turning red. "Ain't this just a damn thing."

"Life is a damn thing, sergeant." Devon motioned for Darnell to stand. "Now, if you will, I would like to meet with my clients in their holding area. In private. We have much to speak of."

"As you wish, *counselor*," the sergeant growled, and took a small bow.

Devon led Darnell back into the hall towards the holding area, the two of them escorted by a pair of armed guards. Eager, Darnell tried to ask questions, but Devon put a finger over his lips, forestalling any. There was so much he wanted to know.

They reached the holding area, and the few other prisoners who were not part of their group had been moved, leaving Devon alone with their crew. Keelin and Captain Cho had been returned, patched up and looking well, all things considered.

"What's going on," Lexi asked Darnell. "I got worried after you were gone for a while. Who's this character?"

Before Darnell could introduce the man, Devon tipped his head and spoke, "I am Devon Wainwright, and I will be representing each of you in the impending trials as the custodian of the Lindvall Family."

Captain Cho leaned forward where she sat, Keelin helping her. "Shut—up. The message, it went through?"

"The message you sent the family was received, yes. It sat in an inbox for nearly six weeks before an intern uncovered it during a routine clean up."

"We thought you had chosen to ignore us."

"Hardly." He dismissed the idea with a wave of a hand. "But how often does one receive messages from deep space? Hmm? Especially of this importance. Outside of Earth, time tends to move a bit slower, what with travel and all."

"Nice suit," Atticus said, smiling at the lawyer. Devon nodded his approval.

"So you got the message," Keelin said. "What does that mean for the rest of us?"

Atticus pointed at Keelin. "Yes, exactly what *does* this mean for the rest of us?"

"I hope it means getting out of here," Sarita mumbled, and Sarah agreed.

Devon began pacing the room in thought, his unengaged magnetic boots clinking against the metal floor. "While we do have some legal challenges before us, I am confident much of this will go away. Do you have the letter?"

"From the Slipstream?" Darnell asked. "That one?"

Devon nodded.

"It's on the *Peridot*, yes."

"Very good. What do you say we make a trade?"

"A trade?" Lexi asked, her eyes wide. "What do you mean?"

"I have spoken with the family over this matter, and we are grateful that despite the Slipstream's destruction, it did not fall into the hands of a private collector like Carlisle. To be honest, it's remarkable the car was not space dust in the first place. As it stands, this man's agenda does not align with our own. Despite his claims to revere Lindvall's vision to advance our species, he seeks to turn the clock back. He seeks to plunge humanity, or at the very least America, into a less *enlightened age*. I am not sure if this one artifact would have changed that. On the other hand, it did succeed in getting Carlisle caught in the act. As the lead counsel for the family, I will make sure he is prosecuted to the fullest extent of the law. That includes not just the Slipstream, but all other items discovered in his possession."

"Are they not inadmissible?" Atticus mused. "We entered the warehouse illegally."

He pressed a fist against his chin to consider this. "While you might have done so, the UEI Security Forces did not. Carlisle has become a bit of a thorn for the authorities on Luna. They will be happy to co-operate."

Lexi let out a long sigh, eyed Darnell, then turned back to Devon, arms crossed. "So what are you telling us? You'll send Carlisle away for a long time, and just get us off?"

"That is the short of it. You were coerced into an impossible situation. Carlisle had a hostage. What else were you to do?"

"This feels way too easy," Atticus mused, turning to the group, his face compressed with worry. "Here comes the magic wand, the Fairy Godmother to make everything okay. We've been there before. Did not turn out well."

"No kaching, kaching," Keelin echoed, her attention falling on her bandaged leg. "Got shot in the leg as payment."

Logan frowned. "And we didn't know about that aforementioned situation of coercion and hostage taking until Saturn."

They were right. This felt too easy. In their experience, easy had not turned out well.

Devon shrugged at their concerns. "I'm sure that your timeline of yours is not accurate. It will need to be revised."

"Oh," Lexi said, her arms falling to her sides. "I see."

"Does this mean we can go back to work?" Captain Cho asked. "Soon as it is all settled, I'd love to know I have a life that didn't involve pan handling."

"What do you say we come to a new agreement?" Devon smiled and this time it was genuine. "I have more than enough work to go around, compensation for people with your skills, so long as you wish to get out of this place."

"Work?" Keelin piped up. "You mean I don't need to become Luna's little night lady?"

Captain Cho reached for Keelin's hand and squeezed. "Compensation?" she asked the attorney.

"And more," Devon went on. "The family's holding company has quite a significant benefits package. Since this mess began over a piece of family property, it seems only fair that we pay you back for all you have done."

From the look on her face, it was clear that Lexi was dumbfounded. "You would get us out and give us jobs because of what happened?"

"And why not?"

"Yes," Darnell said. "Please. I'm sorry how what happened, happened. We did our best given the circumstances."

And it was true. He might have guilt over how a few of the events had gone down, but what were his options? The only one he could see would have been quitting on Stratus Base after this haphazard deal had been accepted, but he knew he wouldn't have done that. His loyalty was with the crew of the *Peridot*. For good or ill, he was with them. No matter how he felt inside, he was a ride or die friend.

God help him.

"The family understands," Devon said. "Economic challenges can force many a good person to make less than admirable choices. This is your opportunity to prove you are good people at heart."

"So how much do these jobs pay?" Atticus ventured. "I'm curious is all. Working for KTS hasn't been the best."

"More than you'll need for any research project you wish to pursue, Mr. Prescott."

"Enough to build a clinic?" Logan asked.

"And a staff to run it for at least twenty years." Devon removed a hand terminal and pressed a few buttons. "I even have positions for Mrs. Conyers and her wife. If they wish."

"We just want a quiet place to live out our lives," Sarah replied.

"Yes," Sarita agreed. "We've had enough excitement for one lifetime."

"Then you shall have your peace," he said, "while using your talents for the good of all mankind."

And this was the dream. To get the things that matter but to get them while helping everyone. It was all Darnell ever wanted, to offer his life in the service of others and receive a small reward for that service, not just a paycheck, not just a steady meal.

He wanted a life he could look back at and be proud of having lived it.

Darnell extended a hand to Devon, who accepted it after only a slight hesitation. "I'd be honored to work for the family, sir." He turned his head and scanned the rest of the group. "Anyone else with me?"

There was a moment of silence while they processed this.

Was it really over?

Were they safe?

"Yes," they each said in turn.

Lexi nodded at him. "I'm with you."

And with that, the world felt right again.

It was over.

[epilogue]

After the mess of a situation over Luna, the *Peridot* needed a serious overhaul. Many of its maneuvering systems were shot. Its backup solar array was in tatters. There were several hull breaches. It would be months before the girl would be flying again. Fortunately for Captain Cho, she didn't own it anymore. Between insurance, the KTS contract being bought out, and a "mysterious purchaser", this liability had been removed from her balance sheet. The crew found it sad to see her go, to crawl into her belly and clear out several years' worth of memories, but better days lay ahead for them all.

"Got everything?" Lexi asked Darnell, a wry smile on her face. He rolled a cart full of duffels and boxes across the crowded concourse of Luna base. Darnell's wrought iron Texas Star stuck out the side, as did Lexi's paintings. Passersby gave them a funny look. A ground car would have been easier, but they'd have to wait several hours for one to be available, and they were, well—impatient.

He paused, bringing the cart to a halt, and one of the bags fell off its side. "Could use some help here."

She shrugged. "Looks like you got it," she said, then patted the bag slung over her shoulder. "Come on, old top."

They wheeled their personal belongings away from the *Peridot*, leaving the old girl to new owners and new adventures. It would never be the same, and that was okay. It was okay. What happened there should stay there.

As they entered the food court, belongings towed behind them, Captain Cho waved from a table. Lexi gave Darnell a look and he nodded. They walked over to her.

"We always have more things than we thought," Captain Cho said, eyeing the precarious stack of personal belongings on the cart. "Got my stuff moved out just a few hours ago." She offered them seats at the table then began to dig back into her food, which was a steaming bowl of pho with meatballs. This food court had one of the best noodle joints in existence, *The Raging Chowby,* a favorite stop for their crew since being released from holding.

"It's quiet on the ship," Lexi said, resigned.

"Empty more like it," Darnell said, plopping down into a seat. He dug out his hand terminal and began to order. "I'm hongry."

"Is that even a word?"

"Hell if I know, and don't rightly care. You want something, babe?"

Lexi nodded, leaning over to look at his screen. "You know what I like. Just so long as it's not Exo-bites."

This made Captain Cho chuckle. "I still say they're good."

Captain Cho. Was that the right name for her now? She was a captain, yes, but not *their* captain.

He pressed a few keys on his hand terminal, producing a chime. Their order was made.

"Talked to Devon and Sarita this morning," Cho went on after a slurpy bite of noodles. "We have a couple more court appearances via uplink, but that's it. Most of the charges have been dropped outright. Devon was able to make a plea deal with the UEI for most everything he couldn't make disappear. Be warned though, looks like the group of us might be facing down a few hundred hours of community service."

Darnell's eyebrows narrowed. "Community service?"

She nodded. "A bit of work in the gardens. Maybe a couple short hop runs and hard vacuum work. Nothing you can't handle."

"And what about for yours?" Lexi asked.

"Me? I'm a flyer captain. I just sit in a comfy chair, bark orders, and talk to people over comms."

The corner of Lexi's lip curled, not quite a smile. "How's Sarah?"

Captain Cho shrugged. "Bad things happened while we took our time. She's seeing a therapist. Processing it."

"Oh? That's good."

"I'm not so sure, given the doctor."

"Why's that?"

"I think you know him." She took another bite and sighed. "Mmm. These are the best damn noodles, I swear. It's nice having real food."

"Be careful, now," Darnell said, patting his belly, "it can stick to your bones."

"At this point, I don't care if I end up turning into a roly-poly."

"Pill bug's a good look," Lexi said, waving at the confused server looking for them. They came over and set a tray down with two bowls: one filled to the brim with noodles and broth, pho khong thit for Lexi; the other, spicy beef teriyaki, Seattle Style, for Darnell.

"I'm hungry as a hostage in a holdup situation," Darnell said, picking up his fork and digging in.

"Say what?" Lexi whirled on him.

He smiled back.

The three of them ate their lunch and chatted, laughing about old times and speculating about the future. Cho wasn't their captain anymore. She'd been given a new ship, a new job, working direct for the Lindvall family. Due to the nature of this assignment, she had not been permitted to say where she would be going, or what she would be doing. It was for the best. Still, there was a sense that everything would be okay.

"Will you visit?" Lexi asked as they were getting up to leave, their meal nothing but a rapidly fading memory of spices across the tongue.

Cho nodded. "Yes. I'll be back here, hopefully not too far in the future."

Darnell cut between them and reached out his hand. "You'll always be my Cap."

"Katia," she said, taking his hand. "You can call me Katia."

"Yes, Cap."

Lexi took a deep breath and tossed her arms around her. The two of them squeezed one another tight enough it made joints crack as if they'd been put on a chiropractor's table for an adjustment.

"Go see your sisters," Katia whispered in her ear. "You won't regret it."

They held onto one another for a long moment, then let go, each dabbing the moisture from their eyes with the backs of jumpsuit sleeves, before laughing about it.

"She's right," Darnell said, leading them away.

"I know." Lexi let out a long sigh. "I know."

As they reached the edge of the food court, entering the tunnel connecting the space port to the rest of Luna Base, Logan appeared up ahead. They were talking to a group of friends, then broke off at Lexi and Darnell's approach.

"Catch up with you later," they said, then took off at a jog to fall in line. "How are you guys?" A glint of something metallic flashed by their hair line on the back of their neck.

"Doing well," Darnell said, head cocking. "I see you got a, em, upgrade." Was it a miniature version of the gas converters used on suits to turn CO_2 into breathable oxygen? If it wasn't, it sure looked like one.

Logan blushed. "Well, you know me. Certain upgrades are more than aesthetic, they can increase our chances of survival. I'm not sure this flesh thing we all wear is what makes us human anyways." They tapped the side of their head with a finger. "We live up here. Seems only fitting to make a few changes, we are traveling out into the stars."

"Maybe."

"Where'd the reprobates get off to?" Lexi looked around as they walked. "Figured we'd have come across them by now."

"Where do you think?" They asked, a sly smile on their face.

As the three of them reached the end of the tunnel, they came upon a light commercial district with clothing shops and general goods. At the corner of the dome's outer transit line was a dark, open alcove fenced in by waist high metal rails. Within this space, people sat at dimly lit tables and a long bar, a red, LED glow making them each appear like demons in the dark. Occult symbols hung on the walls beside magical sigils and the skulls of horned animals. This made Darnell roll his eyes and pray for the souls of all within.

Dark rhythms oozed their way into the halls, infecting the air with mischief.

"God save them from their evil ways, for they know not what they do," he whispered.

"Fook off!" a red-headed woman screamed from the railing of the bar, *Dust Devils*, a full glass of frosty beer raised in her right hand. "Get over 'ere, bastards!"

Lexi chuckled under her breath and walked over, Logan and Darnell following.

On the other side of the fence sat Atticus, leaned back with legs crossed, a tumbler of whiskey in his right hand. He swirled the amber liquid for a moment, stuck his nose deep into the mouth of the glass, then took a sip.

"A pleasure to see you," he said, setting down his drink and standing. "I must say, the accommodations are far better on Luna than they were on that cramped flyer. For one, I have some real privacy."

"As if you need any," Keelin said, slapping him on the back. Beer ran over the edge of her glass, and she licked it off the side before too much was spilled. The action was a bit—suggestive.

"Looks like the party is already getting kicked off," Logan commented.

"Richardson? Carver?" Keelin said, her tone inviting. "Come on. You know you want to."

Darnell raised his hands, then gestured at their cart. "We need to get settled. Living out of a suitcase is for the birds."

"Get a few drinks before you ship out?" Lexi ventured, taking hold of Darnell's arm and hanging onto him.

Keelin stuck out her tongue and pouted. "Count on it. Going to need as many as I can get if this arsehole is comin' with me."

Atticus rolled his eyes. "I swear this bitch is going to push me over the edge, you hear me?"

"You're headed to Stratus, right?" Lexi asked.

"Head engineer on contract," Keelin said, tossing a thumb at her chest. "Good job to 'ave. Extra benefits from the family, for the family."

"What she's telling us," Atticus started, his words a bit slurred, "is that her mother no longer—"

"Hush your cock hole," Keelin said, shoving Atticus back. The two of them laughed at one another.

"See you guys tomorrow then?" Darnell asked.

"It's a date. A four-way, perhap." Keelin made a suggestive dance, grinding her pelvis against open air, then laughed at herself.

Logan hopped the railing to join them. "Later, love birds." They held up two fingers in a side-ways peace sign.

Darnell and Lexi left them to their own devices, hopping the nearest transport and rode their way up to the fifteenth floor. As they stood before the entrance of their new home they sighed.

1527 Dome 2 – The Gardens of the Moon, the sign read.

With a swipe of a key card, the door opened. They looked at one another, took a deep breath, then nodded and stepped over the threshold to a new life. From this moment forward, everything would be different. They'd gone through fire together and come out on the other side. They were better for it. Better together.

Lindvall's custodian had been true to his word. Their new positions as private contractors and consultants for the family had benefits—excellent pay, health insurance, powerful friends... and a great place to live.

Their new apartment was larger than most on Luna, close to two thousand square feet in all. It had a massive, open concept kitchen and living room, expensive, top of the line appliances, genuine leather furniture, and dark, luxury flooring. The style of the space was modern, sleek angles and neutral colors with plenty of natural white light running along the edges of the room. But these features weren't even the best part.

Darnell abandoned the cart before their kitchen and led Lexi, hand in hand, to the main window at the edge of the living room. He called to the computer, and the blinds opened, revealing the gardens beneath them. From the fifteenth floor they could see all the way to the other side of the steel and glass dome, a thick forest of green trees and trails, of burbling streams and grassy knolls before them. Birds flocked in the open air, tweeting songs never meant for such a place. Small animals scurried around in branches. People walked the trails, pointing up at the sky, groups of families, groups of friends... lovers enjoying life. This was a paradise among an ancient wasteland. A perfect place to raise children beneath a sky of black and a globe of blue at the edges of human exploration.

It was paradise.

Lexi turned to Darnell, her eyes filled with appreciation and longing. She took hold of his hands, interlacing her fingers with his. "You ready to get started on that family of ours?"

He swallowed the rock in his throat and gave her a smile. "Yes, ma'am. I do believe that I am."

They closed the blinds, and the room went dark. Their lips met in this self-imposed void, soft and silent, a breath held too long.

For the first time in years, they were truly alone, no one else to interfere, left with nothing but one another's happiness to occupy their time.

It was their dream. It had always been their dream. And no matter what the world might say, no matter what judgement may come, they knew that they deserved every moment of it.

AFTERWARD

This book has been an adventure to write. If you haven't figured it out by now, the core heist was one that was inspired by real-life events, though shifted into narrative forms. Those real-life events are less the political drama part, and more the "hey we're gonna shoot a car into space" part. In 2018, Space X launched Elon Musk's roadster into space as a publicity stunt during a test of their Falcon 9 faring module. And it worked. As the rockets burned, the Space X crew blared David Bowie's classic, "Space Oddity". Star Man, the roadster's driver looked forward as the words DON'T PANIC, a reference to the Hitchhikers Guide to the Galaxy, appeared on the screen in the center console.

I watched it take off, the car released into interplanetary freefall, and put a note in my iPhone to write a short story about a group of space miners who recover the car in space for money. In between writing some other stories, The Foundry, and more, I sat down and tried to cram this narrative into 3000-4000 words. Let's just say it did not go well. A short story soon became a novella, then in revisions, it became a novel without an ending. And so, I wrote the ending. In editing I realized the focus of the story was in the wrong place. I had placed the historical journey of this car on the shoulders of Space X, when I realized that some of the events I set up in the main Foundry series might fit nice if we made some changes.

I went back for a 3rd draft, removing the 1:1 historical comparison and created a fictitious rival to Tesla, Lindvall. I surveyed everyone I could get my hands on to see what range in miles it would take before they would buy an electric car. At what point did range anxiety end? Take all the political calculus out of it, the dangerous materials needed for the batteries, and most said that number was over 600 miles. So, I decided to double down. Well... triple down. And we ended up with the Lindvall Slipstream, an electric car which runs on a graphene supercapacitor (a theoretical "battery" that would likely be environmentally safe) with a range of 2000 miles. Enter the polar opposite to the Tesla CEO, and we have, Matteo Lindvall, who pulls the same stunt as Musk but in the character's mind "a better stunt".

Now, let me be clear. I wrote this version of the story starting 2 years ago, 2023, and finished editing in mid-2024. I have made no edits to this novel other than a few copy-edits for typos. Any events that happen to line up with current world events are purely coincidental. I have no crystal ball. And I have no agenda: save one.

I wrote this story to highlight that for most of us, political or spiritual divides do not serve us. And that for most of us, especially those not in power, how we show up and how we treat one another is far more important than doctrine or dogma.

This was one of the most fun, most challenging stories I've ever written. It took a lot of reflection, soul seeking, and research. I hope you enjoyed it. And perhaps next time, before you react to those in the world (or mostly on the internet) with only anger or hate, do yourself, and your fellow neighbor a favor—take a deep breath. Remember, they are human beings, just like you, and just like you, they have fears and concerns that have not been developed solely by their personal observations but bred into them by an imperfect system. They are just as much the victim as you are. So, show some love, live in the moment, and give each other a helping hand.

Safe journeys, Cosmic Traveler. And thank you.

J Fitzpatrick Mauldin, March 2025

THERE IS MORE TO THE FOUNDRY UNIVERSE.

IF YOU ENJOYED THIS BOOK, BE SURE TO LEAVE A RATING/REVIEW.

BECOME A COSMIC TRAVELER

THE FOUNDRY

NOVELS AND SHORT STORIES

J Fitzpatrick Mauldin is a science fiction writer based in Atlanta, Georgia, best known for the hard science fiction first contact series The Foundry, which was featured in Kirkus Reviews. A technology expert and nationwide business leader by trade, he serves thousands of professionals in achieving their dreams while nurturing an insatiable passion for world-building and fiction. A father of two, husband, and lover of role-playing and strategy video games (though he's terrible at Baldur's Gate), he is also an amateur scientist with aspirations to pursue a PhD in an undefined, esoteric field. His fiction aims to offer readers immersive worlds to escape the noise of everyday life and inspire them to see the best in their fellow humans who ride alongside on this cosmic journey.

GET YOUR FREE E-BOOK & AUDIO BOOK, SIGN UP FOR OUR EMAIL LIST:
www.jfitzpatrickmauldin.com
"A cunning young girl comes face to face with an interstellar threat when her mother and grandfather are murdered aboard their ship while making contact with a mysterious entity. Alone, and with no way home, Bellamy makes a deal with an alien intelligence to chase the signal of her mother's soul to a facility light-years away, in the hope she might be resurrected and the two of them reunited." – Chasing the Signal (The Foundry 0.5)

Follow on:

 facebook.com/jfmauld  @jfitzpatrickmauldin

@jfitzpatrickmauldin

www.ingramcontent.com/pod-product-compliance
Lightning Source LLC
Chambersburg PA
CBHW050009120726
47903CB00006B/1705